Teleportnation

Copyright

Chapter 1

She was gone.

I had never lost somebody before.

Vaguely familiar faces surrounded me, buzzing around in an almost practiced form of faux panic.

'It's OK, Leon. Just stay put, we'll get you sorted.'

'It's OK, Leon. Nothing you can do now.'

'It's OK, Leon. These things happen.'

Comfortless remarks played on repeat from the flurry of people now involved. It seemed less like a panicked worry and more like an inconveniencing embarrassment.

'Hiccup?' I heard someone say.

'Yep, looks that way,' another followed, now scanning through my station's interface. 'It's been a while, I guess. Damn, bound to happen sooner or later.'

I just sat there, staring straight ahead into the now vacant area surrounding my gate, slowly slumping down into my seat under the weight of what had happened. I was just speaking to her—face to face—alive and well, only a few minutes previous, but now?

Now who knows.

Could it have been me? Did I do this?

I found myself trailing back over my entire day, wondering if anything could have been off, or wrong. It was an unusual day, granted, but it was still as mundane as most. Nothing went wrong.

But it didn't matter. No amount of thinking or hindsight would help now.

She was gone.

***

February 29th, 2072.

'What a day,' I groaned to myself as I took up residence at my terminal at Hub 29, finally glad to be out of the suit I had been coerced into wearing all morning. It had been a while since my last wedding attendance, and the fit did not feel flattering anymore. *Less muffins*, I thought, knowing I already had several at home I wouldn't allow go to waste.

'What a day, what a day,' I continued as I ran my hands through my hair, awaiting the start of my shift.

The morning had not begun well.

To be invited as a guest at an MIT lecture was an honour typically reserved for only the elite alumni, those who had either contributed greatly through excellence in their fields, or those with money. To be forced into attending such an occasion as a non-vocal participant because you were caught tampering with the company's coffee machines, again, was slightly less of an honour.

Just a case of wrong place, wrong time, wrong manager, I guessed.

Sure, I was an alumnus. One box ticked at least. Three years had passed since my graduation, yet still I felt unease passing through the crowded hallways.

I brushed through the masses, eyes straight ahead, not visiting any of my old haunts. It wasn't a social visit, and I wasn't early. The opposite actually. There wasn't even an excuse for my tardiness, just regular old disdain for the situation I'd found myself in.

Mikey, a PR rep I had the misfortune of having met several times before, was my liaison on the day, and was stood waiting for me at the lecture hall. He was not happy. But then again, he never was. So maybe he was actually sort of content in his own weird way.

'Leon! Where the hell—' he began, immediately ruining my idea of his contentment. But knowing what was to come, I cut him off as I pushed the large door to the lecture hall open, just a crack. Heaven forbid any of the students heard him reprimanding me. The perfect 'mute' button for a PR rep.

Begrudgingly he fell silent and forced a smile while ushering me into the hall. A full house, just as I feared. There must have been over 300 people in attendance, the air heavy with a constant hum of idle chat.

The microphone had screeched awkwardly into life right as we entered. Wincing a bit, I turned and followed Mikey from a few steps back as he positioned himself at the seat closest the lectern. I made my way to the only seat remaining, at the end of the small line of chairs where my other punctual colleagues took residence.

After a short and mostly inaudible introduction by the Professor, who looked to still be mostly asleep, Mikey took to the stage and began the charade on behalf of our gracious employer, WormWhole Inc.

I knew exactly what he would say too. It wasn't the first time I had attended one of these recruitment seminars. Just never from this side.

'Now students, we have a special set of guests for you today. Firstly, allow me to introduce Leon, a Saint working at Hub 29 in Central Europe...'

Saint—I always felt—was too grand a nickname for slipway technicians. News reporters originally coined the term, a play on our abbreviated designation as STs. An obvious joke, but it had stuck almost immediately.

Traditionally, Saint was a term used to describe a person who exhibited an exceptional degree of holiness. Someone who displayed such overwhelmingly positive personal traits during their lifetime that they were posthumously revered to a high degree.

How anyone could be considered somewhat superhuman or otherworldly just because they performed acts of kindness and bravery was beyond me. Was that not how most of us tried to act?

Or more truthfully, how we imagined we would act if given the right circumstances.

I had been a Saint at WormWhole Inc ever since I stepped foot out of MIT. It may have only been a few years, but it felt a lifetime already. Their "internal hiring policy" was yet to pay off for me, as moving up the ranks to the engineering department seemed to be just as far off as when I began. Slogging through my engineering degree was feeling like more and more of a waste every year.

'Leon attended this fine institution only three years ago...' Mikey continued.

I felt my reddened cheeks divulge my immediate discomfort. I didn't expect quite the level of introduction he was giving me. Why somebody cycling through the details of my life embarrassed me so much, I don't know. It wasn't like I didn't know the details already. I was there for all of it, after all.

It was as basic a biography as could be given as an introduction, yet Mikey preached my short résumé with some serious zeal. I had to hand it to him, he was a great public speaker. But I always hated people who were overly preachy, about anything. It made my skin crawl. And I feel my tardiness may have been part of why he was hamming it up so much as he looked at me several times during with a sort of side smirk.

But he eventually relented and moved on to the other, more impressive, colleagues of mine. We had someone from the engineering core, a professor in experimental physics from one of the company's research centres, and even a Hub junior manager.

It was not a group I would ever expect to be involved with again.

The talk went on, word for word, just like it had

years before for the talk I attended. If it ain't broke, but is still daydream inducingly boring, why fix it.

It was all very basic, painfully so at times, exactly what you would expect from a big multinational company coming in and trying to entice the next generation of the workforce to join their ranks.

Mikey covered it all. Right from the inception of the slipway technology, a revolutionary transportation method developed in 2026, all the way through to the mass adoption of the gate network in 2031 and beyond. It was mostly all very common knowledge, but some parts of the speech did generally interest me still, even though I had heard them many times over the years.

It was hard for me to imagine that every country was divided and crisscrossed with the worldwide highway systems, a method of enhanced travel dating back to the Roman Empire. Only once had I ever driven an automotive vehicle, and that was a birthday present for when I turned 21. Automotive travel in general was, at best, a hobbyist pastime. In fact, even gaining access to any of the petroleum-based fuels to run the machines was a difficult ask.

But thanks to the disuse and removal of these networked roadways, the sudden and drastic reduction of fossil fuel combustion, and some feverish tree planting initiatives worldwide, the planet had recovered. And more rapidly than anyone could have predicted.

Worldwide oxygen levels rose, desertification was reversed in places, species on the brink of extinction were allowed space and time to begin regenerating. Entire ecosystems on the cusp of disappearing were preserved. Nature was a commodity that had long been in decline due to negative human influences. But that was not the world I was accustomed to. Towns, cities, hamlets, all were surrounded by lush greenery and wildlife. That was the world I grew up in.

Personally, I could have done without all the constant greenery. It didn't exactly do wonders for those of us with hay fever—an unpopular and selfish opinion in the grander scheme of things.

And this entire "new world" was attributed to one person, Dr Meribel Sterne.

A brilliant scientist, and a personal hero, I had no problem listening to the amazing facts about her life rifled off in vivid detail to the lecture hall. In fact, if that was the only topic of the day, I imagine I would have quite enjoyed the whole obligatory affair.

But of course, it was only a side note, a namedrop of sorts.

The final few minutes of the talk were spent detailing various historical landmarks in WormWhole's growth as an industry leader. In other words, the boring indoctrination segment of the lecture. Mikey detailed the more obvious improvements the slipway network made over early stage teleportation technology, as well as rattling off the details of the symbiotic relationship between WormWhole and the BioDev corporation. After the bioterrorism attacks in the early 2030s, each gate was fitted with their small scanner devices to ensure nobody ferrying containers of harm-ful pathogens or microbes could pass through. An important technology, and one I hoped I would never witness in operation.

He wrapped up the speech with a recap on how WormWhole was the "World leader in developing and supplying gateway stations to every corner of the planet." They were also known for brutally crush-ing potential opponents financially, but that never appeared on the script somehow.

Funny that.

A quick round of seemingly voluntary applause rounded off the event, and we all stood for a moment to give a slight nod and a wave to the crowd. The in-tention was that we would stay behind and answer any of the students' questions, but thankfully for myself, and the students' sake, that was impossible. My atten-dance was a sort of hybrid mandatory-extracurricular activity, so no time off my usual shift, which was get-ting very close.

I had all but ran to the campus gate station to get me back in time for my shift.

'But WormWhole really did care about us worker bees, right?' I said to myself as I sat, still rubbing my hands through my hair, yawning. I had finally given in and powered up my workstation, so I needed to shake the morning's fatigue. 'It's not like they would add that to a speech and not mean it.'

I had spent enough time replaying the morning's activities in my mind, it was time for my actual shift.

And my piping hot—and mediocre at best—coffee had just about cooled enough to be of some use.

The second my gate began powering up a queue had formed. It was going to be a busy day.

At least everyone looked just as jaded as myself. Solidarity.

Although passing through a gate for the several-hundredth time was nothing to write home about, I still got a small flutter of excitement in my chest on occasion. Travel felt almost instantaneous, although actual times varied from two to five seconds, gate to gate. Something to do with slight time distortions at such speed of travel, or so I was led to believe.

The only way you would even realise you had passed through a gate was the momentary refocusing of your vision. It was like walking from a dark to a light room; it just took that split second for you to react.

Most people just passed through the gate at pace once they gave me their destination, never breaking stride or pausing to acknowledge they had just travelled at a speed akin to a superhero.

But not me. I enjoyed it. I would pass as slowly as possible, much to the ire of other travellers.

I always thought that maybe, just maybe, if I found that sweet spot right in the middle, I could exist in two places at once. To me, it was as enjoyable as attempting to fight an anaesthetic. I always thought I could do it, but it was quite impossible.

Physics be damned.

As usual, every transition was incredibly smooth. Instantaneous travel from point A to point B. Perfect.

Boring even.

I had even blinked on my way back to the Hub that morning, missing the slight blur of light that appears in your peripheral vision if you move slowly enough. A distortion of light coming from either end of the slipway, I guessed. To me, it always appeared as streaks of blue and green flowing like water around me, seemingly independent of the gate's ambient light. It was beautiful to be wrapped momentarily in pure colour.

The Hub was busy that day, as expected, and throughout my shift people appeared and disappeared all around me as the gates buzzed with activity.

The larger Hubs resembled an apiary, with each beehive-shaped slipway gate a constant source of motion and activity. There was no reason for the gates to be beehive shaped, but the inventors had been huge fans of a classic sci-fi movie about teleportation apparently and opted for the retro look. The Hubs themselves were about as contemporary as they could be. They were huge and had an open hexagonal floor plan. The glossy white walls and floor clashed with brushed metal railings and furniture at every turn. It looked sterile, just as they liked it.

As usual, the people passed quickly but the hours moved slowly. A group of elderly ex-nurses on a trip to Las Vegas had kept my imagination flowing. I wondered what type of shenanigans they might have gotten up to in the city of sin.

Commuter in—Ping.

Commuter out—Pong.

A repetitive rhythm playing out from my computer daily, matched with a visual pop of pixels on my display. Ping, pong. Ping, pong. Ping, pong. A continuous serenade of acknowledgement. I was so used to the sound that it almost seemed strange if I found a moment of silence at my station. "Institutionalised" seemed a fitting description for my auditory affliction.

Nearing the end of my shift, watching people ping from one dot to another on my display, I stole a quick glance at my AMI, the shiny, brand spanking new arm-mounted interface—colloquially called Amy—now adorning my left forearm. It was almost quitting time. Boredom levels may have been at a record high, but I was excited for the night ahead.

I had always loved to celebrate Leap Day, February 29th. A meaningless day to most, but to me and my older brother, Dan, it was fantastic.

When we were teenagers, Dan and I decided that anything that rolled around only once every four years was worth some sort of celebration. And what better way to celebrate than a box of semi-legal fireworks and a twelve-pack of the cheapest beer we could find. Each.

It was our longest standing tradition, and I had spent much of my shift daydreaming of impending inebriation.

'Only a few minutes until freedom,' I told myself as I began cleaning up my station. The other gates close by had already finished up. The closest gate to me was operated by Samantha, or Sam, as she demanded she be called. She had already clocked out and flipped me off while dancing her way through the lobby to head home, already sporting her after work "out out" wig. She was my only real friend amongst the other less-than-social Saints, and my sanity was often held together by her and her endearing nonsense. She had even been the person to show me how to improve the coffee machine's barista talents with a little algorithm change, so I was forever in her debt. Even if it did often cause me to be reprimanded when caught tinkering with the machine.

Looking up from the screen of my AMI, the newest purchase that I was just dying to show off to Dan, I locked eyes with a beautiful young woman approaching the gate.

I wasn't finished just yet.

'Hi there, destination please?'

'Hub 3, please.'

A strange request considering the Hub-to-Hub automated gates. Typically, they were favoured by commuters to avoid interaction with us Saints.

'Sure thing. Eh, is there an issue with the automated gates?'

'No,' she replied with a slight smirk, 'I just thought you looked like a trustworthy Saint who would ensure my safe travel.'

An obvious exaggeration of my duties, but I enjoyed the playful compliment.

'I wouldn't be so sure. I once sent an old married couple to a rave in Tahiti. Not a hint of a complaint though, heard the wife loved it. Who wants an average diamond anniversary anyway, right?' Absolute fiction every word, but it was fun to josh around a little. 'Any accidental holiday destinations pique your curiosity?'

A growing smile showed my wit had landed. If only for a moment.

'Don't tempt me. I'm late enough for dinner with my parents as it is; they'll be ordering without me.'

'Of course, we can't have that. Hub 3 straight away.'

Our moment cut shorter than I would have liked, I sent her on her way with a small wave.

Commuter in—Ping.

Commuter out—

. Nothing.

Silence. I scanned my monitor for evidence of an arrival. Maybe I had actually sent her to Tahiti in my flirtatious haze.

Blank. The display showed normal operation, simply awaiting a further command. The system remained idle, the speakers hushed.

My gut tightened as I felt a slight tremble run up my right arm.

Grabbing my headset, I hastily input the code for a line directly to Hub 3.

'Hub 3, David—'

The calmness of the receiver did nothing to reign in my fear as I cut him short.

'Has a commuter just arrived from gate 29-810 in Hub 29?'

He paused for only a few seconds to check, but I had already chewed my lip hard enough for a slight iron taste to appear in my mouth by the time he answered.

'No, sorry, nothing on this end. Are you sure—'

I hung up.

Nothing.

The screen was blank. No record. No trail. No woman.

She was gone.

I had never lost somebody before.

Chapter 2

A hiccup.

A mild annoyance. A momentary disruption to your day. By definition, nothing more than an awkward gulp of air, an involuntary contraction of your diaphragm. In no way harmful. Everybody gets them, and everybody has a fun or quirky method of how to treat them.

A hiccup. An unexciting term for a run-of-the-mill irritation.

WormWhole article 2.7 of the employee handbook also referenced hiccups.

"A hiccup is a momentary disruption to a slipway, generated by a wide variety of complex and uncontrollable events, including but not restricted to: momentary power loss [at either gateway], 'ghosts' in the plotting course computational code, excessive radiation expelled from the sun (coronal mass ejections)."

A soft, almost personal term, likely chosen to ensure the minimal public backlash when a commuter is reported as lost in transit.

Hiccups were rare. I had only been aware of three

incidents at other gates in Hub 29 since I began working. I had no idea how many occur yearly in other Hubs, but the numbers could hardly be much higher.

But, on several occasions over the previous 30 years, relatively large-scale losses had been recorded in a short space of time.

A couple of hundred people were lost in each event, all travelling to separate destinations from unrelated origins. No real causes were ever attributed to these mass malfunctions, at least none outside of the textbook excuses.

Media attacks on the system's safety record were never long-lived. Families would campaign, petitions would be signed, and local government would puff their chests. In retaliation, WormWhole would, in turn, promise perfection of services, hire additional temporary engineers, and compensate those affected. But outside of this, nothing changed.

If it wasn't you, or somebody you knew, why worry?

An ignorance born of historical comparison.

Automotive travel—the old standard of transportation—had come with a heavy cost of life. Typically, over the course of a year in the early 2000s, hundreds of thousands of people lost their lives in automotive accidents. It was an inconceivable death toll by today's standards.

Compared to this, occasional accidents on the slipway were considered negligible.

The gates were the safest, that was a fact. After all, it was in the handbook. And handbooks don't lie.

Especially not handbooks published by the very company responsible for the gates.

A near flawless system, with just an occasional hiccup.

That fact wasn't lost on me. I knew the safety of the gate network was unparalleled, and I had no fear of travel myself.

But that didn't help me feel any less unhappy.

Four days of paid leave and counselling was my sentence. It may have only been for an hour each day, but it was monotonous enough to feel like a full nine to five. Company funded of course. Funded, and mandatory.

"Hiccup."

It played on a loop in my head as I crossed the bland brown waiting room to attend my each "therapy" session.

Dr Singh was the therapist I was referred to. She was an older woman, with a kind and motherly demeanour, and an obvious perfume addiction. I specifically inhaled through my mouth when she was near.

But after it all, I still questioned my attention to detail that day.

We had reached the end of my attendance, and as she ran through her recap of our sessions, I positioned myself upright on her brown faux leather couch to appear engaged. But my mind still wandered.

Could I have made a mistake?

Unknown to the general public, the inputs I had actual control over were basic. A gate's interface is

designed to be streamlined, graphically controlled using gestures as opposed to physical keys. A selection
of maps, similar in design to the old London Underground schematics, linked the world's array of slipway
gates. Our roles as Saints were almost superficial;
people just wanted the personal touch to their commute. Maybe it was a trust thing.

Making any important mistakes was impossible for
a Saint. But how could I be sure?

I hadn't mourned the lost commuter, not really. I
didn't know her, and I never would. But the situation
had left me deeply unsettled, despite what I relayed
to the therapist.

And, as selfish as it was, I couldn't stop feeling
sorry for myself too. That this had happened to me. It
was my gate, my responsibility. My duty. I had failed.

I didn't dream about her, even though I felt like
I should, after what happened. But I missed enough
sleep thinking about what happened to consider my
fantasies akin to nightmares. I simply lay in bed every
night since, playing out a variety of possibilities in my
imagination before eventually succumbing to fatigue.

What could happen to somebody lost in transit?

Were they simply disintegrated, destroyed in an
instant, ignorant of any dread or impending doom?

Were they catapulted into the molten core of our
planet mid-journey, suffering a moment of extreme
pain and horror before being crushed under the weight
of an entire planet?

Maybe they were simply still there, in the slipway.

Stranded, but unaware. Exempt from time as we understand it. Perhaps they could re-emerge one day, hundreds of years from now, assuming the world to have waited with them.

Alive or dead, none of the spiralling fabrications of my imagination gave any real answers. The young woman was gone. Her family, devastated. They couldn't even cremate her, just hope instead that through some divine intervention she would miraculously arrive at her destination someday. Yet they must use the same gate network that stole their precious daughter, sister, and niece to go and pay their respects to her.

They knew these things happened. Just no one ever thinks it will.

My few days offline were finished, and I would soon return to Hub 29. I didn't feel any anxiety towards returning to my station. At least, not yet. I felt more focused, if anything.

Not on work. I had a plan, and like most of my previous work, it would be better to seek forgiveness if I got caught than to ask permission.

As I left Dr Singh for the last time, shaking hands and signing waivers, my mind was happily distracted, a welcome change to the more recent daydreams. Tonight was the "final hurrah to the mid-twenties" as Dan called it. He was turning twenty-nine—not exactly mid-twenties, but he refused to acknowledge that. He had a deep hatred for aging, and preferred to live as young at heart as he could. We had skipped our leap-year festivities due to my lost commuter, but

I felt like now I could at least enjoy getting out and meeting up with our friends.

No parents, however. Not this year. Even with almost instant access to the world, they rarely ventured outside of their country home in Galway. They preferred their world to be within walking distance, even though technically our whole planet was.

Possibly for the best. Our parents were a bit elderly, and loud parties weren't their style. When they visited, on the rare occasion, they would almost time their interactions. The deadline was always 5 p.m., always. It didn't matter what stage the conversation was in. When the hour struck, that was that. Up and out at a speed you would have thought lost to people of their age. Crumbs and lukewarm tea were the only gifts left behind.

I arrived home in what felt like an instant, thoughts of Dan's party dancing in my mind. I was headed straight for the shower, anxious to be rid of the remnants of bioweapon-grade perfume that still clung to my skin and clothes.

My apartment was never well lived in. I liked to lead an active life so was hardly ever home. But as I crossed the main lounge area, disrobing as I proceeded, it was obvious a clean was long overdue. A healthy amount of air freshener gave it the veneer of cleanliness, for now, but I had to confess even that was beginning to fade at this point.

'Future Leon's problem,' I sighed to myself.

It didn't take long to get ready for the party. In fact,

most of my time was dedicated to drawing a hat and a monocle on the glass to class up my reflection in the bathroom mirror. Dan always thought I was weird keeping markers beside my toothbrush, but I doubted his bathroom routine was as entertaining as mine.

I had planned my arrival to be suitably late, so as not to be one of the first attendees. It was mainly to toy with Dan, who was always a bit worried people wouldn't show, but also I loved a party to be in full swing on arrival.

Once I was ready, having teased my hair into a precarious mixture of messy and kept, I threw on best shirt and trousers, doused myself in an aftershave Dan had bought for me the previous Christmas, and left.

I floated through the gate network as slowly as possible, forcing my eyes to stay open to catch the waves of colour rushing around me as I commuted. Mint and azure ripples, swirling only for a moment before reality regained control.

Appropriately late, I could hear the music as I approached Dan's doorway. A distinct smell of finger food wafted from beneath the doorframe.

Dan always had terrible taste in food, and the smell did nothing to encourage a different mindset.

I entered, brushing past several people congregating near the doorway. Busier than expected, but, then again, Dan was the popular one.

I slid through the room as stealthily as possible, making sure to gain a surprise advantage on the man of the hour. Sneaking up on Dan, tiptoeing like a cartoon villain for effect, I hit him with a combo bearhug-tackle. Then, in anticipation of his reaction, I spun off and headed straight for the kitchen. After all, the alcohol was there, and Dan was only so important. I heard him as I slunk away: 'Yeah, you're a funny man, Leon. Spilt my damn drink...'

The night couldn't have been more perfect. I chatted. I drank. I revelled in the oily glow of Dan's retro, green neon beer sign. Long had I coveted that foolish purchase. Several of our mutual friends from home were also in attendance, and we spent the guts of a few hours regaling one another with tales of Dan's time in boarding school.

Every story started with something similar. "Oh man, do you remember," or "I know it was technically illegal," or my favourite, "I don't fully believe it, but apparently."

I always thought the refurbished chemistry laboratory should have been named after him. After all, a freezer was a difficult place to cause an explosion.

Deciding it was time to put in a bit of one-on-one with Dan, I left our friends to their increasingly slurred anecdotal one-upping.

I had always felt Dan's apartment had quite a grand appeal to it. It felt huge. An open-plan design with a cream interior, but barely any furniture so as to maximise the floor space. Only the furniture attempted to upset the colour scheme, as the black leather couches stood out boldly against the soft surrounding. He could thank his last partner for the decorating, because Dan was about as useless as me at such things.

As I made my way through the crowd, I spotted the merry host in the corner. But just as I was about to reach him, a sharp tug on my collar from behind stopped me.

'Hey, Leo!'

Caught off guard by the surprise attack, my drink slipped from my grasp. A last-minute correction allowed me to grasp the slimmer neck of the bottle as my beer preservation instincts appeared to be intact still. It would not have been a good time for embarrassment.

I spun to face my assailant.

Standing a good foot below eye level was Jessica, the crown jewel of Dan's inner circle of friends. Her hair was auburn with a shine of crimson, and the green hue of Dan's neon sign positioned behind her gave Jess an extra-terrestrial glow. She was smirking of course, her eyes big and wide as always, highlighting their brilliant sapphire.

She looked both mischievious and angelic. I had just finished my seventh beer, so it was hard to decide which was most prevalent.

But one thing never changed, she was stunning. I rarely got flustered when it came to the opposite sex, but even I could recognise the severe lack of cool I had around her.

'Hey Jess. I was wondering when you were going to pop your head in; took your sweet time.'

'I thought you of all people would appreciate a late entrance, Leo.' Her dimples flaired as she teased me.

Nobody called me Leo, but I was flattered by her need to shorten my already clearly lengthy name.

She continued, 'I'm only here a few minutes, very strict hours in the zoo you know.'

'Oh right, Dan said you'd upgraded your BioDev geek status to Supreme Chancellor. His words, not mine, of course. I'm surprised they let you out at all.'

Jess tried her best to force her face into a frown from a smirk, but my tease had hit home.

'Neither you nor your brother can ever call anyone a geek.' Her tone was full on mocking and accompanied by erratic hand gesturing. 'MIT nerds the two of you... But yes, the almighty BioDemons enjoy their funny work schedules. Feels like we slave away solstice to solstice most days in there.'

I wouldn't know anything about that. I clocked out the second my shift ended every day. Overtime was not a thing for a Saint—in fact, they actively discouraged it.

'But I see Dan is moving up in the world at least,' she added. 'Computational epidemiology department in London, he was saying?'

I had almost forgotten Dan was starting in his new job the following day. He would definitely be feeling the party the next morning, one-part regret and two-parts nausea no doubt. He had a hangover scale he would text me every morning after a large night out. Everything below 70% was acceptable, anything above meant no ability to eat for the day. And 100% meant most likely unable to hold down even water. I always enjoyed his post-night-out morning text; it made my own hangover feel better.

'I know, he's really been looking forward to it, I think.' I hadn't actually asked him about it properly yet. I hoped it didn't come across as disinterest. 'But you're in Brussels, right, in tissue regen?'

Before she could answer, I could see a glimpse of impending doom. I could tell immediately by the staggered gait and slouched shoulders. Disaster Dan was approaching.

'Jess, how the hell are you!'

A bouquet of whiskey aromas accompanied every word.

'Took your sweet time I see. Typical.' His eyes darted between Jess and me for a moment. 'But I see my little bro found you quickly enough. Funny that...'

No matter how much I focussed, I lacked the telekinetic ability to shut Dan's mouth magically.

'...I'm sure it has nothing to do with him pining on about you, as usual.' He swivelled his head towards me, smirking from cheek to cheek. 'Just get on and seduce him already, would you? He's easy.'

And there we had it. A dose of instant awkward, straight from the grinning birthday boy.

Not that Jess would ever have had to seduce me. Seduction involved a certain initial unwillingness from the involved party, a resistance against the incoming affection. I, on the other hand, was prepared to skip all normal courting practice and give her a key to my apartment.

Maybe hiding those markers wasn't the worst idea, in hindsight.

Jess was quick with her rebuttal, 'Actually, Dan, speaking of seduction, isn't that Damian over there talking to James?'

It took several seconds for him to process the information, but once he had, Dan spun on his heels and was mobile once more. Had Jess just figured out Disaster Dan's off switch? And who was Damian? Questions for another time, I told myself as I turned back to Jess. She was contentedly sipping on her wine.

I let a slight chuckle out in appreciation of her lightening of the mood.

'Let's grab a drink and head out to the balcony, it's a bit warm in here.' I gestured towards the kitchen, where we grabbed some drinks before heading outside.

I didn't want to let Dan's outburst get the better of me. I had always genuinely enjoyed Jess's company, and romantic interest reciprocated or not, I never saw that changing.

We chatted for hours, with only minor interruption by an increasingly drunk brother. I told her about my time at MIT, what young Dan was like, my family in Galway. She filled me in on her beginnings in BioDev, her time spent at the Technical University of Berlin, and her love of travel. I knew everybody could travel to most of the world on a whim, but I don't think I had ever met somebody who was so well travelled.

Every story she told was accompanied with wide eyes and a smile. I could see she was almost reliving each adventure through her stories.

When we returned to the party, it was beginning to wind down. Dan was no longer present, likely comatose in bed.

I offered to escort Jess home, so we said our goodbyes and made our way out. I avoided travelling slowly through the gates on the journey to her home. I thought it best not to appear overly eccentric just yet. It took only a moment to reach her apartment block, the journey too quick for my liking.

I sensed our time together was running short.

As she reached to open the door I slightly closed the gap between us. She turned back, smirked, and hugged me around the chest, unable to reach any higher.

But instead of then breaking away, she moved back but kept her arms by my side. Her eyes shone in the bright amber glow of the corridor lighting as she quietly leered at me, her dimples creeping slowly back into show.

Quick as a hare she popped up and gave me a peck on the cheek.

'I had a fun night, Leo. We should do it again sometime soon.'

'Me too.' I was surprised I could articulate through my smile. 'And yeah anytime.'

Nothing else needed to be said. She smiled, and disappeared into her apartment.

I stood for several moments, smirking to myself, before turning to leave.

I floated back through the slipway, green and blue highlights washing around me as I travelled.

Too tired to get undressed I threw myself onto the bed. My head spun from excitement, and possibly the remnants of alcohol in my system.

I wouldn't forget that night anytime soon. For many reasons.

***

I woke in a daze, my familiar array of alarms dragging me from a deep slumber.

The familiar taste of an alcohol fuelled night still clung to my lips. The stale, hops-infused breath was an unwelcome morning trend I was probably too accustomed to.

A message flashing from my AMI brought reality crashing back into perspective. A reminder of a plan set in motion two weeks previously. In my revelry, I had almost forgotten about her. About my lost commuter.

Almost.

I proceeded with my typical morning routines, pausing for a moment to admire the previous night's artwork on the mirror in the bathroom.

It wasn't long before I was out the door in my usual semi-punctual fashion.

Arriving at Hub 29 stung of familiarity. No anxiety,

no nerves at my return. My activities the night before had served to settle my disposition more than expected. I didn't feel like I had really been away at all.

Grabbing a quick snack and some much-needed coffee, I ventured casually over to my idle gate station. It was several minutes to go until operation. Perfect.

I was on the early shift today. None of the usual characters occupied their stations yet. I rotated in my seat nonchalantly, scanning my immediate area for any potentially unwanted guests.

All clear.

Shooting below my gates console, I pulled out the small stash of tools kept there by the ever-elusive engineer core, spreading them across the floor. Quick access to them would be required.

As steadily as I could, while attempting to keep one eye on my surroundings, I began removing the small panels lining the area under the workstation.

Sam, although cautiously intrigued by the request, had mailed me a detailed explanation of how to remove all the panelling. And there was only one thing to watch out for really, if Sam's wealth of knowledge was any use. Each panel had a removable sensor, installed to activate an alarm if a panel was unexpectedly removed. A security device to stop criminals from accessing internal components we were told. What would criminals possibly want from our stations though?

I didn't have the clearance to disable the alarms

through the console, so instead the painfully slower pulling-teeth method would have to suffice.

The panelling was quite intricate. It took several moments per panel to carefully navigate a pin to disconnect each sensor, an easier process than I predicted, but time-consuming. Sam's knowledge was proving infallible, no doubt she had first-hand experience.

Finally, through patience and dexterity, the panels were removed. I sprung like a meerkat from under my console, scouting my immediate area. Business as usual still.

I may not have been able to join the WormWhole engineering department just yet, but my education as an engineer was proving useful. The console's innards were a maze of wires, ports, LED-lit processing units, and liquid cooling tubes. It would have been intimidating to someone who had never seen it before, but for once the detailed schematics in our textbooks had come in use. And also, what I needed was luckily housed at the closest point of the circuitry. A small port with a generic connection, likely used for simple diagnostics.

A small vibration from my AMI warned I only had a minute left until gate activation. Finally, and unwelcomely, my anxiety began to arrive.

Soon my absence would be noticed.

I plugged my AMI into the port. The display lit up with a variety of options on the holoscreen, but only one cluster of information was needed: the operational source code of the gate, a simple, constant stream of data comprised of the processes the gate performs while under use. The code consisted of the exact inputs, outputs, and computational calculations required to deliver a commuter safely to their destination. Engineers often used the data in assessing the need for system re-calibration.

I, however, was not running a diagnostic. I didn't need raw computational data to better calibrate my system. I needed a clue as to what goes wrong during a hiccup. Everything is logged by the system. Every process is monitored, every output or input catalogued. Every feature of the slipway and the commuter would be tracked and stored.

The answer had to be there somewhere. I could think of no other way I could possibly figure out what had happened. What had really happened. And I couldn't go through official channels to access the information either. Sam had made that very clear.

I found the appropriate date almost immediately. It helped that my station had been inactive since my departure. A few gestures and the download began. Despite the unusually large size of the data being transferred it took only a moment to complete. I couldn't help but slap myself on the knee in celebration of my achievement. It was all going to plan.

'Are you alright there, Leon?'

I launched myself out from underneath the console, smashing my head off the underside of my station as I went.

I was caught.

Falling back to the floor in an uncomfortable slump, I shot a glance up at my discoverer while feverishly trying to rub the pain away from the back of my head.

It was Gerry, one of the Hub security guards. He was a nice guy, but I didn't know him very well. I knew him to take his job seriously though. Not the person I wanted to see right then.

'Sorry, Gerry, just hit my head there.' I continued rubbing my head, attempting to keep his focus on me as opposed to the station. 'What's up?'

A small trickle of moisture ran down the back of my neck. I hoped it was just sweat.

'Yeah, I heard that, sounded like quite the bang.' Gerry released a loud guffaw. 'You alright?'

'Yeah...yeah sorry, was just in my own little world there.'

'Sorry I startled you, but you have some visitors, and I was just making sure everything was okay. You know, after...'

I knew what he meant, but I chose to ignore it. Peering around him, several commuters were stood waiting just beyond the gate. They displayed a variety of irate expressions, not accustomed to being delayed for the slightest moment.

'Oh right, sorry about that Gerry. One of the engineers must have left his tools lying about. I was just putting them away.'

From my vantage point, it appeared Gerry couldn't

see the removed panels or the opening to the system core. I hoped my poker face would boost my bluff.

'Yeah, they're a strange bunch, those engineers. Come in like a whirlwind and rarely clean up their mess. Do you need a hand?'

I slammed the toolbox shut, despite its occupants still littering the floor beside my feet.

'No no, I'm just finished. Sorry for the delay, I must have been daydreaming or something, lost track of time.'

'That's okay, Leon.' His voice was softer all of a sudden. 'I don't blame you for being a little distracted, all things considered. I'll tell these people you were just setting up a little late and they'll be on their way in a jiffy.'

'Okay perfect, thanks, Gerry. I'll boot up now, and we'll be good to go.'

Disaster averted. No alarms. No arrest. Just a sore head and a moment of panic, but I had what I needed. I hoped.

After powering up my gate, I began ushering forth my commuters. A sweet symphony of pings and pongs began to ring out from the system. I hadn't expected the sound to be so calming, but it was a relief to hear.

The day quickly became mundane, indiscernible from all that came before it. All but that one day.

I focussed on the future, that day was gone I reminded myself. I had the data now. And with it, maybe, just maybe, I could figure out what happened that day.

At least, that was the plan.

Chapter 3

Three weeks I spent sifting through that damned hiccup code I stole. Three weeks of frustration after frustration. All that time, every free minute of every day, wasted.

The missing commuter seemed more lost than ever.

I isolated what familiar processes I could in the code, but hardly scraped the surface of the monstrous data cluster. I couldn't believe my eyes when I first extracted the file. Typically, gate processes were logical, based on dynamic commuter specific variables and established operating instructions. Volume, mass, destination, all the information needed to form the slipway in that instance.

But not this.

Although the disappearance of the commuter seemed instantaneous to me, the system appeared to have fought the corrupting code a near endless number of times before being overcome. Line after line of recalculations, screens upon screens full of redundancies attempting to correct the festering breakdown of the slipway.

But it was all for nought.

I grew to appreciate the system's various attempts to protect its traveller. I wondered how often commuters had been saved by the system's robust backups.

Apart from the initial inputs, and subsequent attempts at rerouting, the code was alien to me. Gibberish. But I wasn't alone in my frustration. I had spent the entire Friday in Sam's apartment after I acquired the code. Sam always leapt at the chance to fool around with WormWhole tech. It almost seemed like she had a personal vendetta against her employer at times.

But this time was different. I had planned to work the project alone, but Sam knew something was up when I asked how to remove the gates system panelling. She became insufferably involved almost immediately.

'Let's do this!' A simple message that I received hourly for the days following the code's extraction, accompanied by an exponentially increasing amount of exclamation marks per message.

I swear, at times it almost felt like she had tricked me into the whole idea somehow, she was just that pushy.

Resistance was pointless.

But to be fair, you couldn't have asked for a better partner. Sam's home computer setup was beyond belief. How in the world she ever could afford it was beyond me, but it made the job seem infinitely more achievable with all that processing power. And even though we were both on a similar standing as Saints, Sam always just had an air of confident intelligence about her. It really made the task appear more achievable.

At first.

We scanned through the entirety of the code together, taking almost a full 24 hours one of the days, with two rounds of fast food fuelling our endeavour. We tried to match every segment of code to standard system processes. We even tried matching it with older slipway coding, unused beta coding, basic textbook coding, everything we could think of trying. It didn't matter how obscure the plan, we tried them all. We worked on it together, we worked separately, we worked hour shifts on and off. Anything to keep us fresh and focussed.

Nothing.

It was like trying to solve a single colour jigsaw. We would find a random assortment of pieces that seemed to fit together perfectly, but the further we went down those rabbit holes, the more apparent it became that we were simply matching pieces up at random. Nothing truly fit together. It was nothing more than wishful thinking bridging the gap between useful information and utter garbage.

Our eyes could hardly stand to look at the constant stream of figures by the end of our third marathon session, and our perseverance remained unrewarded.

'We're probably not the first to try to sort this, y'know,' Sam said when I left her apartment. 'If it were easy, I guess they would have just sorted it themselves by now. Don't beat yourself up about it, it ain't over yet.'

It was easy for her to say. She was just being a good friend.

But I had let my commuter down.

Again.

Regardless of our failure, I had kept the code with me, on my AMI. I thought that patterns would begin to emerge if I knew the hiccup code well enough. But the data packet was humongous, and without a real structure to the gibberish, the code still seemed almost as random as the first time I laid eyes on it.

As I finished the third week of trying to make sense of it, I could feel my focus drifting. It was becoming hard not to get disheartened at the lack of progress.

At MIT I learned all about the coding used in gate-to-gate slipway generation. We were educated almost to become a jack-of-all-trades when it came to gate operation.

Hell, I could probably build my own.

There was always a great call for well-educated graduates to take up a Saint's role. The public preferred the idea that the gates were all managed by competent staff. I guess the general populace didn't like the idea of just anyone having control over them as they slingshot around the world. Overeducation was a standard for most Saints.

Internal hiring was how they managed it. You could only join their engineering ranks if you started somewhere else in the company. You had to do your time as it was. But that didn't stop "a waste of talent" being a common phrase thrown around during family visits. Not everyone was happy that upon graduating I "settled" with a position as a Saint. But they just didn't understand what needed to be done, so I tried not to take it too personally.

But even Sam and my combined knowledge couldn't crack the code. Not even close.

I couldn't help but feel foolish. I risked my job to get that code, and for what? A chance at solving an unsolvable issue? Why did I discredit that pamphlet information so quickly, where did the self-assured hubris come from on that day that I decided I could solve this problem?

I needed to purge. To get away from it all and have a night without obsessing.

Thankfully, my attention was being pulled to another pressing matter. One just about a foot shy of eye level.

Jessica.

I had been in near constant contact with Jess since Dan's party—of which he has only partial memory, but luckily only registered a 60% on the hangover scale for his first day in the new job. Although Jess remained under a heavy workload, we had managed to carve out a plan for a trip to a great coffee bar in Palermo that Tuesday evening. I had no idea how she had come across this "hidden gem," as she called it, but I was promised a detailed report on more of her travels when we met.

I woke up before my alarm that morning, excited by the prospect of seeing her again.

My morning routine had returned to normal. The mirror drawings had even gotten more intricate, spurred by the addition of a few coloured markers— borrowed from the unwitting duty managers in my Hub. I was sure they wouldn't be missed.

I made my way to the Hub earlier than usual. Sam had messaged me to come "say hello" before the shift started. An unusual request, but I had spent more time with her than usual over the last while, so I was warming to her multitude of quirks.

After picking up some liquid energy from the coffee dispenser, I sauntered over to Sam's station.

'The Hub looks a bit busier than usual right?' I asked.

'Yeah yeah yeah. Holiday season or something. Small talk, small talk. But check this out!'

She could hardly contain her excitement. She pointed towards her AMI, wrapped tightly around her left forearm. It looked slightly less comfortable on Sam than on me, bits of her forearm ballooned out at either end. She really needed a fitted version, not that child-sized bit of tech. Hers even looked like more of a battle-worn gauntlet than a modern AMI, especially compared to my sleeker contemporary model.

As I rounded her workstation, the projected screen caught my eye with its web-like interface.

'What's this?' I was almost hesitant. I knew Sam refused to explain anything without feeling that you were at least a little drawn in already.

She chuckled with excitement. 'It's taken me almost a year, a full bloody year, but I nailed it. I finally reverse engineered that protocol band I got from Lucy in Hub security last year.'

Protocol bands were another level of security within the WormWhole hierarchy. Instead of requiring a Saint to program their destination, anyone with a protocol band simply had to approach a gate and allow the system to react. The bands put out a constant low-frequency signal that assumes momentary, but dominant, control over a gate's system, plotting their own course. Once the signal was gone, the gate reverted to operator control.

It was a two-pronged safety measure, ensuring that the Saint on duty knew nothing of the destination, and making sure the commuter could not be followed easily. To me, it was overkill, but the people who possessed the bands must have been very important.

'What do you mean, reverse engineered?'

'Here, link your AMI to mine. It's easier to show you.' She rushed the words, her eagerness running high.

I allowed Sam to transfer the program files, although I was wary of her intentions. She had once installed a midday alarm on my AMI, which, when activated, played some rather erotic-sounding music files. And loudly.

I was at my parents' house when the alarm had gone off the first time.

Once the transfer completed, I booted up the program, and a projection similar to Sam's appeared immediately.

'Recognise the layout?'

Of course I did. I had only been looking at that same schematic for several years. It had just been less apparent on Sam's old-school AMI as her projections had started to look pixelated and discoloured.

I preferred my displays to be fully legible.

'Is this the gate network?' I figured I would continue playing dumb in light of her impressive accomplishment.

'Bingo! I've mixed and matched the protocol algorithms with my own little version of our gate network interface. Awesome right?'

'Wait, how did you get access to the gate interface?'

She grinned wide while pointing under her station's display, 'Oh you know, a little bit of tinkering here and there.'

At least that answered the question of how she knew so much about opening up our stations security panels.

'Wow, Sam, that's actually really cool.' It was pointless to try and hide my genuine fascination.

'I know, right? The protocol bands don't even let you pick a destination, they're all just useless, preset armbands. But with this...'

Sam snapped from excited to serious in the blink

of an eye as she laid out her demands for my participation in beta testing her new application.

'Just don't let any of the upper echelons find you
playing with it, alright? Or anyone for that matter.'

She was right. That little piece of stolen tech could
land us in some hot water. Hotter than I think even
she realized. The managerial presence at Hub 29 may
have been pretty lacking, but every gate in the entire
network was under constant surveillance.

And with that realisation, I looked up, locking eyes
with the camera pointed right back at me.

'Oh, shit...' I let slip, as I tried to move my arm
behind my back subtly and out of view.

Sam, however, simply burst out laughing as she saw
my face drop.

'What's so funny?' My mouth hardly moved while
I tried to remain still. I could only assume that at that
moment I had imagined the security camera to have
vision based purely on motion, like an ever-watchful
T-Rex.

'You don't really think that still works do you?
Please...' Sam continued to giggle.

It was then I noticed the cable running from the
back of the unit. It wasn't noticeable at first, but it
ran the length of the wall, cleverly matching the walls
shaded colour, over to the next closest station.

'Why do you think I never get in trouble for being
late? A slight video feed delay, and voila.' She pointed
over at the next station. 'Susan over there is my stand-
in. Not a perfect match I know, but who are they to

know? They're hardly gonna come down and try to say I was looking a bit slimmer on the security camera last week.'

I didn't even want to question how that could ever have worked. So instead I just sighed heavily, only hinting at my mild disapproval.

That brief moment of fright would do me for the day.

I waved Sam off and returned to my gate.

Only that one shift stood between me and my first proper date with Jess.

It was building to be a hell of a day.

***

The day moved on slowly.

The constant crowd of people appeared bland, even more so than usual. Too many to take note of any outstanding features or clothing. Just a constant stream of the same repetitive small talk and subsequent ping-pong melody.

I was definitely back in the swing of work, for better or worse.

'Hi there, destination please?'

A few moments of unexpected silence snapped me out of my bored haze. The queue of people had been redirected, and only four men remained.

The first of the group had ignored me and moved towards the gate, while one approached me head on.

'Eh, I'm sorry, sir, but the gate won't activate until you've given me a destination.'

He shot me a blank glance before turning back, fixated on a point on the gate.

I turned back towards the other three, wondering if I had missed something.

Just as I turned, the second man was rounding the dividers to my side of the station.

'Sorry sir, but you can't come back—'

Pain ripped through my cheekbone as two quick blows connected, followed swiftly by a third with something cold and incredibly hard. I shifted my weight to try and turn away from the attack but was pulled and shoved back into the chair by the collar of my shirt. I could feel the same cold metal pushed against the side of my right temple as he held me by the back of my neck, half choking me in the process.

'Shut up, kid. This will all be over soon.'

His voice was calm, almost unassuming. It didn't match the violence that he had just demonstrated. It was hard to understand him as my face throbbed, the pain overloaded my other senses tenfold.

'Now, I want you to give me access to the systems admin account.'

He forced my head down towards the system's display as he talked.

'Do it, and do it fast, kid.'

I hesitated, still confused and terrified by the situation.

He pushed the metal object harder against my

head. I began accessing the systems administrator login, the swelling around my eye slowly growing and obstructing my vision. Just as the eye began to close completely, I shifted my gaze to try and catch a glimpse of the man, and what he was holding against my face.

I couldn't get a clear look at it. But as I looked back to my display, the reflection off the gloss black finish of the workstation betrayed the identity of the foreign object.

It was a gun.

I didn't know what to think. What to feel. I sunk in the seat, frozen. I had never had a moment of complete pause, to be totally blank. No thoughts, no feelings.

Panic and terror seemed inferior emotions for the occasion. The first semblance of a reaction came as a trembling in my legs, now independent of my motor functions.

As my senses slowly returned, my hands were damp with cold sweat.

'I... please, just take it easy—'

'Shut the fuck up,' he whispered, almost hissing the words at me through his teeth. 'You scream, you dream, kid.'

I heard a large thud close by, something metal hitting the floor, but I couldn't look as my attention was firmly on my work console and trying not to get shot. I could see from my peripherals that the first man was returning from the gate, mumbling to himself.

I felt the hard press of metal against my face once again.

'Now listen closely, *Saint*. You are going to give me access, and I am going to watch you. One slip, one flinch, one stray input, and I decorate this screen with your deepest thoughts, get me?'

His threats were almost meaningless by then. I don't think I could have been pushed further into fear. I could almost feel my clothes becoming heavier with the damp of my cold sweat.

Instead of nodding, or making any noise, I slowly gave a thumbs-up gesture from my console.

'Excellent, so we understand each other. Now be a good kid and hurry the fuck up.'

I fought to regain access to minor motor functions and got to unlocking my systems admin privileges as fast as my fingers allowed. I still didn't understand. My personal account was privy to hardly any actual admin rights on the system.

I looked momentarily to the other two men, still actively shepherding commuters away from my gate. They had worn clothes similar in design to the WormWhole technicians' uniform. The outfits looked homemade, something regular commuters probably wouldn't have noticed.

The first man stood separately. He appeared uncomfortable in his attire, however, shuffling something under his jacket and still mumbling.

'Don't fucking mess with that, you ape!' The

warning seemed to ring with genuine panic from my aggressor. 'Do you want it to go off?'

I threw my gaze back to the screen, my fingers beginning to cramp and seize up hard as I tried to finish my task.

I knew exactly what he meant. I didn't have to see what was under his top to know what it was that was making the man uncomfortable. It was a bomb.

A bomb. In my Hub, at my gate.

Small black dots began to fill my vision as my head began to lighten. Somehow the thought of being turned to a purple mist had further affected me for the worst. Was it silly to be more panicked, considering the similar outcome to a bullet in the head?

My predicament had not technically changed, and yet everything had just become a thousand times worse.

Another glancing blow from the weapon returned my wits, but now I could feel a warm trickle of something running down my neck.

'Hurry the fuck up, you prick!' He was now openly shouting at me. 'Unlock the damn system!'

I continued as best I could. The process would usually only take me a few moments, but my mind was awash with nonsense and scattered thoughts, each coming and going faster than they could be processed, making it nearly impossible to focus.

I recalled glimpses of seemingly futile induction talks, aimed at training us how to deal with dangerous situations. A laughable exercise I had thought, like so many others. There hadn't been a terror attack since the early days of the gate network.

"Always appease," we were told. "Always agree. If in danger don't put yourself in harm's way. There are security protocols in place to protect you and others..."

The scanners!

The scanners detect any incoming hazardous materials. Although primarily for biological threats they all come equipped with measures for detecting a range of dangerous materials.

In the event of explosives or other accelerants attempting to cross the threshold, it catapults them directly to a quarantined area. No exit terminals—only incarceration would await them. They would never achieve their target.

I finish unlocking the station, spurred on by the thought of their impending failure.

But before my momentary smugness could take hold, I found myself reeling from my seat, collapsing hard to the ground. The blow had no doubt been intended to incapacitate me, but instead, I lay sideways on the floor, still conscious, a small crimson pool of blood forming under my cheek.

As I lay in the slowly forming puddle of blood, I was eye to eye with the gate's security scanner, bent and broken, and most importantly, no longer on the machine. The last line of defence, useless. I guess that answered the question of what I had heard hitting the ground previously.

The system began powering up.

'Right, boys, hurry the fuck up, we are out of time.'
The voice was low but panicked, coming from one of
the men dressed as a technician.

'Nearly finished, slow them down.'

After a few moments of quiet from the men, a conversation started up close by, adding another voice. It
was brief but seemed relaxed.

It's hard to describe what happened then. I'm not
sure if you can describe a scuffle based only on
sound. It was rubber screeching and struggling to get
a grip on the floor, followed by muffled shouting, and
a final thud as something soft but heavy hit off the
tiles floor.

It lasted only a few seconds, then silence again.

'We gotta go, now!' Panic saturated every word of
the man.

Without much movement, I bent my head back
around to try and see what was happening. As I looked
up I saw my assailant, now frantically bashing in-
process code. He was locking the system so that the
gate stayed permanently open to some destination.

From his peripheral, he must have noticed my
prying.

'Just in case you get a dumbshit idea and feel like
playing hero,' he announced, quietly enough so that
only the two of us could hear it.

I wasn't sure what he was expecting, I was definitely not moving from my position on the floor until
they had left. Even if I wanted to, my whole face
was on fire with the pain, and I was physically weak

from the blows to the head. I could feel my blood and sweat-soaked shirt was sagging slightly under the added weight of moisture.

'Come on!' another voice shouted from outside my view.

'Nearly there...' he mumbled to himself.

I turned away from the screen as something caught the attention of my one good eye. My AMI was awake, likely activated by my fall, and flashing dimly. I brought my arm closer to my face in an attempt to hide the light from any unwanted attention. Unexpectedly, as I brought it closer, I was suddenly facing my console's system layout.

I must have left Sam's programme running in the background, and it was automatically interacting with the closest gate, just like a protocol band.

Everything was being displayed. His destination, the sequence of operation inputs, every single bit of code was being duplicated on my screen.

Not that it mattered. What could I do but lie there, frozen in panic and pain?

In an almost cruel twist, my mind began to recount the story of the lost commuter as if rubbing salt in the wound of another painful day spent at my gate.

I couldn't help but think, why now? Why heap these negative memories on me now? If fate was fair, these guys would be the ones to disappear into oblivion...

The code!

I had forgotten completely about the code. The

code of a lost traveller. The code that beat Sam and me. The code that makes people vanish into thin air, good, bad, or indifferent.

I still had it.

'Finished! Fucking move, boys!' A quick kick to my right leg gives me another burst of pain, nothing compared to the war zone that was my face. 'Have a nice day, *Saint*.'

There it was again. I thought it was just my hearing the first time, but the way he said "*Saint*" was so...hateful.

Several shots rang out. Not all of which were from close by.

I don't know if it was the new burst of adrenaline from the kick or his derogatory use of the word "Saint," but before I knew it I was half upright, livid, and frantically bashing commands into my AMI.

One thought ran through my head. Would a Saint have allowed these men to continue unchallenged? Not a gate Saint, not a slipway technician, but a Saint. How many people could be hurt, or even killed, and what did I do to try and stop them?

I couldn't have saved that commuter's life, deep down I knew that. But maybe I could do something for someone else.

Before I even knew what I was thinking, my task was finished. I sat back and watched my display as the foul code was injected right into the heart of my gate.

Their safety net, locking the outgoing slipway,

would be their undoing. That evil little man, with all his hate and aggression, had sealed their doom.

I heard the men's boots squeak and thud towards the gate. They fired off a few more rounds, maybe in celebration, or maybe to keep pursuers at bay. I sat, eyes focused on my display, hands trembling.

Sam's program may have been lacking sound, but the melody from my station was unmissable.

Ping. Ping. Ping. Ping.

Those few moments felt like hours. I waited, I prayed, I begged for this to have been worthwhile. That maybe I didn't allow four men to deliver their hatred to some unwitting populous.

The screen remained blank. The speakers, idle.

'A hiccup,' I whispered.

Chapter 4

I could hear the screams now.

The screech of rubber soles echoed all around me, as people fled from my direction. The Hub was deafening with the activity. The alarms were no more than a droning buzz, drowned out by a stampede of panicked commuters.

I had propped myself up against the cold metal of the gate station. Sam was already there, kneeling beside me. She had appeared almost as quickly as the men had disappeared.

The Hub was ringing with ambient noise, but Sam's words were clear and stern.

'Hold still,' she said. An order more than a request.

'Ow, what the hell,' pain again visiting the blinded side of my face.

'Quit squirming, Leon, just hold still.'

Bloodied bandages lay just out of reach at my right leg, as the first aid kit that had gathered dust for so long on the wall had been split open as it was thrown down beside me.

'Jesus, Sam, ease up would you...'

'Just be cool, I know what I'm doing.' Her words seemed only partly directed at myself. 'You've lost a bit of blood, but it doesn't look too bad.'

I looked down. My shirt was unrecognisable, the plaid design now smeared all over with dried maroon.

'Stop dropping your head, Leon, look at me.'

I turned my gaze to Sam. She looked intense. Her eyes scanned me.

'Look, I'm fine, okay?' I gingerly tried to push her back a little. 'Just, help me up or something.'

'Woah, that guy did a number on you. I foresee no beauty pageants in your immediate future.' She didn't even snigger or stutter, so I assumed her cutting remark was more factual than playful. 'Just quit being awkward and let me clean you up.'

I reached a hand up to feel her work. My head was well wrapped, she had done a good job from what I could tell, having not seen it.

'Thanks, I guess, what happened to—'

Before I could get the words out Sam grabbed at my AMI. With a quick gesture she was gliding through the gate program.

'Hey, watch it.'

'Shut up, Leon. What did you do?' Sam's eyes were wide and intimidating.

'What do you mean?' The coordinates from the attempted attack were still being displayed on my AMI. It looked like they had been attempting to travel somewhere just outside Nagoya City, Japan.

'What did you do?' She pulled my arm up to my face, my AMI firmly in her grasp.

Her anxious demeanour made me feel uneasy.

'I used your program,' I said sheepishly.

'To do what?'

'I used the code, Sam. I uploaded it directly to the gate, I made them disappear just like that.' I tried to click my fingers for effect, but the blood on my hand made it too slick.

I expected praise from Sam, but instead, she looked back towards the crowd forming around the two un-conscious security workers. It seemed, so far, we were unnoticed behind my station.

'Look, Leon, you have to delete the code.'

'Delete it? But, why? We've been trying for so long-'

'Just fucking delete it, okay! You can't let them find it. You can't tell them what you did.' I looked at Sam, and she stared right through me. It wasn't anger in her eyes. I couldn't tell what it was really. 'They'll know. Once they come over here to check out the station, they'll know. We're screwed if you still have that hiccup code on you, do you not see that?'

It all came flooding back. The code, the program, the stolen protocol band. Sam was right.

I hadn't even paused to consider the implications of being caught, despite in my mind having done the right thing. We wouldn't just be fired; who knows what they would do to us.

'But...' I had exhausted my excuses. I couldn't jus-tify keeping it.

Sam moved her face closer to mine, and whispered, 'Look, they won't ever see the good of this, Leon. Just trust me, okay? Delete it. Now. My program is deeply embedded and hidden well enough, but the code has to go.'

I didn't know why I felt somewhat protective of the code all of a sudden. I had felt such disdain for it not even an hour ago.

Sam turned from me and began interfacing with the system through her own AMI. Her fingers gestured at speed, and I could see her mumbling.

Just as I hit the delete command, clearing my device, a man stepped around the barrier.

'Mr Murphy?' He turned back out to the crowd, 'Hey, we've got another one! Are you okay?'

The security team had finally come to check on my station, but their timing wasn't welcome. Sam slinked away quickly as the team of first responders rushed around me.

'Here, let us get you over to the med bench.' It was no more a choice than a statement as they whipped me off the ground, away from my puddle of sweat and blood, and bundled me over to a small bench covered in some white tissue-like material. The rapid movement was not exactly standard protocol for someone with a head injury I imagined.

Blinded by the several lights they continued to shine in my face, I couldn't see much of what was happening around me.

'Your friend must work well under pressure, she

covered your wound up nicely.' The female officer poked at my bandages, a little harder than I would have liked.

Who would have thought Sam would be Ms First-aid, I had always assumed her talents lay solely grounded in technology.

'Yeah, she's something else alright.' I rubbed at the bandage again. 'Could have been a bit gentler...'

'No need worrying now, just lay back and take it easy. Somebody will be along to sort you right out soon.'

And with that semi-comforting comment, the officer was gone.

I looked out at the large open foyer of the Hub. People were pushed as far to the extremities as they could manage. The Hub must have been on lockdown if they couldn't leave.

Close by, several people were lying on the floor, but there was no blood that I could see. They must have been hurt in the retreating stampede of panicked commuters, or maybe it had just been shock.

The screaming had stopped, and in its stead soft sobbing filled the air as people attempted to wrap their heads around the recent activity.

I leaned back against the wall, upright in the make-shift cot. I was still feeling the effects of the attack, and my eye was still throbbing and swollen.

I was sat close to the windows of the security office; the people raced back and forth in the room at a speed I could no longer follow. And then they all stopped, and the televisions in the room burst into life.

I shifted to get a closer look with my remaining good eye.

Scrolling messages in a large bright red text filled the lower section of the screen, as newscasters mouthed an inaudible report from my vantage point. So I stood, unbalanced and uneasy, and made my way to the adjacent doorway.

'...explosion ripped through the city, leaving hundreds injured with many predicted to be dead. A coordinated attack such as this has not been reported...'

I stood, mouth agape and hands trembling. The screen was full with imagery of collapsing buildings, fires raging out of control, people covered in burns and blood.

How? I thought. *How did they make it through?*

That damned code. I felt so stupid. How could I have trusted it, it was a complete unknown, a weapon in the hands of a fool. How could I have been so foolish as to think that gibberish could ever have been of use to anyone?

'...Madrid suffering the worst of the blasts. In London, an explosion underground caused huge structural damage to...'

I couldn't get my head around it for a moment. Two locations, two explosions. My attention fell rapidly to the scrawling details below the presenter.

Madrid, Minsk, London, and Seattle. Four different

explosions. I struggled to comprehend what I was witnessing as it unfolded on the screens.

All the death. All that misery.

No mention of Japan though. At least not yet.

Maybe it just hadn't been reported yet. Or maybe something far worse. Could I have duplicated the bombers somehow? A ridiculous hypothesis, but my brain struggled to comprehend the situation.

People still moved frantically around the Hub. Repair crews and other WormWhole branded people filled the space now.

The repair crews congregated mainly around my gate. I could see they were investigating the dismantled security scanner. The other corporate-looking crowd had gathered around my access point, probably trying to figure out anything they could.

I snapped out of my delirium for long enough to remember Sam's warning. I needed to make sure the code was gone.

I looked down to my AMI. It was alight with notifications. Feeling the need to solve my more immediate issue, I dismissed them without a second glance. It took only seconds to check, but the code and every trace of its existence was gone. Most likely alongside my chances of ever solving its mystery.

I sat back down on my makeshift medical bench. My nerves were officially shot, and I was ready to sleep for the rest of the week.

My AMI, still flashing from the sheer mass of ignored notifications was annoying me by now. Just as

I was about to power the whole unit off for a moment of peace, a new message came through. It was from my mother, but not nearly as grammatically coherent as usual.

"HAV U HERD FROM DAN?"

I stayed sitting for a moment, wondering about her intent. Why would I have heard from Dan?

I backed out from the message and into the home screen of my AMI. The mass of messages was overwhelming but most intimidating of all was the missed calls from my mother. She had tried to call 43 times.

If I had learned anything as a child, I was in some serious trouble.

I returned the call as quickly as my AMI would allow. The display picked up just as I began to speak.

'Mam? Hey, sorry I—'

She was unrecognisable. Doubled over, tears and makeup streaming down her face. She wasn't just crying. She was howling.

'Mam? Hey, what the hell is going on? I don't know what you've heard, but I'm okay, it's fine—'

She cut me off, mustering what control she had left to form a coherent sentence.

'Dan...' She struggled the words between fits of sniffling, 'My God, Leon, Dan was in that building.'

***

The funeral wasn't until the following Saturday.

The building in London that had been attacked,

the one that was mostly rubble in the news report, it was the London BioDev headquarters. The building wing Dan was in had collapsed completely.

It had taken days to exhume the bodies.

There were hundreds of people in the BioDev complex. Very few escaped with just injuries. Many bodies were too badly damaged to identify.

The death toll was in the hundreds.

The attacks had all taken place within minutes of one another; there was no chance for escape. It was completely undetected.

Emergency staff arrived at the London site within minutes. But it was useless.

The explosion had come from a lab area underground that the terrorists had somehow accessed. Dan was on one of the upper floors as the building's support gave in and collapsed. The coroner told me we were lucky in a way, that we were somehow blessed that we actually had something to cremate, unlike many other families.

I wanted to hit him.

The weather suited my mood. Dark and still, deathly quiet outside the crematorium, not as much as a rustle of leaves. I stood in a daze, staring out at those in attendance.

Our family was small, but Dan had many friends.

Jess was there too. She had abandoned the others on arrival and had been firmly grasping my arm ever since. I was grateful to her for the gesture, but I knew it wasn't just for my sake, it was for us both.

My mother, draped in her black clothes, clung to my father like an extra shadow, never parting from his arm for even a moment. He stood strong, ever the stoic example of how to act, acknowledging the condolences.

It was all an act, a stance of strength for the benefit of the others in attendance. But even the greatest actors break character. And as the casket moved into the incinerator, my father's limits were reached.

It was the first time I had ever witnessed him display any serious emotion. I turned to him, right as the casket was engulfed, looking for him to ground me.

But instead, he stood there, streams of tears running unchecked down his face, dripping from his chin. He was distraught. Frail.

It shook me to my core. I don't know what it was about seeing my father cry, but it cut deeper than I could have imagined, deeper than I could protect against.

It wasn't that I held archaic family values, or that he had stood as my hero or something to aspire to in life. If anything, that's more how I regarded my mother. But I had always just respected his ability to stand firm, no matter the situation. He was always a constant before now. Logic over emotion.

But this was uncharted waters.

It wasn't until Jess rubbed a tear from my cheek that I realised I was crying too.

You often hear people speak of moments so intense, so visceral, that they appear to endure for an impossible length of time, where in reality it was a mere few seconds. But not this.

In a flash, he was gone.

And I was alone.

***

After the ceremony, we returned to my family home. The few relatives we had took their place in our small house. I had remained sitting in the dining room for an hour or so, shaking hands with the convocation of locals and friends passing on their condolences.

Jess had hung around and was helping my mother serve out the several hundred sandwiches that had been brought by friends and neighbours.

At the first break in the melancholy procession, I escaped to Dan's old room.

I sat on the end of his bed, face in hand, trying to calm the slight quake starting in my right leg.

I could feel the collar under my chin had lost almost all its rigidity and had become slightly cold to the touch from the tears that dampened it.

Still, it felt good to have a few minutes to myself, even if it was just for a solitary weep.

I lay back on the bed, kicking up just the smallest plume of fine dust. It was all so familiar. Dan's room had always had a unique quality to it, from the odour to the decorations. I never did get his novelty troll doll obsession, but he had an army of the things across the window sills. As for the smell, it could only be described as lavender and gym bag. He had stayed a few nights at home only recently, so the scent was still present.

It was misleadingly comforting. Like he had simply stepped out and would be back any moment.

How many times had I snuck into his room as a kid, scared of the dark, just to sleep beside him? It was my comfort zone, much to his indignation having to share a single bed.

But just as the fatigue of the day started to creep up on me, a polite knock came on the door.

It was Jess, petite and proper, poking her head through the cracked door. 'Hey, can I join you?'

I tried to be subtle wiping the mostly crystalised tears from my cheek as I sat up to face her. 'Yeah, sorry, it was just getting a bit too...blah down there, if that even makes sense.'

She made her way over to the bed, sitting down beside me.

'So, this is Dan's room?' She looked around taking it all in. 'What's the deal with the hairy punk Smurf dolls?'

I couldn't help but smirk. 'You know, I never once thought to ask him. Don't think I really wanted to know. Weird, right?'

I could feel her grinning as her face was pressed close to my shoulder. 'Dan was weird.'

'I know.' I let just the slightest wisp of a chuckle out. 'He liked to call himself "limited edition" if I ever made fun of his quirks.'

Almost in unison, we both laughed, then sighed, then fell silent again. I was glad of the company; conversation wasn't required.

After a minute I felt her hand on my chest as she sat upright. 'I think your mother is looking for you.'

With that she stood up, lightly tugging at my left arm.

I gave in without much struggle. I knew it was time to return to the family. I didn't want to be selfish and act like I was the only one in this particular state of mourning.

'Come on.' As I stood, she pulled my shoulder down, giving me a quick kiss on the cheek. 'It'll be fine.'

I knew it wouldn't be, but as we left the room, she knotted her hand in mine.

It was nice for those few moments. The warmth of her hand was comforting.

Dan always used to tell me, "Not every day will be good, but there is always a little good in every day."

I tried to believe that.

Chapter 5

I always found it easy to forget that WormWhole was a faceless corporate entity, only pretending to value their staff above productivity.

I received only a week of time off after Dan's funeral. Safe to say this left a bitter taste in my mouth.

I had spent a lot of the time at home with my parents, although we were mainly grieving alone. We were not the most emotive family, especially now that Dan was gone.

I had travelled up to the northern tip of Donegal several times over the week. It was a scenic area I often visited when wanting to clear my head and have time to myself. I had many fond memories of being there when I was younger. The summer school myself and Dan had attended, although on separate occasions, was long gone, but the countryside was possibly the better for it.

It was wilder now and looked almost untouched by humanity.

I thought back to those days of summer. Improving our language skills—the main focus of the courses—

was of little importance to us then. Instead we treated it as a sort of summer retreat. Although subjected to schooling in the mornings, from the afternoon on we had all sorts of activities and trips. Cliff diving, kayaking, football, hiking, swimming, and the occasional choreographed dance session in the evenings.

I met some great people, some of whom I was still close with, albeit mostly through social media. I had even met my first real crush there.

I couldn't help but romanticise the memories of those summers.

I always returned to the same place—a small rock formation beside the old cliff diving spot. It jutted out far into the Atlantic, dipping down to only a few feet above the water.

As I sat at the extreme of its reach, with no land to be seen in my peripherals, my perch on the watery pedestal felt like I was marooned on a piece of rock, standing alone amongst the waves lapping off its thin base.

It was nice to be in a familiar space, accompanied only by some of my fondest childhood memories.

But the thoughts of the attack were never too far from my more pleasant memories.

The news had reported that all bomb-making materials and accomplices were seized within a day after the attack. A small group, it had taken them months to transport their equipment, mostly travelling on foot to avoid the gates' security systems.

It was well planned and mercilessly executed.

They were cowards, whatever their reasons.

Despite the round-the-clock coverage of the events, I had escaped the public eye. The team of "advisors" that accosted me the day before Dan's funeral made sure my role in the incident was swept neatly away. It turned out the surveillance camera couldn't see me on the ground, so they edited me out of the transgression.

Covering the company more than myself of course.

But with wounds of that day only partially healed, and thoughts of Dan still filling most waking moments, I was returning to work.

I decided to get in early to visit Sam before my shift. She had been a ghost since the attack and had only paid a glancing visit to the funeral, so I hadn't had an opportunity to thank her for the triage.

I made my way across the foyer of the Hub, receiving subtle nods and waves from other Saints acknowledging my return.

As I arrived at Sam's gate, I wasn't greeted by her "business" hair piece or cheeky smirk. Instead, I was greeted by Luke, a less than favourite fellow Saint.

He eyed me up as I approached, sighing slightly and shifting back into his seat.

'Is Sam around today?' I asked politely.

With raised hands, he took a long and studious look around his immediate area. 'Does it look like she is?'

'Okay, well do you know if she's in at all today?' I struggled to maintain my initial politeness.

He just looked at me, shrugged, and sat there.

Prick.

I wasn't in the mood to engage further with him, so I left him to stew in his miserable existence.

In a small and unusually cruel twist of fate, my employee discount at the coffee stall didn't work either. A most heinous and unforgivable personal attack by the villainous virtual barista. It would require another personal "upgrade" it would appear.

Begrudgingly, I paid and marched away to my station.

The site of the incident appeared perfectly bland. If anything, my gate looked brand new, but with one glaring mistake. My chair was gone, and a bastard chair of unknown origin now sat in its place.

I wasn't sure what constituted a petty workplace grievance, but I'm assuming I would soon find out.

With half an hour to the start of my shift, I pulled up my new chair and threw myself into it.

I couldn't help but wince a little though; the last few times I had been here my life had taken a couple of drastic turns for the worse. I had been offered a relocation but thought forcing myself back to the scene of the altercation would be therapeutic in some strange way.

Every gate was pretty much a carbon copy of one another anyway. No matter where I sat, it would likely feel the same.

I looked to my AMI and returned to the most recently opened gallery.

I had been looking through swats of old pictures,

mainly of Dan and me. But the one that was getting the most attention was of Dan and me as caricatures. We had it made a few years back when we visited a friend who lived next to the world's largest amusement park, Sky City.

A funny name, considering it was in a canyon, and a hundred feet below sea level.

It was a fantastic trip. Their rollercoasters, in particular, were amazing. They had one of the fastest in the world too, the Bullet Bus. I had managed to keep it together during repeated rides, but it had enough twists and turns to force Dan into losing most of his partly digested hotdog.

That only seemed to make him hungrier somehow.

But just as I began to lose myself to the memories stored on my AMI, my alarm sounded, warning me that it was time to reassume my duties.

For the best maybe. I welcomed any distraction.

I powered up my gate like I had a thousand times before. It lit up and hummed into life just as the first commuter approached.

Headphones on. Hands in pockets. Relaxed gait. Neutral expression.

Clothes hung naturally, no room for anything underneath.

'You're fine,' I whispered, both a comment about the man and a reassurance to myself.

I just needed the first day to be over.

***

I couldn't quite put my finger on it, but the first few days back at work had been unusual.

Maybe I was a bit more sensitive to my workplace than before, or maybe people were just tiptoeing around me, but there was a definite shift between myself and the management.

They had never had such a heavy presence before, not to mention the multitude of security personnel now in a constant parade around the Hub. It was still the same managers, but they were just more present. And they were even less interested in interacting than usual.

I suppose it was to be expected. Maybe they felt their slack operation of the Hub was partly to blame for what happened. Maybe they needed a show of force.

But I felt like a pariah. I caught them watching me on several occasions like they were afraid my bad luck would somehow become contagious, and I required some sort of minding or surveillance.

As my fourth straight working day was coming to a close, and I began powering down the gate system, my AMI sprung to life with a notification.

It was Jess.

She had been ever-present over the previous few weeks. Some of the only laughs I had had in what felt like a lifetime were thanks to her.

It was good to have someone to talk to.

I still allowed myself to drift into romantic daydreams, remembering our kiss often, but I couldn't fathom beginning any courtship in my current state of mind. She had become accustomed to leading me around by the hand when we were together, so I felt we had at least grown closer, and that was good enough for now.

I decided I would pay her a visit. The message had reminded me that there were still several personal effects of Dan's that she had at work. Dan hadn't even had the time to unpack his few office decorations in London before the attack. Jess secured the items before the cleaning staff cleared his previous office space, vehemently erasing all vestiges of the previous occupancy.

I arrived at the BioDev lobby in Brussels promptly, progressing quickly through the gateway due to the heavy level of rushing commuters. The gate station was alive with activity.

The glass and bare metal building was a spectacle. Massive twisting metal beams formed gothic style flying buttresses on the outside, holding in place the clear glass dome in which I now stood. It was raining lightly outside, and what stray beams of sunshine managed to break through the clouds sent waves of rippling light across the lobby floor, creating the illusion that the white granite flowed and ebbed beneath my feet.

After a lengthy exchange with the building's security, and a quick but personal scan and pat down, I was allowed into the office spaces. Luckily, I had joined Jess for lunch here once and recognised the security officer, who was a friend of hers. Otherwise I would likely have never been granted access with their tighter-than-ever security.

I traversed the maze of corridors to Jess's lab, a less trivial task than I had remembered.

Approaching her door, I heard two distinct voices engaged in muddled conversation, both from behind the frosted glass wall. I couldn't help but feel my impromptu visit may have required a call ahead, or just better timing.

Unfortunately, this wasn't the type of environment you would linger in aimlessly. At least not without drawing unwanted attention.

An awkward interruption was my only course of action.

'Hey Jess,' I knocked while pushing open the door, making it seem I was oblivious to her guest's presence.

'Leo? Wow, what are you doing here?' She stood up from her seat and greeted me with a kiss on the cheek and the slightest squeeze of my hand. It was enough to cause the faintest of flutters in my chest.

But as I looked back to her guest, the flutter was quickly quelled. I had locked eyes with the imposing frame of Dr Josef Ross.

Jessica's father.

'Sorry, Dad.' Jess spun around, placing her hand on his elbow. 'This is Leon who I told you about—you know, Daniel's brother.'

'Ah yes.' He put down his binder and stretched out a hand to me. 'I'm very sorry for your loss.'

The mention of Dan stung, but I shrugged it off as best I could and reached out, making sure to engage firmly in the handshake. 'Thank you, sir.'

Sir?

I hadn't called somebody sir since school.

Dr Ross was a world-renowned bioinformatician and was famous almost to the same extent as my idol, Dr Sterne. Although, famous may not be the right descriptor. Scientists, no matter how renowned and influential, were not fawned over like the typical "celebrity" by the general population.

He ran the entire R&D department for BioDev on Human Epidemiology and Immunological Monitoring. He was also one of the original three creators of the Artificial Organic Experimentation system, or AOE for short, which was hands down the sole reason BioDev became the world's largest medical and pharmaceutical company.

The AOE system was immense. An artificial human body, created using incredibly intensive computer modelling. You could test the impact of anything on a person, from physical injuries, to drug side effects and bioweapon attack, all within a permanently evolving computational system. Every variation of ethnicity and genetic predisposition present on the planet could be assessed by altering the base parameters.

It had already helped lead to the complete

eradication of a range of diseases and spawned various successful cancer treatments.

I was still waiting on a hay fever cure, but I assumed my wants might be classed as "petty" in the grander scale of the system's accomplishments.

Snapping out of my awed daze, I realised I had held his hand for too long, his raised eyebrow revealing he too had noticed.

'It's nice to meet you.' I pivoted towards Jess. 'Sorry, I should have called ahead before showing up. I just thought I'd pop in for a quick visit, are you free for lunch maybe?'

'Oh, sorry Leo,' she said with a genuine ring of disappointment to her voice. 'I'm actually just about to run out. Maybe we grab a bite later?'

Disappointed, yes. Delighted with her offer of meeting later, also yes. But before I could leave, my original mission needed tending to.

'Do you mind if I just quickly grab that box? You know...Dan's box?'

'Oh shit.' She held her hand to her mouth, looking apologetically at her father, albeit jokingly. 'Sorry Leon, of course, I completely forgot. It's with the other boxes in my dad's office. Would you mind?' She turned on her heels, grabbing up several binders, the question directed to Dr Ross.

'Of course, dear.' The gentlest of sighs escaped as he spoke.

And with a quick wave, she was gone, vanished through the door and into the labyrinth of corridors.

Dr Ross and I followed suit, passing along the string of identical offices, all sporting the same sterile frosted glass exterior.

'Jessica tells me your brother was a fine scientist. It was a real tragedy what happened that day. So many lost, needlessly.' The way he spoke was extremely matter-of-fact, even stern. Exactly how I expected he would sound.

I didn't feel the remark required a response or that the conversation needed extending, considering the topic.

'Do you mind me asking, what is it you do, Leon?'

I felt a slight air of discomfort to the question. Not because it was an uncommon inquiry, but because typically people with any knowledge of my education looked on me with confusion or bemusement when informed I was a Saint.

Or in their eyes, "just" a Saint.

'I work in Hub 29, I'm a Slipway Technician,' I hesitantly explained.

'Oh.'

And that was that. The usual judgement. I didn't even bother trying to expand upon my career plans any further, instead remaining silent for the rest of our walk.

Dr Ross's office was immense. It was a completely contained unit, covering a sizable block of the office space. From outside it looked like it was bigger than my entire apartment.

He placed his hand on the door for a fraction of a

second before a greenish halo appeared around his fingers. With that, the door unlocked and swung open.

From inside the office looked even bigger.

It was no wonder he chose to avoid the all-glass enclosure of his subordinates—everything in the room screamed of excess. It was a collage of leather and stainless steel, a strange mixture I had never encountered. Polished metal shelves, frames and fittings, all lined neatly by a soft burgundy leather. It looked sterile yet comfortable, with the reflective metal surfaces giving the entire room an oddly reddish glow.

A huge map of the world hung behind his desk, with a numeric digital display of some sort fixed into its frame at the top. The numbers were small, and I couldn't make them out from my position just inside the door, but the red number on the left appeared much shorter than the pale blue number on the right, which took up the majority of the space.

Some longitude and latitude coordinates, most likely. Maybe he had a secret island hidden away somewhere in the tropics.

But before I had time to investigate further, Dr Ross blocked my view of the map.

'Here you go.' He pushed the small box into my chest. 'These are the items I believe. My apologies, but I will have to run.'

Before I could reply he had ushered me back out the door, with a little bit of force it must be said. I had only stepped a short way into the room to get a better look at the strange decor, but this seemed to have perturbed him a little. I guessed he just didn't want someone like me wandering around his pristine environment, possibly leaving a fingerprint on a glossy surface like an animal.

'Can you find your way from here?'

'Yes sir, I'll be fine.'

Sir, again? I needed to get a grip.

And with a split-second handshake, he disappeared down the passage of opaque glass walls.

Not an entirely unsuccessful trip, I assured myself. I had the box, and possibly even more face time with Jess.

Just as I passed along the outside wall of Dr Ross's office, my AMI vibrated. I pulled up the display, but there was no new message.

Instead, in the top corner, there was a small web-like notification.

I was hooked into a gate, or at least Sam's program was. I hadn't touched it in days, but every time I approached a gate it automatically associated itself.

But I was nowhere near their gate station; how could the signal possibly be carrying this far?

I chose to ignore the faulty notification, but it did remind me of Sam.

She'd been too quiet lately, so a visit was due.

The view above the foyer's glass dome was now sparsely dotted with bright clouds, and the sky was showing the first sign of nightfall as the colour drifted from blue to lilac.

I joined the slight queue at the only gate now operational.

The hustle and bustle of earlier had receded, but it was still busy.

Amongst the constantly shifting crowd, however, a solitary figure caught my attention for the slightest of moments. I recognised the man, but I wasn't sure from where.

I would probably have ignored him. There was nothing off about him other than the fact that he was the only stationary person outside of security personnel. Or at least was stationary until I looked his direction.

He turned almost too quickly. It was not a natural pivot, more of a rushed alteration. But still, he didn't walk away, choosing instead to remain in his place, but now looking out at the foyer.

How strange. I didn't feel I knew him, but he just had a recognisable face. Maybe from TV or work or something.

It didn't matter—places to be, people to see. I reached the top of the queue and dictated my destination to the local Saint.

I hoped Sam would welcome a spontaneous visitor.

Chapter 6

Just one quick stop before Sam.

I had intended to grab lunch with Jess, and part of that plan was to skip all prior eating to ensure I would enjoy the lunch all the more.

But instead, I was just famished and desperate for something to at least tide me over until dinner. And I knew just what the perfect fit would be.

Hub 1 was a monster compared to my workplace. Apparently, it had been an old airbase, and outside was surrounded by nothing but desert for miles. It wasn't just a standard Hub either, much of Worm-Whole's research and development laboratories were here. A rotating observatory above the main foyer also allowed for a brilliant night viewing experience; due to some clever light insulation of the building, it was designated one of the world's best dark sky locations.

But I wasn't there for science and sky. I was there for muffins and pie.

The smell would hit you the moment you arrived. I had hardly exited the gate when the alluring aroma of

Bakery 51-A had me hooked. It wasn't even just the smell of the baking; the air was also warm and homely.

Irresistible.

I got in line, envisioning the caramel-smothered glory that awaited me. I trembled just a little. I got far too excited when I knew a treat was on the horizon.

I arrived at the terminal end of the queue just in time for a new tray of huge caramel drizzled muffins to emerge from the kitchen. The smell was intoxicating. I couldn't believe my luck.

My day was definitely being upgraded from passable to good.

I paid for the treat and briskly moved across the dining area to a secluded corner, like a squirrel hiding away with his food so as not to be disturbed.

After carefully placing Dan's belongings in the seat beside me, I turned my attention to the guest of honour. I wolfed down the muffin, taking as few bites as possible to do so.

If my mother saw me do that, she would be disgusted. And rightly so.

Napkins, I thought as I struggled to separate the sticky caramel from my fingers. *I always forget the damned napkins.*

I was glad nobody paid me any attention as I licked and sucked the confectionary from my fingers. How uncouth they would have found me.

As I sat back, content in my choice of grub, I peered out into the collection of commuters gathered in my immediate area, likely also ensnared by the passing scent of baked goods. The hum of a hundred conversations radiated through the air. The noise added to the peaceful feel of the starkly white surroundings.

I leaned forwards, the beginning of my lazy standing motion. But just as my weight shifted to the front of my seat, I paused. An old woman was dining alone, only a few tables away. She was familiar but not obviously so.

It took only a moment for my brain to catch up with my eyes. And only a moment more for my brain to freak out just a tad.

It was Dr Sterne. It had to be her.

Years had passed since I had seen her in person. She had given a free talk at the Hub's conference centre about the ethical implications of a completely autonomous network system. It was an amazing talk, highlighting both the implications and limitations of complete commuter-based control over systems.

As far as I remember she was brilliantly unbiased in her assessment, which no doubt went heavily against our employer's viewpoint.

It was strange to see her sitting alone. I would have expected an entourage of research fellows, professors, even postgraduates seeking to share her company, if only for a short snack.

And with that, a strange thought made its home in my head. An opportunity had been made possible.

Nobody could know the gate technology like her. She knew everything there was to know.

Maybe, just maybe, she knew more than a golden pamphlet's simplification of tragedy.

Before my train of thought had finalised my plan of broaching the subject, I found myself almost at her table. I would have never approached her so brazenly like this before. With everything that had happened in the previous weeks, anything that might help me understand at this stage was worth at least a little embarrassment.

'Excuse me, Dr Sterne?' I felt like a child, introducing myself to an adult for the first time.

She peeked up, just over the rim of her glasses. 'Yes?'

Don't panic, play it cool.

'I'm sorry to bother you, doctor, but I was wondering if maybe I could join you for a moment?' The request must have seemed odd, as her raised brow bunched the wrinkles of her forehead.

I clambered to come up with an additional reason for joining her company. 'My name's Leon. I'm a Saint over in Hub 29.' Still not a good reason to join her, but she smiled politely despite my awkward introduction.

'Of course, young man,' she replied after a moment. 'Please, pull up a seat.'

'Thank you, Dr Sterne.' I pulled a chair out quickly and threw myself down across the table.

'No need to be so formal at lunch...Leon, was it? You can call me Meribel.'

'Oh, yes, sorry.' First name terms? I couldn't appear

too giddy, but if I had a diary, it would refer to that moment on most pages from then on.

Meribel, it was such a nice old-fashioned name.

'You're a Saint, yes?' She spoke through her napkin while wiping the last of her food away from the edges of her mouth. 'In Hub 29? I hope you weren't there on the day of those ghastly attacks?'

'Oh, eh yes, I was actually pretty unlucky on the day...' I turned my head, showing the hairless mark of the small scar left by the man's blows. She reached out and positioned my head with her hand to get a better look before inhaling through her teeth to show her acknowledgement of the injury.

'Ow. That must have stung...'

I neglected to mention it was my gate that was attacked; better for her just to assume I had somehow been hurt in the commotion. I was still under strict direction to refrain from divulging what really happened that day.

'It's okay now.' I quickly shifted the focus from that days happening, in case the questions became too probing. 'I hope you don't mind, but I was hoping to ask you about the gate network.'

'The network?' She seemed confused. I needed to elaborate.

'I'm sorry, I mean...a short while ago one of my commuters disappeared.'

'Oh...oh well I'm very sorry to hear that.' She removed her glasses, wiping them with her napkin. 'A hiccup?'

I could sense the slightest bit of indifference from the word as she spoke it. Maybe that was something we agreed upon.

'Yes, my first hiccup actually, and hopefully my last. I was just wondering if maybe you could give me some insight about what a hiccup really is?'

She looked at me with the slightest of smirks. 'They cover this in the employee handbook, no?'

'Yes, they do, to an extent. They listed off the most "well-known" causes, but they're kind of...nonsense really. Seems like an excuse to me, just a page filler. But if they don't know, why not just say it?'

She smiled bigger this time, almost releasing a laugh at my apparent scepticism of our employers.

'Well, which would you find scarier? That you could disappear, in the blink of an eye, for absolutely no apparent reason, at any moment? Or that the chance of you ever disappearing is controlled by a set number of variables that are "understood," making them more real, and therefore more likely to be manageable, even if you don't really understand these variables your-self?'

I hadn't thought of it like that. A random, unpre-dictable end, versus a seemingly avoidable but equally final fate.

She continued, 'You know, a lot of work goes into mimicking the conditions that could throw off a healthy slipway. You're not wrong to be sceptical—that's the sign of an inquisitive mind, you know. But all you or anybody else will ever be told is carefully worded by lawyers, not scientists. Just rewording un-deniable factors and disprovable theories. A placating placebo to distract, really.'

I hadn't expected her to be so...honest. I was a stranger to her, but she spoke so candidly. I was be-coming more enamoured with every sentence.

She leaned back and paused for a moment, taking in a wider view of the cafeteria and surrounding space, settling on looking out past my right shoulder.

'To tell you the truth, we don't know why it hap-pens.' Her expression shifted slightly with the revela-tion, a pang of disappointment ringing in her words.

'For years the network was infallible, perfect. Never a problem, never an unstable slipway. The network grew and grew unabated. The technology was univer-sally accepted almost overnight.' Again, she removed her glasses, wiping them with her napkin while peer-ing my direction, but still slightly off over my shoul-der, as if purposefully not making eye contact while regaling me with the story of the network's incep-tion. 'It was well over a decade before we heard of a lost commuter. Sure, the gate network was misused by countless people before, we knew that. Politicians, dictators, terrorists, religious leaders. But the network itself was perfect. Until it wasn't.'

I had read her books, I had seen her speak, but I had never heard about the networks roots in this light. I couldn't interrupt, even if I wanted to. She enthralled me.

'It all just...changed.'

She stopped, taking a final sip from her coffee and straightening herself in the seat.

But that couldn't be all there was to it.

I snapped out of my silence, trying not to be over-zealous in my questioning. 'It changed? How? Why?'

She chuckled, her mood seemingly improved by what I thought were reasonable questions. 'Old questions. Old questions I used to ask myself every day. How and why. Both, I'm afraid, are answered one in the same. Volume.'

'Volume? I don't understand...'

'The only factor that ever changed, from the beginning of the gate network to today, is the sheer volume of commuters and interlinked gateways. What other reason could there be?' I felt from the way she asked the question, that she was almost genuinely looking for my opinion.

She continued, 'In a way, you could say the planet is overloaded.'

Her words brought back memories of early morning classes at MIT. Equations, theorems, Laws, all attributed with the names of those who discovered them. I was very bad with names, but I knew the principles behind them. Slipways were generated through the planet itself. The solid mass of the earth was a major stabilising factor for them. That's why space travel was still impossible. Interstellar plasma had a density far too low to generate a slipway. "Mass passes through mass," as we were always reminded.

'But...is that even possible?' My mind tried to wrap

around the idea of the earth struggling under the weight of its travelling populace.

'Well, consider this. We developed the gates in the mid-20s. Back then there were around 370 gates deployed in Europe. But the number rose exponentially within a short space of time. Do you know the total gate population now?'

I didn't. I shook my head, feeling slightly embarrassed. As a Saint, should I have known that?

'Well it's somewhere in the range of 790 million, between WormWhole and all the others. There's not a village, town, or city on the planet without at least a pair of gates. Major cities have gates in almost every building.'

790 million. I had never really thought about how many there might be. Anywhere I had ever wanted to travel had a gate. It just seemed normal. There was no reason to take note of the expanse of the network.

So many gates, so many commuters. A staggering number for sure, the safest mode of travel ever known to man.

Almost perfectly safe.

At this revelation, I was reminded of my original reason for approaching Dr Sterne.

'Do you know what happens to them?'

I could see I had hit a sore spot. She slumped back into her seat, letting out a faint sigh. I backtracked immediately instead of pushing for the answer.

'I'm sorry, Dr Sterne, I've taken up enough of your time.'

I still thought of that one girl I had lost, but I was just an operator. This was her technology essentially; maybe she similarly felt responsible, albeit on a much grander scale.

Anyway, how could she—or anyone—possibly know what happened to a person who was never seen again?

I noticed her checking the time projected across the wall above the bakery.

She smiled, again looking out past me, still fixated somewhere beyond my right shoulder, making me feel I was definitely holding her back from something going on in the background. 'Oh please, it was nice to have some company during lunch; it's usually so monotonous.'

Her eyes flicked back to me for a moment. 'And it's Meribel.'

'I'm sorry...Meribel.' It still didn't seem right, like I was being disrespectful by using her name. 'But thank you, you've given me a lot to think about.'

She slowly positioned herself upright in the chair, still not engaging in eye contact, sliding her arm out towards mine as if to shake my hand. But at the last second, she corrected her trajectory, grabbing instead the AMI on my left forearm.

I looked at her confused, before noticing my AMI seemed to be under duress. What little of the screen I could see went bright green, and then off.

I didn't want to create an awkward moment by pulling away abruptly, so instead, I broke the silence. 'Em, is everything okay, Meribel?'

She looked back at me, and then down to my arm, 'Oh, sorry, you'll have to forgive me, I was a million miles away.' She repositioned her hand to a gentle embrace with the back of mine instead, grabbing me firmly in a sort of backwards handshake.

'I must be going, but it has been tremendous meeting you Leon.'

I could feel something cold and hard in her hand, not the expected warmth of skin on skin contact. But before I had a chance to think what it could be she removed her hand and stood, picking up her tray and smiling one last time before turning away from the table.

I stood quickly. 'No the pleasure was mine...' but she was out of earshot.

I had outstayed my welcome it appeared.

'Piece of junk,' I muttered to myself as I restarted my AMI system. 'The battery must nearly be dead.'

As the AMI system struggled to come back to life, I packed away my rubbish and moved towards the travel zone with Dan's box safely in tow.

Back to normality now. I knew Sam wouldn't believe the story of my lunch companion, but I was already working on how best to rub it in when I reached her home.

***

Sometimes I wondered if humans still possess any remnant of animalistic instinct or natural subconscious awareness of our environment beyond what visual markers littered the landscape.

Not a sixth sense per se, just some last vestige of our connection to our deep ancestry, built into our DNA originally to give ancient humans an early warning against the unknown.

Or maybe we couldn't, our baser instincts made redundant by human advances in technology and science.

Not a bad trade for the most part.

I had arrived and now stood at the threshold of Sam's apartment.

The door was slightly ajar, allowing a projection of thin blue light stream out into the harshly lit hallway. The light was static, an unresponsive ghostly illumination cutting across my feet.

I nudged the door open with an outstretched foot.

Leaving Dan's box in the hallway, I proceeded, my bemusement slowly turning to worry. Sam wouldn't just forget and leave the door open.

The apartment I knew was gone. What remained was more of an electronic waste disposal. Everything had been thoroughly flipped and scoured, with no regard for the fragility of the computers and components.

I ventured in quickly, but stealthily, eyes wide and scanning, driven now by fear for Sam's safety. The eerie quiet lead me to believe the perpetrators had since vacated.

My skin tingled with the static in the air as I proceeded. The silence was broken only by the whirl of several cooling fans, still powered, but struggling. A faint hint of coffee still touched the air, the remnant of a morning brew no doubt.

I made sure to keep my hands to myself as I sleuthed through. I couldn't contaminate the scene, that's what the many crime dramas I had watched as a teenager had taught me. All of this would be needed for evidence no doubt.

I scoured the small apartment, as thoroughly as possible.

Nothing. No sign of Sam. Everything had been pulled apart and thrown around. Even the kitchen drawers were in various states of open.

Sam's bedroom didn't even look lived in. The minimalistic decorations had the look of a brochure showcase, simply faking occupancy.

I'd seen enough. Sam wasn't there, and this was not a place I wanted to spend more time in.

I stepped outside, attempting to call her. Nothing. I appeared to have full signal, but I couldn't seem to connect. Of all times for my AMI to start acting up.

I hoped she simply hadn't come home yet.

I could mail her from my home terminal, ask her to come around or tell her not to go home at the very least. I could contact the police from there too if that hadn't already been done.

I approached the building's lobby, changing my hurried step to a casual stroll. Ahead the area was busy, so I decided to pause a moment and ensure I was fully composed. The last thing I needed was to look like I was making a quick exit.

As I stood at the boundary of the area, only able to peek slightly around the corner, I could see the mass of people coming and going as freely as ever. I would blend right in. Nobody had a reason to notice me.

But from my vantage, I immediately picked out a character from the edge of the foyer, his crisp suit highlighting him from the general populace.

It was the man from earlier, the man I had noticed in the foyer at BioDev. I couldn't get a clear shot of his face, but it was him. He was talking to the building's security officer, and the conversation seemed somewhat animated.

I didn't like coincidences. Was I paranoid? Perhaps, but I would rather live with a paranoid mystery than spend any more time in that building.

I walked through the centre of the room, making a direct line to the nearest automatic gateway, blending in with the masses. The line was small, and my wait was only seconds.

I steamed through, worry weighing heavily on each step.

I hoped Sam was alright.

Chapter 7

Back to the safety of my building, and away from whatever had befallen Sam's.

I needed to call her again, and I bounded up the stairs to my floor. The extra weight of Dan's box made the climb a little more tiring than usual, making me think that my distrust of the old-fashioned elevators was somewhat misplaced.

Slingshotting around the world fifty times a day from a gate—fine. Riding a moveable room held aloft by cables, counterweights and a bit of prayer—no thank you.

The front door of my apartment slid smoothly open as I approached, allowing me to keep my hurried pace. The customary welcoming chime was still ringing as it quickly shut behind me, with a heavier than usual thud.

But instead of the typical pouring of LED lighting, I stood stranded in darkness.

The lights were out, and only then did I become aware of just how sealed my apartment was from the outside world. Not a single beam of light squeezed through the blackout phasic window panes. I hated the red standby lights on electronics, so I made sure to cut all power to sockets when I left in the mornings.

I regretted my energy saving morals at that moment.

I bent to rest the box safely on the floor beside my feet.

Straightening up, I slid my hands across the wall, searching for the apartment interface panel next to the entrance. The near frictionless motion of my hand traversing the slick wall surface created the only sound in the vacuum that was currently my apartment.

But as I paused for that moment, questioning how the darkness had rid me of any sense of positional awareness in a place I had lived for years, a faint noise caught my attention.

I ceased all movement, focusing on the distant sound, hoping it to be a beacon I could use to position myself in the darkness. A neighbour dragging a piece of furniture, the whirl of an old air conditioning unit, Mrs Langton blending that godforsaken excuse for a smoothie. I knew all the neighbours' theme music by now.

I listened intently, hands cupping my ears to gather and amplify every vibration.

Again, a faint whisp of air, minute in duration, just faintly distinguishable from a natural breeze. Only this time, it brought with it a wretch in my stomach.

It wasn't a reverberating wall, nor was it footsteps from the ceiling above or a creeping draft through an unsecured window. It was in the room.

I raised my guard instinctively, bending down ever so slightly and squinting my eyes in an attempt to pierce the blackness somehow.

My ears pumped under the heightened rhythm of my heart, hindering my most vital of senses in their moment of need. I reached behind myself, carefully searching for anything to hold as a weapon. I could feel the early stages of perspiration beginning to form on my palms.

Silence, and for a longer moment than last. I held my position, scanning as aggressively as I could using my limited senses.

A small clunk of cardboard and glass was all that was needed, as Dan's box was clipped, betraying movement a mere foot to the left of my position.

Springing from my stance, I launched at the source. But just as I lunged, the lights burst into life, momentarily blinding me as I crashed headfirst into both the small figure of the intruder and the side wall, sending Dan's box sliding across the floor.

My body contorted as my face hit the wall, half pinned, half off balance. I twisted to turn, arms straining to be released from the vice-like grip I was now being held in.

Kicking off the wall I seized my chance, throwing my right elbow back around my body. The momentum I put behind the attack became my undoing as I was tossed like a ragdoll, crashing down on my back and immediately being pinned by a knee to the sternum.

'Leon, calm down!'

The words were shouted directly into my face as both my arms were restrained, one by a tight grip and the other under the second leg.

I grimaced, winded and struggling to move, before opening my eyes just enough to come face to face with my attacker.

I don't know what I expected. A scar above the left eye, a hook for a hand, several missing teeth, a T-shirt with a slogan displaying a general disdain for good manners.

But instead, there was a set of pearly white teeth, half smiling, although panting mildly. Two earrings in the right ear, perfectly smooth skin, hair tied up in a bun, and just a whiff of coffee breath.

'Oh, for fuck's sake.' I allowed my head to go limp, bouncing slightly off the hard floor. 'What the hell, Sam?'

She smiled wider now, releasing my arm with her hand and giving me a small double slap on the cheek. 'Oh you know, just hanging out, kicking your ass. A normal Tuesday night.'

She stood up and released me, dusting herself off. Obviously it was more for show, my apartment was messy but never dusty.

Groaning heavily and still winded, I raised myself into a seated position on the floor.

Sam made her way towards my kitchen, almost a skip in her step. She had on occasion pointed out that if needed she could kick my ass. And although I felt she had an unfair advantage in this instance, it was safe to say her predictions weren't totally inaccurate.

'Any beer?' she called out from the kitchen, accompanied by the clinking of glasses and slamming of cupboards.

I didn't need to reply as I got to my feet, holding my chest as I moved. A long 'Bingo' joyously rang out from the kitchen as I heard the familiar hiss of carbonation escaping from a freshly opened bottlecap.

I threw myself down on the couch as Sam heroically re-entered the living room, frothing glasses of amber goodness in each hand.

She also had two coasters, how thoughtful. Possibly the world's most subtle apology, considering what had just transpired.

I reached out, accepting the beer.

'Drink up, buddy,' she said as she double tapped the glasses together. Clink with the top, then clink with the bottom. Dan had the same habit.

She sat down directly across from me, savouring every moment of the first chug of beer.

I stared at her, over the glass, as I indulged in just a sip, expecting her to say something.

But she was content, sitting back with her head resting over the back of the seat looking up at the ceiling, not a care in the world now that she had a drink.

'Are you shitting me?' I hissed at her. 'Care to elaborate on, oh I don't know, pretty much everything? What are you even doing here?'

'Me?' She perked up, placing the beer down beside the coaster. 'Where the hell have you been, you were supposed to be here, like, an hour ago.'

'Supposed to be here? What the hell do you mean by that? What are you even doing in here? No actually, HOW did you get in?' There were too many questions, too many confusing occurrences in my day that I could hardly form a coherent interrogation.

'Whoa, whoa there Sherlock, take a beat. Jeez, you're worse than my mother.' She took another quick gulp of beer, again missing the coaster as she placed it back down. 'Ok, fine. I'll confess. I broke in, slightly. But I swear, I only enjoyed it a little bit.'

Always a joker. But whereas I typically humoured the nonsensical blurbs Sam gave out daily, I was not in the mood.

'Where have you been, Sam? I was actually starting to worry.'

'Pfft, worrying about me, that's rich. I'm not exactly the damsel-in-distress type you know. Exhibit A.' She pointed towards the door, hinting at our recent alter-cation. Or rather, my ambush.

'Enough, Sam!' I slammed my glass back down onto the table. 'Stop deflecting, I'm not kidding okay? What are you doing here?'

The smirk left her face in a disappointed flash. Ex-pressionless, Sam straightened up in the seat, staring right across at me.

'Okay then, Leon, let's talk. You want to know why I'm here. Fine, I'll tell you. I'm here because we have a lot to discuss. You're not going to like half of it, and you're probably not going to believe the other half.' She slid forwards, right to the edge of her seat. 'Just try to relax, okay?'

Relax? I was starting to think relaxation was the least likely thing I was going to experience with her.

'Okay, let's get down to it. First things first I guess, how was your muffin—'

Electronic bells rang out to my left, cutting Sam off. The front entrance was pulsing teal lighting.

'Are you expecting company?' Sam asked, now standing.

'No.' It was always a strange occasion when guests arrived unannounced; I didn't have many friends of the spontaneous variety.

I moved to the door, activating the visitor camera once I reached the wall panel.

I may not have recognised him before, but repetition was the key to a good memory. Once again, I was confronted with the suited man. Taller than he had appeared at a distance, suit pressed to perfection, this time sporting a pair of thick dark rimmed glasses.

'Shit...' Sam whispered, just over my shoulder. She had approached with such stealth I didn't realise she was behind me. 'Where were you, Leon? Before now.'

'What? What does that have to do with anything?'

'Just...I wish you'd just answer my damn questions.' She reached over and activated the door panel.

Without a moment to breathe, I was face to face with the man, perfectly at eye level.

'What?' Sam's question had a not unfamiliar hint of venom to it. But it wasn't directed at me as usual.

'Nice to see you too, Sam.'

The man pushed his way past me and into the living room, as Sam closed the door behind him.

'Sorry to interrupt this little party, guys.' He picked up the glasses, took a drink out of mine, and carried them and the coasters to the kitchen. 'But we have to leave.'

'Leave? Who the hell are you? Why are you following me?' I couldn't hold back the frustration in my questioning. It was all getting too out of hand for my liking.

He exited the kitchen, looking to Sam. 'Is he always like this?'

'Pretty much, but in his defence, you're an asshole, Frank.'

'Frank?' I knew that name, and I half recognised his face the first time I saw him. 'Frank, Frank...as in, your Frank?'

'He ain't my nothing. He's just a walking buzzkill. Isn't that right, Frankly?' Her joking tone hinted that Frankly might not be his favourite nickname.

'Well as much as I love a walk down memory lane, I don't think now is quite the time, do you? Orientation can wait.'

Orientation? I was officially on the brink of just checking out and leaving them in my apartment.

'We need to be gone, like, five minutes ago. Mr

Curious over here has nearly wasted our window trying to visit your fortress of solitude.'

'Ha!' Sam pointed directly in my face. 'I knew you were somewhere fishy.'

'Sam!' Frank wasn't joking around this time as much as he was indulging Sam's idiosyncrasies.

'Fine, fine. Shit.' She turned to me, putting her hand on my shoulder, 'No time to pack. I'll explain soon, but you have to follow us. No questions, okay? I'll fill you in, just please Leon, trust me.'

I don't think Sam had ever sounded or looked as sincere as she did in that moment. She hadn't blinked, she hadn't smirked, she hadn't tried to turn it into a joke or a play on words. She just stared deeply into my eyes, longing for me to trust her in this obscure situation I had found myself in.

"They're on their way up, time to go." The words echoed out from Franks earpiece, barely audible and possibly not meant for me to hear.

'That's our cue, guys, we are out of time. We have to leave right now.' He moved towards the door, Sam in hot pursuit.

What else could I do? I had no idea what was happening. Sam was a friend. She had no reason to be messing with me. But I was so in the dark I would have followed any slight bit of advice just to get to the bottom of things.

I shifted to follow, picking up Dan's box as I moved, placing it on the table beside my doorway and out of harm's way.

Franks' hand shot out in front as an inaudible conversation continued between him and someone else.

'Elevator three, that's our route,' he stated to nobody in particular as he opened the door.

I went to move, instinctively thinking the opening of the door was the indication to progress. But Frank kept his hand up blocking us, listening to the ambient sounds of the corridor.

We both paused, looking at him and waiting for instructions.

I had tried to ignore the situation I had found myself in, a usually easy task when everything around you is progressing so quickly. But this pause had given me a moment to assess.

Frank had been following me. He was at BioDev, and he was at Sam's building too. But somebody had ransacked Sam's apartment. And now he was here, telling me we had to leave immediately. And Sam wasn't questioning it.

I grabbed Dan's box off the table, clutching it tightly, ready to move.

'What are you doing?' Sam whispered to me, not taking her eyes off the door.

'If my apartment's going to turn out like yours, then I'm saving this.'

Sam straightened up slightly. 'Wait, what about my apartment?'

'Go!' Frank bolted ahead. Before Sam had a chance to continue her train of thought, she followed. And so did I.

We ran past the two elevators adjacent to my next-door neighbours' entrance, and then past the stairs I would usually take. It was only a few moments before we were at the elevator, which Frank had already called.

It arrived just as I could hear footsteps echoing from the stairs. We had timed it to perfection.

I tried not to hesitate getting in, but I must have had a visible stutter in my gait as I moved towards the elevator doors. Sam grabbed me, pulling me inside as the doors closed. I kept my eyes shut for the entire unnatural journey down.

Within moments the doors opened, releasing me from my building sense of claustrophobia. We walked out, Frank leading the way with purpose, and headed directly towards a gate with no queue, unusual at that time of day.

'Sam?' It was obvious Frank had given an order without needing to elaborate, as Sam immediately brought up her AMI and starting gesturing rapidly.

The gate came to life as we approached.

'Perfect timing, guys.' The voice came from behind as another woman joined our little marching group.

Just keep going, Leon. It'll be fine.

I repeated that to myself as I followed, not making a sound. I had no idea what was going on, where we were going, or who this other person was. She must have been the one feeding Frank his information.

My willingness to comply with these people was

based entirely on the sincerity of Sam's request, and I trusted her.

And it was her sincerity in that moment that was making me sick to my stomach, more so than the elevator.

What the hell had she gotten me into?

Chapter 8

I emerged from the gate into the unknown.

Several large lights surrounded me, causing me to raise an arm to block what I could. Intensely bright, with sort of an off-yellow glow, they were obviously old halogen lights. Not a common feature of any building I had ever been in.

'Where the hell am I?' I spoke softly under my breath, arm still raised to block the glaring light.

I couldn't put my finger on it, but the commute had seemed longer than usual. The fact it didn't seem instantaneous at all was strange.

I walked out past the gate's immediate area, clearing the lights and moving towards where Sam and the others stood. As I passed the welcoming lights, the rest of the room came into proper focus.

Although "room" may not have been the best way to describe it.

The large domed area was a cold grey of rough cement. Large girders stood as supports for the huge roofing, giving a cavernous feel to the interior. Some of the walls had partially given way to age or physical trauma, as a mesh-like metal skeleton protruded in several places. The entire structure looked like it was once an impenetrable fortress, but time was taking its toll.

The floor space, however, had an entirely different appearance. Poorly kept cream marble tiles were all but hidden under the mass of electronics strewn across the area. Computers, wiring, flashing conduits, holo-displays, and even some parts and pieces I couldn't recognise littered the floors and bench space. The air felt alive with static, vibrating with the hum of so many computers running at once. I guessed that was the reason the air was so warm and stuffy. I couldn't place the source of the sweet scent occasionally float-ing past me. Somebody must have had a penchant for potpourri. It smelt like the downstairs bathroom in my parents' house.

I hadn't noticed Sam standing at my side as I took in my new surroundings.

She nudged me, snapping me out of my survey mode.

'You all good, Leon?' A hint of appreciation rang from her words, happy that I was not questioning everything. But I wasn't in a forgiving mood just yet, and Sam had a lot to account for.

'Yeah, I see that look. We'll get settled in here, and then we'll have our deep and meaningful. Deal?'

But before I could react, a new face came towards us. A taller athletic woman, half a foot smaller than myself, with blondish brown hair and lightly tanned skin. I thought she was going to walk right through Sam at first, but instead, she used her momentum to land a playful but knuckle cracking punch on Sam's shoulder.

'Ow!' Sam winced from the attack, 'What the hell, Styx?!'

'You know why.' She raised her finger to Sam. 'Every day until I get it back, your punishment doubles.'

I couldn't help but recognise the similarities between the two, which lead to a worrying train of thought.

Oh great, I thought. *There's two of them.*

'Introductions?' She twisted towards me, eyebrow raised, looking me up and down twice.

I decided to let Sam off explaining.

'I'm Leon.' I rebalanced the box to reach out a hand. 'Sticks, was it?'

'Yep, that's Styx with a y and an x.' She grabbed tightly on my hand, just giving a single but firm up and down. 'Sam's told me about you alright. And you came in with Frank there?' She smiled, showing off her brilliantly white teeth. 'You guys must've been coming in hot.'

'Yeah well, timing wasn't always my speciality.' Sam had recovered, her gripped fist showing she was contemplating some swift retribution. 'But Frankly came in handy this time. Our little guardian angel.'

With his back turned, Frank raised a single middle finger towards us, obviously still within earshot.

'Okay, Leon, let's get you acclimatised.'

I followed Sam through the maze of computers and electronics, with fans spinning heavily in all directions and a concert of monotonous beeping melodies ringing out from across the dome. It was truly a Luddite's worst dream, but from it was Heaven for my inner nerd.

She walked me to a room at the far end of the area, where a small kitchenette lead into a sleeping area scattered with bunk beds and footlockers.

'Just throw the box there.' She pointed out an empty spot beside the closest bed. 'It'll be fine for now.'

Was she expecting me to take up residence here or something? There weren't nearly as many beds as there were people busying themselves all around the concrete dome, so clearly this was just meant as a respite area.

She waved me onwards, walking me back out into the clutter of technology.

'Where are we?' An appropriate first question I felt. My AMI was flashing on my forearm, signalling a complete lack of network connectivity.

We had cleared the taller machines and could again see across most of the domed expanse. Sam stopped and raised an arm out towards the busy hive of activity. 'This is Achterhuis, our little haven from the world above.'

I honed in on the exact wording. Sam was very astute in her descriptions, and nothing was ever by mistake or chance.

'What do you mean, "the world above"?'

'Well, you don't think buildings like this are easy to come by, do you? Look at it!' She swung her arms up and around, pointing with no real direction. 'It's a relic, a bunker for some forgotten purpose underground. How far underground is anyone's guess, but Styx said we're under Kavir National Park somewhere. Can't exactly look out a window to check though...'

Kavir didn't sound even vaguely familiar, and my raised eyebrow likely betrayed my internal geographic struggle.

'We're in Iran, Leon.' Sam scoffed, acting as if I should have been aware of the fact.

I had never been to Iran. It was one of the few places in the world that didn't allow unrestricted gate access to everyone. Not for any mysterious reason—after all, it was one of the world's largest tourist destinations, but they had laws limiting extensive gate installation and use outside of the major cities. Protecting the country's landscape from "excessive human interaction" I had read before. Even a Saint's passport meant nought out there. I had always meant to apply for a visa but had just never gotten around to it.

We continued walking towards the back wall while I brooded about not following through on plans made by a younger more adventurous self. When had I started just letting plans get away from me?

As we approached the wall, it became obvious that the concrete didn't cover the entire surface of the dome. White glossy paint covered the walls in both directions, the bold black writing on them fooling my eyes at a distance into thinking them grey.

'What is that?' I pointed out at the expansive white banner, heavily filled with indiscriminate scrawls. I moved around Sam to get a closer look as she began to answer.

'That's the List.'

As I approached, I could make out some of the writing.

Siena Di Pasqua – 47 – 19/08/2065

Kacper Singh – 66 – 02/06/2059

Alan F.S. Harrison – 26 – 14/12/2070

Margaret Lyon – 43 – 14/02/2068

Sam had followed me to the boards, standing in solemn silence beside me as I read.

The names and numbers continued in both directions across the boards, messily spaced and with erratic, interchanging writing styles. But all were the same format.

Name – age – date.

It was like a war memorial. The longer I looked, the more the unease twisted and turned in my stomach. 'What is this?' I asked, unsure of whether or not the answer would help alleviate the growing discomfort.

'It's everyone.' She paused, licking her thumb and using it to remove a piece of dirt from the board in front of her. 'Everyone that has gone missing from a WormWhole gate in the past 30 years, we think. We've compiled all that we can, but we're bound to miss a few here and there. It's not kept on any database that we've found. No running tally in any newspaper archives. No backup missing persons list on a city council's memory drive. Just scattered information from every corner of the globe we can get hold of...'

Sam's words had drowned out to white noise amid the deafening weight of the board's information. It was an obituary.

I was transfixed. But not on the board in general, or the sprawl of names and numbers filling my peripherals. I could see nothing but a single entry, directly in my eye line.

Ada Jensen – 9 – 08/10/2058

Nine years old.

Nine.

My soul sank, and a chill rubbed its tendril-like fingers down the length of my spine with every character I read, and reread, hoping I had made a mistake. Hoping it was just an error by a careless person filling in the blanks of information. Hoping a preceding or following digit was hiding from my vision.

I didn't know why it had never registered with me before.

Of course, it wasn't just adults. Of course, a machine wouldn't discriminate. Of course, that blighted code couldn't show mercy to those deserving of it.

It occurred to me then that in all my hatred I had humanised the problem in the system. I was a fool, assuming it could feel pity or adhere to a code of morality for those too young to understand the greater realities of life, or loss thereof.

Nine years old.

Sam, as usual, was the one to break the silence. 'Pretty grim, eh?'

Grim didn't begin to describe it. I had had no idea that many people had gone missing. It made perfect sense considering how long the gates had been in use, and how many people used them every day. But I just hadn't sat and gave it any real thought. I had lost a commuter, and outside of that, I had remained completely ignorant, almost blissfully so.

Even my attempts to help had been completely self-centered in a way.

'Oh, I almost forgot.' Sam got busy gesturing at her AMI. 'There you go, just in case you missed it.'

A package of data popped up on my display. It was the blighted hiccup gate code.

'What? How did you get this?' I asked confused.

'You really think I wouldn't steal a copy once you had it? Ha, please. But no point in trying to solve a mystery without all the clues, right?'

She was right. As much as I hated that damned code, even more so now that the tombstone of a wall stretched in front of me, it was important information. I was sure of that.

'Is she here?'

'Who?'

'Her. The woman from my gate...'

'Oh, yeah, over here towards the side.' Sam walked off to the right, scanning an area beside where the boards remained blank.

'No. No, it's fine.' I called down to Sam. I didn't need to see her information. I was there. I knew enough.

She returned without questioning my change of heart.

'Come on, we have a little bit more to go.' She ushered me away from the wall.

'Now you see why I was so eager to help you get that code, Leon? We haven't been at this very long, but that was the first chance we had to get a hold of it. Sheer luck it was you really.'

There was nothing lucky about it.

'Did you ever...?'

'Lose a commuter? Yeah, a long time back. A woman around the same age as myself. Rachael was her name. Scared the life out of me. I wasn't even paying full attention on the day, just pottering around as usual. I had no idea she never arrived until the following day when she was listed as missing.'

Sam didn't seem fazed talking about her missing commuter. 'You don't sound too cut up about it.'

'Why would I be? I was for a while, maybe. But it's just like that poem says, "Living displaces false sentiments." I know I did nothing wrong, I know she did nothing wrong. It just sort of...happened.'

Despite her cavalier attitude and tone, I didn't believe her. Not fully. She was hard as nails, granted. But her answer seemed rehearsed.

We made our way back towards the gate area, where I could see Styx and Frank in deep conversation.

Seeing them by the gate reminded me of the

strangeness of my arrival here. I had, for the most part remained quiet and tagged along thus far. It had all happened within the last hour, and still my main confusion hadn't been addressed, and likely would not be willingly.

'Why am I here Sam?' I stopped short of where the others were, turning my back on them to face her. I wanted a straight answer, without external influence. I had so many questions whirling around in my mind, but I had to be direct with Sam, and give her no chances to deviate. 'Who or what were you guys avoiding at my apartment?'

'Ah, shit. Thought I could put that off just a bit longer.' Sam stopped, half sitting on one of the only empty bits of desk I could see in the structure. 'Right, where to start.'

Sam looked genuinely confused as if picking the most relevant chapter of a story to tell somebody who hadn't as much as heard of the book.

'Look, Leon...I did this for you. And for me, kinda. The people on their way up to us, they were Worm-Whole security. But not a version of the security you're likely to have seen before. It was all in our files, I didn't believe it until I saw it myself. They put you under watch because they were already watching me. But then, out of nowhere, you were all over their radar, I mean you really lit up, and we don't know why. But they had you linked to the attacks that day. They have us both marked as conspirators...'

'Conspirators?!' I had noticeably lost my volume

control, as several people stopped what they were doing close by. 'You mean they think we're fucking terrorists!'

The thought brought my blood to a boil.

I was nothing like those men.

'There must be a way to clear this up.' I could feel I was floundering but couldn't hold back. 'If I just go in and talk to them, I could clear us. I was attacked, I didn't help. For fuck's sake, I tried to stop them!'

'Leon, just try to calm down for a moment.'

'Calm down? Calm down!? Are you fucking kidding? This is your fault, you said it yourself. I wouldn't be involved in any of this if they weren't watching you. Why the hell were they even watching you, what the hell did you do, Sam?'

Frank had approached with Styx and the other woman from my building.

'Leon, just hold up for a minute.' Frank was perfectly calm in his tone, which didn't help my wildly spiralling mood. 'There's no need to fly off the handle. You're safe here, and there's nothing they can do about that.'

'Safe? Who gives a shit about safe? You don't understand do you. Dan died, my brother died, and they're going to say I helped? That I was somehow to blame for this?' I could feel the salty sting behind the bridge of my nose as my tear ducts became ready to betray the devastating turn my thoughts had taken.

There was mumbling from behind me, but I paid no

attention as I looked at the faces of each of the four gathered in front and beside me.

They were all mute. Not one willing to push further after seeing how I was struggling to cope. Apart from Sam, none of them were even looking at me, instead focussed elsewhere beyond my shoulder.

But just as I readied to inform them of where they could stick their depressing bunker of rubbish, a hand came up onto my shoulder from behind, softly squeezing me.

Although agitated beyond anything I had ever experienced or could remember, I turned slowly. A response to the delicacy of the contact from behind.

In that instance, my anger and frustration drained, replaced with a sort of embarrassment, or a need to appear collected and in complete control of my faculties.

Standing there, with a kind smile, peeking up just over the rim of her glasses, was Dr Sterne.

'Hello again, Leon. How nice it is to see you.' She reached out with her other hand, offering me a large caramel-drizzled muffin. 'We have a lot to discuss.'

Chapter 9

Was any of this really happening?

There I sat, looking directly at the two. Sam, my recently more mysterious, and obviously physically capable, friend from work. And Dr Sterne—or Meribel—the poster child for the contemporary world and a distinguished scientific powerhouse. On any other day, I would have expected this to be not only a dream, but an obscure one at that.

But sometimes reality can trump even the most whimsical screenplay of a resting mind.

There they sat, brimming with intelligence and confidence, looking over at me, lost in the new world I had been cast into.

'I hope you understand, Leon?' Dr Sterne was so calming and authoritative in her speech that I found myself sitting with perfect posture whenever she addressed me. 'That's why Sam and Frank had to bring you in.'

Her story wasn't that different from Sam's. I was more than just a person of interest for WormWhole now, as crazy as that idea was to me. And our chance

meeting in Hub 1, although unplanned, had only compounded that fact.

Even more worrisome was the revelation that my
AMI had been bugged, and I was likely being tracked
and listened to for who knows how long. Ignoring the
blatant illegality of that breach in privacy, my immediate reaction to the news wasn't to go and call a lawyer,
considering recent events. They must have heard me
asking about the gate network, divulging how I didn't
believe their corporate nonsense answers on hiccups.
I probably sounded like I was fishing for information
about the gate's operations from Dr Sterne herself.

Which I absolutely was of course. But still.

Unbeknownst to me, it was Dr Sterne who had
saved me in a way. She had somehow managed to
scramble my AMI while we spoke, disabling its capa-
bility to send or receive data. I don't know how she
did it, but that was why I couldn't make contact with
Sam after visiting her apartment.

I had dropped off WormWhole's radar just long
enough to make it back to my apartment and leave
with Sam and Frank, leaving no trace we had even
been there.

I was grateful. Or, more honestly, I felt like I had
to be grateful given my lack of understanding. Trying
to wrap my head around all that had transpired was
becoming tiresome. But there was still a question I
needed to ask, one that gnawed at me from the moment of Dr Sterne's arrival.

'Why me?' I was still unsure of what role I was

being cast in amongst the rabble of people swarming around the bunker. 'Why help me?'

She sat up in her seat.

'Sam has spoken very highly of you, Leon. It was by her request that you're here, and she has assured us you will be invaluable to our efforts. Plus, if I remember correctly, you were very curious as to why these people keep going missing, right?'

I looked at Sam, stretching her arms out over her head, looking away so as not to connect with my gaze. I knew she wouldn't like being outed as being overly complimentary of anyone.

But Dr Sterne had just reminded me of what I thought was a salient piece of information from earlier.

'Sorry, Meribel, but didn't you tell me that the gate network can't take the commuter load? That the planet was just too strained, and that was why hiccups happen?'

She smiled at the idea. 'Purely fictitious. Did you think I would simply disclose all to a stranger with crumbs clinging to his face? Not to mention an AMI outputting so much private data you could practically hear the audio packets divulging our conversation.'

At that moment, I felt foolish. Not just because of the crumbs remark, but her jocund tone made it appear I should have come to that conclusion myself.

In my defence, she could have told me that the slipway was accidentally turning people into seahorses and I would have believed her. She's Dr Meribel

Sterne. And I was just a fanboy, blinded by respect and admiration.

She continued. 'From all my research, and everything I have put into finding out why people disappear, I have come to a single conclusion.'

I braced myself for the bombshell that was about to come, the answer I had been striving for since that damned day several weeks ago. I leant forwards, chest swelling with anticipative breath.

'The reason is, Leon, that there is no reason. The network is perfect. Nobody should ever go missing.'

It was less of a bombshell and more of a cluster bomb.

'Perfect? But, that's impossible. How can people still go missing if it's perfect? That makes no sense.' My internal monologue had spilt outward, giving voice to an avalanche of doubt. 'The wall, your List. Isn't that proof enough that it's not perfect?'

Dr Sterne looked to Sam. And so did I. Sam had her head in her AMI, gesturing a series of commands too quickly for me to follow. 'Here we go,' she spoke lowly to herself before standing from her seat.

Projecting out from her holoscreen was a heavily scattered document of some kind. It wasn't redacted as such, it just seemed damaged or incomplete. A corrupted file.

'You see the List over there, Leon?' Sam pointed over to the memorial wall once again. I had hardly gone a minute without glancing in its direction. It was morbidly distracting, a constant siren call of despair.

'The only thing they have in common, that we can find, is that they disappeared. And that's where their story ends.'

My curiosity was piqued. Not by what Sam was saying, but by how she was saying it. It was always obvious with her when a "but" was lying in wait.

'That was until five months ago. Incident 3761-37, Mr Garvan Doherty, reported lost to a slipway hiccup around the same time. This document you see here, it's an internal memo, sent from a director in one of the biopharma wings of the BioDev research centre in Arizona. The memo is dated two days after his disappearance to a hiccup. It's pretty badly corrupted as you can see, so we're trying to read between the lines. Apparently, Mr Ghost, as we've been calling him, managed to assault several employees, leaving two of them seriously injured and requiring medical attention.' Sam barely took a breath. 'It didn't say what he was doing there, but it seems he was trying to break into a highly restricted area of the laboratory, specifically a level four biohazard lab. And that was it. We haven't found any other information about the incident. If they're covering it up, they've done a damned good job. The lab isn't even registered. It's a figment of this file's imagination, and nothing more.'

She allowed a stage-worthy pause before continuing. 'He's the first and only proof that we have that someone can come back.'

I tried to talk but found my mouth bone dry. I had

been slack-jawed the entire time, dazed by the revelation, and mystified by the possibilities.

Someone who disappeared had actually reappeared.

'Yep, there's an appropriate reaction.' Styx laughed behind me.

Several more people had gathered upon seeing Sam's projection, although they didn't seem fazed by it. Not their first viewing, I could tell.

Frank approached from the side, patting me on the shoulder as he passed by. I could tell this was his version of support; perhaps he was seeing similarities in my reaction to his own.

'Problem is Leon, that's all we've got.' Frank kept walking as he talked, squeezing past Sam and Dr Sterne, but stopping at a terminal just beyond them. 'A name. And nothing more. How many Garvan Dohertys are there in the world?'

'Thirteen!' Styx had shouted out the answer before anyone even had a chance to contemplate the statistical probability of name sharing globally. 'Oh wait, I know this one. Fifteen? Damn it Frank don't you dare tell me, seventeen?!'

Several others chuckled as they began to disperse from the crowd. Even Frank had a smile creep across the side of his face.

It wasn't the most common name I had ever heard, but by the law of averages, there was bound to be a few.

'So what if it's a bit thin on information, Frankly,

it's something.' Sam seemed upset by Frank's dismissive attitude. 'You know full well it's worth it. Why else would you be here, asshole?'

'Who knows, Sam.' His voice was low, but for the slightest of moments, and unknown to Sam, Frank turned and looked at her. He was too far away for me to gauge his expression accurately, but the look implied he had a specific reason in mind.

'So, what do we do with that information?' I addressed the question to the four still left in my immediate area. Frank, Styx, and Dr Sterne let the question pass over them, seemingly giving it some thought. But Sam's face lit up unexpectedly.

'What?' I asked, noticing her change in expression. 'What did I say?'

She spoke through her smile, with an eyebrow raised.

'We.'

***

I stood at the gate once again, thankful to finally be done with my orientation. I had a lot to process, and it was difficult to think.

And on top of it all, there were too many introductions. It was like the first day of school.

I was bad with names on a good day, but there must have been two dozen other bunker dwellers pottering about and working on various tasks. I repeated the names in my head over and over so as not to forget, but with every repeat, I lost another name.

There was Amal, tall and smiley, the supply guy. You want something, he's got you. Raleigh, short hair and nose ring, computer salvage. She mainly was seeing if any of the old equipment lying around was of use. Christian, short and quiet, something to do with cables or cable management? Or maybe he was the one doing supplies? His coat was vibrantly red, far louder than he was, so at least he had that going. But to be fair, he had probably been the friendliest when I arrived.

'Leon, was it?' Christian asked the first chance he could get at me. 'That's great, and you know Sam? Oh you worked with Sam, oh that's great she's the best. So another Saint, eh, and a WormWholer, you guys are great, good to have a few of you around. Put it there.'

I swear Christian's handshake was so thorough he was trying to get my pulse, or lift my fingerprints, or maybe he had just read a book on how to be the "Alpha Male" with new people and really long uncomfortable handshakes was the way to go.

But at least he was friendly, so I hoped that would help me to remember his name. Christian, Amal, Raleigh, Frank, Styx...

And that was about it now.

I cursed my brain, but it was too late. I would have to be re-introduced to everyone.

The lights at the gate were turned off now, allowing my retinae the luxury of remaining unburnt. I hadn't noticed it on the way in, but the gate was modified. Heavily.

'Frankenstein's monster.' I read the label above the entrance aloud.

Styx, who had been giving me the breakdown of the mostly useless technology scattering the bunker, was stood beside me, beaming.

'What's the story behind this?'

'Oh, you mean this old thing?' She slapped the frame of the gate firmly, immediately regretting her decision as her hand reverberated off the hard metal structure. She continued, feigning a pain-free demeanour. 'She's a beauty, right?'

'What's up with all the...extras?' I couldn't make sense of the many cables spreading to various machines surrounding our position.

'Well, we do like our privacy down here amongst the rubble. And what's more private than our own floating gateway?'

I paused for a moment, looking at her with stunned disbelief, but then turned back to the mass of tentacle-like cables coming from the system.

A floating gate.

Custom gates were relatively easy to build. But only if you had a tonne of money, access to fabrication facilities, and an in-depth engineering education coupled with cutting-edge gate physics knowledge. You know, real run-of-the-mill stuff.

But as soon as a gate went live it was tagged by whatever company controlled the district you fell under. You'd be lucky to take a single trip before you were taken offline and slapped with various legal pile-drivers. That type of private personal access to the slipway network was considered just a little too un-restricted, and dangerous. They were illegal the world over.

But floating gates, from what little information I could lay hands on in MIT, were designed to remain undetected permanently. You could go anywhere, any time. Nobody could find it. Nobody could stop you. The gate was a needle in a haystack, if the needle was designed to look like a piece of hay.

'Woah...' Amid all the troubles, and the unforeseen vacation to Iran, I was utterly amazed.

'Exactly.' She spoke while circling the system, per-forming a simple visual scan. 'Took us a few weeks to get everything we needed, hard to secretly move around so much tech with those damned cameras watching every gate. Definitely a team effort. But now we're free as a bird to come and go as we please, for the most part.'

'For the most part?'

'Well, yeah. WormWhole and all those other com-panies have cameras on every single gate on the planet. You think those universal privacy laws really matter? They see everybody come and go, everyone is on their radar. So, we have to use it sparingly. Can't have too many people travelling through gates with-out ever appearing on another end.'

It made sense. Groups of people couldn't just be

seen to be entering gates and never showing up at another, only to appear again several hours or days later to repeat the process. Faking a hiccup would be hard.

I stepped slightly closer to the gate, only to be greeted by a vibration from my AMI. I had no coverage down in the bunker, so it piqued my curiosity as I activated the interface. No new messages, no mails, just a small web-like notification in the top corner. Sam had successfully unscrambled my AMI it would seem as it was now able to interact with the gate.

'Hmph, good to know it's not completely broken,' I murmured to myself as I ignored the notification.

'Something up, Leon?' Styx was back by my side, having completed her evaluation of the gate.

'Oh, nothing. Just thought this program of Sam's had gone bogey on me. It kept giving me the same notification when I was nowhere near the gates at BioDev. Thought it was just—'

Styx held her palm up directly in front of my face, hushing me. Bit rude, but effective.

'You were in BioDev?' The pitch of her tone had dropped several bars. 'When?'

'Eh, I don't know, maybe half a day ago by now?'

'Are you sure it was trying to connect with a gate?' Again, her friendly tone was all but gone.

'Well, yeah. I was passing through the offices, after visiting a friend, and it went off. Why?'

Again, she hushed me, looking away for a moment to gather whatever thoughts were flooding her mind. The hand disappeared from my face, and she was bounding towards Sam and the other woman that had joined us when we were fleeing my building. I still hadn't been properly introduced to her, despite the role she played in bringing me here.

Lucy was her name, and I congratulated myself on remembering that.

Styx immediately ingrained herself in the conversation between the two, aiming the majority of her speech at Sam, while pointing at her AMI. She became more animated the more Sam responded until eventually she turned and stepped quickly back towards me, both of the others in tow.

'Give Sam your AMI, Leon.'

I disengaged the AMI from my forearm, handing it over without question. My arm felt cold as the sweaty skin from under my gauntlet met the air. The triangle of women in front of me were deeply engaged in something, but I couldn't see properly past Styx with her back turned.

I didn't appreciate being left out, so I decided it was time to become more proactive in my new surroundings.

'What are you doing, Sam?' I demanded, pushing my way into their little rabble. 'And what does my AMI have to do with it?'

Lucy looked up and spoke first. 'Where exactly in the building were you when you synced with the gate?'

I was a little taken aback that it was her that responded, but I wasn't about to let it derail my demands. 'Look, either you guys fill me in, or you can hand back my AMI and—'

'Bingo!' Sam yelled out as a projection sprung from my holoscreen.

The web-like interface was familiar, but the focus of the projection was an obscure departure from the central Hub of gates at the BioDev building. A display of the building was being generated floor by floor as the projection grew more detailed. I recognised some of the layouts as the hallways and lab spaces were populated in the display.

'Lucy?' Both Styx and Sam said it at the same time, turning to Lucy with wide eyes.

'That's Dr Ross's office,' she said, a little taken by surprise.

'Yes,' I interjected. 'I was there collecting some stuff. What of it?'

'You were in the room, with him?' Lucy nearly boiled over with anticipation.

'Eh, well I guess.' I recalled all the detail I could from my short visit, trying to decipher why this may be exciting news for them. 'I was only just inside the door. I don't think he wanted me to step in; he seemed a bit flustered when he noticed I had followed him in. He kind of pushed me out pretty quickly.' I hadn't thought about it at the time, but Dr Ross did appear to rush me out of the room once he had noticed I stepped inside. It was a bit rude really.

'Holy shit, is that a private gate in his office?' Styx interjected, clearly only catching up with the others line of thought, but still a step ahead of myself. 'Fancy prick...'

Sam chuckled to herself. 'Just visiting a friend was it, Leon? Well, who would have known your lusty wandering would come in use some day.' Her chuckle turned to a full laugh for a moment before she composed herself. 'Looks like you're going to prove your worth to us sooner than expected.'

'I hope you made a good impression, Leon.' Lucy was again talking directly to me, excitement filling her every word. All three were now looking at me, wide-eyed and struggling to reign in their excitement. 'Because we're going to need you to make a pretty bad one now.'

Chapter 10

The bunker had become a frenzy of excited chatter.

Sam and Styx were in a full-on war of words at the terminal a few feet away from the gate. Dr Sterne and Frank were talking to several of the other underground residents, giving out cups of coffee and snacks in equal measure. Lucy was joyously singing to herself as she operated the nearest computer at lightning speed. I couldn't keep up with her finger movements, let alone the display's staggered response.

And there I sat, in the middle of it all, the catalyst of this newly assembled plan.

But what was expected of me, was a little troubling.

Lucy had become extremely excited at the revelation I had stepped foot inside Dr Ross's office, and this was what made me the lynchpin of their newest endeavour.

It turned out Lucy was a good friend of Frank's, both having worked in the BioDev security firm for several years. More directly however, Lucy, ignoring the possible repercussions upon Frank's request, joined the group on nothing but Frank's word that she wouldn't regret it.

And it was her in-depth knowledge of the security systems in BioDev that was the basis for this mission.

According to her, Dr Ross, and any other high clearance members of BioDev's elite, had an ARC security system installed in their offices. ARC, or Ambient Recognition Charter, systems were designed to perfectly recognise guests through a variety of physical and chemical characteristics. Basically it sized you up and "smelled" you on entry. It was a literal electronic guard dog.

One advantage of this? It would technically "remember" me as a verified guest for a short period of time. So, should I, for some reason, choose to appear out of thin air in the middle of his office, I would not set off the alarm system immediately. I couldn't get through the doors' combination of biometric sensors, but I didn't need to now.

And access to an office in BioDev, let alone such a senior office, meant possible access to records. Records like the uncorrupted version of the re-appearing hiccup man. A record to prove that maybe, just maybe, they don't all just disappear into the ether.

Even though I had only briefly peered into Dr Ross's office, I had not spotted any sign of a personal gate. The room was immaculate in its burgundy and silver. A gate should have stood out.

But the coordinates were there, no doubt about that.

I rose from my seat, slowly making my way towards Dr Sterne, who like me was now enjoying the lively debate going on between Sam and Styx.

She turned to me, looking out over her glasses as usual. She seemed to welcome every exchange, no matter who approached her in the bunker. She was an open book. It was like she had developed the perfect expression for inviting conversation.

Or maybe that was all just in my head, the delusions of a fanboy. I still wanted her to sign my copy of her autobiography, one of the only paperback books I had ever bought. I was beating myself up a little that I hadn't brought it from my apartment.

'Enjoying the show?' She pointed back at the other two, who now were in a different argument about something. I knew Sam's moods could swing like a sail, but Styx didn't seem one to back down from a good fight.

'Oh, very much,' I replied. 'I always get a bit of enjoyment out of Sam, whether she realises it or not.'

We shared a light-hearted chuckle. I was feeling more and more settled surrounded by these new acquaintances.

'It's a brave thing, Leon. I hope you know we really appreciate what you are about to do.' She placed her hand on my forearm, sincerity pouring out over every word. 'I hope what we have asked of you isn't too much.'

It almost felt as if she had been put up to saying this to me. That Sam or the others knew I wouldn't be able to show any regret or nervousness in front of her. That I would perform the task out of some strange wish to avoid disappointing this person I barely knew but respected more than most.

If they had put her up to it, I was in trouble. Because it worked.

'Breaking and entering? Nothing me and my brother, Dan, didn't do a hundred times to the school cafeteria years ago. It'll be fine.' I was lying, hard. A lump was almost forming in my throat as I thought about the mission. 'Lucy has me fully prepped. I walk in, I walk out. No problems.'

No problems outside of possibly being caught breaking into an extremely high-profile researcher's office, where untold company secrets may well reside. Oh, and I was apparently somewhat of a wanted man too. And there was no guarantee what we were looking for was actually there.

Nothing but positives on the horizon of the adventure so far.

'Ok, all set.' Lucy cut between myself and Dr Sterne, clutching something small in her hand. 'You two done bickering?'

With a joint 'hmph,' Sam and Styx turned back to us.

Sam spoke first. 'We should at least try to get more people in there. When will we ever have a chance like this again?'

Styx's reply was quick. 'We already went over this.

We need to keep a low profile and just get what we need. He's the only one that can go.'

'But—' Sam's rebuttal was cut short.

'You two can be truly useless sometimes.' Lucy rolled her eyes. 'Here, Leon.'

She handed me a data key. I rolled the small object between my fingers. It was small but felt durable with its rubber and metal combination overlay. The type of device you would use to back up your backups, just to be sure you were covered.

'Sam, your plan is the right one,' Lucy said, not directing it towards the group. 'Leon can't be expected to do everything. So, with this key Leon now holds so firmly, we can fool the security system for long enough to get what we need. That means we need some volunteers. And by volunteers, I mean you two.' She pointed to both Frank and Sam. A match made in Heaven, unless you're the accompanying party.

Styx let out a little chuckle.

'No debating. They don't know about us, and we want to keep it that way. In and out, don't touch anything you don't have to, and we'll be safe as houses.' Lucy spoke firmly and with great aplomb. She had clearly been a figure of authority in her previous occupation.

'Lucy is right.' Now it was Dr Sterne's turn. Everyone that had gathered immediately hushed their silent micro-conversations, coming to full attention. 'This is the greatest opportunity any of us will have to get to the bottom of these mysterious events, maybe the only opportunity. I know you all have a variety of reasons for being here and have sacrificed in a multitude of different ways, but I hope you trust that what we are doing here is worth all of it. We will get to the bottom of this, one way or another. I promise you that.'

A short speech, but it was rousing enough that I would have sprinted through the gate there and then. But that made me uneasy, just a little. I don't think anyone else noticed it, but the way Dr Sterne spoke bordered on a call to arms. Almost as if she was aware of what the information we would find could lead to.

It was just a feeling, and a small one at that. But it was still there.

'Boot the monster up, Styx. Let's do this.' Sam had brushed past Frank, acting like a child and sticking her tongue out as she passed. 'Leon, you're up.'

With those three words, my fate had been sealed. I just hoped it would be a good fate.

***

I didn't sprint through the gate, desperate to see what lay on the other side. I eased into the journey, as I had done so many times in the past, slowly stepping into the event horizon of the slipway.

The journey to the bunker had felt unusually long, so it was reasonable to think it would be the same leaving. I hoped I would get more time awash in the blue and green aura that had so often made my journeys that bit more spectacular in the past. A calming build-up to the daunting task at hand.

But I was left disappointed.

No streaming blue lights, no shades of green swirled around my extremities. Just nothing.

I arrived quicker than expected, continuing my stride through to the other side, but was met immediately with resistance. I bounced off an unseen, solid obstacle, face and nose first, knocking me back into the entrance of the gate. Normal gate travel worked on burst single direction traffic, so instead of landing butt first back in front of all of those I just left, I instead rolled back and hit my head off the hard-metallic surface of the gate's back wall.

Not an ideal start, but not totally unexpected.

If I hadn't seen the gate in his office, it meant it was hidden away. Likely so nobody knew he had the power to come and go as he pleased. So, if it was hidden behind a wall, there was a good chance it would not be open on my arrival.

And you would think knowing that information that I would have come through with my hands raised, as opposed to using my face.

Nope.

I stood up, dusting myself off, looking around to ensure that nobody had somehow seen my embarrassing tumble. There had to be a switch here somewhere, or a simple lever. There was no need for a proper security lock for something secretive like this.

My hands searched the wall up and down, sliding

along the cold, hard doorway. It was perfectly polished.

Down to the right, just by the frame, and almost exactly where you would expect to find one, my hand made contact with a handle. One simple turn and push and I was no longer steeped in darkness.

The large door swung effortlessly out into the room, requiring no real force on my part. But what greeted me wasn't what I had remembered.

The whole room was alien. The beautiful modern décor of daytime transformed into a ghoulish, unwelcoming darkroom at night as the red leather had turned a murky blood shade in the low light. Each metal surface reflected only small sprays of light as I stepped in, making it appear there was movement all around.

I wasted no time getting acclimatised, unsure of how long the security system would assume me a colleague or welcomed guest. I walked to Dr Ross's impressively large desk, where, just as Lucy had told me, a small flickering interface was built into the wooden top.

I found the port for the key, pushed it in, and watched for the lights to stop flickering as it did whatever it needed to do. From what Lucy had explained, it was going to add Frank and Sam's details to the security system, just like I was. It wasn't a hack as such, which could have caused a security backlash, just a few additional bits of information. It would be short-lived but effective.

Once the lights had stopped, I removed the key, breathed a sigh of relief, and made my way back to the gate. I spun up Sam's gate interface on my AMI and input the custom address I had been given. Once engaged I threw the key drive back in. That was our very advanced and highly thought-out way of showing I had completed my task.

It was only seconds later that Sam arrived, with Frank a few moments after. Both silently patted me on the back as they passed me by and moved directly to their intended targets.

Frank was to ensure, as best he could, that the fake details allowing him and Sam to be in the room would not stay logged on the security system. As I had been there already, it wasn't necessary for mine to be erased.

Sam had the more pressing task of breaking into Dr Ross's terminal and searching for any information about the event with our Mr Ghost.

And I was a lookout. A task given to me most likely because I had to stay behind to activate whatever Frank set up to delete their involvement. It reminded me of when I was a child and I would keep watch for our parents while Dan made a midnight raid on the treats cabinet.

None of us said a word. I felt I wasn't the only one brimming with two parts excitement and one-part terror. I moved towards the frosted windows, trying to find a way to peer out. But the office was self-contained; nobody could see in or out. My duties of keeping watch were finished before they had even begun.

I couldn't help but wonder what we would find. It was baffling to think about. Why would this man, who apparently disappeared years ago, all of a sudden be breaking into somewhere like this? And also, how? It didn't seem like these guys were lacking in security.

It was probably best not to speculate on what happened to him, or who he really was. We would hopefully know soon enough.

Gingerly leaning on the window, I turned back towards the desk, looking up again at the whitish blue and fiery red numbers above the giant map. The combined purple glow made that side of the room all the more alien. I wished now that I had taken note of the numbers earlier or paid closer attention. They had changed, or at least I was pretty sure they had changed.

There went my theory of it being a secret map to their hidden family island.

Unless it was a hidden family zeppelin, constantly on the move. That made it seem even cooler.

Frank was finished and was looking over Sam's shoulder quietly as she calmly executed her plans. 'Stop breathing so close to me,' she whispered without moving her gaze from the computer's display.

'Okay, okay here we go,' she said, standing up from her seat. 'It's working, I don't know what we're getting, but we're getting something.'

'Well download it and let's go, there's no telling

how long this security blind spot will last.' Frank, now making his way towards the gate, was beginning to sweat. 'Leon, all you have to do is press enter once we leave, okay? The security override will do the rest.'

'Of course,' I replied, hoping it really would be that simple. My unease wasn't dissipating the longer we stayed here, and the adrenaline and thrill of our brazen operation was starting to decline.

'Got it! Frank?' Sam detached a small cable connecting her AMI to the computer, shutting it down as she moved away.

Frank was already activating the gateway, which silently whirled into action. In a heartbeat, Sam had disappeared. 'Be quick,' Frank warned as he reactivated the gate and jogged through.

I had already moved to the back of the desk, ready to enact his final command. Once the room was empty again, I activated the code and moved to my extraction point.

I stepped into the small alcove, turning to pull the door behind me when several small bright green lights caught my attention.

Accompanied by a distinct latching sound, much more obvious from this side of the wall, the door to the office swung open.

I leapt back, pinning myself to the inner wall of the gate, crouching instinctively.

'Shit, shit, shit,' I whispered as I tried to peek out. I was trapped.

The lights flickered to life as someone stepped into

the room. Thankfully the gate remained mostly in the dark, but the panel was still open, and more light than I would have liked seeped in around me. I pinned myself to the darker wall of the gate, just to the side, hoping the shadows would conceal me further.

I couldn't activate the gate, it would be too obvious. I couldn't close the door, the movement would be noticed. I couldn't run, I was on the bad end of a highly secure facility. I couldn't do anything but hide, and even that seemed foolish.

'You know he'll still kill you for coming in here, right?' I didn't recognise the voice, but it was deep and obviously a man.

'You're all so afraid of my dad. You know he would respect you more if you were less timid.'

The second voice, however, was unmistakable. It was Jess.

'Oh yeah, sure. "Hey, Dr Ross, what's hanging, my man? Are you coming out later for Dave's retro movie night? *Groundhog Day,* it's gonna be off the hook! You'll bring the nachos, right?" You're right that does sound like a good idea.'

'Oh, hardy har har, very funny. You should do stand up. In fact, why don't you just stay standing out there and don't come in. The last thing we need is a lockdown.'

Jess's wit was just as sharp as ever. Usually I would have chuckled at such a quick put down, but with my back pinned against the wall, literally, and trying to keep myself as quiet as a church mouse, there was no time for amusement.

I could hear her footsteps as she moved about the room.

'What the?'

The footsteps got louder.

She must have noticed the panel being open. There was no time for a plan. I still couldn't activate the gate. She wouldn't know I was a fugitive, if I even truly am. At least not yet. I would have to confront her, even though it would be impossible to explain why I was there.

I held my breath as the footsteps got closer. Shifting my weight, I got ready to push myself out from my barely concealed hiding spot.

But instead, she stopped.

'I guess that explains why I didn't see him leave this evening. He's getting very lazy in his old age with this damned gate.'

Her voice was close. I could feel she was almost right beside me, close enough to reach out and touch, but the curvature of the gate's internal quarter lent me enough shadow to remain inconspicuous.

A sheer fluke, my position had made it impossible for us to see each other. Another step maybe, or another inch, and we could have been locking eyes.

'Come on, we don't have all night you know.' The voice from across the room allowed for me to let a small exhalation escape without notice.

'Oh, I'm sorry, am I holding you back, Stavros? Well,

we can't have that now can we.' Her voice started to lower as she turned and walked away from the alcove. 'God forbid I hold you back from your precious mass spectrometry for another moment. BioDemon must have their precious data before daybreak, lest the company come crashing down.' She had added a dramatical tone to her voice while berating the mystery associate. 'Oh, and you now owe me two coffees.'

'Yeah, yeah. You know that's the only prize you ever ask for? You got a problem, Jess.'

They shared a small laugh, and I could hear her riffling through some paper on the far side of the room.

And just as quickly as they had arrived, they were gone. The door latched itself once more, a flash of red filling the room for a moment to show it was now on lockdown.

I slumped to the ground, palms sweating and breathing heavily.

In that instance, only moments ago, I wanted nothing more than just to step out and talk to her. To even just see her face.

I was so utterly drained from the day. Everything since I had last seen her had been a rollercoaster of emotions. Just seeing her for a moment, dimples flaring, eyes wide and beautiful, would've gone a long way to cheering me up. To making this all okay.

But I couldn't. And the revelation that I mightn't see her again for quite a while left me even more diminished.

It was kind of sad. She wasn't my partner or girlfriend, she wasn't someone I used to be involved with. She was only slowly becoming more than a friend. How could she already have such a strong effect on me?

I always felt I was a naturally jovial person. Optimistic to a fault was what a friend in MIT used to call it, but I was never sure if it leant more towards an insult than a compliment.

But not now. Not in that moment. It was easy to be perpetually optimistic when everything in life was simple, and nothing too terrible ever happened. But that life seemed further and further away with each new day.

I dabbed the sweat off my brow with a sleeve before standing.

Pulling the door shut, I locked it neatly into place, and once more plunged myself into pitch darkness.

With my back pressed against the door, I lifted my AMI, already paired to the gate, and activated the secret slipway coordinates.

I looked at the distorted light of the event horizon.

'This will be worth it,' I assuredly said to myself, as I stepped back into the previously unknown.

Chapter 11

I arrived in a split second, unsure of what was awaiting me in the bunker.

Would I be returning as part of a conquering threesome, successful in our espionage, cheered on by our peers? Or would my delayed appearance have been the cause for undue worry, for which they were already in the process of forming a search and rescue?

'What the fuck, Leon?'

It appeared neither. Sam stood ready to scold, inches from my face.

'What part of a quick in and out didn't you understand?' Her words weren't worrisome. She seemed genuinely angry at my tardiness. 'Did you hang around just to take in the sights, or were you too busy staring at that damned digital clock on the wall you seemed so fascinated by? We had a job to—'

'The panel jammed, okay!' I snapped at her. A fabrication would suffice. 'Would you rather I just left it open? Maybe left a little bit of extra evidence behind, a note to thank him for his hospitality perhaps?'

I instantly felt I had overdone it.

Sam furrowed her brow and stepped down her assault. I could tell I had lashed back a little too hard, but I was still feeling raw from my near miss with Jess, and the day's fatigue had shortened my fuse immensely. I must have been awake nearly twenty hours straight.

'Fine, Jeez, sorry for caring.' Sam turned her head to the others, waving to Styx. 'Come on, get it done before Frank cracks the security on that chip.'

Styx came jogging over sporting a huge grin, overjoyed with our success. She ignored us both, instead pushing through between us, and headed straight to the terminal closest to the gate.

'Get what done?' I asked, pausing between each word, barely holding back the first of what I felt was to be many yawns.

Sam took a quick breath, her expression softening as she turned back to talk. 'She has to re-float the gate. Have to keep anonymous you know.'

'Re-float the gate?' She knew I didn't understand, but she thrived on knowing more than others, so I asked the question as a sort of apology for my short fuse.

'Well everyone that leaves here leaves with the gate address, right? And thanks to my nifty little bit of gate interface software, you can gain access from anywhere. But,' she raised her index finger up close to my face, 'once everyone returns, or time runs out, we re-float the gate, taking us off the network. Every gate can store a commuter's destination code, so anyone with a hint of intelligence would be able to find us here pretty quickly if they wanted. And when we re-join the network, we'll have a brand-new address again.'

Like a big game of hide and seek, even a child would realise staying in the same place would be counter-intuitive. It was all very logical, or at least nearly all of it.

'What do you mean, "time runs out"?' I felt she had glided over a fairly crucial fact.

'Oh yeah, we re-float the gate if a person doesn't come back soon after they're supposed to. Can't be too careful you know. Styx's rules.' She pointed over to Styx, who was working away and humming to herself but still managed to give us a quick thumbs-up in acknowledgement.

'But what if you get stuck on the other side? How do you find your way back?' I fought the question out against another building yawn.

'Hasn't been a problem yet, so just try not to get stuck, okay?' The answer came from Styx, now finished her job and ushering us towards the group. 'Come on, come on. Frank will be ready any minute.'

The three of us made our way back to the group. Everyone in the bunker had taken up stations around Frank, making it easier to get a head count. There looked to be just over the two dozen people from earlier, give or take. Not a bad little ragtag group size, but the bunker was big enough to house hundreds if they wanted.

'Is this everyone?' I whispered to Sam as we found a place to sit.

She took a quick look around the group. 'Looks about right.'

It was like sitting around a campfire. Half on the floor, with legs crossed, and half standing at the back with arms crossed, a funny group of opposites. All had eyes on Frank, and most were giddy and whispering to one another, making sure to stay quiet so as not to interfere. A few were not as visibly excited, their faces adorned with a stoic blandness. A sort of "here we go again" attitude.

I didn't know if they were all privy to the details of the mission, but I felt that maybe these few had had more than one let down before.

'I think we have something here.' Frank spoke up from the group's focal point, rapidly gesturing through the holoprojection filling the air in front of him. 'Just another few moments...'

Everyone hushed, the purr of electronics replacing whispers. Hardly anyone budged while Frank neared completion of decoding our spoils.

But in that instance of pure pause, with fatigue held at bay by the overwhelming curiosity of our discovery, a shift in my peripheral shook me from the communal daze.

Just for a moment, a flash of pale red pulled my attention from the group, and back towards the gate. The sombre grey of the machinery and surroundings had dissolved that sector of my vision into nothing but white noise. But now a spark of movement in the void had stirred me. I snapped around to see but was met with emptiness.

Shaking my head, I turned back, cursing my drooping eyes and overworked mind. I refocussed on the possibilities of the impending reveal while shifting from my now uncomfortable table top perch.

But again, a flash from my right stole my attention. Except it didn't seem like movement this time, more of a flickering of light.

Curious even more on this occasion, I stood and approached the gate. It had lain dormant since my arrival a few moments ago, but within a moment it flashed again. A burst of orange from the large LED panel directly above the threshold of the gate. I had never seen it pulse before; I didn't even know it could go orange. Solid green was engaged, solid red was offline. It was a simple traffic light for commuters and Saints alike.

It pulsed again, and then again, a few seconds after. And then again, a double pulse this time. It continued pulsing, only seconds apart, and seemingly erratic, but definitely quickening.

'Eh, Styx?' My voice was low and inquisitive, almost as if I had asked myself without any real hope the others heard it.

It pulsed, in groups of flashes. 1, 2, 3, pause. 1, 2, 3, 4, 5, pause. 1, 2, pause. There didn't seem any pattern to them, even the pulses had incoherent durations.

'Hey, Styx?' Again, my voice hardly reached a

normal conversation level, the flashing light was a confusing fascination, something I didn't know could occur with a machine I was supposed to be supremely familiar with. Although my voice was failing to break through to the others mere feet behind me, a response of sorts came. But not from another person, from the machine.

As if reacting to my voice, it stopped. Abruptly and without sound.

The moment lasted only a few seconds, long enough for me to feel the whole thing could have almost been my imagination, just sleep deprived machinations.

Then with a momentary high-pitched ringing, the unmistakable hum of an active gate emerged, and the LED panel beamed a solid green light out into the bunker.

I swung to the crowd, this time roaring as I turned. 'Styx?!'

Everyone turned, shocked at the sudden outburst.

I raised an arm and turned back to point at the light as if needing to highlight the source of my worries.

But between myself and the gate stood another man now, slightly familiar. He was short, wearing a vibrantly red coat.

The friendliness in his expression long gone, Christian had his arm raised towards me.

Something hit me. Not too hard, but hard enough to force me to take a step back. In front of me, his outstretched arm now sported a small holographic crosshair floating above the device wrapped tightly around his hand.

I ran my left hand down my torso.

My whole mid-section was distended and getting worse. It felt surreal. Like I was being inflated.

I strained not to look down as my left leg began to tremble in panic.

But from nowhere, a bolt of lightning. A thunder-bolt of divine intensity.

Crashing to the ground, I screamed from the agony pouring out from my left side. It burnt as I spasmed, causing me to lash out in all directions. I was being shocked and torn apart at the same time; the pain spread out in every direction along my side, drawing an unending scream from my lungs.

I couldn't stop. The disorientation of the pain left me with no alternatives but to scream and writhe on the floor.

Somebody was trying to hold me down, two people possibly, but I couldn't twist to look. My senses were in overdrive. The harsh floor was cold, but I was on fire. I couldn't move my arms, but still they spasmed at my side. I tried to form words, but only screams escaped. It sounded like the whole bunker was full of yelling, with shots ringing out again and again.

'Hold him still!'

I tried to help, tried to comply with the command of whoever was on my back, but my body couldn't stop convulsing. The surges of muscle spasms from the epicentre of pain in my side were unrelenting. I was being shocked to the point that my body was about to tear open.

'I'm sorry, Leon, this is going to fucking hurt!'

I felt a hand go around my side, under the shirt, and straight into the heart of where the pain was emanating. It was excruciating, to the point I could no longer scream. It had rendered me mute. I couldn't even take in air to vocalise the torturous procedure being performed on me.

But within a moment the convulsions stopped, and the pain eased from crippling to severe.

'Pick him up, get him out of here!'

The bunker was ear-popping, with the echoes reverberating off every solid surface all around.

'Freeze!'

'Get back!'

'Shut it down!'

'Don't move!'

It was hard to pinpoint their origin as I was hauled across the floor and thrown down behind a large cabinet.

'Leon! Leon, focus up! Can you stand?' It was Frank, pulling me up and leaning me against the firm backing. He had a gun in his hand, his free hand holding me by my collar, making sure I couldn't fall over.

I pushed myself up properly, the pain in my side was intense, but not debilitating as it had started. It felt shallow but spread halfway across my side.

'Y-yes. Yes, I think I'm fine.' I patted myself down, wincing at the soggy section of the shirt above my hip.

'Just stay here, okay? Don't move.'

With that Frank burst out from our cover, disappearing from my sight at full sprint.

I stood with my back pinned against the cabinet, listening to the orchestra of voices ringing out from beyond my view. They were shrill and panicked, unintelligible for the most part.

I twisted to my side, trying not to contort my mid-section as I turned. Peering out from behind the cover, I got my first glance at the chaos.

Although my view was partially blocked by the many desks and hunks of elderly machines, it was clear people were lying by the gateway.

It looked like three bodies, dressed in heavy black, lying motionless just past the gate entrance.

Another two lay almost out of sight, convulsing on the ground and howling. I couldn't make out who they were, but they must have been some of the other bunker occupants.

More shots rang out, accompanied by more shouting.

I moved around to the other side of my cover, trying to get a better view.

Frank was now kneeling behind a chest-high container, with Sam sitting beside him frantically doing something with her AMI. They were in a heated screaming match.

But before either of them budged, an explosion rang out from the corner of the bunker, knocking over several large server blocks and shaking the floor under my feet.

The power failed, plunging the entire facility into dark red emergency lighting.

As my eyes readjusted, Sam and Frank had gone.

What the fuck is going on?!

Who were those bodies, clad in black? Where did everyone go?

Was I shot? The realisation finally settled in, and I clawed my shirt up from my stomach. How was I even still standing if I had been shot?

There was very little blood, and most of it had begun to dry. There was only a small trickle still coming from the obvious wound at the centre. I poked at it, biting my tongue as the outburst of pain spread around my side. But I still felt...normal. Fine even.

It didn't feel like there was a gap or a hole of any kind behind the wound. It was almost superficial. But the pain I had felt, the intensity of the convulsions, the uncontrollable muscle spasms. I had never been shot, so I had nothing to compare it to, but nothing about it seemed right.

I readjusted my shirt, making sure it was pressed against the wound to halt the last of the bleeding. It seemed the action had left my immediate area, as the shouting was mainly on the far end of the bunker.

I stepped out of my shelter, moving towards the bodies on the ground.

The three bodies—although hard to make out in the deep crimson of the scene—seemed to be wearing heavy armour of some kind, as the padded clothing made their bodies bulky and disproportioned.

I stepped over them, taking just a quick glance towards Christian in the red jacket, lying motionless on the ground. I had forgot most names of the other bunker dwellers, but not his. And I definitely would never forget it now.

Just past him there were two others on the floor. I recognised the faces from only a few minutes earlier, casualties from our side.

I kneeled in between both, turning first to the man. As I placed a hand on him, I could feel his body was still convulsing slightly, but he was silent and clearly unconscious. The woman was completely still, but she was warm, and I could feel her breath when I put my hand in front of her mouth.

It seemed both had been shot with the same weapon as myself.

I rolled them into the recovery position, something my father taught me. I wasn't sure if it would do any-thing for them, but I couldn't just leave them sprawled so awkwardly on the hard floor.

I stood as a final shot rang out, followed not by silence, but a quietness that allowed for the carrying of other sounds. There was heavy panting, sobbing, and crackling. There was also a fierce debate going on in the direction of the last few shots.

I walked slowly, peering around each corner as I moved. The air grew smoky the closer I got, and the flickering light of a small fire was reflecting off the curved roof.

I reached a small opening, just short of the bunker wall, where several people were gathered around a flaming hunk of metal.

'I told you we should never have let him come!' Frank was livid and shouting at Sam.

'He wasn't with me; you know that. Sterne brought him. He was one of her researchers.' Sam wasn't shouting back. Instead she was stood talking into the fire, holding a large cable, a defeatist tone to her voice. 'He must have been a plant. Meribel was always wary she was under scrutiny...'

'Is everyone okay?' I asked, stepping towards them.

Only Sam turned, recognising my voice. 'Us? Shit, are you?'

I patted my side again, the shirt now thoroughly stuck to my skin. 'Yeah, I'm fine, I think. The others? Dr Sterne, Styx?'

Frank turned, walking over towards two more bodies lying off to the side.

'Styx will be fine, don't worry about her. I imagine she will just be pissed off once she comes to. Same for the others they got closer the gate' Frank said as he knelt down beside her. 'But Sterne, she's old. I don't know. We need a doctor. But...'

'But what?' I asked, wondering what more could possibly go further wrong.

A large clank rang out as Sam threw the cable into the dying flames.

'Power's gone Leon. We're trapped.'

Chapter 12

I awoke to the harsh garnet glow of the bunker's emergency lighting.

Stirring from my sleep, I rubbed the crusted deposits from my eyes while trying to stretch my legs in the less-than-average length bunk. 'How long was I out?' I asked the back of the person perched on the adjacent bunk removing their shoes.

'About four hours.' The reply came just as he stood and walked to a separate bed to lie down. It was Frank. He rolled to turn his back on me, clutching the pillow to his chest.

My sleep hadn't been planned but was desperately needed. We had moved all of those still unconscious to the rest area, where they could be easily looked after. Frank had been standing watch over Dr Sterne's bed, replaced now it seemed.

As for those uninjured, many had curled up on the other empty beds, too shaken to talk or partake in any problem-solving activities. I had only planned to sit for a moment too, but fatigue got the better of me once I was down.

The muscles still ached all down my left side, and it was an ordeal just to sit up.

Rising from my bed, quietly so as not to disturb any others, I made my way out to the small kitchen-ette. Everybody had gathered there after the fire had been taken care of, but it was deserted now. The area was far away from the smouldering wreckage of the generator, but the air was still smoky. Thankfully the fire was short-lived and small. Whatever passive ven-tilation system the bunker had been built with was helping, but slowly.

It seemed everyone was either asleep or still wan-dering the bunker hoping a miracle escape route would fall into their laps.

Looking out from the kitchenette, I had a direct view of the powerless gate and the bodies that still surrounded it.

There were six members of the assault team, all wearing the same armoured getup in head-to-toe tac-tical black. Three lay by the gate and three were by the wreckage of the generator. The explosion seemed to have been a mistake, not intentional sabotage. Frank had said one of their rounds must have ignited the battery cell, but I thought a stray bullet from our side would have been a more likely culprit.

Luckily, I guess, Frank and some others had some-how managed to bring weapons to the bunker. Or the weapons were already there possibly. I didn't want to pry as to where they got them or why they felt they needed weapons in this previously impenetrable top-secret facility of theirs.

As for my attacker, it was Christian who had shot me, the red-coated bastard. Styx guessed that he had somehow supplanted her security settings and dialled out for a connection to an unknown source. He had waited for Styx to re-float the gate, knowing nobody would pay it any attention once it was offline. But without power to the gate, it was pure guesswork as to where these few people may have come from, or who they were.

There was nothing on their persons to hint at a specific allegiance or organisation, but we all had our suspicions, considering our recent espionage.

The only clear thing about their motives, I felt at least, was that they weren't there to kill. The weapons they had were called "shotputs" according to Frank and Lucy. Non-lethal crowd control weapons.

The projectile would immediately expel a rapidly expanding conductive foam upon penetrating the skin, anchoring in surrounding tissue but not damaging internal organs or blood vessels. Once embedded, the core of the projectile would begin releasing a burst set of shocks to the target. Ten thousand volts, right on top of your muscle fibres and nerves. Although non-lethal, it was definitely not designed to be painless, and most people lost consciousness after several seconds.

The only reason Frank and Lucy even knew about them was through things they heard working security for BioDev. Apparently, the company had deployed them on several occasions to deal with "unrest" at clinics in some of the poorer regions of France.

I hoped that would be the last time I would see weapons like that. They often say you forget the pain, but not the experience, of injuries. I didn't think it would be possible ever to forget the pain I experienced for those few moments.

I threw myself down into a seat at the small dining table. A few biscuits were scattered on a plate and I ate them. I didn't think anybody had even stopped to consider our food stores in the crisis. They were well stocked, but there was a lot of us, and no more food would be coming our way anytime soon.

Sighing heavily, I put my head in my hands, crumbs falling from my mouth onto the rough cement floor. I tugged at my hair, mashing my face and head with my hands, one leg shaking not from cold but from a habit of fidgeting. All my nervous ticks were getting their moment in the spotlight as I tried to wake myself.

Still, I didn't believe the situation I found myself in. My life was dull but safe before. Now it had speedily turned 180, landing me in this miserable scenario. Every decision I had made that led me there was brash and reactionary, foolish even. I told myself I needed to grab the bull by the horns to regain some control of my situation. But it was too late. The bull had long died.

'Hey.' I looked up just as Styx was pulling a chair towards mine. 'You okay, super spy?'

I gave out a small exhalation of acknowledgement at her levity.

'Yeah...don't know why I asked really.' She slouched down into her chair, hanging her head back and looking up at the roof. 'Up shit's creek without a paddle, right?'

Understatement of the century. Our boat had already sunk to the river bed, with us thoroughly anchored to it.

We sat in silence for a few moments, both thinking of something worthwhile or constructive to say. But I didn't know the bunker as they did. In fact, I had only seen a fraction of the floor space since I arrived.

A simple question came to mind first as I lifted my head from my hands.

'How did you guys even get down here?'

Styx sat up straight and looked out past where the gate was. 'Sam got us access. Don't ask me how the hell she did it, but she somehow got the destination codes to this place off a "friend" of hers.'

'So, what, there just happened to be a gate lying in this old bunker, off the grid and ready to go?' The idea seemed preposterous. Who would just leave something like that unused?

'Kind of. Not exactly.' She paused for a second, her eyebrows raised and eyes rolled up as her head tilted ever so slightly from side to side. 'Actually, screw it, show is always easier than tell right.'

She popped up from her seat, not quite as spritely as usual, but much livelier than myself. She was obviously a hardy person, not showing any signs of pain or weakness despite having had a similar electrifying moment to myself only hours before.

'Chop chop,' she commanded, walking towards the lifeless gate.

I followed suit, hoping the walk would clear my head if nothing else.

We paced by the gate, Styx running her hand along its cold metal frame as she passed. The bunker was now a wasteland of random electronics. Some of them still survived off their backups, and most were already inactive before the power loss, but the bunker felt like more of a void as the constant background hum of electronics was all but gone now.

We approached a large battered metal doorway at the back of the bunker. From what I could tell we were on the exact opposite side to the wall covered in names.

The door was slightly ajar, and I could hear someone talking inside as Styx lead me through.

The lighting became a tad more bearable, the sombre red from outside diluted by a weak white portable spotlight.

Lucy was standing just inside, alone, deeply engaged in her AMI, and mumbling to herself. I hadn't seen her since I had stood in the crowd of bunker dwellers, right before the attack. She looked a little different than before. Not just stressed, more like weary. She had the look of an overworked research student, hair held precariously together by a few pins and random

extra layers of clothing. I hadn't noticed the temperature had changed in our underground dome but looking at her made me feel under-insulated.

Styx grabbed her softly by the shoulders, shaking
her from her daze. 'Get some rest, would you? You're
long past running on empty.'

Lucy's eyes were red. It was obvious she had been
crying only recently, or maybe just hadn't blinked in
a long time. I didn't want to ask but gave her a hopefully comforting pat on the arm as she walked past,
still mumbling to herself.

With her gone, Styx repositioned the spotlight, activating its accompanying bulbs. The room was large
and continued with the bunker's harsh concrete decor.
In it were various large canopy-covered somethings, a
foot or more taller than myself. They all formed a grid
of sorts, each perfectly placed in rows and columns,
just leaving enough room it looked to walk between
without squeezing.

Styx walked up to the closest mystery figure and
pulled off the large khaki covering with a quick jerk.

Dust filled the air and whipped all around us. I tried
my best to bat away as much as I could with one hand
covering my mouth and nose, but strained to keep my
eyes open.

The mysterious curtain dropped to the floor, and
in its place now stood a pristine, although somewhat
unusually designed slipway gate.

I stood and gazed at the hulking machinery, much
broader than a normal gate, and more pointed at the

top. Several small lights flickered on the front panel, showing it wasn't just for show.

'Eh... What's going on?' I queried as I peered around at the mass of likely live gateways that filled the room. There was no point in getting excited, or allowing my usual runaway imagination take hold of the moment. If the gates were in any way useful the general demeanour of the bunker wouldn't have been so distraught. 'All broken or something?'

'No, not broken, but not exactly useful either.' Styx began her explanation while she tore the covering off of a few more gates. 'This bunker is just an old wartime relic. Sturdy, strong, hidden. Ticks all the boxes for the perfect place to just dump a few more unwanted bits of military tech. All the gates you see here, in all their unmodified hulking glory, they're just deployment gates. Hardware locked into one-way traffic only.'

My assumptions to not get excited had been confirmed. I didn't really know anything about these gates, just a little about their short-lived history. They could be deployed anywhere, and their onboard battery allowed for a few minutes of one-way traffic. You could step out of your barracks right into the front line anywhere on the planet.

The only problem was, they weren't helpful in the case of a retreat, so they didn't have a very prestigious service record.

Styx had continued inspecting the individual machines, kicking up clouds of dust as she went.

'Lucy's been driving herself a bit mad, trying to work out if all these old batteries could power the gate.' She slammed her palm on one of the gates panels as she continued to explain, it flickered to life in response, but only barely. 'Problem is, these guys weren't exactly designed to share. Quite the opposite really.'

She returned to my side, standing with her back to the gates, looking out to the central bunker. 'It's a pity there's no signal down here. We could get everything we need delivered through one of these, no problem. The Monster was just a sort of maintenance gate until we got our hands on it, but we had to use these bad boys to sneak in in the first place. Sam's contact somehow got an address for one of these, and we were in. I don't think whoever owns this place even knows we're here, and I made sure to change all the incoming addresses on these so that we wouldn't be disturbed. Lot of good that did us...'

They must have been dead set on absolute secrecy to go to such extremes to stay out of sight. A lot of good it had done them indeed. They had simply claimed squatter's rights to a tomb.

Styx shut down the lights as we both left the gates' storage space. The possible answer to our predicament, sitting idle and useless, tempting the imagination with what might have been.

It was rare in my life I had ever been in a situation where my AMI simply had no mobile coverage. I couldn't even remember a time before now. But as opposed to a lack of signal causing a momentarily delayed email or social media update, this lack of connection was building to be my doom.

Our doom.

'Fuckin' Christian...' Styx muttered under her breath as she went to move off in another direction to myself.

'Wait,' I called after Styx. 'How long is it since Christian came here?'

Bemused, Styx came back towards me. 'I don't know, a couple of weeks maybe. Sterne brought him in. He was quite eager apparently. Why?'

My mind rocked around the isolation of the bunker, and how nobody could have noticed any odd behaviour from the Judas in our midst. Or maybe they had and ignored it. Wasn't even being here odd behaviour to begin with? But something seemed amiss to my understanding of the situation.

'If none of us can communicate with the outside world, how did Christian?' I quizzed Styx. 'I don't know a lot about how this would work, but I highly doubt a corporate security team, or whatever those people were, just sat by a gate for a few weeks on the off chance that they would be needed. He must have found a way to tell them when we left to break into Dr Ross's office.'

Styx stood facing me, a blank expression on her face.

Just as I was about to reach out, to check for some

signs of life, she slammed both her palms hard on my chest, and shouted, 'You fucking daisy!'

I stood as steady as I could, playing possum instead of revealing just how winded she had made me, while she broke into a sprint towards the gate. I followed suit as soon as I could fill my lungs again, with only minor pain to accompany the breath.

When I arrived, she was already rifling through the dead man's jacket pockets. Three others, including Sam, had begun to close in, clearly intrigued by the burst of energy Styx had just displayed.

'Bingo!' Styx shouted out as she pulled out a small item from the inner breast pocket of the red jacket. 'That sneaky bastard! Here, look at this.' Her words were to everyone within earshot.

The small item appeared to be a connector of some kind. One end, the male connector, was a standard AMI connector. But the far end, extended by a short cable, was an unfamiliar interface.

'Sixteen pins, symmetrical on both sides, roughly one and a half centimetres wide, half a mill thick, copper plated.' Styx described the unknown connector in detail to the small group that had gathered.

She jumped up, holding the connector in front of her. 'Everyone, look at this. Pay close attention to the size and number of connection pins.'

'What the hell are you talking about, Styx?' Sam didn't appreciate being left out, but Styx's enthusiasm clearly had her excited.

'When Christian came here first, he was looking for

something to do, right? He wasn't overly skilled but said he would do some cleanup and cable management of the bunker wiring, see if there was anything of use to us down here.' Styx was talking almost too fast to comprehend, her words chasing her thoughts at an awful speed. 'I bet that sneaky fucker found a way to get a signal out. We need to look for the matching female connection to this one. Look for the cables coming down from the high walls, look at any set of cables that's been tied up or stands out in any way. I would bet my life that this will let us get a signal out.'

Without as much as a reply, just simple nods all around, we turned on our heels and ran in separate directions.

I sprinted off towards the furthest wall, the one adorned with the painfully large number of names. But I didn't have time to delve into a depressing read through. My eyes darted above the white text-filled sections of wall, looking for any sort of cables running vertically from the domed roof.

I jogged the length of the wall, looking roof to floor, roof to floor, roof to floor, between every break in the whiteboards. I reached the end, almost running into Sam who had been doing the same.

'Nothing?' I asked.

'Nothing...' she replied, still looking past me as if to check my work. I couldn't blame her. I was doing the same. This wasn't a time for complacency or hurt feelings to get in the way.

'HERE, HERE!' The screams came from behind

Sam, about a quarter of the way around the curved wall from our position.

Everyone converged on the source of the yelling.

As we arrived Styx was already hooking her AMI up to the mystery conduit, sitting in the middle of a gang of similar wires, all gathered together in an attempt to hide the source of our interest.

We all remained totally silent, even Styx, as we crowded heavily in on top of her.

The AMI was connected to the wall. The screen was on.

Nothing for a few moments, tension levels rising higher and higher by every beat of our collective hearts.

The vibration was sharp and sudden, almost frightening Styx into a fit, as a section of the top right of her display shifted pixels.

"(3) new messages received."

Chapter 13

Things had taken a turn, and for the first time in recent memory, it was a turn for the better.

Almost everyone had gathered in the small kitchenette.

The scene playing out in front of me was similar to Dan's birthday. A jocund gathering of people, revelling in a communal win. There were even a few laughs, and the hidden stash of whiskey was helping. It mightn't have been very good whiskey, but it more than did the trick.

Myself and the others who had become target practice earlier were extra pleased for the alcohol, as it helped take the edge off the last of the waning muscle pains.

The air of tension had almost disappeared altogether, although it wasn't hard to see people's occasional glances in the direction of the newest gate, cleverly being referred to as the "life preserver."

Some others had helped Sam and Lucy to load the chosen gate onto a heavy-duty stacker and had moved it next to our powerless unit. Those few chose to enjoy their drinks while seated around the object of our deliverance, eagerly awaiting our supplies.

We had taken it in turns to check on Dr Sterne since the attack, who was unfortunately still unconscious. Styx had some basic first aid training, but aside from that we just did whatever little we felt we could, which in my case wasn't much more than checking her pillow was fluffed.

We couldn't tell if she was improving, but her vitals seemed stable, and we took that as a good sign.

Frank hadn't budged much from his bunk, despite our improved situation. Sam told me he felt partially responsible for the attack, as if he had some way of predicting such an outcome. But he was once a security officer, and a damned good one from what I was told, so I understood where he was coming from.

Maybe I felt a slight kinship to his current state of mind. The whole reason I had wound up involved in this mess was that I believed I was somehow complicit in losing my commuter. "Shit happens" as they say, but that sentiment means little when it happens to you.

And it didn't even happen to me. It happened to her. In the aftermath of the hiccup, I was selfish, feeling sorry for myself instead of for her.

Even though it probably wouldn't help, I thought I would attempt to raise Frank's spirits. After all, he had been a sort of guardian angel when he was watching my comings and goings back at BioDev, something that I'm sure came with a hefty amount of personal danger to himself. He may have had the help of some IR blocking facial augments to stop security cameras from recognising him, but if he'd run into someone he knew, it could have been a different issue altogether.

I filled two tumblers with an indulgent amount of whiskey and made my way into the rest area. He was sat in a seat beside Dr Sterne's bed, keeping a watch on her while the rest of us blew off steam.

I pulled up a chair and reached out with the glass.

He didn't even hesitate, shooting back the whiskey and placing the glass back in my hand before I had even pulled away my arm. And without even the slightest hint of a gag reflex or wincing from the strength of the spirit.

Frank had just become my drinking hero.

But envy aside, I sipped on mine and kept quiet for the first few moments.

'How's she doing?' I eventually asked.

'Same.' He spoke lowly, still looking at her.

'Good.' I took another sip before putting the glass down beside my foot. 'And you?'

Frank looked at me from the corner of his eye, not turning his head. I knew a disapproving look when I saw it.

'Okay, sore subject, I get it.' Back to silent whiskey sipping it was, I guessed.

A few minutes passed, sitting in complete silence. I continued to sip away at the whiskey, but the poor quality and lack of a disguising mixer was finally getting to me. I took one final gulp, simply with the aim of being rid of the dark oaky liquid.

It turned my stomach ever so slightly, and I couldn't fight back my disdain as I let out a big "eww-h-hew" as my mouth became excessively watery and I wrestled away my gagging response.

But it turned out that was exactly what the situation needed, as once I opened my eyes again, and retracted my tongue, I caught Frank's smirking face.

'We can't all be a professional like you, y'know.'

'Hmph.' He shrugged the comment off but was clearly building up to saying something.

After a few more moments of silence, he continued, 'I wasn't very professional today.'

'Ah would you stop, you had nothing to do with earlier.' I was prepared for this turn in conversation and had my response practised. 'Those guys were packing—hell the fact we're not all waking up in some cell or worse is almost a miracle.' I poured sincerity over every word, which was easy since it was the absolute truth. I hoped it was exactly what he needed to hear.

Frank shifted the chair my direction so that we were now both head-on.

'I don't think waking up in a cell would've been the worst of our worries.'

'Why? What do you think they would they have done to us?' Frank's insight into the company may have given him a deeper well of knowledge, so I pried a little more. 'Has this sort of stuff happened before?'

'No. At least not that I know. And not like this, at least not exactly. I don't know.' Frank, a bit unsure, seemed to be questioning what he was saying as he said it. 'It's different now. I don't know what to think. Those people were in full combat armour, they weren't joking. Small units like that are common, but not the gear. Somebody high up must have signed off on that. Makes sense after that report we found, I guess. But we got lucky, and that stroke of luck nearly trapped us here for good. It's just all so...fucked.'

I paused. 'Sorry Frank, rewind there a moment. Report? What report?' He had more than just glossed over what seemed an important fact.

'What report? Are you joking? The one from Dr Ross's office. The one we stole.' He seemed just as confused as I was.

'I... you...when the hell did that happen?' How I had missed something like that was beyond confusing. If it hadn't been for the look on his face I would have assumed it a joke.

'It decoded, right before the attack. Everyone saw it. You were there.' Frank was now looking at me as if I was playing a stupid prank on him, and he didn't appreciate it.

I thought back to the moments before the attack. I was there, in the group sitting and waiting just like the others. But not really. No, my attention had been pulled away, drawn to the pulses of colour at the gate.

At that moment it became clear. Clear how nobody had heard me the first two times I had called to Styx, despite the relative silence of the bunker in those few moments. They were all so absorbed by the information on display that I needed to scream to stir them from the haze.

But nobody had mentioned it since. Why would they? Why would it have mattered with our impending doom creeping closer?

I hadn't even thought to query if we had made any progress on the decryption. The whole event was stolen away in a blaze of pain and terror.

'Show me.' The curiosity I had felt in the moments leading to the attack burst into the foreground of my mind again, this time stronger than ever without fatigue dulling my thoughts. It was the information we had been searching for, a possible clue to help our efforts.

Frank looked at his AMI, activating the holodisplay and performing a quick search.

With a flurry of light, I could see a plain text document was isolated on his wrist, and with a single wave of his hand, it hung itself in the air between us.

I took a deep breath as I started, the anticipation bringing on a slight tremor in my right hand.

"FWD: Incident Report 341-1, test site amber, sublevel 11, Induction Zone A

Greetings Director Ross,

At approximately 7.17 a.m. GMT, an incident occurred at the AOE amber test site, location—Phoenix, Arizona. A single Variable (#11437) escaped decontamination, injuring several members of the laboratory staff and two security personnel. The incident was resolved within 14 minutes, and no damage to AOE servers or hardware is reported.

It is worth noting that attempted entry to the contagious disease storage (BioHaz L4) was attributed to the Variable's own disorientation and is not viewed as intended sabotage.

Due to your recent overhaul of the standard operating practices in place across all AOE test sites, it is hereby put forth that we resume previous operations until further notice.

It is also my duty to inform you that all database records and references to Variable 11437, Mr Garvan Doherty, will be redacted in accordance with Act C39, clause 3, and all reference to his biometric data will be wiped from the AOE double-blind database.

I will be in touch shortly regarding review and reinstitution of your new processing scheme, but only after the root cause of this breakdown has been unearthed.

Best regards,

M. Scaife

Director of Blacksite Security"

I wasn't sure I even understood the document in its entirety. I read it, and then I read it again for good measure, each time from the very beginning to the sombre end, stressing over every sentence as if each was more important than the last.

But it didn't feel right. This man, the version of our "Mr Ghost" from this memo, wasn't trying to break into somewhere. He wasn't some rogue combatant,

fighting his way into a secret and potentially dangerous wing of a laboratory, sticking it to the man.

'He was trying to escape.' The words came from
behind the floating document as I remained stunned
and glassy-eyed at the projection.

We had been wrong about hiccups. I had been
wrong.

Horribly so.

Mr Ghost, this unknown ethereal figure who disappeared one day only to re-emerge in a corrupted
text document months later, was trying to escape.

These people weren't going missing. They were
being abducted.

My mind bent to the possibilities this information
had produced, my wild imagination creating multi-
tudes of arrangements of facts that tried to lend sense
to these findings. My thoughts were muddled and
misleading, from the most innocent machinations to
the most deplorable. I just couldn't grasp the reasoning for any of it.

I was still processing, internally debating the only
questions I felt were relevant. *How could this be true?*
And if it was, *Why is this happening?*

'Bit of a bombshell, right?' Frank said as he turned
off the holodisplay. 'I don't know how anyone is processing that info, or if they've had time to. Maybe
they're just trying to ignore what they saw, considering what happened. I don't think most people out
there ever considered things may get violent by helping us.'

I know I hadn't. Before then I had clung to the fleeting hope that we would somehow find a problem in the gate system's coding that would help to stop hiccups, or that the answers lay in the code I had stolen from my gate's database.

Never once had I thought that maybe, just maybe, this was being done on purpose.

I pieced everything I knew together loosely in my head as I stared at the empty glass in my hand. The timing of our attack was too coincidental to be pure fluke; it had to be BioDev that sent them. A fact now compounded by this new evidence. Of course they wouldn't want people knowing what we now knew, and they were willing to go on the offensive to stop it from getting out.

Maybe they had underestimated us slightly, trying to disable the group as opposed to a more "permanent" means of keeping us quiet. Conventional ballistic weaponry wasn't commonplace, so it made sense if they assumed us to have none. But that would not be the case the next time around. And since their squad never returned, they would likely go to even further lengths to shut us down.

We had just taken on one of the largest corporations in the world, and I had been more than complicit. Not only that, but WormWhole already considered us terrorists, contributors to the attacks a couple of weeks back.

There was nothing else to it. We were in deep shit.

'Oh man.' I shook my head as I placed it in my hands. 'This is...a lot to take on, Frank.'

'Yeah. Yeah, I know.' He sat back in his seat, letting out a long sigh. 'We're through the looking glass now alright. But we can't flounder just yet.'

I looked up at him. He had turned slightly again and was checking on Dr Sterne.

'You see, this whole thing was set up for a reason. To stop people from disappearing in transit, right? But it was Meribel here who really got the ball rolling. Hell, she bankrolled a lot of the stuff you see out there. Only she could be able to get her hands on so many high-tech gate augmentations without anyone batting an eyelash.' He pulled her blanket up slightly, making sure she was fully covered up to her shoulders.

He then stood, encouraging me to follow suit, and continued. 'But out of everyone here, who do you think would be the most likely to know anything, no matter how small or insignificant, about why people may have disappeared?'

'Dr Sterne.' He was baiting me for an answer instead of just saying it outright, possibly to ensure we were on the same page. 'So?'

'So, when all the cards were on the table, and we finally see that this whole thing is actually by the design of BioDev, who do you think should have been the most outright enraged?'

I didn't answer straight away. Of course, someone like Dr Sterne was going to be distraught at the thought that her technology, her pride and joy, could have possibly been used for something so nefarious. We still didn't have a definitive reason as to why they were being abducted, but for now, that didn't matter. What mattered is that we had answered the first, and possibly most important of the mysteries, and that was "where did they go?"

I imagined she would have been livid.

'Dr Sterne, obviously.' I still didn't follow.

'Exactly.' He walked past, leading me by the arm to leave the sleeping area, but stopping just short of the kitchenette. 'I don't know how you react to bad news, but I tend to display a slight hint of shock or dismay.'

'Why are you telling me all this?'

'Because she didn't flinch.' His arm was stretched out, pointing at our patient. 'Not only did she not flinch, she hardly reacted to the assault. As soon as that document went up, I looked straight to her. She simply shook her head and looked straight back at me, without a hint of emotion in her eyes.'

'Why are you telling me this?' I felt uncomfortable that we were within earshot of her, unconscious or not.

'She knew, man!' he hissed at me. 'Maybe she didn't know the minutiae of what was going on, but there's no way she could act so disjointed facing that. Not if it was a complete surprise to her. She had to have known something.'

Just as I felt the beginning of anger build in my chest, a cheer from out in the bunker redirected our attention.

'About damned time.' Frank walked away from me at speed, clearly more excited about the escape plan than he had recently portrayed.

But I didn't budge. Not for a few moments. I was trapped between loyalty born of personal respect for someone I hardly knew, and the offhand—and possibly misinterpreted—feelings of someone I had no reason to distrust.

Maybe I just didn't want to believe Dr Sterne— Meribel—could possibly have allowed something like that to become a reality without fighting back.

There was no point in jumping to conclusions just yet.

I took a long look back at her, so small and fragile in her current state in the bunk.

'No,' I said to myself as I turned to head back into the uproarious crowd gathered around the two gates. 'There has to be another reason.'

But for now, it was time to get to work.

Achterhuis was soon to be back up and running, and our new enemy had made the first move.

The ball was in our court now.

Chapter 14

"This should suffice. Do not contact me again."

The message was stapled to the crate that appeared through our favourite new gate, the only one of the automated gates with enough battery power to truly do anything. I guessed whoever had been contacted for help was unhappy to be involved but had come through for us nonetheless.

Wasting no time, Lucy, Styx, and several others loaded the crate onto the stacker and jogged off towards the defunct power generator, eager to install the new source.

I felt like following, to revel in our deliverance. But as I turned heel to follow, Frank and Sam began walking away in a different direction, Frank leading Sam by the arm in a less-than-gentle manner. The unfriendly body language gave me pause, and I decided to follow them instead.

I closed in as much as I could so I would be within earshot of them. Peering from around the corner of a large metal container, I witnessed the standoff.

'Sterne said not to contact him, no matter what.

What the hell were you thinking?' Frank's voice was low, but he was all but shouting in Sam's face.

'The hell did you expect us to do?' Sam wasn't backing down, matching his tone and flailing her arms out by her sides. 'You think just anybody would have something like that lying around? Or would be willing to give it to us? Get a grip and drop down off your high horse, we were screwed without him.'

'He's a liar and a damn psychopath, in case you've forgotten.'

'It doesn't matter. Now we aren't going to spend our last few days huddled around a dead gate telling ourselves "at least we took the moral high ground," give ourselves a nice pat on the back while we're at it.' Sam's decibel level was slowly creeping upwards. 'Don't be a fool.'

'What did it take? What did you have to give him?' Frank stood back, stepping his assault down slightly in exchange for curiosity.

Sam stopped for a moment, refusing to answer verbally, but her defiant stance seemed to be enough.

'Oh for...are you serious? Do you have any idea what he might do with that information?' Frank rolled his eyes and rubbed his face with both hands. 'Why couldn't you have at least asked what I thought beforehand?'

'Eh, because of this reaction?' Sam replied, her arms now crossed.

'You're...you... I just...' He shook his fists in frustration.

But in his moment of contemplation, likely weighing his options regarding a follow-through insult, the lighting of the bunker burst into a stark white brilliance. The sound of multiple electronic cooling fans hummed once more through the air.

'Save that thought.' Sam pushed past Frank and headed back in my direction.

I spun, and as quietly as possible, snuck back towards the gate area. I doubted they would have welcomed my prying. Whoever had been our saviour didn't sound like a particularly popular person. But I agreed with Sam. Who here would possibly care where the generator came from?

I adopted a relaxed stance beside some of the others, trying to look as natural as possible so as not to arouse suspicion from Frank or Sam as they returned. Everyone was on tenterhooks as Styx returned and began powering on the gate system. It was a longer process than expected, but I assumed the augments were the contributing factor.

Unhappy with the delay, Styx gave one of the closest subsystem enclosures a swift kick. A purely symbolic attempt at hurrying the system up, but her timing was impeccable as the panel on the front of the gate sprang to life in a blaze of pixels.

The cheer was infectious as we all roared and displayed various levels of affection to those closest us at that moment. A heavy pat on the back, being shaken by your shoulders, or just grabbed in a less-than-gentle embrace, it was a moment of pure happiness and relief.

Even Sam gave a playful nudge to Frank's arm in her excitement, and he didn't seem to mind it too much. He even smiled.

'Hell yeah!' Styx shouted, patting her machine hard on the side. 'The Monster's back in action.'

A few of the others went so far as to shed a tear. Most people don't ever have to deal with their own mortality in such a way, so it was completely understandable. We were no longer trapped, we could go wherever we wanted now.

But not really.

The cheering didn't last long, as the crowd slowly calmed down, waiting for someone to speak up and say what they were all thinking.

It remained silent for several seconds, nothing but the familiar hum of the bunker's electronics and the heavy breathing of the exhausted few who had high-fived and hugged with such zeal as to actually build up a sweat.

'What now?' I decided to break the silence and get the conversation started. I wasn't going to be a passenger anymore, that hadn't been working out for me.

'First things first, Leon.' Frank stood out into the centre of the group. 'We still have a patient back there. Did we get any medical supplies?'

'Just a few bits, not sure if it's enough though.' Styx had a small shoulder bag with her from the crate. 'Does anyone know how to set up an IV drip?'

A slight murmur from the crowd didn't build confidence. But after a moment a hand was timidly raised from one of the other men. 'I could probably do it,' he said sheepishly, not willing to divulge where or how he may have got the practice with a needle.

'You'll do.'

The two headed off to the sleeping area. The rest remained.

'Right, back to the point.' Sam was aiming the conversation at me. 'You're right. We've been hit hard, in more ways than one. I suppose we just need to know where everyone's heads are at.'

Again, the crowd remained mainly silent, eyes to the ground, submissive.

'Yeah,' she continued, 'I thought as much.'

'I don't think we can go home,' I noted as if this wasn't apparent already.

'True, but I don't think staying here forever is a crowd-pleaser either.' Sam didn't seem thrilled with my honesty, but we were far past unnecessary pleasantries or placation. 'Frank, how about those IR facial recognition augments, how many do we have?'

'Not enough.' He scanned the group. 'Not for this many of us at least. And we can only use the automatic gates. The last thing we need is to get past the security cameras just to be recognised by some random Saint.'

'But we're not trapped at least. So, we should be able to get supplies if we're careful, food and water and the like.' Sam was thinking aloud.

'We need to talk about BioDev.' The statement came from Lucy, still looking dishevelled and over-worked. 'I know we're all thinking it.'

I didn't want to jump straight in on that specific conversation until everything had calmed, but it was burning a hole in my mind trying not to bring it up every second since I saw the report. I could only imag-ine how the others were feeling, having known about it for hours. Had they even had a moment to process it really? Now that there weren't more immediate prob-lems facing the group, we couldn't just ignore what we had discovered.

'Yeah, I suppose we do.' Sam walked to the cen-tre of the group beside Frank. She paused, taking a deep breath before continuing. 'Anyone have any thoughts?'

The group remained quiet. We were mostly Saints from what I knew, not in any way prepared for an eventuality like this in our lives. Would any have even joined if they knew the now very real outcomes of our investigation? My own joining had only been partly voluntary.

Sam sighed. 'We're all on the same page. Let's just make sure the place is back up and running. Frank and I will see if we can wake Sterne; she tends to be an idea box. Maybe she'll have a clue as to what the hell we should be doing.'

Everyone seemed to like that idea. Dr Sterne was no doubt the de facto leader of the group, so everyone seemed comfortable leaving the decision-making to her.

And with that the group split once more, feigning a business-as-usual demeanour as they went about turning on various systems and light sources, making themselves busy so as not to allow the crippling weight of their predicament to affect them too much. Not just yet at least. Not until Dr Sterne was involved.

I stayed behind as I saw Styx returning.

'Hey Styx,' I said as she approached. 'The gate still operates mainly like a normal one, right?'

'Yeah, for the most part. The augments just supplement the control system, they don't replace most of the operating processes.' She tilted her head and eyed me up. 'Why?'

'Just curious.' I thought for a few moments about what had led to the arrival of our "guests." 'The gate was floating, right? So, we were off the grid. But Christian made contact somehow without us having an address to connect to. Think we can find out how?'

Styx smiled at me, her perfect white teeth standing out against her tanned skin. 'Great minds think alike, Leon. That's exactly what I was coming here to do.'

We pulled up two seats beside the gate. There was no controlling terminal powered on, just the status and diagnostic screens, as Sam's interface program was all that was needed to interact. And thanks to the protocol band algorithms built into the program, whatever security systems may have been in place were completely disabled as we probed into the system's memory.

It wasn't as "clean" as what I had remembered from my own gate. Instead of a normal system waiting for the next input, this gate was constantly running processes to keep it afloat on the network. It wasn't ever truly off the network but instead used a jumping address. It could change several times a second, making the system's memory heavily loaded with torturous amounts of nonsense code.

Luckily, I was with Styx, the gate whisperer. She glided through the code with ease. I was hardly able to keep up with what was happening on her holo-display. It was a spectacle watching her work. I found myself drawn to her kind of greenish eyes, enthralled by how quickly they darted from side to side, top to bottom, keeping up with the overwhelming mass of text flying by.

I hadn't taken note before then, but Styx was quite beautiful.

'Eh, Leon?'

Her words snapped me out of my trance, and I was left red-faced as I realised I had just been sat staring into her eyes for the past few moments. Gawking really. I hadn't even noticed she was staring back.

Very smooth.

'Right, shit, sorry.'

She laughed, shaking her head at me.

Rekindled focus on the data, she was isolating a

gigantic stretch of code. Within seconds it had been extracted and downloaded to her AMI.

'There, I think this is it. Can I tap your display?'

I quickly unlocked the local grouping on my AMI. 'Yeah sure, it's good to go.'

When I held my arm out close to hers, both holo-displays burst into action, creating a large projection that hung in the air before us. It could only fit a fraction of the code at once and still be legible.

'What the hell is that?' I questioned. 'It's like an aggregation of gate addresses, except...they're off slightly. Too short. But the destinations are there.'

Styx sat squinting at the code. 'They're a bit abnormal alright. It's like they're pinging each address, but not trying to engage a slipway. They're all missing the engagement variables.'

I shook my head.

More confusing gate codes, I thought. *That was all this day needed.*

'Why so many though?' Styx continued. 'There are thousands of them.'

'Can you go to the end?' I asked.

With a swift gesture, she sent us into a long stretch of repeating code. It seemed to be mostly gibberish. A single address was embedded and repeating, but there were hundreds of nonsensical characters forming no discernible code between each copy.

'That must have been where they came from,' Styx remarked, as she clipped the small section of code from the muddled mass of text. 'Let's see where our friends come from, shall we?'

She brought back up the interface of Sam's program, keeping the dual holodisplay engaged to include me. The familiar blue web of the gate's transit system was crystal clear when given such a large area to project onto.

'If we put the code in as is, keeping the engagement variables out, it should just ping to the address I'm hoping.' Styx didn't seem certain, but she proceeded anyway.

The blue mesh remained unchanged, however. Typically, an engaged slipway would form a red journey pattern through the blue labyrinth, but we had hoped for at least some form of feedback, even knowing the code was partially incomplete.

'Did you see that?' Styx asked, curious as to whether or not she had imagined something.

'See what?' I replied.

She zoomed in on a section of the gate network, somewhere in Western Europe.

'Keep an eye out here, I'll try again.'

She input the code again. I had been waiting for a red connection out of habit, but what we saw instead was a simple pop of colour, almost indiscernible from the mass of blue all around it.

'There!' she shouted. 'That's England. Hold on we'll zoom in a bit more.'

She expanded the region it seemed to emanate from. The area was large, encompassing most of the southern half of England and some of Wales and France.

'Just one more...' She again injected the code into the system, and surely enough the shifting pop of light in the display betrayed the location we had been looking for. One quick gesture and we had focussed perfectly on the source of the feedback. It was a mass of blue interconnects, the largest conglomeration of them for miles. 'There! Right there, look. Just outside of London.'

She was right. In fact, I knew the area well. We had just focussed in on an installation close to where Dan had worked.

'Are you sure?' I quizzed, grimacing at the memories of my lost brother.

'The code can't lie, Leon, it's there.'

I looked down at what remained of the blood stains on the floor from earlier. The bodies had been moved, but the clean-up had been haphazard at best. And in that instant, I felt remorse for contributing to these six people's deaths. Seven with Christian included. No matter how small my part was in what led to the incident, I was still complicit.

They were someone else's brother, sister, family member.

I tried to shake the thoughts from my mind. It was them or us, and I knew that. But it was a strange feeling to know you had been a part of something so violent.

I thought back to the day of the attack, confused as

to how anybody could get into the state of mind that they would be such willing participants in causing so much death. Hell, they had even celebrated before running through the gate, albeit foolishly. Little could they have known I had hijacked their destination.

'It still doesn't explain it.' Styx broke me out of my internal monologue. 'They shouldn't have been able to get here. The gate was clearly communicating with theirs, but we never engaged a slipway. All the sub-processes were still running. Our address wasn't static. I just don't get it.'

I knew she wasn't asking for my input. She clearly understood the workings of a gate far better than I did. But at this stage, it seemed she was just reaching for even a wild theory that she could dispute to get her pointed in the right direction.

'Maybe flooding the system with the constant pings stopped the gate from shifting addresses,' she continued. 'No, it couldn't be that. Maybe they could predict the addresses? Maybe Christian has somehow circumvented my coding. No, that's even stupider. Come on you should know this.' Styx was in a full-on argument with herself, and she was winning neither side of it.

'Maybe it's like a flare?' I hypothesised, trying to come up with a remotely feasible idea to break her out of her loop. 'You know, like when someone gets stuck out on a boat. If you can't find your rescuers, you send up a flare and they find you, right? Maybe the gate was calling out to their gate, asking for a connection instead of making one itself.' I paused, thinking of the right example to make sure my point was easily understood. 'It was a beacon.'

Styx thought for a moment.

'Yeah,' she eventually came out with. 'Yeah, you could have something there. I won't be able to tell just from our side, but that makes sense. He didn't dial another address. He couldn't have used the gate without knowing how to ground it. But it could be forced into operation from the other side. Hmph, clever.'

I knew she wasn't calling me clever, but referencing how they had somehow outsmarted her.

But I still sat upright, chest puffed slightly in pride. Not because I may or may not have helped solve a small mystery, but because my three months of yachting classes when I was thirteen hadn't been a complete waste of time.

Suck it, Mr Rosenberg. Most likely to get lost at sea my ass.

'Not much good that information does us now anyway,' Styx said as she closed down the projections, checking the gate was still afloat. 'We shouldn't have that problem again; gate controls are locked until I say. I'm gonna head back over to the kitchen, you coming?'

'Yeah, I'll follow you in a minute,' I replied.

Once she had left, I activated my AMI. The new '*flare*' code as I called it was still displayed. With a quick gesture, it was side by side with the original corrupted gate code. I still felt a pinch of unease every time I looked at it.

It was just a hunch, but I scrolled through the mass of codes, haphazardly jumping to large seemingly important segments.

But they weren't the same. No repeating sequence, and no address-related segments. In all but a few minutes my hunch had fallen flat.

But I couldn't shake the feeling they were related.

Somehow.

Chapter 15

Describing the mood in the bunker was hard.

So much had happened, and so much lay on the horizon, that nobody could quite nail the appropriate demeanour. Maybe it was the effect the bunker itself was having on us. I had heard a lack of natural light could get to people over time.

That, or the realisation that one of the most powerful companies in the world was abducting people and probably now wanted us all dead.

Probably the second one.

But nobody wanted to give in to the mounting worry, at least not yet. We were all still clinging to the hope that everything would be fine, like the last life ring of a ship that seemed destined for the sandy seafloor.

"Dr Sterne will know what to do." The sentiment circled the crowd that had gathered inconspicuously right outside the rest area.

The medical pack we had so generously been donated sported the BioDev logo on the side. Not a very welcome sight, but whatever was in it seemed to be working. Those of us who were brave enough to peer around the corner into the bed space could see Dr Sterne was now sitting upright in the bed, simply sipping on some water in silence.

Sam, Styx, and Frank sat in front of her, each leaning in slightly, clearly waiting for a moment to bring up their individual ideas, but fearful they may overwhelm her in this new frail state.

For now, the fact she was awake was a win, and so all of us outer circle inhabitants retired to the kitchenette to wait.

I stood to the side of the table, allowing Lucy to take up the closest seat. She looked exhausted, but still managed a smile in recognition of the gesture. With her head in her arms on the table, she let out one large sigh before drifting into a heavy sleep. It wasn't that she had been up for days, but the stressful events had drained her of whatever stamina she had clung to during our time marooned in the grey dome.

I leaned back on the counter top, looking around at the group. They were in various stages of dishevelment, and all focussed primarily on keeping their coffee cups topped up.

I took a moment to pause on every face as I scanned the crowd. Despite what we had been through together, and how much I'd contributed to the group by now, they were still mostly alien to me. They could have been double agents, swapped out while Styx and I remained to inspect the gate, and I don't feel I would have noticed the difference.

Was her name Alison? Is he Benji? I couldn't place any names to faces, and I was unsure if I had just fabricated the names from thin air.

It reminded me of my first few days in boarding school. I was shy then and hadn't made a great start with introducing myself to anyone. Dan had spent extra time with me during breaks and after classes to make sure I wouldn't be alone.

But that memory of Dan and the gathering of unknown faces left me feeling alone, almost as much as at his funeral. Maybe it was the accumulation of everything that had happened, or specifically my thoughts about Dan, but I couldn't fight back the tear that trickled down my cheek. I quickly removed it with my sleeve but ducked my head just in case anyone would see.

It was a low moment, but luckily it was short-lived. 'Leon?'

I looked up to see Styx, her hand on my shoulder. She had such an infectious and kind smile, immediately lifting my spirits.

She signalled towards the rest area, so I followed, trying to ignore the whispers and looks from the others, likely confused as to why I was the one being involved.

As I entered they already had another seat positioned for me, creating a small semi-circle around Dr Sterne's bed. Frank and Sam on her left, Styx on her right. I joined them eagerly, intrigued to find out what they'd planned or decided.

'What do you think, Leon?' The question came from Sam.

'Think about what?' I replied.

'About all of this. BioDev, the missing commuters, the attack. We need an unbiased insight, and you were unanimously voted as our new mediator.'

I was torn between being honoured that this impressive group of professionals chose me to break their apparent stalemate, and fearful that I was about to pick a side.

'I don't know.' I decided honesty would be the best response. 'I don't really know where to start thinking about it. I'm anxious, like everyone else, but there's still too much we don't know. We have the who, but not the why or the how. That's what's important.'

Frank scoffed, but it seemed to be more disappointment than disapproval of what I had said.

'I didn't exactly come here thinking this was how anything would go. Hell I don't really feel like I was given a huge amount of choice in the matter.' My retort wasn't just directed at Frank and Sam. 'But we have to find out more. There's no going back now, not after what happened here, after what we did.'

I felt it better to say "we" instead of "you" at Frank; I knew the incident was still weighing heavily on him.

'Exactly,' Styx proclaimed, unbreakably positive as usual. 'We have to push on. We have to dig deeper. How was it you said it? The why and the how, that's what matters.'

'It's not that simple,' Sam interjected. 'We had

anonymity on our side before this. But now, after that damned rat Christian, they probably know every one of us. Nobody out there can come and go as freely as before.'

'Why don't you just call up your mystery knight in shining armour?' Styx said to Sam. 'Get him to send a few more care packages our way?'

Styx's words were the first thing to stir Dr Sterne from her silence.

'Who?' Her tone was tired, almost laboured, but had a sting of accusation about it.

Sam immediately launched into her defence, but not before cursing under her breath and throwing Styx a nasty stare. 'Okay, before you and Frank mount your high horses, we were dead without him. Even you have to realise that. He came through, you're awake, we have a gate again, and he can go do whatever the hell he wants with that memo about the incident at the BioDev facility. He just wanted proof that some-one didn't truly disappear for once.'

'That information is dangerous. And dangerous in-formation in the hands of a dangerous man is never to be taken lightly,' Dr Sterne said.

Sam and Frank shared a quick glance before lower-ing their heads slightly.

'Who is it?' I asked.

'Aribert,' Dr Sterne answered without missing a beat, clearly anticipating the question. 'Professor Aribert Borza, an old colleague of mine. He was a very trou-bled man. He lost his brother to a hiccup at a young age; that's what drove him to throw himself into slipway research. He was brilliant, an absolute prodigy, but always had a sort of...cruelty to him. I pitied him at first. I tried to help him, lead him away from his spiralling theories. He never trusted that people could just "go missing" in the slipway. Eventually his conspiracies consumed him. He threatened a lot of people saying he would figure out the cause, including myself. When they came to take him away he injured three security personnel and a lab technician. He's unstable. Dangerous. And worst of all, unshakeably believes he is the only one that is right.'

I didn't want to poke holes in the story but being referred to as a "troubled man" didn't quite match up with Frank calling him a "liar and a damned psychopath" before.

Dr Sterne continued. 'He contacted us a while ago, ranting about how he was going to take WormWhole down a peg, and that he and his group were getting close to some real proof of something. I guess someone kept tabs on him.' Dr Sterne peeked over her glasses at Sam, who was still looking at the ground. 'I'm afraid he may feel validated and justified with that information and do something reprehensible.'

'It doesn't matter now anyway, okay? We aren't changing anything that's done, but we need a plan, and nobody out there is looking to me for it.' Frank addressed Dr Sterne directly.

'Ah yes,' she replied. 'What to do now. I think Leon is right, the how and the why are what's important.'

'Well maybe we have an answer for the how,' I interjected. 'It has to be the code.'

They all contemplated the statement, but Styx was the first to speak up. 'You said you used it on your gate, and it sent the men...somewhere?'

If you said anything in the right tone it could be made to sound foolish, and her words dripped with doubt.

'Yes. Why?'

'Well, we've tried to use it a few times, and it's never once made a connection. It didn't even ping an address, it was just nonsense.'

I was horrified, not just by her lack of faith in what I had told them, but also in the notion that I hadn't really stopped those men.

'Sam was there, she'll tell you.' I struggled to keep my tone lowered, but I had to defend myself. 'Right, Sam?'

The discomfort was apparent on her face. 'I didn't actually check...' The look of betrayal must have been obvious on my face. 'I only had a few moments once I knew what you did, so I just wiped your gate's memory core and left. The situation was too volatile. And you'd been hit pretty hard.'

'That's bullshit. I know what I saw, what I heard, when those men went through the gate. There was no pong off the speakers, no delivery notification, nothing.' I could see everyone's discomfort.

But sometimes actions speak louder than words.

'Styx,' I commanded, as I stood and stormed off towards the gate.

All eyes were on me as I breezed past the kitchenette. I arrived, Styx on my heels, while the other two helped Dr Sterne follow along too.

Styx didn't need direction; she immediately got to work on grounding the gate. Once it was online, my AMI buzzed with the usual syncing notification. It took me only a few seconds to bring back up the corrupted code, glad that Sam had saved it and given it back to me upon arrival at Achterhuis. And with a single gesture, I injected the core of the system with it.

Nothing.

I gestured again, and a third time to make sure it was accepting the command. Maybe the gate's augments were slowing down the slipway's engagement.

But still, the gate sat idle.

'I don't understand...' I couldn't believe what I was seeing. Had I really imagined the incident? An illusion brought on by the blunt force trauma to my skull, exacerbated by the moment's fear? It seemed so real, I had been so elated, how could it have possibly been my imagination? 'Could the code have been corrupted? Are you sure the code you had was the same, Sam?'

Sam shook her head. I knew she wouldn't make a mistake like that. No chance.

'We don't know enough to dismiss the idea just yet,' Dr Sterne spoke out, aware that everyone in the bunker had gathered behind her, 'But for now we must be practical. We have few IR facial distortion clips, but we have to get more information. It's a big risk, but we will need people to go out and bring back some essential supplies so we can get started. But first, just by looking at you all, everyone needs to rest. Doctor's orders.'

The crowd chuckled, spirits lifted just by seeing Dr Sterne up and about. But she needed rest just as much as anyone, if not more. And I wasn't far behind.

Everyone retired to the sleeping area, with only a few, including Dr Sterne and Frank, choosing to stay and eat something beforehand.

I plonked myself down onto the edge of my bottom bunk, stretching my arms out. It was funny how comfortable sitting down can be when you are properly taking a load off. Knowing proper relaxation was around the corner made it feel so much better.

But beside my foot, just under the bed, was something I had almost completely forgotten about. I reached down and pulled out the box from Dan's office. I smirked to myself. It had been the only thing I had brought from my apartment, and it wasn't even mine. It was mostly nonsense too, snow globes from different parts of the world, a few notebooks, and some strange version of a Newton's cradle.

But there was one piece, just a single item, that made me think I'd made the right choice in what to save from my likely ransacked apartment.

The matte black frame stuck up out of the box. It

was a prized possession of Dan's, given to him from my father upon handing in his PhD thesis. I pulled the frame out of the box, blew some dust off, and gazed at the sprawl of text for a moment.

I could recite the piece from memory from a young age, as my father had a similar poster years ago in the loft. "The Great Dictator" was scrawled in large text across the top. His poster had met a mysterious end, timed oddly close to when Dan tried to turn a local feral cat into a house pet.

I began reading, hoping to relive some of those fond childhood memories.

"...the aeroplane and the radio have brought us closer together. The very nature of these inventions cries out for the goodness in men—cries out for universal brotherhood—for the unity of us all..."

It always amazed me to think of what these technologies must have meant to people then, and what this Dictator might have thought of the slipway network now. He considered radios and aeroplanes, archaic technology by today's standards, to be allying factors for the world. By his very definition, the introduction of the slipway network should have been the single greatest unifying advance in human history.

In many ways I guessed it was, at least in a very literal proximity sort of way.

I continued reading. "...the misery that is now upon us is but the passing of greed—the bitterness of men who fear the way of human progress. The hate of men will pass, and dictators die..."

The hate of men, something I had only recently been witness too. My mind flashed back to the attack in the hub. Evil men, performing an evil task. But was I actually mistaken about what had happened, like the others had implied?

The text had taken on a new meaning for me now. Originally, I had considered it an optimistic speech about human capacity for goodness through advancement. But now I realised, as much as that was true, it was also a warning. There will always be those that work against the common good, in one form or another. Those men, BioDev, Christian, who knows how many countless others, self-elevation or worse driving them to perform hateful deeds.

'What's that?' Sam interrupted my philosophising.

She sat down beside me, making sure to elbow me over just a little in a playful manner. She would've been a pest of a sister, of that there was no doubt, but her levity was always welcome.

I showed her the framed print.

'*The Great Dictator*? What's that?' Sam quizzed.

'It's a movie, from who knows when. But my father had always loved it. He bought this in some auction years ago, apparently a page of the original movie screenplay, but I always doubted that. I'm pretty sure they didn't have 120 gsm glossy laminated paper back then.'

We both shared a laugh, as my father was well known to be easily swindled into a sale.

'But me and Dan always loved this speech. It's

just so...powerful.' I would usually feel roused after reading the speech, but my fatigue kept me in check this time.

'In what way?' Sam clearly wasn't sold just yet, despite having worked her way down through a significant portion of the text, her finger tracing the edge of the frame.

'Just read it.'

I waited to be sure she had finished, sitting wide-eyed looking at her face, waiting for the expression to change from bemusement to...well anything but that really. An emotional response of any kind would be welcome.

'I really don't get what the whole point of this is.'

Sam was clearly just not getting it. She was wrong, and I was right, and it was time I changed her opinion.

'Okay, look here.' I cleared my throat and began reading with as much bravado as I could muster. '"I'm sorry but I don't want to be an Emperor. That's not my business. I don't want to—"'

'Stop.' She held her hand up to my face. 'Reading it out loud to me won't change my opinion, you know that right?'

She was just being awkward now.

'I know, but if you just—'

Again, I was shushed, this time with a single finger placed over my lips. 'I'm too tired, Leon, and you're a huge nerd, so I'll leave you be with your little puff piece.'

I could hardly react, instead allowing my irritation to simmer as she got up and walked away.

It was impossible to civilise some people.

I took one last glance before I returned the framed speech to the box, focussing in on one part in particular.

"The way of life can be free and beautiful, but we have lost the way."

How history seemed to be repeating itself. My understanding of the speech wasn't well informed. I know it was to do with wartime. My father was taught about the great wars in school, but that was largely left out of history books in my generation. I never figured out why; maybe people just wanted the world to forget.

I slid the box under the bed with my foot before swinging both legs up onto the mattress.

The last thoughts I had were of the attack in the Hub. I ran through it step by step. It was flawless in my memory.

The others didn't know, but I knew what I saw. And I would show them.

Chapter 16

I awoke to a slap on the forehead.

'You really are a heavy sleeper.' A second slap connected before I could raise my defences. 'Come on, get up.'

Sam would make a good alarm clock, if a short-lived one that would likely get thrown across the room upon first use. I took an extra minute to lie in contemplation, just to wind her up, before moving. The sleep area was beginning to smell...lived in. And I was just as ripe as the rest, the pungent air wafting up through my shirt as I moved.

Clearly, I had pushed my 72-hour antiperspirant to its limits.

Everyone was taking turns using the small bathing area, an old-fashioned detoxification station, with questionable water pressure and even worse privacy.

I chose to have a personal "shower" in the closest sink, using some of the soap left unattended by the others. Quick and efficient, what more could you need.

I ventured out to find Sam, feeling refreshed from

the cripplingly cold water of the makeshift shower. She had gathered with a few others, clearly discussing something laid out on the table in front of them.

'About time, Leon. Get in here.'

A small gap appeared in the group to let me in. Scrawled across the table was a shopping list of items.

'First team's gone out already, their job is to pick up a few odds and ends to try build upon Christian's sneaky satellite link in the back. Second team's job is to pick up a few essentials, water, non-perishables— you have the lists, so I'm not going through it again.' Sam was clearly in charge of delegating the tasks. I took a quick look around and saw no sign of Frank or Lucy, but Styx and Dr Sterne were sat with some others beside the gate.

'Am I included in any of this?' I assumed I was, but best not to assume Sam would fill me in without a push.

'Yeah, you'll be going out with me.' Sam rolled up the list and waved on the others. 'We have a bit of snooping to do.'

'Snooping? Where?'

'Well, we're flying blind down here. We need access to some sort of network outside the bunker, but not just the mobile service Christian used, we have to assume they'll be monitoring our AMIs.'

'Okay, but what can we use instead?'

'Aha, that is the right question. That's why Sterne is coming along for the ride. It's time we made use of our employer's freakishly vast resources.' She flashed a lanyard out of her pocket, WormWhole clearly printed across the top. 'We're gonna tap into their encrypted satellite feeds, and cha-ching.'

Cha-ching for what I hadn't quite figured out yet, but I followed up with what I felt was the more obvious question. 'Why the hell do WormWhole have their own satellites?'

'Doesn't everyone? Hell, doesn't your fancy MIT?' she scoffed. 'Classic big company paranoia. Why bother sending your private internal information over someone else's network when you have enough capital to just build your own? Sterne was filling me in; it's quite extensive considering they're a transportation company.'

She was right. MIT actually had a small triple threat of satellites they used for all sorts of different experimentation. None of which I had studied or dealt with, but they were very proud of their system compared to other institutions.

'Okay, but I'm assuming their fleet of satellites aren't exactly up for rental. What's the plan?'

Sam stretched out her interlocked hands, cracking all her knuckles in the process. 'Sterne has a guy.'

'A guy?'

'Yep, a guy.'

'Okay, so Mr Guy, what does he do?'

'Beats me!' Sam let out a little chuckle. Clearly she was on my side of scepticism. 'But Sterne says if we can get her into the labs in Hub 13, this guy will hook us up with some method to privately access the satellites using a proxy server in their data centre. As long as we don't overuse the service, it shouldn't flag us as anything foreign or abnormal.'

'So, we're flying blind?' I couldn't hide the distaste in my voice.

'Pretty much. Just a pair of bats, reacting to what we come across, blind as hell.' Sam acted like she was enjoying the prospect, but I sensed her playfulness was masking some genuine dislike.

No more being a passenger, Leon, I reminded myself, frustration building at the thought of again blindly following requests.

I decided to cut through Sam's crap talking. 'First off, bats aren't blind. But that's beside the point. Does Sterne not trust you enough to properly fill you in or something?'

The turn in her expression was swift. 'Oh, fuck off, Leon, don't be such a smart ass.'

'What? It's a genuine question. You guys are way more clued in than me, but this is getting ridiculous. You know how much I admire her, hell just being in her vicinity still gives me goose bumps, but it's getting a bit cultish the way everyone looks up to her.' I surprised myself. Had I actually just said something mildly negative about my personal hero? My younger self would've been disgusted.

Sam paused for a moment before retorting in a low and calm voice. 'We need info. She says she has a way to get us some info. I believe her, so please, trust me.'

Trust me.

The last time she had said those two words I left my apartment, and my life, behind me. But given everything I had witnessed, she had been spot on the money so far. I didn't want to be distrustful of her, and I never wanted to think Dr Sterne didn't have the best of intensions.

But something was gnawing at me, something from before. What Frank had said about Dr Sterne's re-action to the attack, to the report, to everything. It was beyond being perpetually calm from what he was saying.

Maybe he had shaken my faith a little.

'Okay.' I decided I had no real grounds to disagree with the plan. We were in a bad position, and any-thing that gave us an edge would be put to good use. I wasn't even sure what sort of information we could glean from accessing the WormWhole private net-work. They weren't our enemies in this fight, BioDev were. There was definitely an angle I was missing. Dr Sterne would know WormWhole's practices inside out, so she must have a plan.

And there I was, right back into the "trust in Dr Sterne" mindset. That didn't take too long.

'When do we head out?' I queried.

Sam answered as she packed up the rest of the table's scattered occupants. 'As soon as Frank comes back, we'll need their IR blockers to get past any secu-rity. Well, the auto surveillance gate security anyway, bit of magic needed by yours truly after that.'

My raised brow hinted at my next question.

'Well the cameras mightn't recognise us thanks to the blockers, but do you really think we'll be able to walk Sterne through a Hub without anyone noticing us?'

A valid point—hell Dr Sterne's face was probably on advertisements all over the Hub.

'So, what then? We make our way in, find a gate a bit deeper in the complex, and just send her a friendly invite?'

Sam laughed boisterously for a moment. 'Word for word, Leon, word for word. Did you steal my notes? See, you're learning already, super spy.'

Me and Sam, the perfect people to sneak into any WormWhole facility. Who better than two Saints after all. Most Hubs were near carbon copies of one another, so we would be able to blend right in with the rest of the workforce. We just needed to act cool.

But could Sam even act cool? I guessed I would find out.

As soon as Frank and the first team returned we suited up and got ready to move out.

Dr Sterne was left waiting by the gate as Styx powered it up. Sam used her AMI interface to dial up the Hub, and the moment the large green panel above the entrance lit up she straightened up and proceeded with a quick but natural gait.

She disappeared, and then it was my turn.

I tried to calm my breathing as I brought up the gate interface.

Although it was BioDev who had us in their crosshairs, we still had reason to fear WormWhole. Both Sam and I had been flagged as possible conspirators in the terror attacks, a thought that infuriated me more and more. I didn't imagine any harm would come our way if caught, but we would definitely be arrested, and who knows what BioDev could do if they got word we had been found.

It wasn't a calming thought.

'Just act natural, you're just passing through, you've done this a million times,' I repeated under my breath.

Nobody said anything, maybe afraid that even some positive reinforcement might put me off my game.

I engaged the destination. As the green light indicated a connection, I walked through, still repeating my calming mantra.

And with that the humdrum grey interior faded away behind me, and for the first time in what seemed weeks I was once again bathed in the familiar and welcoming blue and green flared light of the slipway.

It was a fleeting moment of relaxation.

I stepped out in mid-stride, focusing hard on maintaining progress as I was thrown into the bedlam that was a busy Hub. It was near deafening, the rabble of a thousand micro conversations from all directions as people made their way from A to B as quickly as possible. The lights were piercing, but it wasn't artificial for once. The sun cascaded through the glass panels on the roof, further lightening the white matte aesthetic of the Hub's interior. There were smells of perfume, smells of food, even smells of something slightly "recreational" off the men that pushed their way past me.

It was gloriously overwhelming, and I made sure to take one of the deepest breaths of my life as I continued across the foyer towards our rendezvous point.

It felt like I had been trapped in the bunker, and I only now had to ability to really stretch my legs and move about unhindered. It was funny to think that anybody could take for granted the simple ability to walk around among other people, but that's exactly how I felt.

But we weren't there for fun. Hubs weren't fun places. And today was no exception.

I continued moving, as Sam simply joined my side, her stride in perfect sync with mine.

'Door over by auto gate 15 there, that's the spot.'

Luckily, I was still wearing the same clothes from when I left work a few days prior, complete with the lanyard I had kept in my pocket. I had coated myself in deodorant to hide my building musk, and the material was an anti-fatigue poly blend, so it still looked freshly washed. It just didn't feel it. I would blend right in with the other Saints, as long as my ID didn't require closer than usual inspection.

We both approached the door, "Employees Only" written clearly above, and proceeded through. It was only a back way to the staff toilets, so no security was involved.

We passed several other Saints returning from what looked like a communal toilet visit, but they were unfazed by our presence, which helped calm my nerves immensely.

Passing the two sets of toilets we reached the end of the corridor, where a large metallic door stood, complete with staff card access.

Sam rustled through her pocket, pulling out another WormWhole card, and swiping it without hesitation. I had seen this card several times before. It belonged to the mystery chameleon employee who had racked up a sizeable coffee bill in the canteen, but never seemed to do any work. An exploited problem in the personnel system Sam had told me. A self-replicating malware infecting the database created a new employee every time the card was used. It wasn't untraceable but wouldn't flag anything for days. It was pretty obvious Sam was the culprit who introduced the malware to begin with.

The door unlocked with a nearly inaudible click, and we pushed our way through, pausing only to make sure the door shut properly behind us.

The familiarity of the environment was helping to keep our nerves in check and being there with Sam had the disarming feel of a normal day at the office.

'Okay, next up, block 8A is where we're headed. We just walk with purpose, and nobody will question us.' Sam kept a friendly tone throughout, as if afraid we may be under surveillance. Everything she said just sounded like a jovial chat.

I grabbed a datapad from a cradle just inside the

door, hoping holding it out in front of me would further add to our deception.

Luckily, nobody could see the display, as it turned out to be the cleaning crews schedule. It looked like a few of their toilets had had some catastrophic failures of late.

The photographic evidence was a bit much in my opinion.

We continued on, still slowing as we neared corners, making sure not to take a wrong turn. The signage was lacking, but the hallways were not overly populated. Every time we passed someone, we would repeat the same conversation.

'Did you see Carli Gandhiraman last night on that Vocal Smash replay? That woman can sing.' Having no actual clue what was recently broadcast, we stuck with generic nonsense that Sam loved and had watched before our exile. I didn't know the performer, or the trashy reality show she was speaking about, but I played my part. 'Oh yeah, she has to win it for sure, with that range? No competition.'

I hated myself a little for the looks some of the people gave me as I pretended to like the less than popular show, but it seemed an effective ruse.

The closer we got to block 8, the more obvious the security was. Doors that littered the corridors now had both retinal and card-based access, with some even looking similar to the advanced doorway into Dr Ross's office in BioDev. Luckily the hallways that circled these highly private blocks were open to walk freely, just the occasional camera to contend with, but our faces were protected from automatic detection at least, and anyone watching the hundreds of security feeds was unlikely to take any notice of employees wandering around.

Before long, we turned a corner and saw a large "8A" above a wide metal double door at the far end of the hallway. It was the last entranceway of the entire track, just like Dr Sterne had told us, and I assumed therefore that it was the most important.

'Now what?' I asked, not wanting to approach the door in case the security system took it upon itself to scan me from head to toe.

'We need to get closer. Our AMIs need to sync with the gate that's meant to be in there.'

'How close?' I feared to ask.

Sam just looked at me, 'Closer.'

We each took a step closer to either side of the wide hall and began slowly walking forwards with our arms awkwardly held to our fronts, to give it every chance of getting closer to any gates in the vicinity. Luckily my new datapad made it a more natural posture, whereas the way Sam moved made it look like she just had an awful itch somewhere unsavoury.

We crept along the wall, trying our best to act for the cameras like this was a normal way in which people would move. Every noise from the corridor behind us made my heart flutter a little, afraid someone would round the corner and find us both loitering ahead of one of their more secured areas. If we were caught now, we were too far away from the exit to escape. Sam awkwardly attempted to whistle away her anxiety.

In a flurry of recognition, the doorway lit up once we got within ten feet of it. I stumbled back a bit, fearing I would set off some sort of safety feature. Several screens blinked into life, awakened from their standby settings. Clearly the doorway wasn't used enough to warrant them being left on all day—energy efficiency was king in WormWhole.

'Just a sensor.' Sam pointed out from her side. A nice way for the electronic bouncer to further illuminate the hallway, a reminder to prepare yourself for an invasive security examination.

I edged forwards, now only a few short steps from the doorway.

It was expected, but it still scared the life out of me when my AMI finally sprung to life. I had almost gotten used to not receiving messages or emails. And now that we were out, we had to keep the AMIs offline to make sure we weren't tracked or found.

'Sam. Here.'

She walked as calmly but quickly as she could to my side as I interfaced with the system, pretending something of interest had grabbed my attention.

'Send it,' she commanded.

In a fitting act of subterfuge, I instructed the gate to send a remodelled code, based on that which Christian and BioDev had used to find us, to ping our gate back in the bunker. Styx had been worried that the entire time we were out the gate would be grounded, but the likelihood of someone stumbling across us in that time was deemed negligible. But no doubt she was on tenterhooks waiting for us to reach out to connect.

With our gate still grounded, it would force an outgoing destination from the bunker to whatever lay beyond the doorway.

And with that, our role in the mission was finished. It was up to Dr Sterne now.

We continued our charade of discussing what I had stumbled across on the datapad, but after a few seconds we were both starting to sweat.

How long is too long to just stand around in a place like this? I kept asking myself. The guiltier I *thought* we looked, the guiltier I likely looked.

'We have to leave,' I whispered to Sam after another few seconds passed by. 'We've been standing here for too long, we need to go.'

She nodded in agreement, and we both casually took a step or two back, gave a final look to an un-impressive section of bare wall, shook our heads and turned to leave. I kept my head buried in the datapad to continue the illusion, but the speed at which Sam moved gave me a reason to believe our little act may not have been as natural as we had hoped.

We easily began retracing our steps through the corridors, this time struggling to keep to a conventional walking pace. The hallways were empty. Not a single soul passed us as we counted down the areas we'd gone through.

Section by section we moved through the Hub. Section 7, section 6, section 5, large red painted numbers counted us down.

It wasn't until section 4, this time emblazoned with a large green number, that Sam stopped and pulled me back.

'Where the fuck is everyone?' she asked, more to herself than me.

We both peered around the next corner, into one of the longest sections of corridor, and again saw nobody.

'It's too quiet,' I whispered. 'It's not lunchtime or anything, this place should be busy.'

Sam took a few steps forwards into the hallway. After a split second, she moved towards the closest door, with a card access terminal to its side.

Again, she pulled out her fake employee card and held it up to the doorway.

It doesn't matter what variation of buzzer sound, or coloured lighting a company would use, a "Denied" reaction was universal.

She tried it another five times in quick succession, all with the same confidence shredding result.

I stepped away and peered through the small slit of a window on the closest other door into a pristine laboratory space. It was faint, and almost out of sight, but the flashing yellow light was undeniable.

'It's a silent alarm,' I muttered, hardly audible, fear nearly robbing me of my voice.

But it wasn't until we turned at a far-off noise that my stomach really sank. It was an undeniable sound, creeping closer every moment. Metal doors slamming against walls, and boot stomps echoing off polished hallway floors.

They were coming.

Chapter 17

No audible warning rang in the hallways, but my head was full of alarm bells.

The heavy rubber boots could be heard screeching and stomping on the laminated floors as they seemed to be homing in on our position.

'Here.' I grabbed Sam, ripping her away from the escalating feud with the doorway's card reader. 'There's no time. We have to hide.'

She begrudgingly gave in and charged with me through the doorway back into section 5A. None of the lab or office doorways would give us access now, but I wasn't about to give ourselves up so lightly.

Not here, not here. I quickly scanned each of the small nooks and crannies as we ran through into section 5B. *Camera there, camera there, camera there.*

'There!'

I pushed Sam towards the left side of the corridor with force.

'What the fuck are you doing Leon, we need to get out of here!'

I didn't reply. There was no time.

With the datapad still in my hand, I reached out to an innocuous panel that blended near seamlessly with the pale aquamarine of the wall around it. I hooked my fingers in, clicked it loose, and a small panel popped out from the wall next to us.

'In, now!'

I pushed Sam in first before squeezing in behind her, unable to properly stand upright in the space.

The panel shut slowly, the built-in dampers creating a wholly unnecessary delay. But I didn't let it close completely, painfully using my fingers to block the lock from engaging.

The map on the datapad had shown every ventilation shaft and exit on our route, but it also clearly displayed every storage cabinet. This one luckily wasn't within range of any of the cameras from what I could see, and hiding seemed our only option as they approached.

We both froze. My half-hunched-over position was incredibly uncomfortable, but I forced myself to grin and bear the burning in my legs.

We held our breath as we heard the doorway into our section swing open with force.

The panel wasn't open enough to peer out, but shadows flashed across the bit of light that seeped in. Judging by the sound and the shadows, there was likely five people in total.

The radio was alive with instructions as they progressed. "...in custody. Proceed with caution. This is to be quick and quiet. Extract via internal gateway..."

They passed, and the voice on the radio was too muddled to hear within seconds.

Unable to hold my position any longer, I burst out from our position, falling to the ground alongside several mops and a bucket half full of lilac-scented water.

Sam leapt out from behind, gasping for fresh air.

'Did you hear that?' she asked, her words tinged with panic. 'They weren't talking about us. It must be Sterne, we have to help her!'

'Help her how? We need to get the hell out of here!'

'And how do you suppose we do that? You think they nicely just left all the exits open for us back there? For fuck's sake, we can't even get out the same way we got in, my card is useless. Come on!'

Sam turned and dashed off down the corridor in the same direction as the security troop. I stood in awe of her bravery for a moment, charging off into the unknown for Dr Sterne. But I stumbled, mounting fear gripping at me and forcing me to consider other, less crazy options. They clearly weren't looking for us. We should be able just to leave as we came once the alarm was lifted.

'Leon, come on!' Sam shouted from the far end of the corridor, an unusual panic tainting her voice.

That was all it took for me to make up my mind.

Sam was charging right into captivity, and the thought that she may come to harm, and I didn't do everything in my power to help, stamped enough of my fear down that I could move again.

I ran after her, easily catching up.

We quickly but as quietly as possible glided through the corridors, making sure to not crash open the doorways in case we alerted those ahead of us.

We neared the last corner of the track, knowing the intended section would soon be around the corner. We both came to an abrupt halt as we reached the intersection of 8A. Peeking around the corner, I witnessed the last of the security forces enter the doorway.

Without hesitation, Sam sprinted down the corridor, gracefully enough that she made almost no sound.

I took off behind her, knowing exactly what she was doing. Every single door and panel in the place had some sort of damper so that they would close evenly and slowly so as not to slam. Sam realised that she would have to catch the door before it closed if we were to have any chance.

Passing her at full sprint, I could see we weren't going to make it. Not without something a little drastic.

With two short springy bounds, I dove at the doorway, slamming down hard and sliding the last few feet before crashing shoulder first into the unopened side of the doorway. But the gamble paid off, as my arm managed to brace the door before it shut completely. The doorway was so solid that it didn't even make much in the way of noise as I crashed into it.

Instead, my body just exchanged the noise for double the agony. It became all the more apparent as I tried to lift myself using my free arm, only to give up immediately as the sharp stabbing pain from my shoulder shot down my arm like a rolling ember.

'Woah, Leon, what the hell? Are you okay?' Sam pulled me up from the ground, making sure to pry the door open first.

'Yeah, fine,' I lied, peeking in through the doorway. 'What now?'

'Follow me. No diving please.' She pushed past, leading me into the new corridor that now lay ahead. The door closed softly behind us, followed by a large clunk as the locking mechanism trapped us in the bowels of the facility.

The hallway was just as wide as before and followed a similar green and white aesthetic, but it was littered with doorways.

We crept along, peeking through each glass viewing panel as we went. Every laboratory was empty. Just like any alarm, be it fire or otherwise, the researchers probably all begrudgingly left through the nearest emergency gate to the assembly areas, waiting for whatever nonsense had set off the alarm this time to pass. It was likely nobody even knew there was a real problem.

The gate must have been close as my AMI had been alight since we approached the entrance to the section.

The laboratory was quite noisy. The hum of air filtration systems was echoing through the area, and each lab had a hiss of air passing under the doorways.

Just over the thrumming air systems, we could hear

a voice. It wasn't far away, sounded like it was just in-side one of the adjacent doors in the section of the corridor around the closest corner.

We approached slowly, trying to locate the sound without stepping out from our cover. It wasn't Dr Sterne, but a male voice. Two even, it was hard to tell.

After a few moments, it was quiet again.

We stayed still for a few seconds, bracing ourselves to confront the men as they left the room. But nei-ther came.

I looked at my AMI as it buzzed twice in short succession.

'Shit!' I struggled to hold my pitch in check as I sprinted around the corner and burst into the room.

Nobody and nothing. Except for a large emergency gateway, bright red and yellow in case you would somehow miss it.

'Damn it.' Sam joined me, peering in over my shoul-der. 'They're gone.'

I pulled up the gate interface on my AMI, trying to decipher where they had gone. But it was blank, noth-ing out of the ordinary. Just a self-repeating address for the default assembly point.

'Protocol bands,' I said to Sam. The same tech our gate interface was based on, only theirs didn't leave a trace.

'Shit, shit, shit. Right, let me think.' Sam circled the room like a vulture.

'Do you think she managed to send the uplink back somehow?' I asked, optimism stretched to its limits.

'No, no way. The alarm went off too quickly. We were hardly a minute from sending the coordinates before we were in that damned smelly mop cupboard of yours.'

'How could they have known she was here?' I racked my brain for a moment. 'You don't suppose there's another mole in the bunker, do you?'

The realisation hit Sam hard as she stopped in her tracks and stared blankly into space for a moment.

'Not a mole, no.'

But the answer hadn't come from Sam, whose eyes were wide with fury and looking back over my shoulder.

It was a man's voice. A familiar one.

I swung around in the doorway, recoiling to gain valuable distance between myself and the origin of the voice. But Sam flung herself at the imposing frame that filled the doorway.

'You bastard, what did you do!' she screamed as she crashed into Frank. 'What did you do?!'

He grabbed her by both wrists, holding her out in front of him.

I took that as my moment to strike, shoulder still aching and hardly mobile, but willing to lead with my weaker fist.

But his reactions were too good, and his knowledge of me too personal. He simply stepped back slightly and moved Sam between himself and me, using her as an outstretched shield. I couldn't reach him but through her.

'Will you two calm the hell down. This isn't the time or place, I have orders, and if I have to, I'll drag you both kicking and screaming back through that gate. This was all Sterne's plan, so stop looking for a fight and get with the program.' He released Sam gently.

But not gently enough, as she landed a large slap across his face.

'Are you done?' he asked. 'We need to go before they flip the switch on this gate and all the disgruntled lab rats come piling back through.'

'Fine.' Sam added, 'But you first.'

He smirked and made his way to the gate. Pulling up the gate interface, he activated the bunkers address and disappeared into the slipways event horizon. Sam was quick on his heels, but not before mumbling 'Lying piece of shit better have a good excuse for—'

Not wanting to waste any time, I followed suit. I wasn't glad to be returning to the bunker, but this place had quickly turned into another type of prison, so I didn't delay.

The commute to the bunker again felt longer than normal, and there was no comforting display of mixed mint and azure photons to calm my nerves. It was just bland. There was a perfect semblance between the journey and the destination in that way.

I emerged to the sight of Sam already tearing into Frank. But it wasn't just Frank, as Styx appeared to be by his side backing him up.

'Her plan? What? Did we not pass the fucking polygraph today or something? Why the hell would you keep this from us, we nearly got stung out there!' Sam was livid, employing every dissatisfied arm gesture she could think up.

I approached Sam's side, ready to join her in dis-agreement to whatever the hell had just transpired on the other side of the gate. But as I reached them, Styx peeled off and intercepted me.

'Reason isn't going to win over there. Please, let me explain.' She attempted to push me in the other di-rection by my shoulder, but I recoiled from the touch, so she stood her ground instead.

She clearly thought I was coming in hot too, but I hadn't shifted gear just yet from panic to anger.

'Frank was only doing what Sterne told him to do,' said Styx. 'This was all her plan. The guy in Worm-Whole, the one she was going to meet? It was her son, Damian. We knew they would be monitoring him in case she contacted him, so she decided to use herself as bait.'

She barely took a breath between explaining, maybe afraid I would interject if she had any downtime.

'Frank left the moment you guys sent the address and made his way to Damian. He was the one with the access codes we needed, but we also needed him to remain anonymous to WormWhole. So, the second Sterne stood through the gateway, we had Damian report to security that she had arrived, showing he had nothing to do with her. Frank already had the access codes by then, and just had to hide out until they had taken Sterne away. He must have called it in too quickly if you guys didn't make it back to the gates in time, but Sterne never meant to get you guys wrapped up in the second part of the plan.'

I reeled for a moment, struggling to take it all in. What an info dump.

We had been successful, but were we really? Dr Sterne was gone. The one everyone looked up to for guidance in this increasingly bonkers situation we found ourselves in.

'Please understand,' Styx said as she retreated to the gate, preparing to ground it again now that everyone was back. 'She couldn't stay here, she needed to do this. I can't tell you why, but it's much better for her to be out there than in here.'

Sam didn't seem to understand though, as she just shook her head at Frank.

I walked back over to them, seeing as the conversation had simmered to only a mild disagreement.

'Look,' he began, 'at the end of the day, Sterne needed a hospital after the attack and you knew that. They'll have the red carpet out for her at the damned place. She barely made it through the gate walking, she's far sicker than she let on. So what if they keep her under lock and key? She's better off with them for now. And it'll keep her away from BioDev—she's too high profile, and too many people saw her in the labs.'

Sam, ever defiant, simply spun on her heels and went towards the rest area.

'I'm sorry, Leon, I would've told you if I could, but

she knew Sam would never have let her go through with it had she known.'

He wasn't wrong, but I didn't appreciate being kept in the dark again. 'From now on, Frank, if you guys want my help, I know everything, right?'

He smirked. 'Fine by me. Just, maybe try and calm Sam down a bit first. I think she nearly knocked my tooth out with that slap.'

He left me, rubbing his face as he went.

Well done, Sam, I thought as I followed her.

She didn't take long to find, sat over the edge of her cot, hair hanging down over her face to hide whatever angry expression she was making.

I sat down beside her, thinking I could at least join her in a moment of mutual frustration.

'Dr Sterne, eh? Crafty old coot,' I joshed.

She didn't speak. Instead, all I heard was a low sniffle, as she moved her hand to her face, rubbing it on both sides. She then reached over and took a tight grip on my hand.

Another sniffle and she turned to lay sideways down on the bed, still holding my hand. I shifted to allow her to swing her legs up, but still she held on lightly.

I sat in silence, with her lying in the foetal position, facing out into the room, her hair still partly covering her face.

It was a few minutes before her grip became slack, and she drifted to sleep. I stayed for a while longer, holding her hand gently enough so as not to wake her.

She was never overly affectionate, and never showed an ounce of weakness when I was around. Mainly, she just displayed a combination of whimsy and fury, in equal measure.

This was new.

I wasn't sure if the gesture was her looking for a moment of comfort considering how nothing was turning out how we planned, or if it was meant as an apology for embroiling me in this escalating situation. Maybe it didn't matter the reason.

It was hard to tell how long I sat there holding her hand. But it was a nice moment.

Chapter 18

Dr Sterne was gone.

She was lost to a wild gambit, one that could have cost Sam and me our freedom too. Silver linings had become scarce in our lives, but in this instance, we had achieved exactly what had aimed for. The entire WormWhole intranet was now open to us.

Frank and Lucy had gone to task setting up our monitoring system over by the far wall, utilising the external connection Christian had used to our detriment. I had re-joined Styx and some others sitting by the gate, leaving Sam to sleep. She deserved some downtime.

'What kind of info do you think we'll get off their satellites?' I asked, fed up of the silence most people here seemed content to flounder in.

'Hard to know really,' Styx began. 'Files and information stored on their cloud servers are tricky, it's heavily encrypted, and we could set off a security lockdown. But all the live data is easy to watch, so we should be able to follow everything that goes on with any WormWhole gate in the world. And that includes tracking whoever we feel needs tracking. Pretty handy, hey?'

WormWhole wasn't the only gate company, of course, but by far the leader in both volume and coverage. A handy tool was right, so long as we used it appropriately.

'It would keep track of anyone travelling,' I continued, 'even BioDev employees?'

'Sure,' Styx replied. 'Every commute uses passport data as people move around. That's only standard gates though. Private gates are a tad different. We can tell travellers are passing through, but we can't tell who it is if there's no security scanner hardwired into the network too.'

'But there should be travel signatures you could track, right?' I thought back to various lecturers about the physics behind slipway travel. 'Everyone interacts with the formed slipway differently, it all depends on mass, volume, and distance to travel if I remember correctly.'

She took a moment to think. 'There should be a way to monitor for something like that alright. It mightn't be an exact science, but assuming we follow someone from a public gate, we should be able to track similar slipway characteristics from their destination. Assuming they don't gorge out on too much during their stay the slipway, features should remain mostly unchanged run to run.'

My stomach growled at Styx's mention of food. Sushi, steak, a sloppy burrito. The foods of kings, but all out of reach. Who would have thought it possible to have taken their local takeaway for granted all those years?

Food envy aside, this was all positive. WormWhole information would flow through these satellites, thinking themselves stealthy couriers of sensitive data, but we would be watching. Anything they knew, we would know.

And in that instant, with all this new information at hand, a peculiar idea formed. One based on the task which had inadvertantly lead me to this group.

'Do you think we could track hiccups?' I asked coyly, making sure the others nearby weren't disturbed from their own conversations.

Styx looked at me, head slightly tilted and brow raised. 'I think Lucy would be the one to ask about that. She's more familiar with the system than me. But I would imagine so, yes.'

'Okay, thanks.'

The others had openly disputed what had happened on that day. They didn't believe that my use of the code banished those men to an unknown, hinting maybe it was just my reimagining of the situation. They hadn't shaken my faith just yet that the code was important, but maybe the problem was MY code. After all, we had little to compare it to.

That's where spying on the network could really come in handy. All I needed was one hiccup, and I could go and find a new code to compare my own to. Surely there must be some similarities between hiccups, and a comparison could show that. And now that it was in doubt as to whether people ever truly disappeared in transit, it gave me added belief that there was something to be discovered.

I stood up and left Styx's side, heading towards Frank and Lucy. Nobody else had chosen to gather close to them, everyone making sure to give them a wide berth as they got the satellite listener up and going.

They were both standing back from the system as I approached, simply watching the displays scroll through some processes.

'Any updates?' I asked, taking up position beside them and trying to follow the haze of commands as they came and went on the screen.

'It's doing its own thing now,' replied Lucy. 'We're just kind of waiting for it to connect. But we've done everything right from what we can see, so fingers crossed, I guess.'

We all stood in silence, watching the scrolling text. There wasn't exactly a progress bar to contend with, so we had no idea how long the process would take.

It slowed and even stopped on occasion, but only for a moment, long enough to fool us before it began scrolling again. It seemed like it was mocking us, just for fun.

But, as if it became bored of our gawks and antici-pation, it finally came to a halt and exploded into an unfamiliar interface. With a quick gesture Lucy threw the display from the screen into a holoprojection, so we could all have a better view.

'There we go.' Lucy seemed to recognise the layout. 'We're online.'

Frank, ever the solemn figure, even gave her a pat on the back and a 'well done.'

'Right, pay attention you two.'

Lucy launched into her breakdown of the new spy system. It had access to everything in WormWhole. There was limited scope to go digging for information stored in their encrypted servers, but every single bit of live data from the company was up for grabs. She explained how we could filter what we needed using the interface, how to monitor for specific passports, and even how to isolate destination codes that were private, assuming we tracked someone there.

Frank seemed happy with the explanation and left to wake Sam.

Having a moment alone with Lucy and the system, I decided to act upon my plan.

'Do you think we can monitor for hiccups from this terminal?'

Lucy thought for a second on the matter, hiccups clearly something she hadn't contemplated just yet.

'Yes actually, I think we should be able to. Every commute is different, but there are a few basic func-tionalities all gates process during travel. If you travel from A to B, once there are no problems, the system will mark it as "complete." It helps stop people arriving too quickly behind each other. I suppose we could set up something to monitor for oddities like commutes that lack a complete status. But,' she paused to turn towards me, 'why do you want to look out for that, if you don't mind me asking?'

I didn't mind but also thought it best to keep my true plans under wraps for now. 'Well if we're going to keep pressing on it's our best way of staying up to date with missing people, right? Keep the name wall updated.'

'Oh yeah, that's not a bad idea actually. Sure. I'm going to program a few basic monitoring algorithms now so I'll include that. Want me to just hook the alerts directly to your AMI? You can look after the wall then.'

Was there anything Lucy couldn't do? Or for that matter, all of these new friends. Styx, Sam, Frank. Anything we try to do, they do. I was constantly impressed by their abilities. I needed to up my game if I wanted to contribute in a more meaningful way.

'Thanks, that would be perfect.'

It was uncomfortable to lie to Lucy. She was so genuine and friendly. But it was best to keep the idea to myself for now, or at least until I got what I needed. Nobody believed the code was of any use and would likely think it was just a wasteful distraction, so why trouble them with my idea.

The next several hours were a flurry of excitement and wonder.

We chose to track a variety of WormWhole managers as guinea pigs, specifically ones we were less than enamoured with from our time at the company. We couldn't exactly prove it, but from what we were seeing, several of the managers were likely sleeping together.

A scandalous comedic distraction for a few moments.

It was surreal to be monitoring people's movements. Not that I had ever been too adventurous, but to see a map of a person's travel habits could easily paint a life as incredibly droll. I bet mine would have looked no different, but having it pieced together for all to see just made the person seem so...insignificant.

Knowing they would use private gates on occasion, Lucy got started on the task of creating robust tracking measures to ensure we didn't lose them.

While she worked, the rest of us gathered to plan.

'So, we can catch any of these people with their pants down now, what's the next step?' Frank, now attempting to take the reins of the group, stood in front of us all.

A few ideas were batted around meekly, the group's zeal having been drained somewhat by the loss of Dr Sterne. Frank's frustration was apparent, but he remained upbeat and engaging. It wasn't exactly his strong point, but he was doing well. 'No idea is a bad idea,' he kept repeating.

'Let's take a step back,' Sam interjected, having rejoined the group, now fully awake and visibly irritated by Frank's attempted alpha male position. 'We had a simple plan, the why and the how. Who's first on the list of people who might know either?'

The murmurs were unsure, but one name was being repeated. 'Dr Ross.'

And why not? It was his office where we got our most vital piece of intelligence. He was a highly ranked BioDev employee and would likely have his fingers dipped in every pie in the company. Yet, nobody mentioned who I thought would be a much better candidate for our first true tracking test.

'M. Scaife,' I called out, making sure my voice rose above the nonsensical rabble. It didn't stop them debating amongst themselves, but it caught Sam's attention.

'Who?'

Losing the battle to not roll my eyes at her, I stepped forwards. 'M. Scaife? You guys all read the document, right? Completely?'

I could see her recall the memo in her head, her eyes unfocused, darting back and forth as if she was reading it there and then.

'It's the person who wrote the thing,' I said. 'M. Scaife, head or something of their dark site security.'

'Director of Blacksite security?' Frank chimed in.

'Yeah, there, that's the one.' So maybe I wasn't completely correct, but I felt his tone was unnecessary. 'We know Ross is already involved somehow. This person might know even more if they're the one mailing Ross about the incident.'

'Michelle Scaife. It has to be her.' Frank was very

sure of himself as he spoke. 'She ran security for some of BioDev's clinic divisions years back. She was supposed to be...effective.'

'Let me guess.' A painful memory was tricking me into holding my side. 'She was the one who implemented using those shotput guns at clinics.'

'Bingo,' Frank added.

The discussions behind me had shifted to discussing this new plan of attack. The crowd was with me, so I pushed.

'Well, we follow her then.' More murmurs of agreement. 'Why not track Dr Ross too? They're bound to cross paths if they're that involved.'

By adding Dr Ross to the conversation, the other bunker dwellers' first choice of enemy, I had their complete backing. And that of Sam and Frank.

'Perfect.' Sam beamed with delight. She instructed one of the others to go tell Lucy who to start the search for, before turning back to me. 'BioDev may have thousands of employees, but those two should stand out like sore thumbs. We'll have them as soon as they pop up somewhere public.'

And there we had it. Our plan had been formed.

A simple plan for now. Simple was what we needed.

But that was just act one. What good was tracking someone to their lair if we weren't prepared to do something with that information? We were potentially talking about BioDev's most secretive facility, and it would no doubt have formidable security coverage.

We weren't a small army or mercenary group. I didn't think an attack was in our best interests.

But thankfully, we didn't have to enter the lion's den just yet. We just needed our target. Essentially, we needed to abduct the abductor.

If there was anyone we could lean on to try and find out why these people were going missing, it would be this M. Scaife. Information was what was needed. The right information in the right hands could cripple people and companies alike, no matter how large.

But this person wasn't to be taken lightly. She was a big fish, and we were minnows.

Frank waved me over to him as he moved to leave the circle of people around the gate. He led me back to a small area just out of view, one that had started to gather a slight smell of something I couldn't put my finger on. It was like a sterile cleaning product. Two-parts chlorine, one-part vinegar.

As I rounded a large cabinet, I saw several sets of dark uniforms laid out on a table. There was also a collection of weapons beside them.

'I salvaged the tactical gear, and the weapons, before we disposed of the bodies.' Frank didn't seem bothered when referring to the dead infiltrators. I was still uneasy about their fate.

I walked over and picked up one of the smaller weapons. It felt lighter than I expected, as I nearly threw it in the air when I pulled it up, expecting there to be some sort of resistance.

Frank laughed. 'Polycarbonate blend, no metal

parts. The projectiles have small compressed air capsules instead of gunpowder, so no risk of anything melting. Lightweight and undetectable by conventional security scanners, just in case. Not exactly something an above-board company would need to deploy very often, you would imagine.'

It nuzzled tightly into the contour of my arm, complete with a transparent sleeve to anchor it to the forearm. Not only that, but it could fold in on itself and fit snug enough on your arm to hide under a loose sleeve. It was the type of weaponry you would expect from an old fashioned spy movie.

'Six shots max with those sidearms,' Frank continued as he picked up one of the larger rifles. 'The same type of technology as this, only these rifles are pure animals in comparison.'

He cocked the gun, and it lit up along the barrel, humming as it came to life.

'They're a sort of rail gun. It uses a dual laser to judge projectile speed on the fly, depending on the distance to the target. They store about 40 of those electrofoam rounds but have a secondary fire too. Rubber projectiles, large enough and strong enough to break bones if they want. The ultimate crowd control weaponry.'

I cocked my new sidearm and aimed it, focussing through the small plastic sight. I turned it towards Frank just for fun, just to see if he would flinch a little. Instead he just stared me down disapprovingly.

I know he thought me childish, but I had never held

a real firearm before, even a non-lethal one. I couldn't help but feel slightly excited. Being on that end of a weapon for once was good.

'Here,' Frank threw the top half of one of the outfits to me, 'try that on for size.'

'Eh, somebody kind of...died in this. I'd rather not.'

'Don't be like that, Leon. We're not trying to draft anyone this time. But we need volunteers, and by volunteers, I mean anyone who fits these sets of gear.'

I grimaced at the smell of the gear. It had been thoroughly cleaned, to the point where the fumes almost burnt my eyes. Begrudgingly, I tried it on.

And low and behold, it fit. Of course it fit. Was it ever not going to fit? For I was the chosen one. Chosen to be screwed at every possible turn. There was no way Frank had chosen me without knowing I would likely be a perfect match. "No drafting" eh?

'Brilliant,' I murmured.

'Good, it fits. Looks like we're up, so.' Frank smirked just enough for me to catch it. 'And don't worry, the smell will wear off, couldn't leave any blood stains for obvious reasons.'

'Alright, fine.' I took the gear off again and threw it down beside the rest of the death-chic attire. 'So, come on then, out with the plan. Where is it all going to go down?'

'Somewhere minimal, somewhere we can catch her off-guard enough that she doesn't have time to think about it. We go in, pretend we're extracting her for her own safety, and have her walk right through to here of her own volition. No violence, no problem.'

I wish I lived in the same world as Frank's imagination, where all of our plans had a hundred percent track record and this cement bomb shelter we were obliged to live in was actually a five-star hotel.

But alas, I was firmly rooted in reality. Tedious, unfortunate reality.

'Do you not think that, being a head of security and probably very in the know about their botched attempt at shutting us down, she might be sceptical? And maybe, just maybe, have some firearms of her own?' I tried not to sound too condescending, but Frank had clearly starting leaning too much towards optimism. 'All I'm saying is, we need a backup.'

'Okay then, wow me.'

'Wow you? Okay. We walk in, zap her ass, and walk back out again.' From what I had gleaned, she wasn't considered a kind woman, so why gently escort her and potentially put ourselves in harm's way? 'Simple right?'

Frank stood for a moment, surprised that I was suggesting a less civilised method. A bit out of character perhaps, but I didn't remember him being shot and shocked to the point of losing everything but bowel control.

'Maybe that can be plan B then...'

'Fine. But the second she flinches, plan B, Thor style.'

Frank shook his head and grinned.

I took that as permission.

I folded the new weapon in and out from my fore-arm a few more times just for fun. It gave me confidence, like an extra layer of armour.

But like with all firearms, it could prove to be a fool's confidence.

Chapter 19

We stalked our prey from the long grass of our bunker for the better part of a day.

It was only a few hours before we had picked up the digital scent of our target, Michelle Scaife. But we needed more time. Time to find a place she would stay in for more than an hour at a time. Her travel patterns seemed erratic, popping in and out from public and private gates alike all over the world. Wherever the trail ended would likely be her home, or somewhere else she found comforting enough to drop her guard and relax.

The plan was to approach her somewhere away from the general public, somewhere we would garner the least attention. Once we intercepted her, we would explain a fictional situation using real emergency protocols from BioDev. Our outfits would be overkill for a normal security detail, and likely the most unbelievable aspect of the con, but it was better than approaching her head on. Hopefully, as such an important figure, she would be used to more serious security personnel being deployed for her.

Frank, myself, and Lucy were suited and booted in tactical gear. Groups of three were common for small security details, and we fit the suits well enough to complete the deception. Frank and Lucy barely flinched while donning the attire; their experience in the BioDev security would be invaluable to our little abduction. They seemed to be relishing the opportunity.

None more than Lucy really. Her obvious claustrophobia had nearly rendered her incapacitated when we were trapped in the bunker before, but now? Now she was a beacon of focus and determination. Every clicking of a buckle on her gear just seemed to raise her zeal. She was ready for war.

And her understated confidence leached into me as I found myself standing more upright and taller than before. I was a security officer. We were a security team. Nobody would be able to tell we weren't.

As we approached the 24-hour mark of monitoring our target, we were confident to proceed. The information we had was limited, but we were sure she was at home. Her last destination, a private gate in a suburban area, had been quiet since her arrival several hours previous.

We stood ready, the armoured overalls and weaponry giving each of us an uneasy level of pseudo-confidence. We put on our best metaphorical war faces, despite our faces being completely covered, and prepared for Styx to dial up the destination.

Everyone sat around the gate, but not too close.

They were statues, all eyes locked on the three of us. Except for Sam, of course, who was having the world's greatest sulk due to not being included. But I knew she was still angry from our previous outing, and likely unhappy with Frank for keeping Dr Sterne's true plans private, so probably best she stayed at home for the excursion.

With a few gestures from Styx, the light above the gate locked in green.

Go time.

As best we could, we broke into a symmetrical stride. Chests puffed, cheeks clenched, and weapons held like Frank had shown us.

Once more into the unknown.

My breath quickened as I followed in the rear. A single bead of sweat escaped the tight face mask and trickled down the bridge of my nose. I swallowed hard as exhilaration and nerves in equal balance drove me through the gate, hot on the tail of the others.

We arrived in an instant, plunging into darkness and unsure of the layout. The other two had their torches on already and stood by the doorway. The small room was bigger than the closet where Dr Ross hid his gateway. A study of sorts, with the gateway seamlessly blended in between two bookcases.

I hadn't expected us to land right in the heart of the household. Who would want a gateway inside the boundary of their home?

Some unknown person could just walk through some day.

An ironic thought.

We stepped out into the hallway. The darkness was split by a streak of moonlight from a nearby window.

We couldn't split up. We needed to act in control, like we knew exactly where we were going.

We glided through the hallway, heading up the central staircase from the foyer.

The house was dead quiet. Middle of the night, granted. But still, eerily quiet.

Did she live alone? In a house that size?

We moved with purpose, in step with one another towards what looked like the largest bedroom.

A faint beam of artificial light crept out from underneath the door.

Bingo.

Frank didn't break his stride; he simply burst through the door.

Cigar in hand, sitting by a single light at the window, the imposing figure of Scaife greeted us. She didn't seem too shocked by our arrival. If anything, she appeared irritated.

'There better be a damned good reason for you to be here, in my home.' She spat the words at us, vitriolic and sharp.

'Ma'am, you need to come with us.' Frank walked past her and pulled the curtain slightly to the side, pretending to check the perimeter. 'This site is compromised. We are to escort you to the nearest security installation.'

'You need to give me a better reason than that,

because I am not moving.' She was incredulous. I wondered how often she had been pestered by overly cautious security personnel in her lifetime to be so dismissive of our message of warning.

'Ma'am this is not a joke, we should—'

'Don't give me that bullshit.' She cut through Frank's earnest but forceful warnings, taking another long drag on her cigar before blowing the plume at myself and Lucy. 'You think I don't know exactly what's going on here?'

Our collective chests seized up as we tried to not look unnerved by her words.

I started to clutch my rifle tighter, the unease causing my trigger finger to cry out for plan B to be unleashed and to just shock her immediately. I was already sweating profusely due to the heavy gear and mental strain; I didn't need the extra stress.

I couldn't put my finger on what part of our act had lead her to believe the threat was a simple annoyance to be dismissed in a puff of her cigar smoke.

Frank was clearly caught short, freezing long enough for his authority to be brought into question.

One more hail Mary play, then this bitch is getting some shock treatment.

I dug deep and pulled the only name I could think of from the back of my mind that may just instil some level of seriousness, as it did in the bunker only a short while ago.

'We received intel that Professor Borza has this location and is planning an attack.' I brought my voice down low, hoping going to a deeper octave would lend me a greater authority. 'There is no time for debate, ma'am.'

She looked at me, cigar still pursed between her lips but no longer pulling on it.

Both Frank and Lucy also seemed sideswiped by my deception, turning to me, eyes screaming in confusion for a moment before regaining their composure.

It took a moment, but Scaife eventually broke her silence.

'That fucking terrorist...' She extinguished the cigar and stood. 'Well? Earn your paycheque. If you idiots couldn't even take out those toothless fools with Sterne, I don't want to rely on your bodyguard abilities. Let's go.'

Back into our synchronised march, we exited the room, Scaife in tow.

In that instance, as we escorted her back through the darkened hallways, I couldn't have been surer she was the perfect target.

But I also couldn't have been more unnerved.

She knew about us. Not only that, but the remark was on the tip of her tongue, and she passed it off so flippantly. She was clearly knowledgeable about our situation, for better or worse.

We reached the bottom floor and progressed quickly, retaining our stealthy movements to keep the illusion of professionalism.

Our acting skills had been unparalleled.

'NO!'

Frank's muted scream was followed by an ear-shattering crash, as the echoing walls made it feel as if a hundred mirrors shattered all around me.

I swung around, rifle humming to life, fright sharpening my every sense.

The uncomfortable gear and large weaponry had laid waste to Frank's composure, as he stood surrounded by a jigsaw puzzle of vase remnants.

Scaife was on him in an instant.

'You incompetent fool, look what you've done! Do you realise how expensive that was?' She grabbed Frank by the scruff of the outfit. 'I'll have your licence for this you ape, who do you think...'

An unexpected silence, mid-rant. She froze, her grip loosening on Frank's gear. Her hand slid down, to a part of the armour just above the Velcro strap holding the chest piece in place.

Right to a small damaged section of the armour. A single bullet hole.

The gear had been cleaned, but it hadn't been repaired.

Shoving me to the side, Lucy burst past me, rifle raised.

Too slow.

In a heartbeat, Scaife tore the rifle from Frank's grip, using the butt of the stock to incapacitate him. One sharp hit to the side of the head, the only unarmoured section of Frank's entire body, and he hit the floor in a thunderous thump, porcelain smashing under him as he went.

Scaife spun, smooth and precise, down onto a knee, and fired.

Lucy took the rubber projectile right to the chest, knocking her off her feet.

I raised my firearm, just in time to halt her from firing as we locked aim, and eyes.

It was a stand-off, and she knew neither firing mode was lethal enough to stop herself from receiving an immediate and similar fate.

Unblinking, unflinching, I stared down the barrel at her as she slowly stood, keeping me dead in the crosshairs too.

Lucy rolled and groaned as she attempted to get back to her feet. Armour may have saved broken bones at that range but the force was enough to knock the wind from her lungs.

I couldn't stop the slight tremor in my right hand, a symptom of the adrenaline.

'You've never looked down the sight of a weapon and seen a person on the far side. You're green.' She was cocky. 'You don't have the balls.'

She was right. Or rather she would have been right, if the gun was lethal. And if she wasn't a bitch.

Mustering up all my bravado in that moment, I replied, 'Screw it, plan B.'

We both fired.

She had aimed high, hoping to catch me in the face.

I ducked my head. Not fast enough. The projectile ricocheted hard off the helmet, nearly spinning me.

Crashing down on my left shoulder again, rattled

and in pain, I tried to reach out to the rifle Lucy had dropped before she fired again.

But I was safe.

Scaife spasmed uncontrollably as the electricity surged through her abdomen. My shot had taken root just below her sternum, rendering her defenceless and in excruciating pain. But still, she managed to remain standing, albeit barely.

Lucy, now back on her feet, kicked Frank's weapon away from Scaife. For a moment it seemed like she was going to lay Scaife out, as she hung her clenched fist down by her side. But instead, she passed by and helped Frank up. He was holding his face, dazed from the hit and clearly in pain.

I slowly staggered up, using the nearest table to stabilise myself. In the process, I knocked over another large vase. It smashed across the floor just like the first.

A complete accident of course. Not at all a cynical act. Never.

Scaife succumbed to the severity of the pain just as I regained my standing, head, neck and shoulder aching from the blow. She struggled out a final 'fuck you' before losing consciousness.

She really was tough, I'll give her that.

But not as tough as my helmet thankfully. It was the one good thing BioDev had done for me lately.

'You okay?' Frank asked me as he and Lucy helped each other along.

'Me? Shit, what about you?'

He tried to laugh it off, a little show of endurance, but instead nearly fell over again. 'Oh yeah,' he replied. 'I'm peachy.'

His face and eyes seemed swollen and red, blood running down the side of his hairline as he pulled the mask down to spit. 'Bitch,' he growled, before re-adjusting the face mask.

'That could've gone better,' Lucy continued. 'But hey, plan B, right?'

Damned right plan B.

'We better split,' I added. 'Don't want to be here when she wakes up. She probably has this place laid out like the McCallister house.'

'The what?' Frank replied.

'Nothing, forget it.'

Nostalgic explanations could wait.

Frank and I pulled Scaife off the ground, her body no longer convulsing as the charge dissipated. Lucy picked up the weapons and went on ahead to prep the gate.

We pulled Scaife along, closing the door to the study behind us as we entered. I transferred her full weight to Frank, who tried not to grimace slightly under the effort. He progressed through the gateway first, followed by Lucy after a few moments, still cursing and trying to regain her composure.

Then it was just me, as I pulled up the gate schematic on my AMI and engaged the slipway.

But through the holodisplay, hovering out from my wrist, an oddity appeared.

I lowered the gate schematic, looking down at a beautifully kept wooden desk beside the wall. It was bare, aside from a single item.

I approached, lifting the small case from the desk.

I had witnessed my fair share of aesthetically pleasing extravagances over the years, mostly in museums. But what I found on the desk was just as eye-catching as any before.

A fountain pen. But no simple fountain pen. A striking design ran the length of the cylindrical barrel, glistening in the room's faint light. The pinkish wooden base was wrapped in a double helix of near silver metal.

An inscription was etched into the case's inner surface.

"Burmese Rosewood and Rhodium."

And under that, a personalised miniature plaque of some kind, with a second inscription.

"If we are to sign away our souls, let it be for the sake of others—Josef Ross"

A personal gift from Dr Ross. Maybe these two were closer than we had originally suspected. But, as enamoured as I was with the pen, I realised I had long outstayed my welcome. I was starting to make delayed returns a habit, and I didn't want Sam getting another go at chewing me out.

I repositioned the pen and case and marched through the gate.

Nobody but Styx was there to greet me on the other side, and she was only there to re-float the gate.

'Take your time, why don't you,' she muttered as she completed her task.

'Sorry, got distracted. Where is she?'

'They took her to the back. Sam and the others moved some of the larger cabinets around to make a small isolation area.'

A good idea. We needed to keep her away from everything and everyone. She was too dangerous, even while restrained.

I removed most of the armour, placing it back down on the table where Frank had originally laid it all out. I kept the rest of the gear on; my own clothes had become too odorous for me to stomach changing into them again.

It was easy to locate the others. I simply followed the sound of the bunker dwellers, naturally gathering close by.

They had grouped beside the impromptu interrogation area and were frenzied trying to peak in and around. But curiosity wasn't enough to gain them access. Sam stood as a bouncer, with Lucy by her side. Frank emerged moments later, pulling a sheet over the entranceway to block her in.

'Everyone stays away for now,' Frank demanded. 'She'll be out cold a bit longer, and we don't want her to see anyone's face before we know what she knows.'

Disappointment rang out through the crowd, but everyone began to disperse.

'Nice work.' Sam's sentiment was accompanied with a punch to the shoulder. I recoiled slightly in pain, my body still aching from Scaife's shot. Was this what whiplash felt like? 'Oh, don't be such a wuss. Come on, I've got a little treat.'

We returned to the rest area, where Sam pulled out a small box from below her bunk.

She opened it, laughed to herself and turned around with an outstretched hand.

On her hand sat what could only be described as one of the most important things Sam had ever provided me with in my life.

Wrapped around her palm, a long string of red liquorice was on offer and I snatched at it immediately.

Nobody had thought of bringing confectionary to the bunker, why would they? We hadn't expected to be so trapped, it was easy to overlook such a simple pleasure.

I scoffed it down in a heartbeat, relishing the strawberry flavour as bits stuck between nearly every tooth.

Sam chuckled. 'I know right? Completely forgot I had these. What a score!'

My father had always complained sugar was a fiendishly addictive substance, but what child ever really cared? The elation for those few seconds made me think there may have been some validity to his argument, as I instantly craved more. But it was a fleeting treat, and that made it all the more special.

'Oh man,' I spoke through using my tongue to dislodge the last few trapped pieces of liquorice. 'What a treat.'

We both sat at the side of her bed on the floor, revelling in the memory of the tasty morsel.

It helped in finishing to calm my nerves, as the last of the adrenaline from our mission left my system.

'You did good, Leon.' Sam finally spoke after a few glorious moments of peace and quiet.

'Yeah thanks, did Frank fill you in?' I rubbed my neck.

'No, but he didn't need to,' she continued. 'Lucy was wheezing and holding her chest, Scaife was unconscious, Frank himself had blood all down his face. So, it went about as well as it usually does.'

I laughed quietly to myself. Our escapades were definitely not going off without a hitch.

'We're not cut out for this Sam. We've been lucky, a bunch of times. It's only a matter of time before we run out of luck.'

She pushed herself up from the floor and sat on the side of the bed. 'Yeah, I think you're right.'

'But,' I began, a thought flashing through my mind, 'it mightn't have just been luck until now.'

'Oh?'

'Well, Scaife nearly wasn't going to comply in the beginning, we hadn't worried her enough to want to leave her home. And when our gambit was about to fail, I kind of spitballed and said it was your buddy Aribert, Professor Borza, who was the threat. That seemed to light a fire under her pretty quick.'

'He's not my buddy,' Sam hissed back. 'But I'm not following.'

'She mentioned us, the group. She called us tooth-less. She didn't seem bothered by us.' I finished the thought in my head as I spoke, not sure where I had been leading with the conversation. 'Maybe we weren't really lucky till now. Maybe they just didn't care about us enough to really try.'

It was an unnerving prospect.

The trouble they had already caused us was simply them swatting at a fly. We weren't considered impor-tant enough for their attention.

Their full attention.

Not yet.

'She's awake,' Frank called to us. Our prisoner was up earlier than expected.

We both stood to attention.

'I hope you're wrong, Leon,' Sam said as she slid her box of belongings back under the bed. 'Because if you're right, I think we've just promoted ourselves to the big leagues.'

If only Sam had known how right she was.

Chapter 20

Scaife seemed calm, serene, completely untroubled. It was unnerving.

She sat face to face with Frank. Myself, Styx, and Sam stood behind her in the entranceway to the makeshift interrogation area. We had all donned the black balaclavas of the BioDev security team, keeping our identities and expressions a secret for now.

Scaife had sat in complete silence, not bothering to call for help or try to break free of her restraints.

She seemed entirely unfazed by the whole ordeal.

'You're probably wondering why we brought you here,' Frank began.

I moved around to her side, wanting to see her facial expressions as Frank confronted her.

Scaife looked at me, rolled her eyes, and turned back to Frank.

No answer.

'We want information, and we know you have it.' Frank brought up the document on his holodisplay, hanging it in the air in front of Scaife. 'Ring any bells?'

Again, she didn't budge. Her eyes stared right through the image, focussed intently on Frank.

'That's your electronic signature, right?' Frank reached out and pointed to the sign off on the mail. 'Are you pretending you don't recognise it?'

Silence.

Scaife had nothing but tunnel vision for Frank. From the side of her mouth, I swear I saw the beginnings of a smirk. The edge of her lips pulsed slightly, curling upwards.

Frank smashed his hands down on the table between them.

'Right, we can do this the easy way, or,' Frank pointed to the rifle leaning against a cabinet beside him. 'Or we can introduce you to an old friend again.'

This time she couldn't hold her expression at bay. Her eyes narrowed, and the edges of her mouth turned upwards even more.

Scaife was toying with Frank, egging him on.

She was enjoying it.

'You think this is a fucking game, Michelle? You think I won't use that.' He stood up and swung around to grab the rifle.

'Oh? I didn't realise we were on a first name basis, Frank.' Her first words cut through the silence and right into the very core of Frank, who froze dead solid, eyes wide. 'Oh sorry, were you trying to be anonymous? Would you prefer I call you Mr White?'

Frank wasn't the only one sent spiralling. Sam had

grabbed Styx by the arm in disbelief, both staring at each other in confused worry.

My own heart began to race as if my fight or flight instincts were pulling me in two completely separate directions.

'Oh, come now, you're hardly surprised.' Scaife chuckled away to herself, sitting up in her seat and peering around. 'But where's Sam? Not attached at the hip anymore I suppose...'

She spoke with such familiarity.

Frank struggled to reclaim his composure.

'Oh no, did I say something to bother you?' she continued. 'Oh, please excuse me, how dreadfully uncouth of me to make you feel uncomfortable. My apologies, I've never been a very gracious captive.'

Her words rang with a level of sarcasm that I hadn't heard since Dan had once corrected me about the pros of cats over dogs. Clearly, he was wrong, but he was too stubborn ever to see that. And him being the older brother, his explanations often had a level of sarcasm reserved specifically for me.

'Please, do go on with your, ahem, interrogation.' Scaife sat back into her chair, the grin now wide across her face. 'I'm sure you'll do better at threatening me this time.'

Frank was slack-jawed and speechless. Thankfully the mask hid most of this from her view.

'What is that document?' he finally asked, clearing his throat before he spoke. 'Test site amber, sub-level 11, Induction Zone A. What is that?'

'Oh,' she replied immediately. 'That sounds like a captivating place. I do love the colour amber you know, one of my favourites.'

'Okay, screw this.' Sam rounded the table and sat beside Frank. 'You know full well what it is, you snarky bitch. You'd better start talking or—'

'Ah, you must be Sam,' Scaife cut her off. 'Sterne's little puppy. I was very sorry to hear about her illness. She'll be taken care of; we'll be sure to keep her safe and well.'

Sam shot up from her stool. 'Don't you dare threaten her!'

'Sam, stop!' Frank grabbed her by the arm. 'She's only saying that to rile you. They wouldn't dare.'

Scaife burst into laughter. 'Oh my, touch a nerve? You're as easy as they say, Sam.' She continued to laugh. 'Don't worry, she's safe for now.'

For now? The words had a sting of foreboding. She was threatening us, but we had no way of validating whether or not she was lying. Scaife was a formidable woman for sure, so it was best to assume she was capable of anything. We already knew BioDev weren't above deplorable acts.

Sam had been reined in, and again sat beside Frank, quietly this time.

Frank nodded to Styx, who came from behind Scaife and undid the restraints around her hands. A display of compromise perhaps, or a bargaining tool. She rubbed the irritated skin on her wrists before placing both hands on the table in front of her, revelling in the partial freedom.

Frank and Sam both removed their balaclavas.

'How kind,' Scaife joshed to Styx.

'I'll ask again.' Frank's question was firm and forceful. 'Test site amber, sub-level 11, Induction Zone A. What is it?'

'Oh, I'm very sorry, dear, that's a little above your pay grade. But I'd be happy to answer any questions on the types of ice cream we—'

The hidden baton came crashing down with knuckle-crunching force.

Scaife howled in pain, recoiling from the table as best she could.

Frank had come down with such force that it dented the side of the table. In fact, as crazy as it seemed at the time, his blow was so heavy it seemed to shake the lights of the bunker high above our heads.

'This isn't a fucking game,' he yelled. 'We know you're involved. We know you abducted that man, and countless others.'

Scaife held her hand under her armpit.

Frank continued, bringing the baton down to rest on the table, still clutching it tightly. 'What are you and BioDev up to? What is test site amber?'

We waited for her to answer, as she still reeled from the pain of the blow.

Or so we thought.

She groaned in pain, rocking slightly in the chair, head down so we couldn't see her face. But the rocking became quicker, and her shoulders started to bounce as she moved. The groaning had almost stopped, and in its place a low laughter.

The laughter grew as she finally brought her head up to look at us. Her face had a hint of red to it, most likely due to the pain, but she was now nearly laughing uncontrollably. Not even laughing, cackling like a lunatic.

'What's so funny?' Frank raised the baton ever so slightly, tightening his grip.

Scaife let out a long sigh as she finished her maniacal laughter, placing her hands back on the table once more. Her right hand was already looking slightly swollen and had small trickles of blood smeared across it. It trembled as she tried to pretend the pain was no longer an issue.

'You think you're so tough, Frank, striking out at a helpless woman. What would your mother think? Maybe you should undo the rest of the restraints. We can be a bit more intimate with a level playing field.' She had regained her composure and was again taunting Frank.

I couldn't help but think there was cause to bring plan B back into action again.

Frank poked her rapidly swelling hand with the baton. As hard as she tried, Scaife couldn't resist wincing in pain. She was human after all, and that hand was possibly broken.

'Alright then,' she said, surprising us all. 'What is it about Amber you want to know exactly.'

Was she pulling a complete 180, or just toying with us again? I was apprehensive, but Frank pushed on.

'What is it?'

'Oh, you know,' Scaife began, 'just your run-of-the-mill research and development wing where we get to do all the fun stuff. Kind of like this place, except, you know, not appallingly depressing.'

Frank pulled up the document again, allowing it to float in between the two of them. 'What happened here?'

'Someone broke in, attacked a few of our scientists, tried to get out again. Nobody was seriously injured, but your concern fills me with joy.'

Sam interjected. 'Fucking liar.'

'Excuse me?'

'He didn't break in. He was breaking out. Otherwise, why would you say he had "escaped decontamination"?'

'Well, what would you call it? That's the funny thing about breaking in somewhere; if you're caught, you kind of have to break out again. Or, in layman's terms, escape.' Scaife's tone was dismissive, like she was talking to a child she had no interest in entertaining.

'Did you abduct him?'

'Abduct him?' She laughed allowed, 'Have you even heard a word I—'

Again, the baton came crashing down, but she was quicker this time, moving her hand just in time to avoid the blow. The baton reverberated off of the table, and I heard someone gasp from outside.

Sam pulled Frank back from the table. 'Don't let her get to you.'

'Yes Frank, don't let me get to you,' she sneered. 'I'd hate for you to lose your temper, that wouldn't be like you.'

'Tell us where test site amber is,' Sam said, allowing Frank a moment to collect himself. Scaife had touched a nerve with what she said, maybe hinting at something violent in Frank's past that she was aware of. It was chilling how familiar she seemed to be with Sam and Frank. I wondered what she knew of Styx and me as well, or everyone in the bunker for that matter.

'Oh, now you see, I'm in a real predicament. I would love nothing more than to tell you where it is, help you guys and your witch hunt. Unfortunately,' she held her arms up and shrugged, 'I kind of signed a non-disclosure agreement. So, you can see the legal bind I'm in. Damned lawyers, right?'

'We're getting nowhere with this bitch,' Styx finally chimed in. 'Maybe we should just zap her again, see if she feels more honest after she wakes up.'

Styx, Frank and Sam huddled close together and started to mutter a strategy. I kept watch on her from the side.

'Do I get a question now?' Scaife broke the silence.

'What?' Frank responded.

'Will you indulge me a question?'

Frank seemed confused but shrugged his shoulders and reassumed his position sitting across from her.

'Fantastic,' Scaife replied as she straightened up in the chair. 'Where can I find Leon?'

My heart sank to hear my name said aloud.

But no answer was needed.

The unexpected question drew everyone's attention straight to me.

'Brilliant,' Scaife replied.

Even with one hand damaged, Frank didn't stand a chance.

She tore the baton from his loosened grip, cracking him across the face with the handle end.

I raised my arms in defence, mostly in vain.

The baton crashed across my left ribs and chest. It was heavier than it looked, and the momentum sent me crashing to the floor.

A quick scuffle ensued. Sam grabbed her from behind, while Styx dove over the table to tackle Scaife to the floor.

Luckily for us all, her legs were still bound to the chair.

Frank quickly leapt into action too, holding one of her arms down while Sam held the other. Styx worked quickly to reattach her arms to the chair.

But as they sat her back up, now so tight to the chair she may as well have been part of it, in one last act of defiance, she spat at me.

Right in my face.

'Murderer. You're lucky I'm in this damned chair.'

'Murderer?' I removed the mask and finished rubbing her phlegm from the only exposed part of my neck. 'I had nothing to do with hurting your men, you crazy bitch. They attacked me with those fucking cattle prod rifles.'

Scaife struggled for another moment before stopping completely. Instead, she stared directly at me, brow scrunched up and eyes scanning my expression.

I picked myself up off the floor, holding my ribs. The heavy tactical clothing had taken some of the blow, but they ached badly. As I reassumed my position, she spoke. Slowly.

'You don't even know, do you?' She dropped her head and began laughing again. 'You fucking fools.'

'What's so funny?' Frank asked, Sam now tending to the side of his face.

She continued to laugh, head hung and rolling side to side.

'What is it!'

'And here he is, standing right beside me this whole time. It was you in my house too, right? The one who shot me?' She continued to laugh, as abrasively as possible. 'That's twice you've signed someone else's death certificate now. How does it feel, killer?'

Was she mistaking me for someone else? Or had the shock from my gun fried her brain completely?

'What're you talking about?' Frank intervened, hissing the question at our increasingly unwanted guest.

He raised the baton again but restrained himself.

As if in preparation for the blow, I noticed the lights above us were jolted and swaying once more.

'Did you guys see that?' I asked.

As if rehearsed, the lights high up on the ceiling shook and flickered again right as the others looked up.

Again, our prisoner began to chuckle to herself.

'What did you do, Scaife?' Sam's eyes were scanning the roof.

But Scaife's eyes were still targeting me. 'I did nothing, I didn't need to. Leon here did it all for me.'

'What the hell are you talking about?' I cocked the firearm I still had strapped to my right forearm. Maybe I could force her into an honest answer for once.

'I wouldn't if I were you.' She smiled, her face distorted to a sinister crooked image. 'It's foolish to repeat your mistakes you know. The second you shot me in my home, my AMI alerted every BioDev security agency.'

The whole bunker shook; this time small bits of the ceiling came loose and fell.

'You think we didn't know where you were all hiding? That this little prison of yours was unreachable? We knew before you even stole that memo.' She struggled for a moment in the seat, testing the restraints, before calming back down. 'You were merely gnats before then, not really worthy of our attention. But now?'

She looked up to the roof, again a tremor sending lighting fixtures swaying hard. 'Knock knock.'

'Shit...' Sam burst into a sprint, right out of our makeshift isolation area. Frank and Styx were tight on her tale, nearly knocking me over as they went.

Scaife resumed her mocking laughter.

The next tremor sounded like it was right on top of the walled structure, and I could hear equipment falling over.

But I didn't follow the others, not yet.

'You said twice?'

'Sorry?' she replied, only realising then that I hadn't left.

'You said twice.'

'Oh, I guess I did, didn't I?' She shifted in her seat to look directly towards me. 'You know, of everything that day, there was only one thing that stood out to us. Several of our buildings attacked. Hundreds of casualties. Pain. Misery. Terrorist attacks, nothing more. Save for one oddity. Every attack, planned and positioned for maximum damage. Foyers, meeting areas, canteens. All but one. In that instant, in the midst of all the global madness, four men arrived, armed to the teeth, like the others. But they didn't reach their destination. They arrived at test site rowan. In London.'

'London?'

'Several stories underground. In one of the most secure facilities on the planet. And above them, hundreds of innocent civilians, workers, friends.' She took a long pause. 'Brothers...'

'No...'

She was lying.

She had to be.

'How does it feel, killer?'

It wasn't real.

She was toying with me.

She had to be.

She *had* to be.

'How does it feel to know you killed your brother?'

Chapter 21

We scattered.

The old metal entrance of the bunker. It looked invincible. A thick, hulking doorway, separating the world above from our den of operations. We had no idea how far below ground we really were. It didn't matter. We had our gate, and despite some close calls, that was all we needed. We could have been ten feet down, or ten hundred.

They didn't seem to care.

The doors peeled back like paper when they came.

In the seconds leading to the breach, the group was split into various mindsets.

Fight.

Surrender.

Flee.

Maybe turn ourselves in to the police, hoping their cells would protect us and we would get a fair hearing.

Achterhuis was lost. And so were we.

There were destinations scrawled on the board beside the gate. Fall-back locations, outside of Worm-Whole's network. Rarely used, remote.

Not good enough.

We didn't have enough IR facial distortion clips for everyone. And balaclavas would just draw more attention.

Frank and I had our clips already, a lucky addition to the BioDev tactical gear. Lucy too. A fight broke out over who else should have the others. Sam and Styx were obvious choices, or rather were until others became aware they would be left defenceless.

There was no way to decide. Nobody wanted to be judge and jury.

The decision was made for them once the doors caved in.

Whoever could grab one did, but fear took over and most turned at once and ran through the gate. They were like sheep, following the person in front who had chosen a destination. Strength in numbers I guess.

The world was crumbling around us. Around me.

But I didn't care.

I had returned to the group in those last moments, but not fully. I witnessed the fear, the panic. I saw friends scream in each other's faces and attempt to shake sense into one another. Tears of terror and helpless anger ran from their faces.

It was the purest display of emotion you could imagine. Each person's despair was amplified by the mimicry around them.

But I didn't indulge. I couldn't.

What did it matter now?

I had allowed myself to believe I did good. That I

saved some faceless people somewhere from a sudden fate.

That I was a hero on that day.

Instead, I had just shifted the pain. To other innocent parties. To their families. To my parents. To me.

It was me. Dan was killed by my action.

I had hardly even come to terms with his absence. I had just tried to ignore it, to deny its legitimacy. He was only gone for a moment. He would be back. Any day he would round a corner, or return from a trip, and he would be back. He couldn't really have been gone.

But he was gone. I sent him away.

The panic all around hardly stirred me from the abyss I was plunging into.

I didn't realise Sam had been screaming in my face until the thunderous clatter of metal doors echoed around the bunker. Or maybe it was the clash of her palm on my face that dragged me from the brink, if only for a moment.

'What the fuck is wrong with you, Leon!' She was hysterical. 'We have to go!'

She had me grabbed by the shoulders, pleading with her eyes.

'Okay.'

It was all I could muster. But it seemed enough.

Frank was making sure everyone had cleared out and was readying to leave himself.

Styx had been barking locations and orders to people as they left.

We had a destination at which regroup in a day's time, and she was making sure everyone knew it.

Sam waved Frank on, after a quick look around to ensure nobody else was left. She then ran towards the gate herself.

The screen closest the gateway had a timer ticking down. Twenty seconds left. Styx had programmed a failsafe after our last encounter. Twenty seconds until the gate was killed. No chance of tracking us, or using it to get out.

I followed Sam, pulling up the gate interface on my AMI to see where we were headed. Somewhere in the Philippines.

Styx feverishly tore down the rendezvous destinations from the board, stuffing them into her pants and disappearing through the gateway.

Frank followed swiftly.

Then Sam, but not before giving my wrist one more tug and urging me on.

And then it was me.

Ten seconds remained.

I wanted to follow, to protect Sam. Styx. Frank. To protect them all, if I could.

For the split second that I was alone, I started to sink again, the abyss now open in my soul, trying to pull me in. I needed to escape.

Not just the bunker. Everything. Just for a moment.

I just needed to adapt to this new version of things.

The version where maybe I was more villain than hero.

And I knew exactly where to go.

It only took a single gesture to bring up my previous journeys, and without as much as a second thought to the possible ramifications, I injected my destination and walked straight through.

The last sound I heard from the bunker was that of an army of heavy boots stomping quickly through the concrete mess we had called home for what seemed a lifetime.

I was almost sad to part with the place.

Facial recognition blocked and wearing insipid black attire, I strolled out and blended into the throbbing crowds of Hub 1.

A wave of odours blew over me as I moved. Perfumes, baked goods, hints of strawberry. I was back in civilization, for better or worse. But I didn't want crowds, or the obscurity they provided. My destination stood floors above me, away from it all.

I couldn't risk assuming my anonymity was endless, so I moved to my destination without delay. The gate was automatic. It didn't need a Saint. The destination didn't even leave the building.

I stepped through into the near pitch darkness of the rotating observatory. Glowing teal lights guided me along the walkway. Most observation beds were empty, but I continued to those furthest from the entrance.

Throwing myself onto the supremely comfortable leather furniture, I activated the observance pod and it raised up to meet the glass domed roof. The pod's walls sealed perfectly to the glass, sound and light proofing the experience. My own little hideout amongst the stars.

Time had become near meaningless in the bunker, but where I was right now was clearly in the dead of night. Not a hint of sunlight.

The sky shimmered with the starlight. The Milky Way was brighter here than any other observatory. You could see the full breadth of the night's sky.

The most spectacularly beautiful view humanity may ever be privy to.

"Perspective can be a beautiful thing. It can make you feel infinitesimally insignificant or help you to realise the astonishingly astounding effect you could have on the world."

That was what Dan used to say. A bit wordy, and he loved a bit of alliteration, but it always stuck with me.

He loved astrophysics, and everything space re-lated, even if his scientific genius took him on a dif-ferent path. I used to sit in wonder as he explained the galaxy, and our place in it, at great length.

"We are special," he would say.

Humanity had never seen any signs of other intel-ligent life in the galaxy. So, it was not unfathomable that we could be the first true space-faring civilisation. We may have only developed small research colonies on two moons and another planet in our solar system, but baby steps were important.

I loved those theories when he shared them.

I equally hated aspects of the knowledge he

imparted. The universe was ever expanding. We were simply getting further and further from everything else. The longer it takes us to shed the shackles of our solar system, the harder it becomes to reach anywhere else.

Granted, my worries were based on a scale of billions of years. But the universe would get bigger and bigger and more isolated and darker as time ticked on. It was full of sadness, if you allowed it to be.

It might have been those irrational fears of the heat death of the universe I harboured from a young age being rekindled, or more likely the mental toll of the recent revelation, but I could hardly see the stars after a few moments.

I tried to rub the tears away with the edges of my sleeve, but they came too quickly.

I fought against my face, to stop my lip from quivering, to stop my chin from scrunching up, to halt the sting at the back of my nostrils.

It was an uphill battle that I no longer had the fortitude to endure. All I could do was cover my face with my hands as the stream of tears became a flood.

What had I done?

There were no words to describe what Dan was to me. The day he died was the most destructive thing to ever happen to me or my parents.

It was no longer the day he died. It was the day I killed him.

Scaife was right.

"Murderer" replayed over and over in my mind.

What Scaife thought didn't matter. Her thoughts were worth nothing to me. If Dan were there, he would tell me what to do. Or I hoped he would. I couldn't help but question myself as I sat there, tears escaping my hands and streaming down my cheeks.

What would he think of me now?

I had tried to do something good, to fight back, to stand up for any number of innocent people on the day. But in doing so, I killed him and other innocents. Was that ever something that could be forgiven?

What would he say to me if he was here?

He would have been positive. He was always positive. He would know exactly what to do. Compared to me he would have been of much more help to Sam and the others. It should have been me that day.

Would he hate me?

I paused on the thought. I was spiralling again, as I had in various moments since his death, but that thought, that alone, brought me a moment of clarity.

Never.

A single memory came to the front of my mind.

I was ten. A particularly overgrown kid from my school had been relentlessly bullying one of the other children in the schoolyard. He was close to tears, and everyone else, too scared to interfere, had turned a blind eye.

I had never witnessed real bullying like that. Maybe I was too young or too aloof, but the whole situation seemed alien to me. So, I intervened.

I stopped the bully, or maybe it would be more accurate to say I redirected the rage.

I ended up with two stitches on my chin from the altercation.

Dan was there while I received the stitches in the local doctor's office. Though the cut was large enough to warrant stitches, it did not warrant any anaesthetic. I howled and screamed as my mother and father held me in place and tried to calm me. But it was over in an instant, and my feelings of betrayal were alleviated by a packet of fruit-flavoured jellies.

The fickleness of childhood firmly taken advantage of by my parents.

I was embarrassed to leave the doctor's room, however. There were other children in the waiting room, and my face was red and covered in tears.

That's when Dan took my shoulder and repeated something he had said to me several times before in my young life, in similar instances where I had injured myself and tried to hide the fact that I was distressed.

"Big boys don't cry," he said.

My parents were horrified to hear him say this to me, and my father dragged him away to scold him. But my father was mistaken.

Dan wasn't shaming me for crying, or whatever the comment had seemed to imply. It was quite the opposite. He was freeing me to be upset.

What they didn't hear was our rehearsed response. "Men do," I had whispered to myself.

When you're a young boy, all you want to be is a

grown man. To have freedom, strength, no bedtime. To eat whatever you want whenever you want. No rules, just fun. It all just seemed so fantastic to be older.

Ironic, really, that I would have given anything to be a kid again.

Dan was making sure I knew it was alright to cry. That my feelings were to be embraced, good or bad.

But it was always the same with Dan. He was my protector as a child and my closest friend as an adult.

He enabled me to feel and be open. To dream stupid things. To be...me.

So there, even in my dark state, I couldn't bring myself to believe he could hate me. If the roles were reversed, how would I have felt? I'm sure I wouldn't have been terribly pleased, I would be dead after all. But the intention was right. I would have known what he did was right.

What I did was right.

It was BioDev's fault. They were to blame.

The explosion had started a process of events that was quickly leading them to ruin, and they knew that. They were scared. Why else would they try to wipe us out?

I dropped my hands from my face, my inward anger starting to be redirected.

They had ruined so many lives, so many families. Just like mine.

They needed to be stopped.

And we were going to do it. One way or another.

Rubbing the last of the tears from my face and eyes,

I remained on the bed, gazing outwards. The others would have moved by now. I couldn't follow them.

I needed to lay low, just like them. Hide out until we were supposed to regroup.

The observatory was as good a place as any.

It was free, and it was cosy.

I continued to stare out into the night's sky, trying to pick out constellations, mapping shapes across the glass with my finger.

It must have been too cosy, as a vibration from my wrist shocked me into alertness. I had dozed off; I wasn't sure for how long.

The glow from my wrist reflected off the glass dome in front of me.

Our AMIs had mostly been put into a sort of semi-disabled mode, so that connections to the normal mobile network infrastructures were unavailable and we couldn't be tracked, instead piggy backing on the WormWhole system. General connectivity was still available too, that way we could interact with gate systems, etc.

It seemed that Lucy had gone above and beyond in the favour I had asked of her

Even in my groggy state, the reflection was sharp and legible. A single concise notification scrolled across the display. "Incomplete travel."

A hiccup.

The data had been sent from the WormWhole network straight to my AMI. It appeared our listener was still active despite losing the bunker. BioDev mustn't have realised it was anything of interest as they no doubt went about searching the bunker for clues. They would find it eventually, but it would be too late to stop me.

I pulled up the information in the data package. It had everything, just a raw info dump straight from the servers. It even had the name of the Saint online at the time. A tough break for "Zachary"; I knew how terrible he must have been feeling. That's if he had even realised the loss just yet.

I needed to move fast if I was to get the code.

For all I knew, my face, and the face of all the others, was circulating to every security firm on the planet.

I may not have worn out my anonymous welcome in the observatory yet, but that was only a matter of time.

I needed to move.

The pod lowered from the glass, bringing me back down to the dimly lit floor. I retraced my steps, moving through the gate and back into the main Hub area.

I ran over my plan as I mingled with the crowds, ensuring to keep my head down to avoid the gaze of any potential security personnel. Not an easy task at my height.

Automatic gates wouldn't get me where I needed to go. I couldn't easily interact with the gate's system when approaching, not without standing out. I could access the destination early, but I would likely send all those entering the gate ahead of me to the location

I needed too. Would that stand out to the local employees as strange? A bunch of confused commuters, unsure of how they ended up there. Would it be enough for them to maybe call it in?

Saint-operated gates were a dangerous alternative. If I was recognised, I was finished. Caught right in the middle of a huge Hub, they would be on me in seconds.

Decisions decisions.

I eyed the closest automatic gate. The queue was moving and wasn't overly long.

The lesser of two evils.

'Sorry guys,' I mumbled to myself as I used the crowd around me to hide my activity. I locked in the destination, disabled my display, and joined the queue.

In seconds I was at the front, and continued through without missing a beat, ready to act just as confused as the others I had ever so slightly inconvenienced. But as small an inconvenience as it was, you could be sure some people would kick up hell over it.

And just as predicted, emerging from the other side, I was met with a small, but angry, mob.

'Is this a joke or something?'

'Where the hell are we? Did you do this?'

'Where's the manager, this is a disgrace!'

The people were worse than expected. Delayed for a minute at most and they were ready to start lighting torches and fetching pitchforks. Were they really that busy, that late? Or was it just a reactionary trait that had been somehow accepted in society, an instinctual anger left over from the days of "biblical traffic jams," as my father described them.

But the distraction couldn't have worked better.

The poor Saint on the nearby outgoing gate just kept his head down and ignored the abuse while politely asking 'Destination please' through the moaning.

Good on him. It was an example of the shit Saints often had to deal with. He was making us proud.

I stood aside from the gate, making sure the cameras couldn't see me. I was getting better at this.

In an instant, I had the Saint's gate under my control. My flurry of gestures delved deep into the heart of the system, searching for the recent spam of unknown processes, just like before.

And there it was, in all its lowliness. Another corrupted code.

I began extraction without a moment wasted.

But the rabble hadn't died down. I expected the people to be gone after only a few moments.

I stepped out around the gate. The crowd were now even more irate, but they weren't moving, and more people had now joined their mob.

The Saint, standing to scratch his head and waving his arm around, wasn't processing anyone.

Instead, he was complaining to someone over his headpiece.

I edged closer.

'No, it's not like that. I don't know what it's like. I

keep telling it to open a route, and it keeps ignoring me. It's like I'm not in control of it or something.'

Shit.

It was me. I was taking over the operation of the gate.

The transfer was complete, but I couldn't disengage the pairing. I had accessed the core systems. It was locked into waiting for a command or reboot it seemed.

I looked up from my AMI, dead ahead, right into the eyes of the Saint.

His voice was too low, but his lips betrayed what he said.

'It's him. He's here.'

And to think I had been proud of him only a few moments before.

It was seconds before security would arrive, maybe less.

Pushing through the unaware crowd, I brought up the interface, not caring who or what saw me now.

'There!'

I didn't look back to see who yelled.

My gestures were near automatic as I injected the gate with the only piece of code or destination I had at the ready.

I hoped and prayed my theory was correct as the vile new hiccup code surged into the system once more.

The gate responded, and the slipway opened.

I had instigated a hiccup, again, but this time it

was me who braced and burst through the threshold. What lay on the other side could be far worse than being caught.

But the die was cast.

Chapter 22

I vomited upon arrival.

The journey was not instantaneous. Not close.

I hadn't expected to witness the swirling ultramarine and mint light distortions as I passed through, the often-missed visual side effect of slipway travel. If you blinked, you could miss them. But not this time. This time they crashed over me like a wave, swirling all around, wrapping my every limb in their cool brilliance.

It was euphoric.

It could have lasted hours, and I would have enjoyed every moment.

I force my eyes to stay open, basking in the glow, unsure of how long the moment would last. But what I witnessed was an upheaval, as the colours violently shifted palette. The cool colours were wrenched away, diluted and destroyed as deep crimson and scarlet poisoned the light streams.

It was hellish. The shards of light probed and invaded as I flailed in vain.

Everything was distorted. I felt upside down,

spinning, tumbling, hot, cold, stretched, compressed. Every sense was on edge and in overdrive.

One thing I learned, and one thing no one else ever needed to concern themselves with: you cannot scream in a slipway. There is no sound.

But as the demonic canvas exploded out in all directions, I was expelled.

Still upright, in the exact stride I had entered the gate, but completely thrown off balance. I fell immediately, throwing up on the pristine white laminate floor ahead of me.

Small pieces of red liquorice stood out amidst the bile.

Figured, it was my last little bit of happiness after all. Made sense BioDev would take that from me too.

I stumbled to my feet, using the closest surface as leverage.

The room was immaculate. All white. Gate, walls, ceiling and floor. Well, not so much the floor anymore. But it was about as inoffensive as you might expect in a highly classified laboratory if that was indeed where I had landed myself.

The stark blandness would definitely not have been a comforting sight on arrival. Especially after the horror show of the commute.

There was no obvious doorway. The walls had grooves in a sort of netted pattern, but none seemed deep enough to hint at an exit. The only features of the room at all were the gate and an open pod with white bedding and a sort of antennae or light pole at its end. I rubbed my hands on the fabrics, but it didn't feel as soft as it looked. It sort of tingled to the touch and had the look of a hospital bed, complete with disposable bed covers.

I stepped forwards and ran my hands along each wall, looking for a pressure sensitive switch, or a hidden panel, or something.

In a jarring shift, the room switched colour to a pale green.

Leaping back from the wall in front of me, a large door panel appeared and swung open. Stepping into the room was a young man wearing a long white unlabelled lab coat. He was flicking through screens on his large datapad, a look of confusion on his face as my arrival seemed to contradict what he was reading. He mumbled, '...must be a glitch or something, the income beacon should be shut down...'

There was no need to wait for him to figure anything out.

I locked my arm forwards, the forearm mounted weapon latched into position. I wasn't sure the type of damage one of these rounds would have at point-blank range, but when he looked up he was met with the outstretched weapon staring him dead in the eye. The datapad dropped, alongside a small assortment of medical supplies, one of which, a syringe full of liquid, smashed on the floor.

I held my finger up to my lip. He complied, keeping silent.

'Where the hell am I?' I whispered, trying to assert a level of demand in my lowered voice.

'I-I-I...' The stutter seemed to have been brought on by the presence of the weapon.

I nudged closer.

'T-t-test site sycamore. Please, I just work here, I—'

I shoved the weapon square with his forehead. It seemed he didn't realise the weapon was non-lethal. So what if he just worked there? Considering what 'here' was, his guilt was implied by being present.

'The lab coat, lose it.' I spoke firmly, not allowing for any chance of him to doubt my resolve. I was having a tough day, maybe shocking him would be entertaining. He was after all the first contact I had made in the belly of the beast. I'm sure he deserved it.

He took it off without missing a beat. I made him empty his pockets and relieved him of his AMI and identification tag.

Picking up his datapad, and pushing him into the room, I again hinted at his silence using my finger before locking him in. I could have incapacitated him more harshly, but I had six shots max, and the walls appeared thick enough to be mostly soundproof.

I looked both ways down the short hallway I found myself in. It looked like there were four of the arrival rooms in that block. They were all white, aside from mine.

There was no plan. I had arrived in a panicked roll of a die. I couldn't just stand around waiting for inspiration.

I turned and moved towards the only doorway, making sure to keep my head buried in the datapad like he had been, hoping that the camera monitoring the hallway wouldn't immediately pick up on any drastic characteristic changes. I just hoped they didn't see that the datapad had become disabled due to the drop. A backlight still made it seem active, but it was completely unresponsive.

Once I exited the area, I was faced with three choices of perfectly identical looking corridors. The floors had large coloured lines running through them, like a hospital, each directing you to the nearest wing or facility.

Without a legend for the colours however, they were mainly useless to me. The green line ran to the area I had just left, so that was one colour to tick off the list.

Red, blue, and yellow ran alongside one another, occasional arrows hinting at the direction you were to follow.

Red might have been emergency exits, yellow may have been the canteen. It didn't matter. Without raising my head, and attempting to act like this was my route all along, I joined the blue line.

Blue seemed a more authoritative colour out of the three.

I followed the blue arrows, the corridors mostly empty aside from the occasional lab-coat-clad worker, nose buried in papers as they moved along, grunting greetings without taking in who they were addressing.

I wondered how long it would take them to track where I had gone. Could they even track it? I had seen the hiccup code, it gave no information on destination that I could decipher, but could they? From the typical Saint console, they wouldn't have received an arrival notification, so they easily could have accidentally followed the previous commuter to whatever their destination was.

Best not to assume my anonymity to be endless.

I turned down a long corridor, the left-hand side of which was completely windowed. It looked out over a huge factory-sized lab space. A couple hundred opaque pods were littering the floor, all evenly spaced allowing room to walk in between.

They were the same style of pods from the room. White and plain looking, but the antennae were beaming. Most of these rods were a bright red, with only a few the shade of green I had encountered on my arrival. And, although tough from a distance, I could swear one of the pods was pulsing red all over as well. The closest green lit pod had an active holodisplay, projecting what looked like a human circulatory system and various lines of text and numbers that were illegible from my vantage.

This must have been where they took the commuters in their arrival pods.

And they had room for hundreds.

It was in that moment that all of our outlandish theories faded away, and the worst-case scenario became the only plausible reality. The beds, the pods, the abductions, the facility.

These people were lab rats.

This wasn't even test site amber, so there was at least one other area in the world mimicking the work done here.

I tried to drown out the thoughts of what the people who arrived here went through, or if they were even aware. It would seem like arriving in a hospital after a traumatic slipway journey, the perfect situation to get someone to drop their guard. They probably thought they were being taken care of when they were put in the pods.

The thought of what they experienced was disgusting.

I used my AMI to take some detailed pictures, making sure nobody could see me as I stood to the side of the final pane of glass. What other chance would I have to find some damning evidence like this? But images wouldn't be enough. I had to try to get more.

I turned my focus back to the blue line, following it out of the viewing corridor. I couldn't do anything for these people on my own. I felt I was abandoning them by walking away, but there was nothing I could do just yet.

Finally, I reached a set of signs, hanging down from the ceiling of the next intersection of corridors.

"Central – Terminal – Variable Storage – Canteen – Conference Centre"

A bland menu of destinations—the facility clearly

kept things basic in a sense. Again, all were colour coded, and this new area had more lines on the floor.

Had to keep moving. I could hear voices approaching from around the corner of one of the corridors. Central didn't seem like the type of destination I should be running to alone, but it was the other direction to the voices.

The destination was close. I had followed the purple line and was now met with a large purple doorway. There may not have been quite as many cameras as you would expect in a facility like this, but there was enough to force me to keep moving, feigning no hesitation.

The door opened as I approached, possibly reacting to the ID tag I had taken. Stepping into the room, I made sure to take in every detail.

Huge stacks of computer towers stood behind a large glass wall. They all seemed to be submerged in a bluish coolant that bubbled heavily from each tower. The room itself was mostly empty of physical furniture, but holoprojections beamed out from every wall, colour coded to each section of the room. They really loved their colour differentiation. One employee sat at a wide central console, back turned to me, posture perfect in his chair. He was waving me over, not even looking to see who I was.

'You check the pit, Xi?' he asked, boredom ringing through his tone.

'Oh,' I replied, stalling for a moment. I hadn't exactly allowed my welcome party a lot of time to vocalise why I shouldn't shoot him, but he did have something of an American accent. Bluffing was the only option.

I stood tall and puffed my chest, and in my most American accent replied, 'Yeah, just a glitch like we thought.'

It was a calculated risk. But whereas I may have excelled at maths in life, accents, or in this case insulting stereotypical Texan accents, were not my forte.

The man paused, put down the cup he held in his hand, and spun in the chair to see.

'Eh, Xi?'

To his surprise, he wasn't met with a fellow employee, but an outstretched weapon.

Not missing a beat, he swung his hand down, grabbing his own firearm as he went. No peaceful negotiations this time.

I fired the moment he flinched.

The spasming threw him from the chair, as the projectile lodged in his chest went to town on his central nervous system.

The rush, the thrill, the adrenaline.

In that moment I felt unstoppable. Like a cowboy from an old western beating a quick draw opponent. I knew my gun was technically pre-raised, but I wasn't about to let technicalities make me feel like less of a master gunman.

But I had crossed a line now, and this was definitely starting a timer on my head for how long my position here would last.

I moved swiftly across the room to where he lay, unconscious but still convulsing. Grabbing him by the ankles, I dragged him around to the front of the console so he couldn't be seen from the doorway.

Pocketing his gun, I ran around to reassume his position, looking down at the huge open display of his console.

Genomics, pathogen analytics, bioinformatics, variable stock, staff onsite, incoming and outgoing travel. The console had everything. That specific panel may not have run the installation, I guessed the coloured holostations were the heart of the operation instead, but it was definitely the eyes and ears.

I hastily opened a number of tabs.

Variable stock – 7/300

That seemed to tally with my quick count of the green lit pods.

Staff Onsite – 37/82

So far, I had seen about eight people, two of whom were now incapacitated. The facility was either huge, or they were in the canteen or meeting in the conference area. Either way, I was outnumbered.

I pulled open the bioinformatics tab next.

It seemed to be a data stream, with information being churned out at an astonishing rate, likely from the row of chilled supercomputers still bubbling away in my peripherals. The data file designation was RABV GD-SH-04, whatever the hell that meant.

I was near certain, from the limited biology background I had gained through the school system, that

this was the AOE system. Genomics, pathogen analytics, bioinformatics, that sounds like the exact combination of factors you would find when experimenting
with diseases.

Unfortunately, I had no means of exporting the
data to my AMI. The layout was too alien to me.

The others need to see this.

'Hey, where's Mark?' The voice came low and soft,
but it was startlingly close.

I spun in the chair to face my newest obstacle.
About three steps away from me was another man
wearing the same outfit as the one who had previously
occupied the seat. The look on his face said it all, as
his jaw dropped ever so slightly and his eyes squinted
for focus.

He recognised my face. But thankfully, for that split
second, he seemed to get caught deciding whether it
was familiarity from work, or a picture he had been
shown of a person of interest.

Whatever the reason, it allowed me time to fire off
yet another shot of the arm-mounted shock cannon.

I jumped out of the seat, and ran over to the body,
making sure to disarm him lest the shock not completely take his consciousness. I placed the second
firearm in one of my tactical trouser pockets

I was running out of time here. I had to let the
others know what I had found.

Calling for help was impossible, everyone was off
the grid network-wise. All I had was a regrouping destination, but what good was that? This place was too

important just to run out on. For all I knew they could change the gate addresses at will, or just lock them down if they deemed the site compromised.

I needed to send a message, with everything I knew and learned about this place, as little or meaningless as it may be.

I patted down the many pockets of the plain lab coat. Nothing. No paper, or pen, although only quirky enthusiasts used pen and paper. The datapad was dead, the backlight finally flickering out of life as I shook the device. Even his AMI had shut off. Having been removed its anti-theft security measures had likely kicked in.

At that moment, staring at his useless AMI, I knew what I had to do. I would have to leave and hope that I could somehow figure out a way back with the others. I would at least have some useful data from my AMI's automatic data gathering of nearby gate traffic, and of course the pictures of the facility.

Plan decided, I dragged the newest lump of BioDev personnel to my mildly hidden body storage spot, and I left the room.

"Terminal" had been coloured pink, so I rushed off along the pink line.

The hallways seemed busier all of a sudden. People in small groups wandered back and forth as I passed through a small crossroads where the pink mapping was directing me. I kept my head down, but I could feel that one or two people's gazes had lingered for just a little too long.

I sped up at the thought of being caught in the middle of the facility. They would be on me like lightning.

Finally, the doorway to the terminal lay in reach, as the last corner I came through landed me right in front of it and five other people coming the opposite way.

I attempted to brush past them, casual as the breeze.

'Hey.'

I ignored it.

'Hey!'

I continued to ignore it, almost at the doorway.

'I said hey!' I was grabbed by the shoulder.

Whether I was made or not, this wasn't a time to half-ass it. I elbowed back into the person's stomach, spun, and fired a single round, catching him in the leg.

He howled in pain, his outstretched hand holding out a familiar ID tag I had clearly just dropped. A miscalculation again by my part, he was just trying to help. No good now as his colleagues screamed and ran from the scene.

'Shit, sorry,' I apologised weakly while I removed his hand from my shoulder and pushed him back onto the floor.

Three shots left.

I burst through the door into the small terminal. Four gates lined the far wall of the large room. Two security personnel populated the room, on either side of the central area.

The first went down easily, having stepped out

from her small alcove. She cursed as she hit the floor, writhing in pain, hand clutching hopelessly at the firearm by her side.

I swung around, arm gliding through the air into position, but in the blink of an eye he was on me. I raised my arm just in time to block the blow as the baton came crashing down. It mangled the barrel of my firearm; the lights along its length fizzled and popped out of existence.

A second blow ruptured the ammo cartridge, as my last two electro rounds fell to the floor.

He raised for a third.

I swung at him, catching him square in the jaw.

He staggered but managed to bring the baton down again anyway.

With what little structural integrity was left of my firearm, I deflected the blow to the ground.

He dropped the baton and grabbed at me, the rough skin of his now free hands clamped down around my neck. The grip was vice like; I could feel every agonising blood vessel being crushed.

I squirmed back to try escape his grasp, but instead sent us both tumbling over, him landing on top of me, hands still firmly placed.

I tried in vain to remove his hands, but I was no match for him.

It felt like I was going to pass out from the pain before the air loss.

I grabbed the baton firmly, but he was too well positioned on top, I couldn't swing it with any true force.

I gasped, but nothing. Oxygen was finite and about to run out completely as my vision started to blur around the edges.

I clawed at his face in vain. He wouldn't relent.

I reached out in all directions, my time almost out.

My last resort. Maybe it should have been my first resort.

I reached down to my trousers, pulling out the security agent's gun. The sound was deafening at such close range, but my assailant immediately released my throat and rolled back onto the ground, screaming in pain.

I rolled away, gasping for breath.

The man still screamed, blood spurting out from his leg.

Too much blood. I must have hit the femoral artery.

He called out on his radio for assistance. That was my cue to leave. I ran towards the gate, activating the rendezvous destination. It dialled in and opened.

I stood there, hearing nothing but the screams of the man.

I felt sick to my stomach from the blood, but also because I had done that to him. This wasn't some non-lethal electro round. I had shot, and potentially mortally wounded, this man. He may have almost killed me, but it still didn't feel right.

I couldn't but imagine past what he was right now, just another BioDev piece of shit. Maybe he was a father, a husband, a brother.

His bleeding was so intense I didn't see how he wouldn't bleed out soon.

Every muscle and sinew tried to pull me towards the entrance of the gate.

"Murderer." Scaife's words called out in my mind.

"Murderer."

"Murderer."

'Fuck!' I screamed at myself as in one swift motion I removed my AMI and threw it through the gate, hoping to any sort of deity watching that the others would find it.

I'm not like them.

I turned and ran back to his side.

There had to be a way to stop the bleeding.

But there was nothing at hand. No clotting medigel, no cauterising tools.

Or maybe there was?

Knowing the situation was dire, I improvised. Grabbing one of the rounds from my damaged stun gun, I stabbed it down onto his leg and crashed down on the back with the baton to activate the projectile.

He screamed again, convulsing as usual before slipping from consciousness.

But the rapidly expanding gel seemed to do its job. The bleeding drastically slowed. Some of the gel even shot out of the wound. It wasn't a permanent solution, it may not have been much of a solution at all, but it would give him time.

A luxury I was clearly out of. I could hear them coming.

The doors burst open. A swarm of people ran through.

I raised my arms.

The last thing I remember was the butt of a metal rifle accelerating towards my face.

Chapter 23

'Are you sure this is wise?'

Voices.

They were close.

'What would you have us do?'

Two distinct voices. A man and a woman.

But others, close by too. Breathing, behind me.

Maybe three more?

I kept my eyes closed, feigning unconsciousness.

'Put him in a pod, get some damned use out of him.'

One of the people behind scoffed. 'Oh, come on, do you even know how a double-blind trial works? Or if he's compatible? Our entire data set could be skewed.'

'Both of you, quiet down. I feel our friend here may be about ready to come to.'

Someone approached from the front.

I prepared as best I could for some sort of physical assault. Instead, the sharpest smell appeared right in front of me. I could taste it in the back of my throat as it burnt my nostrils.

I recoiled, away from whatever it was. It was unpleasant, harsh even, but did have a positive side effect. I was completely awake now, and aware that I was tightly anchored to a chair.

'Ah, good morning.'

I opened my eyes, struggling against the light to focus on the two figures ahead of me.

'Well hello, sunshine.'

I should have recognised the voice. It made sense that Scaife would be there.

But the other, similarly familiar face, was less expected. And the location.

Ahead of me was the hulking wooden desk of Dr Ross, with him right behind it.

I twisted to try and see those behind me, but the room was dark aside from a lamp on the desk. It softened the room's unusual colour scheme, but only barely.

It was clearly a theme with Dr Ross, considering the style of pen he had gifted Scaife.

'Leon, we meet again.' Dr Ross sounded as stern as when I had first met him. 'Although, you have been here in my office since we last met, correct?'

I stayed quiet. Why answer a question he clearly knew the answer to?

'In fact,' he continued, 'you have been quite busy. Michelle here tells me you even paid her a less than cordial visit in her home.'

He turned to Scaife, a smirk on his face, before looking back at me.

'I'm surprised you made it out at all. She's not known for her hospitality.'

Scaife shook her head. She didn't seem enthralled by Dr Ross's jeering. 'Ross,' she hissed.

'Fine, to the matter at hand.' He stood and walked to my side of the table, sitting on the edge looking towards me. 'Leon, we are not the enemy you perceive us to be.'

In my books, that was exactly what an enemy would say.

'What would Jessica say?' I went right for the jugular, right to where it should hurt him the most. 'How do you think she would react to this, all of this? Knowing what you're all doing, how many people you've taken?'

Dr Ross didn't seem fazed.

'Is that how you see it? We are the boogeymen, stealing children from their mother's arms, hiding them away from the world?' His tone was facetious, only riling me up further. 'Tell me Leon, why did you save Henry?'

'What are you talking about?'

'Henry, the man you assaulted in our facility. Or rather I guess, the man who assaulted you. Couldn't blame him really, you were playing very fast and loose with that weapon.' Dr Ross signalled to Scaife, who activated a holodisplay that popped into life above Dr Ross's desk.

It was me, being wrestled to the ground, kicking and flailing as the man's hands clamped down on my neck.

We rocked back and forth, him on top, in control.

The sound rang out from the recording, making me wince in discomfort. I had always thought gunshots at close range had a cauterising effect, but it was obvious from the recording that was not the case. The blood sprayed across the pristine white room behind him and began gushing from his leg, pooling below him as he screamed.

It was surreal, like watching a movie. The actor simply bore a resemblance to me, that was all.

But the muscle strain in my neck kept me grounded in reality.

'You saved his life you know?' Dr Ross continued. 'The medics called what you did a "work of brutal ingenuity." High praise. I'm not sure how happy Henry will be about the whole ordeal, but at least he will be alive to be upset. And I'm sure his wife and kids would be thankful too.'

I shrugged my shoulders as relief washed over me.

I had done some good in the middle of an extreme situation at least. An act that was turning out to be damning.

'Why?'

'Why what?' I grunted dismissively.

'Why save him?'

I took a moment to formulate my answer.

'Because I'm not like you people.'

Nothing. Not a blink, not a squirm, not a raised eyebrow. Was he really so far gone that he couldn't even react to being insulted like that?

'Oh, and what are we exactly? What is it you think

we do?' Dr Ross looked behind me, to the quiet party observing the exchange.

'I know exactly what you do. I saw the facility. You use them like guinea pigs, for whatever sick experiments you're running there. You're all monsters, parading as paragons of medicine.'

'That's not...completely accurate.' He stood from his perch and moved back around the table, back towards the large map on the back wall. 'We're actually more alike than you might think, Leon. Do you see these numbers?'

He stood below the colour coded numbers above his large map. Again, I hadn't noted what they were before, but it seemed like they had changed from my previous visit.

'This clock. It was a gift from an old colleague. He died many years ago, pancreatic cancer. He helped me develop the AOE system. But this clock, it has a simple message. You see these numbers in red?' He turned and raised a hand towards the numbers. 'That's the amount of people who have been chosen by our AOE system.'

I couldn't quite see it perfectly, the light on the table interfering with my vision. But I could see there were five or six digits in red. A horrendous number. I felt my stomach churn at the thought of so many innocent people, taken against their will.

And they were pleading their case of not being monsters?

'But you see this, the numbers in blue?' he continued.

I followed his hand to the second number.

'This is the number of people the AOE system has saved. The people we have saved with our research.'

The green number took up a much larger area but was still hard to make out. Maybe nine, ten digits long. Hundreds of millions or more. And it seemed to be changing, even as I sat there.

No, I told myself. *Don't let them suck you in, don't let them fool you.*

'I don't believe you, that could be anything. You're just lying, trying to justify your sick exp—'

'Oh, fuck this. Do you have any idea what the world was like before Dr Ross's work, you spoilt little prick?' Scaife had cut me off and was right in my face. It seemed she had finished letting Dr Ross take point. 'You think this just happened overnight, that they just decided one day that it would be fun to do this? How fucking sheltered are you? Have you ever even read a history book? 2033 ring a bell?'

'2033?' I asked, hoping my compliance would get her out of my face.

'Did I stutter?' She seemed genuinely angered by my question. '2033. More colloquially known as the year antibiotics failed mankind. Do you know what it was like back then? This wasn't just another Ebola scare or the resurgence of another coronavirus variant. An outbreak of drug resistant Staphylococcus in the east wing of a hospital in New Jersey lead to 276 deaths in a few days, and not just of patients. The panic was so great that the wing was burnt down and all the bodies incinerated. Do you have any idea the fear that gripped the medical community, knowing that some of the stalwarts of modern medicine were failing? And that was only the beginning; the situation was far more dire than anyone thought.'

Despite the ferocity of her explanation, the tale took root. It did have a ring of familiarity. Like a ghost story, told around campfires and under the sheets at sleepovers.

'A highly virulent antibiotic-resistant Tuberculosis strain erupted across the globe almost immediately after. It had evolved to sidestep the stalwart BCG vaccine so well we thought it was man-made at first. The mortality rates were massive, and to add insult to injury those who survived were left with serious long-term complications. A new vaccine would've taken too long, and all of the experimental bacteriophage treatments were even further out. Slipway travel had already taken off massively, but the safety protocols were still in their infancy. All the predictions, even the mildest, were catastrophic. It was an epidemic, quickly turning to a pandemic.' Scaife's tone had softened. 'BioDev responded to an unprecedented threat, with an unprecedented process. We saved millions, maybe billions. Maybe everyone.'

She leaned in even closer, eyes wide open and burning. 'And you want to call us monsters? Big words, from a murderer.'

Instinct can be a funny thing.

There she was, using that word again on me, reminding me of what it entailed. "You killed Dan," that was her translation.

But I had been through the pain already, the torturous retreat to the stars where I had blamed myself for Dan's death. I had come away knowing the real enemy, and there she was.

Just a little too close.

Scaife had perhaps dropped her guard too much. Something I immediately made her regret as my forehead crashed down on the bridge of her nose. Never in my life had I headbutted a person; I was even shocked I went through with it. But she seemed worthy of popping my figurative cherry.

The rebuttal came swift and hard, the back of her hand crashing into my cheekbone.

'You piece of shit!' She raised her arm, a familiar baton now firmly held in her grip, ready to strike.

'No!'

The shout came from behind.

I wish it hadn't. The beatdown would have been preferable to what came next.

'You promised you wouldn't hurt him.'

My soul sank.

The voice was so familiar, so often longed for. It was almost like a dream had seeped into the ongoing nightmare.

'Jessica?'

A hand appeared on my shoulder. The nail polish

chipped and multicoloured. The scent, so familiar, now gut-wrenching.

Scaife moved away, blood starting to trickle from her nose.

'Not you too, Jess...'

A seat appeared from the side, and then there we were, face to face.

She was even more beautiful than my memory had allowed me to recall. Her sapphire eyes, her auburn hair, her dimples. I had never imagined a situation where I wouldn't be elated to be around her. But at that moment, I hated the power she had over me. It was irrational. Beyond irrational even.

I knew most of what I felt for her was a machination of an over-imaginative mind, full of implausible romantic episodes of nonsense. But we had begun to get close before, and nothing about her character in those instances broke away from the version of her I had created.

Not until that moment anyway.

'Hi Leo.' She smiled, to show she was happy to see me I guessed. But I had seen her smile, seen her laugh. This wasn't it, not really.

I didn't have a reply.

'I just...' she began, pausing to look back to her father for a moment. 'We all wanted to be here, to help you.'

Help me?

'My father isn't an evil man. What he does is

important, you have to see that. What we all do is important.'

'I get it.'

'What?'

'I get it,' I repeated. 'Bring you in, a face I can trust, a face I care for. Someone I might believe. What's next, my mother's secretly on the BioDev board? My dad's the groundskeeper?'

'It's not like that. I do care, we care. We just want you to see the good in what we do. You don't know what goes on behind the veil, what my father does, the reason he's still here.'

'Jessica.' Dr Ross was unhappy. Clearly, Jessica was straying too far from her script.

'How long?' I asked, monotone, looking her dead in the eye. 'How long have you known?'

She didn't want to answer, but after a moment's silence, she engaged. 'I've always known.'

I dropped my head. 'You're just like them.'

'Like them? Of course, I'm like them.' Jess's tone began to shift. 'Are you really going to play dumb, after what they've told you? You can see the clock yourself. For every one person who sacrifices for the system, tens of thousands are saved. I know if the cards were down, and you had to sacrifice yourself to save that many people, to save a single person even, you would do it in a heartbeat. You're a good person, Leon. You showed them that when you saved that man's life.'

I couldn't help but laugh.

'Do you even hear yourself? These people aren't sacrificing themselves for the greater good, you're sacrificing them, against their will. For fuck's sake, Jess, they're innocent people.'

'Willingness to help doesn't mean compatibility to help.' Dr Ross spoke out, now rounding the table to our side. 'This was a waste of time. We're done here.'

Jess rose and moved to her father's side. 'Just, please, can I have some time alone with him?'

He looked to his AMI, then to Scaife, who was already moving towards the entranceway to the hidden gate. Although he didn't seem thrilled by the idea, he nodded, kissed her on the cheek, and left. The mysterious others behind me left too. I caught a glimpse of them as they approached the gate. Unrecognisable walking suits.

More BioDev bigwigs no doubt.

Dr Ross paused for only a moment to look at Jess and me.

And then we were alone.

An ironic situation, alone with a woman I would have given all sorts to have been alone with weeks before. And now?

'I'm sorry about all of this Leo. It's...a lot to take in.' She reassumed her position ahead of me. But I decided not to re-join the staring contest, keeping my eyes low instead. 'But please, believe me when I say my father is doing everything he can. None of us wants this to be a reality, but it is, and we're doing the best we can.'

She reached out and placed her hands on my legs. 'Please, Leo, please believe at least that much.'

Her hands were warm and trembling.

I looked back up at her.

She had tears at the corner of her eyes.

'If you don't want this to be a reality, then why be a part of it?' I struggled again in my chair, wanting nothing more than to use my arms for emphasis. 'You and your father, if you're so against this, then just get out.'

'It's not that simple.' She sighed, pulling her hands away.

'Why then, Jess, why is it not simple? Because from where I'm standing it looks pretty simple.'

'Without my father it wouldn't stop. It would get worse.'

'Oh, come on, you expect me to believe that? He runs the damned thing. He's more to blame than anyone else. He made the system!'

'The system? Do you even know what the system is?' A single tear ran down her cheek, dragging with it the faintest streak of the makeup she wore. 'You're personifying it, making it appear intentionally cruel. Do you even care what it really is, or do you just want to use it to hide behind?'

'Fine then. Tell me. Defend the system to me. Make me see the fucking light you moths all fly to.' It was difficult to talk so harshly to her, even now.

'It's an independent sorting system, that's it. A supercomputer, checking everyone's medical history, genetic data, physical characteristics, religious background, diet, anything it can get its hands on that paints the most complete picture of what and who you are.' She was becoming frantic. 'But that's why you need my father, why we all need him.'

'And why would that be?'

'Because without him, without everything he's fought and begged for, that number, that red reminder of the pain endured by so many people, would be magnitudes higher. That's what he does. He never wanted to be involved, not really. His old partner, Professor Reinhardt, begged him to be involved when the experiments began. He knew my father would never allow it to become excessively cruel, that ethics and morality would at least prevail in some way. The people in charge, those really pulling the strings? They didn't care. They still don't. They would have sacrificed every man woman and child who as much as saw an infected person back then.'

Tears were now streaming down both cheeks. She had given up trying to wipe them away.

I wanted to wipe them for her. But I was immobilised and bewildered by the story unfolding.

'It was never meant to continue. Never meant to do anything other than stop the TB outbreak. But once they saw the potential, and how easily they could get away with it, it was kept almost unanimously. My father had to stay. To refine the system. To decrease the raw...ingredients. To make the system clever enough only to need a fraction of the people. That's what he does.'

I could see from her, that she believed every word.

And the outpouring of emotion, the intricacy of the explanation...I believed her.

I hated myself for it. I had called out their plan to use her against me, and yet there I was, believing her.

What she had said wasn't implausible. The report had stated how his implementation of changes had led to the commuters' near escape of the facility. Maybe, just maybe, her story was legitimate.

'Why should I believe you, Jess? Look at me, look at where I am. I'm here simply because we wanted to find out why people were disappearing. They would have killed us. Hell, they still might.'

'You can trust us, Leon, I swear. Scaife, it was her who ordered you captured, not killed. She and my father are very close. He convinced her. But what happened in the bunker...' She readjusted in the seat.

'I had nothing to do with that, those people attacked us. We only acted in self-defence.' I was incapacitated at the time, it's not like I could have hurt them if I tried.

'I know, I know. But my father's restraint cost those people their lives. He can't do anything for your friends now. I'm sorry.'

I paused for a moment, dissecting her words.

'Now?'

'I'm sorry, Leo, but that's where they were headed. Regrouping with the tactical squad and giving them orders before they move on your friends. Scaife is leading the show. They caught a few of them. They have the location of the others.'

'What time is it?!' I screamed as I pulled against the restraints.

We were to regroup in a day's time from when we left the bunker, at the coordinates Styx had given.

'It's 17:32. Why?'

Again, I wrenched and pulled, tugged and twisted. But nothing would come free. I was a literal part of the furniture.

'Please, Jess, please just let me go.'

'What?' She stood and stepped away from me. 'No way, I can't.'

'Please, Jess!' I roared. 'They're going to kill them! They aren't some militant group. They're just a bunch of random do-gooders. Saints and fucking cooks and nannies, who knows, but they don't deserve that! Please, Jess, you asked me to believe you. If you really are what you say you are, and your father is as good a man as you say, please, let me save my friends.'

She was frozen, mouth agape, reality crashing down hard around her.

'Please, Jess, please. Trust me, none of them deserve this. Just trust me.' My gaze was locked onto hers. 'Just trust me, please.'

She swallowed hard, rubbing her eyes hard with the ball of her hands.

'Fuck, fuck, fuck...' she muttered, as she ran behind me and started undoing the restraints.

It was only a moment before I pulled free, unwrapping my legs myself.

'Thank you, Jess, thank you.' I ran towards the gate, grabbing the baton Scaife had left on the desk as I moved and searching for the gate's system panel.

Within seconds I had it engaged, coordinates still burnt brightly in my memory even without my trusty AMI there to pick up the slack.

I stood back, looking into the gate.

'Leo?'

I turned to see, Jess, standing just a foot away.

'Please, whatever you do. My father's a good man. Just...just remember that?'

'...Okay.'

I spun around on my heels and left her, sprinting to both friends and enemies alike.

Chapter 24

Baton raised, teeth gritted, I emerged ready.

I had expected a battleground of sorts, to arrive at a melee of friend and foe. I was psyched up, full of bravado. But whatever had transpired had moved on by the time I arrived.

Probably lucky for me.

The location was an old warehouse of sorts. Or possibly the back of a factory, as machinery hummed just out of sight. The cinder block walls, a rarity in modern construction, still appeared clean and well kept. The stored machinery, mostly covered in cloth, was carefully placed so as not to obstruct passage.

I stood for a moment—shaking as the unused adrenaline coursed through my veins—taking in the area as best I could.

The gate itself was of an unusual design. Angular, blocky, and with no obvious terminal. It was likely a first-generation model, purpose-built without much emphasis on aesthetics. Its covering sheet lay to my left. It was dust-free, so it hadn't laid there long.

Despite the dullness of the scene, there were a few

unnerving signs. It was clear that there had been some serious footfall recently. The dust was heavy in the air. But far more worrisome was the smouldering black mark on one of the nearby walls. The air had a burning smell, but an unusual one. It smelled...clean. Almost chlorinated, like a swimming pool. It was exactly how Dan used to explain the smell of oxone when they used it in the laboratory.

I was unsure of what weapon would, or could, leave such a mark, but it didn't seem non-lethal. Parts of the wall were still falling away as the scorch mark ate further into the material.

I followed the only open trail I could find through the hulking stored machinery, keeping high on my toes to dampen my steps.

I was only a few feet from the gate when I heard a voice.

But not the voice of a person, not really. The voice had a rasp to it, a distortion, a haze. A digital or radio communication of some kind.

I pulled up short of the first corner, hugging the rough grey wall.

Peeking around the bend, trying to pick the perfect angle where the least amount of my head would be visible, I saw the first sign that I was right to worry.

Two people, perfectly resembling those who had come to the bunker, stood only a few feet away, turned enough so as not to notice me.

I cursed as I looked down at my attire. A few more accessories and I could have just blended in, at least for a few moments. But I was missing the bulk of the tactical gear, having left it behind in the bunker for BioDev to re-plunder.

I couldn't make out what was being said from where I stood, but the voice coming from one of their AMIs was spouting out quick, sharp directives.

Neither of my unwanted roadblocks seemed fazed by the calls.

They were the rear guard, but clearly they hadn't been rear enough to catch me entering the area.

Their rifles were large, considerably bulkier than the ones we had salvaged from their compatriots. Each had fuchsia lighting running the length of the barrel, pulsing to red every few seconds.

How the hell do I get past these two?

No such thing as running in guns blazing when you have no guns. And their gear would likely deflect much of the force of the baton. There was only one thing for it.

I stepped back from the corner and threw the baton with as much force as I could muster at a lighting fixture far off to their right-hand side, behind a few rows of unused machinery.

It was a horribly misjudged throw, as the weight of the baton caused it to fall well short. It didn't matter, however—a split second after the baton disappeared from sight, a huge smashing sound echoed out from the point of impact. Whatever I had hit sounded glassy, and absolutely broken.

The two didn't miss a beat. Rifles were raised in perfect harmony, pointing at the source of the sound.

'Movement,' one of them said and both raced in perfect sync towards the distraction. They stepped fast in their large boots, so smooth they seemed to be gliding away from me, hardly making a sound as they progressed.

I took the opportunity to skulk past, ducking in behind the first cover I could find. I didn't look back as I moved from cover to cover, hoping to remain unseen.

My distraction was likely to bring suspicion, so I didn't stop moving. If the security firm were as good as Frank had given them credit for, they wouldn't assume the noise and damage to be a natural phenomenon.

I scanned the walls and roofing as best I could. The building appeared to have a rectangular shape, despite the labyrinthian machinery manipulating my passage, so I continued towards the farthest wall.

Again, I passed through an area rank with the smell of burning. It was stronger here than before, likely the result of multiple shots even if I couldn't see their points of impact.

I was getting closer to the action, I could feel it. My hair was prickly and standing to attention, my senses ready for anything.

But I had to be careful. No weapons, just my smarts and the element of surprise.

I reached my destination quickly, but was met with

another problem. Or rather three. Two doorways to my front left, and one to my front right.

A decision is easy if given time to assess or investigate the options. That was time I didn't have.

Something had stirred behind me, not too far back, the echoes swirling around the husk of a building. It sounded like a small metal bowl skidding across the ground, rocking and rolling as it went. Followed by light but quick footsteps. It appeared my distraction had done nothing but buy me a few minutes of time; I had to move fast.

Front right door was furthest out; reaching it became more unlikely every second I spent weighing options.

Front left option one had a large double door entrance. Front left option two had a single doorway.

So, I went with front left entrance two. It had one door, there was one of me.

An obvious choice clearly, I told myself.

I bounded across to the door, pulling it open as silently but vigorously as I could and shutting it—but not allowing the latch to click in—just in time.

A shadow flashed underneath the door. Then another shadow, followed closely by some muffled words, a muffled grunt, and again nothing.

I played possum for a few moments to be sure, ear pressed up to the door, hand still firmly holding the door in place.

The door was sturdy, heavy and had no glass or transparent section. There was no way I could know if they were still there. I looked back over my shoulder to the metallic staircase that went up behind me. It was as good a route as any.

I softly released the door. Its own weight would hold it in place for long enough.

I moved up the first few steps of the stairs, tip-toeing as I went. Once far enough away from the door, I began to pick up the pace to the exit at the top. I reached it quickly, no glass there either, but I was on at least a totally different floor to my pursuers by now so there was no need to be too careful.

I emerged onto a sort of catwalk, stretching through the middle of a large room, similar to the previous area. The scorching smell had returned, and with a vengeance, as my nostrils burnt.

I moved along, holding my arm over my nose and mouth, trying to filter the air through my sleeve to mild success. It was more my own overpowering odour that was battling the scent, but I took what I could get.

I had only taken a few steps when I found the source of the smell.

I couldn't say for sure, and I couldn't look again to confirm. A single glance, and I almost vomited off the side of the catwalk. But from that single glance, I became all too aware that I was running out of time.

The body was intact, for the most part. Whoever it was lay face down, with a huge burning hole growing from its epicentre on their back.

They had been shot from behind, probably while trying to run away.

It could have been one of us, or some unfortunate worker. I couldn't look to confirm. It was ghastly, a fate you wouldn't wish on anyone. I just kept my sleeve pressed hard to my face and continued along the walkway.

There were noises in the distance. I just needed to follow them. I wasn't too late to help. I knew that. Not for some at least.

The noises became words, and the speech became shouting the closer I got. My careful steps had turned to a sprint, the catwalk seeming sturdy enough to dampen my bounds.

It took little time to find the source, in one of the only spacious openings I had seen. People were on their knees. Others surrounded them, guns held high and aimed down. A huge group, much larger than I had anticipated. And much more confusing.

Arms behind their heads, looking towards the ground, but unmistakeably wearing the BioDev tactical gear. They weren't my friends. But I didn't see a face I recognised among the apparent captors either.

'We have another two!'

The voice came from right below my feet, and I instinctively ducked down behind what little cover the catwalk provided.

Peeking out from around the metallic side rail, a small group escorted two more of the tactically dressed people to the crowd. They were too generic to identify, but it must have been the two that were looking for me, judging by their difference in height.

They were shoved into the middle of the group, begrudgingly joining the rest of their comrades on their knees at gunpoint.

'Where are the others?' a male voice called out from the crowd.

'Next block over, we're closing in on them now,' shouted another member of the mob.

'Right,' the first man began, 'let's be done with this.'

He stood out from the crowd. There was only one word I could use as a descriptor: unassuming.

Medium height, medium build, medium length brown hair. Not the person you would expect to emerge as any sort of leader.

I shifted to try and see better, but even from my poor position, I could see the look on his face, the only thing that stood out about him. He stared his captives down, eyes wild and unblinking, with a look of zealous fury.

In a flash, he raised his weapon—clearly taken from one of the captives—and pointed the barrel at the back of the closest person.

The rifle hummed as its pulsing fuchsia light changed to a solid dark red.

'Don't do this, Aribert!'

The first familiar voice broke free of the crowd below. My eyes scanned and pinpointed the source of the call. Sure enough there stood Sam, in the thick of the action as always, but not free to move. Two others were holding her.

So that was Aribert?

He pretended not to hear her as he nodded to his other weapon-wielding companions. They each raised their weapons, albeit more slowly and not immediately at their targets.

Their hesitancy was noticed.

'Would they have afforded you the same mercy?' Aribert called. 'Did they come here, to us, to talk of resolution, of an amicable solution?'

They still seemed unsure.

'We know what they do. We've seen the pictures of their facility, of the pods awaiting those who disappeared through the gates. We know it's their fault, that they take these people. How many hundreds? How many thousands?'

He sounded like a preacher almost, like he was working his flock up into a murderous frenzy. And for the most part, his words were building anger in the mob. But even worse than that, he was clearly referring to the pictures I had taken, using them as fuel to stoke his inferno.

A few more people raised the rifles to the intruders.

He seemed content with this, looking back to his victim. His body tensed; he was almost licking his lips, savouring the moment. The colouring on the rifle began to pulsate rapidly from barrel to nozzle as it prepared to fire.

'NO!'

A shot tore into the roof above me, with another splashing across the surface of the metallic cover I had hid behind.

I pushed myself back, small acid-like splatters landing close to my hands from the second shot.

They had fired blindly at the source of the noise. At me. Too trigger happy to see who it might be.

'Who's up there?!' someone screamed.

I raised my hands as best I could, just out over the edge of the catwalk. Luckily, they couldn't yet see me. At glance my mostly BioDev attire would likely attract more fire from below.

'I'm not with them, don't shoot!' I yelled down.

It went dead quiet below as they assessed my reply, just the hum of the weapons and sizzling of the way-ward projectiles filled the air.

'Leon?' Sam's voice broke the silence. 'Fuckin' let go of me, asshole! Leon, Leon is that you up there?'

I was still too stunned to want to raise any more of my body into harm's way so I remained still, only answering, 'Eh, hey Sam.'

A mumble burst out below me, but it was quickly silenced. 'Well! An honoured guest indeed. Why not come down and join us, Leon, we would love to meet you.'

Every word Aribert spoke gave me chills, like he was trying to ingratiate people into a cult.

I slowly stood, looking down to the crowd. All eyes were on me, even those of the captured tactical team. I moved to the side, pushing down a small emergency ladder and working my way to the ground floor. Two people were waiting for me and forcefully escorted me into the centre of the group, right to the preacher himself.

They pushed Sam forwards to join me.

'Well, isn't this a nice reunion. I can feel the love from here. It warms my heart. Take heed all, this is the man who went above and beyond where none of us could.' He began circling the BioDev team, speaking loudly to his followers. 'I told you to believe, and you did, and this man has blessed us with the proof we so desperately needed. Thanks to him, everyone will see just how evil these cretins and their organisation really are.'

The crowd was buzzing with excitement.

He came right around and stood almost face to face with me. His breath was horrendous, and he was a heavy breather.

Before I knew what was happening, he grabbed my hand and forced the rifle into it.

'It's only fair that we let him join this moment of glory too!' he said to the mob.

He forced the rifle up and pointed it at the person closest to me.

The mob seemed visibly excited by this turn of events, as if my participation were the last thing required to allow themselves to join the slaughter.

But it wasn't them that I was keyed in on.

I could hear the slightest sniffle come from behind the black mask my weapon now pointed at, the kind of sniffle not related to sickness. It was a sniffle of terror, the type that comes with weeping. It was too low for anyone else to hear, but it was clear as day to me. These people may be robotic looking, but they were still people.

And this psycho was going to kill all of them. It didn't matter their innocence or guilt. He was trying to play judge, jury, and executioner.

So, in a moment of madness, I turned the gun on Aribert instead.

Maybe a bit too rash a move. Every weapon burst into red glowing lights aimed at my position.

Even Sam squeezed my arm. 'Eh, Leon what the hell are you doing?' she murmured, trying not to make any sudden moves.

A bead of sweat trickled down my brow, between my eyebrows, and gathered at the tip of my nose. My gambit to take the focus off the tactical squad had worked, a bit too well.

'And just what do you intend to do with that, Leon?' Aribert asked, his eyes fiery.

I matched his gaze, if only for a moment, looking for the slightest indication he might falter at the end of a gun barrel. But the man didn't blink. I wasn't sure he even could.

'Nothing,' I said calmly.

I threw the heavy rifle to my side, its lights returning to a comforting pinkish glow as it clunked down. If anything, I possibly threw it down a little too hard.

I had no idea if they had a penchant for accidentally firing.

I stepped forwards, all weapons still trained on me, and in one quick motion unclipped and pulled the helmet and facemask off of Aribert's intended target.

Her short blond hair fell down around her face. Her face was red, her eyes even redder from the tears. She sniffled again, just in time, louder so others could hear. I proceeded to the next captive, performing the same unmasking process. I didn't stop until the whole squad was unmasked; nobody tried to stop me or ask what I was doing.

Aribert stood, eyes locked on me.

He knew what I had done, and why I had done it.

It was easy to point their guns at faceless tin can people. Just a black mask, no emotion, no feelings. Androids sent to kill and destroy.

But now they were people. Scared people. The mob couldn't be fooled into thinking they weren't human enough to care about.

'Escort our guests back to their friends.' Aribert spoke to the men closest him, eyes still locked hard onto mine. 'Tie these up. We'll decide what to do with them another time.'

He had been caught out, his bloodlust stymied. I had clearly made what looked like a lasting impression on him.

Aribert's men escorted Sam and me away.

As we walked, Sam nudged me. 'What the hell was all that?'

'Improv?' I tried to keep the mood light, as if my plan wasn't completely out of thin air and loosely based on hoping they all weren't psychopaths.

'You're some idiot.'

One of the men moved ahead of us and unlocked a door to a large canteen. We stepped through and were greeted with the turning heads of more than a few familiar faces.

The man slammed and locked the door behind us.

'Leon!' Styx ran and jumped at me, wrapping her arms tight around my chest and almost squeezing a groan out of me. 'How the hell did you find us?'

We weren't going anywhere with the doors sealed, so I decided I had time to share with them the entire story of what had transpired.

I settled in, accepted the cup of coffee that Frank handed me, and got into it.

But my story wouldn't end up being the only harrowing adventure.

Chapter 25

The happiness of my arrival lasted shorter than the few breaths Styx had squeezed out of me with her powerful hug.

We were fewer now.

Only eleven of us remained from the original bunker dwellers. Lucy was amongst those missing, alongside everyone who had followed her to their respective fall-back locations. I tried to provide optimism, showing that my arrival could mean the others were also still on the move, but the group had already resigned themselves to despair. But if I could survive, surely Lucy would be fine, right?

Even those that stood before me hadn't arrived unscathed.

Although they had kept on the move, using Sam's gate interface to great effect, it wasn't long before they had problems. The lack of protection against facial recognition software and the speed at which it picked them out was almost everyone's undoing. Frank had left quite a few people electrified and unhappy on his travels, but the use of weapons only exacerbated the emergency response units.

It was a desperate moment that led Sam to reach out to Aribert again. They needed any sort of protection, even security in numbers, anything. But his group was much larger than she had anticipated, and better armed. They had laid out ambushes all around our destination, revelling in using us as bait to lure in some unsuspecting BioDev personnel.

Their plans didn't seem to put our safety at the forefront.

The body I had seen on my way to finding Aribert's group was of one of ours. Gumby, they called him, the nickname showing he was at least friendly with the others. I didn't know him, and in a sorrowful way, I was glad I didn't. He had become separated somehow from the rest of the group during the initial commotion, nobody knew how. But I guessed the details didn't really matter, only the outcome.

His death had seemed to knock the sails out of most. And our current predicament only compounded those feelings.

We were "honoured guests" apparently. I imagined in the same way that incarcerated people were "esteemed vacationers" all around the world.

'What do they want?' I took a moment of silence as my opportunity to address the elephant just outside the room.

'Hard to say really,' Frank began. 'They just kind of corralled us in here once the fighting stopped.'

'I don't think they really have any idea what to do with us,' Sam added. 'I think they just wanted to lure some BioDev people here so they could enact whatever silly revenge crap Aribert has been spouting to them. But you saw what it was like Leon. You saw them out there.'

I knew what she meant. The bloodlust Aribert had displayed, and the hesitance in the crowd to slaughter those people on a whim.

I had also seen them begin to sway, their minds being wrapped and warped by Aribert's preachings. They may not be indoctrinated fully yet, but they could still be dangerous if things stayed on course for them.

'But why keep you all here under watch? Why have us locked up?'

They all just shrugged. Nobody even hazarded a guess.

Before I could push more on the subject, a small ruckus flared up outside the doorway. I could hear several people, their muffled disagreement not quite legible. It lasted only a moment before it quieted back down.

Everyone stood as the door swung open.

Two people shuffled through, arms cradling various drinks and food. Between them, with hands on hips and a look of pure smugness, was Aribert. I had no doubt he had been listening in on us, to what end I was unsure.

'Dig in, everyone. You have had an extraordinary day. It isn't much, but we'll soon be doing far better, of that I'm sure.' He raised his arms outwards while speaking to us.

Nobody budged.

It didn't go unnoticed.

'Please. Sit, eat,' he continued. 'There isn't much to go around. We're doing the best we can for you. We would be heartbroken to see you go hungry, trapped in here.'

A thinly veiled threat. He wanted to look generous, but we had to accept the offering for that to happen, and there was quite a crowd watching outside.

Hunger won out in the end. Once the first person moved towards the table, the group caved and attacked the refreshments.

I moved to join, bu, before I could, Aribert swiftly closed the gap between us and took me by the shoulder.

'If you wouldn't mind, Leon, I would have a word.' He kept his voice low, but I could see Sam perk up at the sight of Aribert's approach.

I knew a disapproving look on Sam's face when I saw it.

He all but pulled me back out through the door, leading me by the arm.

We walked out and through another set of industrial metallic doors. The backdrop was becoming eerier with every passing moment. I had been through quite a bit of the facility now, and I hadn't seen a single soul that appeared to work there. The droning of machinery still hung in the air, but there didn't seem to be a hint of life outside our rabble.

Aribert remained quiet as we walked. His eyes were dead ahead, the edge of his mouth curled up into a smug grin. A controlled expression, one I felt was for show more than genuine emotion.

I had no idea if it was some sort of power play or stupid game he was running, but he said he wanted to talk, and I wanted it done as soon as possible.

'So?' I asked. It felt a bit strange to be outwardly rude to someone I barely knew, but I knew enough to justify it.

'Hmph,' he scoffed. 'You and Sam are definitely similar, I'll give you that.'

We stopped, right before another large set of doors. This area seemed untouched; not a hint of dust in the air and the metallic handles shone in the building's stark lighting.

He turned back towards me, still wearing a relaxed expression. Relaxed apart from his eyes, which were unblinking as always.

'So, tell me, Leon. The facility. What was it?' His accent had shifted slightly. He was talking to me personally now, and the faux preacher twang in his voice was gone. 'We have seen the pictures, but they can be interpreted in various ways. I want to know what you saw, beginning to end.'

He had clearly assumed enough from the pictures but needed his assumptions to be validated.

I didn't see the harm in the story, so I regaled him

with the experience, beginning to end. My arrival, the pods, the staff, the huge area where I took the pictures. I told him about the central hub, how it seemed to be controlling the AOE system. I left out the parts where things had gotten a little violent, he would probably try to convince me we're "more alike than you think," or some other nonsense the lunatics in movies use to ingratiate themselves with people.

He hung on every word. It seemed I was validating everything he had long believed.

'Thank you,' he said. 'This is exactly what we needed.'

He began laughing to himself, looking down at the floor with his hand on the side of his face.

'You know, Sam spoke very highly of you. Out of all your lost friends, she had no doubt you would walk through that gate eventually. At first, I just thought it infatuation of some kind, but maybe her faith is well placed.' He laughed once more, sounding a little more maniacal than before. 'But there is one problem that you have left me with.'

I didn't realise I had been there long enough to have given him any real problems, but I enjoyed hearing I may have inconvenienced him.

'You see, you interfered. Those people deserved their fate at our hands, at my hands. They had come here, mindless drones of a corrupt empire, hunting you and yours down, and they had failed. Make no mistake, we are at war, Leon,' he stepped towards the doorway, his zealous posturing returning, 'and they are the enemy.'

He burst open the doors into a larger area, with a group gathered just a few feet inside.

I followed.

The area looked somewhat familiar, as did the cat-walk that now ran above our heads.

The group was silent but parted as Aribert approached.

In front of them was the badly burnt remains of Gumby, the man from our group that had been caught in the crossfire. The smell had mostly subsided, but was still strong enough make me draw away in disgust.

He wasn't alone. On their knees and wearing the full complement of armoured gear was another BioDev captive. They were quiet, head down and looking away from the charred remains. I couldn't tell if it was a man or a woman, the hair hung down over their face too much. There was a trickle of blood on the floor beside them, a sign of Aribert's hospitality no doubt.

'This is the one?' he asked the closest member of his pack.

'Sure is.'

Aribert walked around to the back of the prisoner, before nodding to the men closest to me.

'Doug, Lenny.'

Before I could react, they had me by the arms.

I hadn't a moment to consider the situation before Aribert enacted his vengeance on the captive with a single gunshot.

Blood sprayed across the floor in front of my feet, light splatters tainting the front of my boots.

The body fell limp, keeling over onto the remains of Gumby.

The gunshot rang all around us and echoed off into the distance.

'What the fuck!?' I roared, wrenching one of my arms lose from the weaker of the two, and trying to lunge at Aribert. 'You fucking psychopath, what the hell is wrong with you!'

The second man regained his grip on my arm, pulling me back in line.

Aribert raised his hands high and preached to his flock. 'An eye for an eye. Meet violence with violence. It is the only thing these animals respond to.'

'You fucking lunatic, they were unarmed!' I fought the words out while still struggling against the two. 'You didn't have to do that!'

'And what of your friend!?' Aribert yelled back at me, attempting to stamp his authority on the situation further. 'Did they provide him with the same compassion? Your friends look to you like a moral compass, but you would simply roll over and let them die to keep your hands clean? What if it was someone closer? Frank? Sam? You lack the will to lead anyone in this fight!'

And there it was. In all his righteous fury, Aribert had let slip a chink in his armour.

I threatened him.

Due to my interference, his followers chose not to kill the others. They had taken my side.

The act wasn't an execution of vengeance against BioDev. He was posturing in front of his group. And he needed me there, vulnerable, isolated, powerless.

I had threatened his authority, and he knew it.

The others grunted in a sort of cheer. It was an almost compulsory expression, an obligation, but it made them sound unsure. But not the two men who held me. They appeared invigorated as they clamped down even harder on my arms.

'Why did you shoot them from behind?' I steadied my voice, seizing on his insecurity. 'Why not look them in the eye, why not let them see you as you pulled the trigger? Why gather all your friends here to see you kill someone like a coward?'

He closed the gap in an instance, pinning the gun to my forehead. The barrel still burnt from the first shot, and he pressed it hard into my brow.

The two men by my side released their grip and stood away.

'Maybe another example of our resolve is needed!' he yelled in my face.

In that instance, my original plan had turned to mush in my head. Here I was, facing down the barrel of a gun, again.

I tried every calming trick I had ever heard of to slow my heartbeat, but I couldn't control the tremor building in my knees or the sweat beading on my brow. There was just no getting used to the situation,

no matter how much it was becoming an unfortunately common occurence.

He was unnerved, and still vulnerable. I just needed
to say something, anything, to appeal to his need to
save face.

'Honoured guests.' I finally spat out the words
through dry lips. 'Is...is this how you treat your honoured guests?'

The murmur in the crowd was the sweetest of
sounds. He had made such a fuss about us not being
prisoners, that we were meant to be allies, and the
others only needed that reminder.

He was threatening to cross a line I hoped even he
realised might lose him their trust.

He slowly pulled the gun away, eyes burning with a
new level of intensity.

I tried to keep my sigh as clean and quiet as
possible.

The mumbling in the crowd grew even more as he
backed down.

'Maybe our guest, in all his infinite wisdom, would
like to share with us his plan to stop these demons
from stealing our families away from us? Our daugh-
ters, our sons, our brothers.' He strained to keep his
sarcasm from overpowering his zealous preacher vibe.
'Maybe you can explain to these people why these
animals' lives are more important than those of the
loved ones they've had taken from them? Where is
their justice?'

I had a quick look around, my first time really

trying to take in the faces of the others. They were a broad mix of everything: age, ethnicity, sex. A crowd that would never pique your curiosity in any other setting.

His headhunting tactics were obvious. Obvious and deplorable.

Find people who had lost someone to a hiccup and radicalise them. But they weren't all converted yet.

It wasn't the time or place to try defend any of the BioDev extended workforces. But I hoped a bit of perspective might be enough.

'I'm sorry,' I began, choosing to look first at the men who had held me only moments ago and then spending a second trying to lock gaze with as many as I could. 'I know what it's like to lose someone. I lost my brother. I know the anger, the want to blame someone. But this?'

I pointed back to the lifeless body in black, now surrounded by a sizeable pool of blood.

'Did that bring someone back?'

Nobody answered.

'They think you're the terrorists because that's what they have been told. They aren't the enemy. They're a tool. A tool used by BioDev, nothing more. They probably know as much as anyone else about hiccups.'

'They came here, looking to kill,' Aribert joined in.

'Yes, they did. I'm not telling you not to defend yourself. I'm asking you to redirect your fury now that they've been dealt with.'

The murmur built up again, a ring of agreement in their voices.

'If we take down BioDev, we stop the problem at the source. No more hiccups. Nobody else has to lose as you have. As we have.' I was stretching the truth by saying "we"; our circumstances were hugely different, but I could see from their faces I was beginning to win over some.

'And I assume you know how to do such a thing?' Aribert interjected.

But his snarky question backfired because, from the way everyone perked up and focussed on me, that's exactly what they thought I was building up to.

I didn't have a clue, of course. Everything I had said was coming from an adrenaline excited state, brought on by fear of immediate death. But the adrenaline was wearing thin, and cognitive reasoning was almost back to full.

'Actually, I do,' I replied.

A lie, but one I thought would buy me some time.

Aribert scrunched his brow, seemingly as bemused as I was at myself for saying it.

'We were just finalising our plans before we had to flee from BioDev, but we know exactly how to take them down in one swift motion. But we could use your help.' Why I kept digging the hole, I'll never know. Maybe I assumed inspiration would just hit me on the fly.

I desperately hoped Sam and the others had a plan, even a bad one.

But at least I fixed my immediate problem. The crowd all but cheered as I talked. All except one. But I had confused Aribert at least, and he seemed less violent when bewildered.

The group began to move in the direction of where the others were being "voluntarily" held.

I joined them, but not before Aribert got one last word in.

'Well let us not delay! Our deliverance from this oppression is almost at hand.'

He didn't budge. I took one last look back as I moved in the relative safety of his mob.

His gaze was firmly locked on me, eyes as cadaverous and unblinking as always.

He was by no means finished with me yet. If anything, I had only further inconvenienced him now. And considering his retaliation for that first minor interference, I would need to be extremely wary of him.

But that was "Future Leon's" problem.

"Contemporary Leon" was on the way to a strategic war counsel meeting, based on a fake premise of a plan to topple one of the largest companies in history.

Simple.

Chapter 26

Well, this should be interesting.

That was the only thing I could think on the walk back to the others.

I felt more the fool than ever approaching the room that had become our impromptu holding area. I had made a dangerous gamble, one I had no real reason to believe would ever pay off.

But I was in it now, and the others would be too, soon enough.

We arrived in a buzz of excitement, Aribert's followers revelling in the thought that this episode in their lives may soon come to an end. I had no idea how long they had been with him, but the thought of a resolution seemed to encourage them greatly. I just hoped Aribert's brainwashing was reversible. His violent tendencies seemed to rub off on at least some of them.

I tried my best to imagine them much like Sam and the others.

Two groups, equal but opposite sides of a coin.

With one flip, we landed with Dr Sterne, and they landed with Aribert.

Fate can be cruel like that.

As the men in front of me moved to open the doorway, I called out to them.

'Wait,' I asked in earnest. 'I think my friends are still a little shaken. Can I talk to them myself first, make sure we're on the same page?'

They seemed a bit unsure of the request, and rightly so. They needed a purpose, a distraction, a direction for their energy.

'You took all the weapons from the assault groups, yes?'

'Yes,' several of them answered in perfect harmony.

'Did you take anything else? Access cards, extra ammo, AMIs?' I knew they wouldn't have. That involved being too close. Aribert probably had the majority keeping their distance, lest they realised there were people behind the masks.

They all just looked at each other, in a manner befitting a class of freshman who had ignorantly left a whole section of an exam unread and unanswered. An expression that wasn't alien to me.

'Well if you can take care of that, I'll take care of my friends. We'll be out of here quick as we can. Does that sound like a plan?' I wasn't exactly well versed in giving orders or acting like a leader, but they needed a bit of direction, and I was making the best impression of my mother that I could muster. Why not, she had managed to all but dictate less idiotic courses of action to three men for the whole time I've known her.

They seemed perked up by the new direction. After agreeing on groups they headed away, splitting into two. One headed back the way we had come from, and one left to deal with the assault team I had yet to come across.

With them all now turned and moving away, I entered the room.

Everyone was standing to attention, aware people were outside and still unsure of their intention.

A collective sigh of relief washed through the crowd as I entered.

That wouldn't last long.

Quickly stepping inside, I closed the door and waved to the group to join me on the table furthest from the entrance, and hopefully away from any prying stragglers.

'What happened?'

'What did he want?'

'Where were you?'

'What do they want?'

All questions I would have asked, but I didn't have time for a rundown. We had a problem to solve.

'No time.' They did not look impressed by my honesty. 'That psycho is unhinged. He put a gun to my head, threatened to make an example of me for interfering with his plans. So, I may have provided a few...alternative facts to get out of the situation.'

Despite the rage flashing across Sam's face at the

idea of Aribert's violent outburst, she couldn't help but smirk at my turn of phrase. "Alternate facts" was something she always used to say when caught in a hilariously blatant series of absurd lies.

Frank, as always, was less amused. 'What did you promise them?'

'I didn't technically promise them anything. But on behalf of the group? I promised that we already had a plan to take down BioDev that we're ready to act upon.'

I didn't have to look. I could feel Frank's eyes roll.

I'm sure everyone's did.

I was no longer the miraculous recovery from the abyss; more like another stone in their shoe.

'Oh, come on! You guys must have had some ideas by now? What did you think once we found out the people were being abducted? Give up? Start an online petition? Meditate on it? Someone must have something at least?' I didn't mean to sound so snarky or panicked but blaming them a little for not having any ideas at least lightened my immediate load and would likely force them to put their thinking caps on.

Styx was the first to speak out.

'We can't fight them.'

Most of the group mumbled in agreement.

'And we can't just report them to the authorities either, they would be expecting that. And who knows how far their influence reaches.' Point number two, just as obvious but no less important.

'We don't know half of how far their reach is,'

Frank added. 'We're probably all on every watch list on the planet. It doesn't matter what we say or do, they'll think we're making excuses.'

More mumbled agreement.

Our options were becoming fewer the more we talked.

'We don't even have enough credible evidence to accuse them of anything.' Sam came down with the final hammer blow.

Groans and sighs began to fill the room. Hands were on hips, on faces, running through hair.

Everyone was just wrecked. Too tired to think, too tired to deal. The group had been on the run nonstop since I had left them. I hadn't slept either, technically, unless you count my involuntary rest courtesy of the Blacksite security team.

The team was just about defeated.

Despite Aribert's previous comments, I didn't feel much like a leader at that moment. Before he had said it, I hadn't even considered myself in the running for the position.

I could imagine him, smirking at our frustration, with those unblinking psycho eyes.

It's a pity he wasn't abducted, I thought. *We could have gone and dragged his tortured ass out of the pods and paraded him around as proof of—*

'Shit,' I whispered.

Eyebrows and ears perked up around me.

'Shit!' I exclaimed. 'Sam, you negative genius!'

'What? Spit it out!' Frank wanted an action plan.

'The pods. The pods in that facility. A few of them were green!'

Silence.

'Oh crap, sorry, I forgot you guys weren't there. When I landed there, in BioDev, the room and pod antennae turned green. It was a kind of "occupied" reaction, I think. But in that expansive lab space, the one I took the pictures of, a bunch of those pods were lit up green too. I bet there is a bunch of people there right now. People who are probably reported missing. And if it was long enough ago, WormWhole would have had to confirm a hiccup. So they would be listed officially as lost in transit.'

I thought what I was selling was obvious by now, but the expressions proved the others needed just a little more spoon feeding.

'We need to get those people and pull them out of there! We go in, grab them, get out, and they're our credible evidence.'

I looked to Styx, the only person who seemed to be grasping my plan so far.

'Yeah,' she said. 'Yeah, that might actually work. We wouldn't need anything else. They would be the proof.'

'Yeah. Yeah. Yeah,' the group melodically joined in.

'That's not too bad actually,' Frank added. 'It mightn't be enough though. We're all on too many watch lists. They could flip it on us, accuse us of kidnapping them.'

I didn't remember paging Dr Killjoy, but Frank obliged none the less.

'Sterne!' Sam screamed, scaring the life out of Styx who stood closest to her. 'We use Meribel. She's one of the most recognisable people on the planet. We need her there, a believable personality to verify what's going on. Like a spokesperson or something, to lend legitimacy to everything we're telling them.'

The swell in confidence of our evolving plan began to grow exponentially.

Everyone began throwing ideas out. I had lit a fire under them, and they adapted immediately to the fluid planning.

'A news station.' The ideas started coming from the group at large. 'Could we take over a broadcast? Would they let us? We could play the "terrorist" card they've branded us with, force them to broadcast? What's the best news station? I love that guy on North West Weekly, he's a dreamboat.'

A variety of puzzle pieces had been laid out at our feet. Putting them together would be the next phase, and to keep the peace we would have to include Aribert's rabble.

I felt uneasy even considering the thought of working anywhere near him. But it would have to work, and fast. I could hear them approaching.

'This is brilliant, guys, absolutely stellar. But one last thing...we have to work with the others.'

'No fucking way.' Sam was the first, but not the last to voice her opinion.

Frank was next. 'Fuck no.'

'No.' I appreciated Styx's politeness at least.

Every head shook. And rightly so. It wasn't the others that we worried about. It was their leader that was the problem.

'We can't trust him,' Sam added.

'Look, I get where you're coming from. I don't trust him either. In fact, I'm downright terrified of what he might do. He's dangerous, possibly too dangerous, sure he put a fucking gun to my head! But we don't have a choice.' I could see nobody wanted to listen at that point. 'The others, they never asked for this. He preyed on them, normal people just like us, because they were angry and lost after a loved one disappeared in transit. They aren't bad people. They were just unlucky that HE was the one to find them.'

Their silence was all I needed.

I moved over to the door. The group outside must not have wanted to interfere with our little session in case they interrupted the planning or something. But when I opened the door, they were all stood to attention, bright-eyed and hopeful.

Mostly.

At their centre was Aribert, now wearing a heavy trench coat and carrying one of the largest BioDev rifles. As always, he had his closest two confidants by his side. They were like his bodyguards I guessed. They had worn clothes similar in design to the WormWhole technicians uniform. But the outfits looked home-made. An odd choice, I felt, that made me uneasy.

'Are you prepared?' he asked, looking past me to the others.

'Yeah, we're ready, but the plan isn't an easy one. Please, sit.'

They walked in, grabbing seats at the nearest table to the door.

I explained the plan in the most coherent way I could put it together in my head on the fly, trying my best to sound like it was always the plan from day one.

The group hung on every word, agreeing and patting each other on the back at the thought of a plan of action that was so immediate.

Aribert scoffed several times but refrained from interjecting. He had no counter arguments worth speaking it appeared.

At least not until the end.

'We need to break into teams,' he added.

'Agreed. We'll have to do this all in one fell swoop if we want to succeed.'

'I shall lead the attack on this Blacksite you have described. We'll save every misplaced soul unlucky enough to have ended up there.' I was quickly becoming allergic to the way he spoke. So pompous. He really seemed to believe he was this exalted leader.

But his phrasing wasn't missed.

'It's not an attack. It's a rescue mission. In and out, as quickly as possible.'

He looked at me for the first time since I opened the

doorway. Expressionless and pale, he simply stared for a moment.

'A slip of the tongue,' he eventually spat out. 'But you're a fool if you think they will just give up those people.'

He was right of course.

'I'm the only one who knows the layout, so I'll go with that group. But you're right, I know that's the most dangerous leg of the operation. We have to be clever. How many of the security passes did you salvage from the tactical team?'

'Sixteen,' one of the men spoke out, holding a small bag out to me. He pulled it back slightly as Aribert shot him a glance, and placed it on the table instead.

'Great, thanks. We can use those. They might buy us enough time. First things first, I guess, we need a way to get back there. Where is my AMI?'

I knew who would have it. There was no need to look to anyone else for the answer.

Begrudgingly, and without taking his eyes from mine, Aribert revealed the AMI from under his coat. He tossed it underarm to me, putting so little force I had to move to save it from crashing off the hard floor.

Prick.

I waved to Styx to come over.

'Think we have any way of getting back there?'

She approached, trying her best to avoid contact with the other group. 'I don't know,' she replied sheepishly. 'If their security is worth a shit, nobody would be able to get in. You would just be redirected. Those passes, they should let you through, but you'll have to enter from a security-enabled gateway.'

I had suspected as much myself. But it was better than nothing.

The gate I arrived in didn't appear to have any security augments at all, so we would have to step out into the public for a short stint to make our way.

But with the speed at which they could find us in a public space, it wasn't ideal.

'We need a diversion.' Sam spoke as she joined my side. 'Something that pulls their attention away from everywhere else. They're likely aware that things have gone south here for them, and it's only a matter of time before they find a way to rectify that, but their security will be on high alert everywhere. Leon has already broken in once, so we need something big, elsewhere, to grab their attention.'

Aribert piped up, smirking at his two lackeys. 'We can take care of—'

'A non-violent distraction.' I cut him off. Knowing how his mind worked, he would have probably marched the whole lot of the captured BioDev team off the top of a building to draw attention.

His anger was apparent, slamming his fist down on the table. Fury perhaps because I had cut him off, more so than me drying up his wet dreams of violence.

I was possibly pushing him too far. The only thing holding him back from striking out at me was likely the people there to bear witness. I needed to give them a reason to believe non-violence was the way.

'If we come out the other side of this, we don't want that on our consciences. The more bodies you leave behind, the more the outcome goes against us. Please, trust me.'

His followers nodded in silence. He did not.

'I'm pretty sure just a group of us showing up some-where public would be a bit of a distraction,' Styx added. 'Do we really need more than that?'

'It's hard to know how surrendering would go,' Sam added. 'If the plan falls through, we could just be handing ourselves over to who knows what.'

'We can't continue as we are; it's only a matter of time before we're caught or worse.' I felt it needed to be said. 'You saw the number of them that came this time. It won't be long before even more come, and their intentions at this stage seem a little more like search and destroy than find and capture. We need this to work.'

Everyone let that thought sink in for a moment. We had been operating on borrowed time almost. The only reason our group seemed to have gotten as far as we did was that they hadn't considered us a true threat. But now that we had teamed up, for lack of a better term, with Aribert's flock, they had no reason to hold back.

We had just created our own endgame, but I had no doubt BioDev's was already in motion.

Sam tugged at my arm.

'I just had a thought. A stupid story you told me a good while back.'

That didn't narrow anything down for me.

'You always go on about that swirl of colour when you moved slowly through the gates, right?'

'Yeah of course.' I had gone on about that at length several times with her. The blue and green twister was my favourite thing about the gate network. But I had thought about it more and more since my trip to their Blacksite. The colour change to darkened shades of red was beyond disturbing and made me wonder about the true source of the coloured streams in the slipstream.

But they were thoughts for another day. I couldn't get distracted now, and Sam had a plan.

'I remember a stupid plan you and Dan had come up with ages back. You would put two gates pointed directly at each other, and just run through, constantly going from one to the other in a loop. You thought you would be able to spend enough time in the slipstream to really experience the effect.'

Apart from being horrified that she had called our brilliant plan stupid, I wasn't sure I was following.

'So, imagine this,' she continued. 'We get everyone loaded up with the gate interface code. Styx can program something that will output completely random addresses constantly, locking gates into a random cycle of destinations. And we keep running, gate to gate to gate. Focus on the Hubs if we can, cripple the system. They shouldn't be able to follow us easily, and even if they did, we would be moving too fast and too random to track properly. That should get their attention. Then we split, each group heading to their intended targets amidst the chaos.'

I couldn't believe what I was hearing. I don't even think Sam knew how perfect her idea was. I grabbed her, hugging tight enough to feel a crack or two.

'Yes!' I exclaimed. 'That's brilliant. Perfect even. They wouldn't know what to think. It would be real shock and awe.'

But that wasn't the true brilliance of her plan.

'It plays into everything we've planned so far. Imagine the public outcry, the anger. You've seen people freak out at a few seconds of being delayed? What if the system wasn't working for them at all, or people kept getting sent to the wrong place. The public's attention would be on the news, trying to figure out what the hell is going on.'

'And that's when we hijack the broadcast,' Aribert boasted from his seat, acting like it was his idea to begin with. But he wasn't wrong, and I would let him have this victory if it calmed him down.

'Exactly!'

'Holy shit, we are actually doing this?' Styx was bubbling with excitement.

There was no other alternative.

'Fuck yeah, we are,' Frank joined in, fist clenched and punching the air.

At last, an element of hope had materialised. It was palpable. Everyone was pumped, the excitement of the plan moving through the entirety of our now extended family.

Even Aribert cracked a smile, but I didn't believe it was in reaction to our plan. He revelled in this war of his, so I doubted he was looking for it to end.

But he didn't matter for now.

The endgame was upon us. No going back, no saving progress, no second chances.

It was all in, now or never.

Chapter 27

The air was electric.

The cocktail of fear, excitement, and anticipation was potent. Nobody could as much as stay still or stay sitting. Everyone was preparing as best they could. Some prayed. Some looked at cherished pictures of loved ones on their AMIs. Some even shared moments of embrace so strong that it was apparent that something had grown between them during our struggles.

It was a perfectly raw display of humanity, beautiful to behold.

I kept mainly to myself.

The idea of what was about to happen weighed heavily on me. Aribert had begun to refer to me as "Instigator." I knew he despised me, and the nickname was very much to remind me that anything bad that happened to these people was due to me.

And he was right, to a point.

"Instigator."

Dan had on occasion called me by this title too, more so due to my penchant for showing up at his apartment with my "Whisky of the Week." Sometimes I'd skip a week only to show up twice in the same week. I couldn't let him become complacent. But as life went on responsibilities and jobs had unfortunately beaten that little tradition out of us for the most part.

While everyone continued their prep, that thought was what I dwelled on.

I had lost nearly all of the stupid traditions I had had with Dan before he died. The only one left really, and our longest standing tradition, was our leap day antics. And on what turned out to be the last leap day we would ever spend together, I let him down.

That was the day I lost the commuter. The day all this began. I was so in shock, felt so guilty. I was in a daze. He came to console me, but I acted out. I didn't need help. Didn't need my big brother to come swinging in to save the day. We were long past that. Or at least I thought I was. I just wanted to be alone. Alone and angry over something I had no control over. And it cost me greatly.

I had let a bad mood ruin one of the last good times I could have spent with him. The hiccups had stolen that moment away from me.

It might not have been the most productive use of my prep time, standing in a corner becoming irritated by those thoughts, but it seemed to work. I was more resolved than ever that we would tear down their whole system, with our bare hands if we had to.

And we would do it now.

A dozen or so of the BioDev team members had been relieved of their tactical gear, and a group of

Aribert's people were now fully combat ready. They would be the team to move on the Blacksite, with Frank and me in tow. We could keep a closer eye on Aribert this way.

Sam was leading the group to retrieve Dr Sterne. I had told Styx that the WormWhole satellite had still been in contact for some time after we left the bunker, and although we had no idea if it was still active, we had never received reports about Sterne moving. So, our best bet was that she was still in the same hospital. One of our surviving members was a patient there before, so he was able to give some general ideas on layout. Every little tidbit of information helped.

Aribert and I were to lead the mission to extract the people from the BioDev Blacksite.

And last, but by no means least, it would be up to a group headed by Styx to prepare for our arrival at the news station. I didn't follow news broadcasts, but most Hubs around the world typically had the ECN broadcast station on all their screens during the day. The European Central News station may not have been a giant in the news industry, but it was a good plan, and the report was going to end up being sprawled across a lot of screens in places where many irate commuters were stuck and looking for answers.

Styx's small group had all been given the same rip-off WormWhole technician overalls sported by Aribert's two henchmen. I still couldn't place what was so familiar about them, aside from the obvious branding, but I ignored the unease they gave me, chalking it down to pre-game jitters. Maybe it just reminded me of work; wouldn't that be typically enough to illicit unease in a person?

'I hope you're right about this.' Styx whispered the words as she passed me, re-joining the group.

I hoped so too.

In the distracted excitement, I had asked her to perform a small task behind Aribert's back. An insurance policy of sorts. We couldn't trust him. I asked for nonviolence, and he agreed. If he were a child, I would have had no doubt he was holding his hands behind his back, with fingers crossed, every time he agreed with me.

But with my insurance policy in place, it was time to act.

I gave the nod to Aribert, knowing he would want to preach a little before we began.

He didn't miss a beat.

'It's time!' he called to the group at large. 'You know what is expected of you. We all have our roles to play, our burdens to bear, to ensure we emerge victoriously. I trust that each and every one of you will do anything that is necessary to ensure our victory. Do not falter, do not fret. We are on the side of the righteous, no matter the outcome. Believe in our mission, and nothing will stop us.'

Not the worst speech really, but it definitely had some defiant undertones aimed at my nonviolence policy.

I just hoped my trust in the better nature of some of his followers was well placed.

But only when I stood out from the wall and looked around properly, did I realise things had become a little quieter.

Sam, Frank, Styx, and all that was left of our group remained silent, looking to me. Even Aribert's group had mostly turned to me now, still stood in the corner by myself.

It was an unusual feeling.

I wasn't overly comfortable with the gazing, but I knew people were scared. Scared like me. I could act a de facto leader no problem, but it didn't mean the terror that stirred in their chests wasn't also tearing into mine. So, I sucked it up. If I was to assume the role of a leader for the time being, I would do my best for their sake.

'We all know what's at stake here. We've known for a while. We're not doing this for us. We're doing it for them. The lost commuters. Knowing what we now know, we can't possibly in good conscience do anything less than tear down this system for good.'

I tried to lock eyes with as many onlookers as I could while I talked, focussing on those that appeared the most worried.

'I know you're scared. Hell, I'm terrified. But not terrified of them, not this time. I'm terrified of just how important this all is. So there's only one way this goes. We're going to win. I don't see any other possible outcome. They were fools ever to have doubted our resolve, and we'll make them sorry they did. We all have a part to play, and I just ask one thing of each of you. Be better than them.'

Heads nodded. The absolute silence of the moment was intimidating, but I had successfully reined in my own anxiety and wanted to be sure they all had too. I was under no grand delusion that this would be easy.

'We can do this. We will do this.'

My call to action had been received.

Everyone cocked and loaded their weapons as familiar neon lighting flickered to life on the firearms.

Our bunker group had been armed with only non-lethal weapons. I assumed Aribert thought this a joke of sorts. But we were more than pleased. Having each seen the destructive power of those other rifles, we wanted nothing to do with them.

The forearm-mounted weapon, an exact match to my previous one, hummed to life on my command. It was comforting to have it back again. One on each arm this time.

I felt kind of badass really.

Everyone was ready, and Styx moved to activate the supplied gateway. No point in turning on the old one, which had been shut down moments after my arrival. BioDev could come flooding through before we even got a chance to leave.

It silently hummed into life.

'Good luck everyone.' It was all I could think to say, and hopefully all that was needed.

It was time to lead by example.

I activated the new gate scrambler on my AMI, took a few deep breaths, and sprinted to the gate. The program was clearly doing its job on approach, as the typically solid green light above the entrance was now flickering erratically.

I could hear the footsteps of the others close behind as I entered the gate's event horizon.

Full steam ahead.

***

It was like a dream.

In and out, in and out, in and out. Rarely did I have to take more than a few steps between each gate. One moment you're in a Hub, the next you're in a tiny rural station. Now it was France. Then it was Colombia. The scenery flashed and changed so dramatically it felt like running through a slideshow.

But the real beauty was the colour streams in transit.

They crashed on me every time I entered the slipway. Split second waves of cold blue and green cascading all around, bringing every moment of the erratic journey to life. I didn't expect to see much if it, travelling through the gates at such speed, but it was almost like they were becoming more pronounced the more I travelled.

It was just how Dan and I had imagined it.

Glorious.

I kept watch of my time as I went. Everything was

to be performed to a specific timescale. We only had a couple of minutes to run through and scramble as many gates as possible.

The world had become a beautiful blur by the time my alarm went off. I just landed in a medium-sized hub as it sounded, and I sprinted for a far gate upon arrival, hoping I could scramble as many gates as possible before heading to my final destination.

'Hey! Stop!'

A sign my time was truly up with this section of our plan.

People scattered out of my path as I ran. A good thing too, because I was struggling to activate the address I wanted, and bumping into someone would have thrown me.

I arrived at the gate, disabled the scrambler, and uploaded my destination.

'Freeze!' The voice was now very close, almost causing me to jump.

I pulled on the BioDev helmet and jogged through.

Our timing was immaculate. The group of sixteen landed in perfect order.

The tactical teams mustn't have been an unusual sight, as the security guards didn't panic at our arrival.

I stood out at the front of our group to meet the guard who had eventually stirred and came to greet us.

'We weren't notified of any arrivals, sir. To what do we owe the pleasure?' He was relaxed, suspecting nothing.

'Have you seen what's going on out there?' I

assumed he hadn't. 'Everything's going into lockdown, sightings of terrorists popping up everywhere across the network. We're going to need you to take these gates offline for now.'

'Oh, right, yes sir, straight away.'

I couldn't believe how casual his attitude was. And now he was going to cover our backs by deactivating the gates. It was a perfect start.

He returned to his station and powered all four gates down.

I nodded at him before signalling the others to move out. On first glance at the group, I couldn't distinguish anyone but Frank. He was the only one taller than me after all, and the new tactical gear wasn't the most comfortable fit for him.

The rest were just faceless team members. But I couldn't relax knowing that Aribert was in there, anonymous and reckless.

We moved through the facility, trying our best to keep an even steady pace to make us appear more professional. I guided us back to the security station I had visited on my previous journey. You could see the entirety of the lab where the people were being held in the pods from there. The few green pods were still lit up, but the previously flashing red pod was gone, the space vacant. I assumed the worst, but tried to block it out.

We would need the security silenced before attempting the extraction.

Frank volunteered, picking another two faceless

team members to join him. They entered the room casually so as not to elicit an early response. Before the doorway closed completely, I heard two bodies hitting the floor. Frank was clearly wasting no time.

The rest of us moved off to the central lab. I hadn't come across the entranceway on my previous journey, so I relied again on the coloured lines directing along the floor.

Eventually, we landed at what seemed like our mark, a huge doorway littered with cautionary designs. Bio-hazards, contagions, carcinogens, acids, skull symbols, they had a logo for everything on the door.

'This must be it,' I confirmed to the rest of the group.

I approached and pushed, but nothing. Not even the slightest bit of give. It was rock solid and standing between us and our target.

'Frank?' I called out over the helmets radio. 'Little help.'

'Hold on.'

It was an uncomfortable wait.

'Frank?'

'Yeah just hold on, it's like a fucking maze this computer system. It should be...this one?'

The doorway made a heavy clunking sound. I placed my hand on it again, and it budged at the slightest of pushes. I leaned in a bit harder, and it swung open with ease. It required so little force, like pushing open a paper doorway.

Engineering envy aside, we were inside.

A small hallway lay in front of us. A disinfection area. We all moved in, trying to remain as natural as possible, but I could feel the others tensing up behind me. The door closed automatically with a clunk.

A whirling sound began, quietly at first, but within seconds the hallways became a miniature wind tunnel. The air smelt strange, but it was impossible to distinguish the odour. A blast of a few seconds of a heavy UV lighting, and the hallways became peaceful again.

We moved on, the doorway at the end opening automatically with the purge cycle now completed.

The laboratory was even more spectacular from the inside. The ceiling was far above us, and the room expanded a good distance in every direction. The pods filled the majority of the space, a couple of hundred of the large oval units sat unattended across the floor, their rods of red light filling our line of sight.

But the lab was not completely empty. A number of people moved about, completely clad in heavy white. They were mainly congregating around the few green lit pods.

We stood out in the all black gear and were already beginning to attract attention.

'There, the green ones.'

I ushered the others to follow.

We made quick work of closing the gap between the pods and us, but several of the researchers had gathered close and were watching us intently.

I stopped at the first green pod. A vibrant orange

heart rate pattern pulsed along the top of the smooth white pod surface, but there didn't appear to be any controls. No obvious buttons or handles adorned the outer surface of the bubble. I looked down to where the mass of cables entered the underside, but they simply ran from a junction in the floor into a small opening on the underside of the pod.

I tapped on the heart rate projection—the plastic shell rubbery to the touch—but it didn't react.

'Excuse me, what are you doing?' One of the white-clad scientists approached me.

The others were trying their hands at figuring out the other pods, so it was just this man and me. He was so heavily gowned it was like talking to the negative of a ninja.

'We need these people out of here.'

He scoffed at the thought. 'You can't be serious? Take them out of the pods, here? We haven't even finished the first round of homeostatic modifiers. We need each of them maintaining an internal temperature of 39.1 degrees Celsius for at least 31 hours before the next round of testing. If you take them out now, they would have no ability to retain normothermia and our results would be meaningless.' He looked me up and down, rolling his head slightly. 'Who authorised this?'

I wished somebody else had been listening because I only understood part of the man's explanation.

Maybe he was right, and taking them out could be dangerous. But no more dangerous than leaving them here. Not that our little conversation mattered. One of the others had already figured out a way to open the pod. A burst of warm, cloudy air escaped from around the central dividing line as the top half of the pod popped open.

'Stop that now!' the man screamed and ran off towards the opening pod. Several other members of his reverse ninja clan moved to join him.

My team raised their weapons.

The lab staff backed down immediately, not as much as uttering a word.

'Put your full palm across the top of the pod to bring up the interface.' The instructions came from the faceless teammate who had managed to open their pod. 'Swipe down to settings and hit "Abort Processes and Eject."'

We all followed suit, and within moments each of the pods was exhaling warm dense air with a hissing sound.

I popped the lid on mine the second it budged.

The woman was unconscious. They all were. It was an outcome we hadn't accounted for, but an obvious one now that we were faced with it. Our plan was showing cracks in its foundation.

'Hurry it up, Leon. We have incoming.' The voice crackled over the headset.

'From where?' I asked.

'East wing it says, normal security personnel. Someone must have signalled them, because from the monitors it looks like they're coming in hot.'

'Right, be ready to move, we're leaving.'

Frank didn't sound worried, but we didn't want to get pinned down on this leg of our master plan.

There wasn't as much as a wheelchair, or anything with wheels for that matter, in the vicinity. Crane-like machinery was hooked to tracks running across the ceiling. They likely only ever moved full pods, not individual people.

'Right, we're going to have to carry them,' I called out as I pulled the limp body of the young woman from the bed. I did my best to make sure her hospital gown retained her decency, the only kindness I could afford her.

Within seconds the seven pods were empty, and those of us who felt capable hoisted the people up and into a fireman carry position.

Coupled with the weight of the tactical gear, it was not comfortable. I didn't know about the others, but I was unsure how far I would make it under this new load. I gritted my teeth, dug deep, and started plodding towards the doorway.

A couple of the unencumbered jogged ahead to secure our exit, with the other free-handed people forming a rear guard.

'Frank?' I called, as we pushed on through. 'We're nearly at the door again. We'll need you to open it.'

Nothing.

'Frank! You still there?'

'We're kind of busy!' he roared back over the mic.

I turned towards the window facing into the security

office. There were several flashes like a strobe light. The sound was dull on our side, but there was a fight going on in the security office; we couldn't rely on their help for now.

'There!' I shouted, encouraging the others to follow me. Everyone had stopped, hearing the same commotion over the radio as I had. 'The glass, somebody break the glass.'

I rushed everyone towards the viewing windows where I had taken the pictures of the facility. The hallway looked empty, but it would put us on the wrong end of Frank's firefight. Or the right side perhaps, if we could get the drop on them.

One of the people at the front of the group raised the butt of their rifle and smashed it hard against the glass fixtures, but it hardly scuffed the surface.

'Get back!' he shouted, taking a few steps back from the window. He knelt down on one knee, lined up his shot, and let rip. Four quick, concise shots, one at each of the corners of the window.

It seemed the rifle had a multitude of firing options, as the projectiles were more precise than those that Aribert's group had accidentally fired at me on the catwalk. Whoever was behind the mask was familiar with the weaponry.

The window cracked and splintered. Only one hit with the butt of the rifle was needed to finish the job, as the glass bent in on one side and caved under the force. The laminated safety glass kept the whole pane from shattering or splintering too hard, and the others pulled it back far enough to create a large opening for everyone.

Looking back to the security window, it seemed the fight was still raging. Frank needed help, and fast.

I looked to the person closest to me. 'Here, take her.'

We swapped weapon for person.

'You guys, follow the pink markings on the ground back to the terminal. Secure our way out, and we'll be hot on your heels. You two come with me.'

I leapt through the now large opening in the window space. The two unencumbered party members followed suit. Once we were all through I lead them down the purple line towards "Central."

We could hear the commotion. Yelling, swearing, shots firing and ricocheting off metal walls.

'Get those gates back online now. We need backup!'

If they got their backup, we were screwed. I hoped the others would reach the gates before we got pinned on both sides.

We pulled up just around the corner from the action.

'We just have to push them back, make an opening for Frank and the others. There are too many for us to take on here, alright?'

We brought our weapons up, each humming, ready for action.

I poked my head around the corner. A group of about twenty people were positioned around the doorway, which was now barely functional and partly closed over. They were in a standoff with Frank and the others, but wouldn't be for long.

'Do these guns have rapid fire?'

One of the others showed me how to access the appropriate setting, and the weapon began pulsing from stock to barrel. They followed suit too, all weapons now harmoniously pulsing, almost in sync with my racing heartbeat.

'Perfect! How about we give them a little shock and awe?'

We spun around the corner.

The projectiles ripped through the air and into the hallway around the group of security personnel.

The noise was incredible as the projectiles tore into every surface. Walls, ceiling, floor, furniture, everything was fair game. It looked like we were going to tear the whole facility down with our hail of firepower.

It sounded like there was fifty of us, raining war down upon enemy troops.

The guards couldn't have reacted fast enough.

They fell back immediately, running to the safety of the next corridor around the bend.

The gunfire was perhaps a bit overzealous though. Several of their units dropped as stray shots ricocheted off the surfaces of the hallway. I could see them being dragged along the ground by their peers, small trails of blood behind them.

But no injury looked too serious at least.

Once the last of their group was safety behind the next turn in the corridor, I radioed to Frank.

'The hallway is clear. You need to get out of there now!'

A few stray shots came back our way from the security forces new cover.

'We need to keep them pinned down, keep firing near their location!'

I let a small burst of fire off in their direction, just enough to make them pull back into cover for the moment.

'Let me try this!' one of my faceless compatriots yelled. 'At full power this thing is insane! A bit slow, but screw it!'

The colouring of his rifle had shifted to green and was now pulsing furiously along the barrel.

He pulled the trigger. It took a second to power up, making three clunking sounds, but with an almighty kickback the rifle fired a fast-moving projectile that splashed onto the far wall of the corridor. The green flame from the impact was intense for a moment before it started burning into the wall.

'Fall back, fall back!' We could hear the echoing shouts of the security force.

It was an effective suppression technique. It probably terrified me as much as them.

Frank and the others appeared through the doorway, which he had now fully pried open. One of the trio was being carried, arms up over both of the other's shoulders, limping on a single functional leg.

'Go, now!' Frank called as they moved past us.

I fired a few more scattered rounds towards the end of the corridor before turning to follow suit.

Even with the incapacitated teammate we made quick work of navigating the hallways and burst in through the entrance to the gate terminal.

The rest of our group, complete with rescued abductees, were present, although it looked like the security guards had put up a fight. Three of our party members were being seen to, and there were splatters of blood around where they sat.

Frank nearly dumped his injured party member on the floor to be tended to—they were bleeding quite heavily by now—and ran to the gate controls.

Both security guards from earlier were still convulsing on the floor, a welcome sign that they had been neutralised using non-lethal force.

It had been a bit hairy, but we had actually managed to pull it off, and almost exactly to plan.

I wanted so bad to resist my urge, but I felt it needed to be pointed out to Aribert that the mostly non-violent routine had worked a charm.

'Aribert?' I asked to the group at large. 'Where are you, Aribert?'

Nobody raised a hand.

'Aribert, I know you're here, where are you?'

Again nothing.

I pulled my mask off. The closest team member to his height had their back turned, so I approached and moved around to pull off the mask. It was just one of his group. I didn't know his name.

I began counting the people in our group. "Two, four, six...sixteen."

We were all accounted for.

'What the hell, does anyone know where Aribert is?'

'He's not here.'

A random voice from the faceless crowd.

'What?'

'He's not here. Neither are Doug or Lenny.'

'What do you mean they're not here? Where the hell are they?'

'I don't know, he just told us to replace them and follow you, that you would be best to lead this mission. That they had a special mission of their own.'

The manipulative fucker. There were so many of us using the tactical gear that it was too easy to remain anonymous, and now he had slipped away to do God knows what.

'We're set!' Frank yelled out.

There wasn't enough time to think about Aribert's treachery.

We had to leave. We couldn't risk the lives of the people we had just saved.

But the growing dread in the back of my mind pulled at me.

What the hell was he up to now?

Chapter 28

Landing in the news station foyer, my blood was boiling.

We had no way to communicate, our AMIs still off the normal network services. But somehow, Aribert had slipped away. For all I knew, that would be the last I ever heard from him.

But I doubted it.

We were building to get our message to a world audience. There was no way he would keep himself in the shadows for such an occasion.

Our injured party members had to suck it up and feign fortitude as we entered the news station. They were patched up, but still walking wounded. A security force showing up in a time of crisis should have been a welcome sign.

And it probably would have been, if it wasn't for the media displays around the foyer, all of which clearly showed a large group of people sabotaging the gate system wearing the exact outfits we did.

We were being labelled in bold red font as "Known Terrorists."

And here we were, arriving en masse, with a few clearly unconscious bodies slumped over our shoulders.

Luckily because of the interruption and moderate suspension of the international gate system, the foyer was mostly empty. The few people that were there, fled. It wouldn't be long before we were reported.

It didn't matter. We were there to report ourselves anyway.

I pulled my mask off again. No need for it anymore.

'Leon!'

The voice came from the far side of the orange-tinted foyer.

'Over here.' We looked over to see Styx and one other waving us over to a staff access doorway, behind the ID turnstiles and now vacant welcoming desk.

We shared the load of the rescued commuters as best we could as we moved, but the injured few could hardly hold themselves up, let alone help. The security alarms didn't even acknowledge us as we passed through. The composite material of the weapons and armour was top class, it wouldn't set off any security features.

'How are we set?' I asked, gently setting my still motionless patient on the floor.

'Fine, for now. I think they've been broadcasting nonstop since the gate issues began; I doubt they know anything going on in the building. Security are tied up down below. These suits really made them drop their guard.' She couldn't take her eyes off of the limp body by my side, propped up against the wall. 'Eh, what's up with the talent?'

'They're all out cold. We'll need to wake them up, but if what the nutty professor in their lab said they mightn't be doing too well either. He said something like they couldn't maintain normal-thermia? Normo-thermal?'

I should have gotten him to write it down.

'Normothermia?'

'Sure, that sounds about right. Whatever they were doing to these people seems to have messed that up.'

Styx pushed me aside and put her hand on the young girl's forehead.

'Shit, she feels a bit cold. We need to warm them all up. They could become hypothermic if we don't take care of them. Quick, move them all back into the employee lounge area and crank up the heating. Find whatever blankets or clothes or towels you can get your hands on.'

I moved to pick my passenger up, but Styx pulled me back.

'Not you.'

'Why not?'

'You're wanted upstairs. Follow me.'

I stood, bewildered, and followed her through a nearby door and up the steps to a long straight hall-way. I hadn't so much as seen a carpeted floor in years. Even my parents had ditched the carpeted floors when we were young. But there it was, as odorous and outlandishly tacky as I remembered. It was like we had stepped into the hallways of yestercentury.

Styx opened the third door to the left, ushering me in.

Sat there, with a flurry of people working on her hair it appeared, was Dr Sterne.

She peeked up over the rim of her glasses. 'Hello, Leon, lovely to see you.'

She was so brilliantly polite, as always. But she didn't look healthy, despite the makeup the others were applying for the upcoming air time. She had to look herself, powerful but kind, and more importantly, completely in control of her faculties.

'May we have a minute?' she asked of her make-over squad.

They all left, still holding onto their cosmetics.

'No, you stay too,' she called to Styx. 'I want to talk to you both.'

We pulled up seats in front of her. I couldn't help but smirk. It was comforting to see her again.

'Sam told me everything,' she began. 'You have both performed admirably in these trying times. I couldn't be prouder. Everything that has transpired, everything you all have accomplished? It is nothing less than astounding. I just wish I could have been there with you, and I apologise for my absence. I started this, I involved you all, and I am eternally regretful that you had to do so much alone.'

It was not a direction I had expected the conversation to go. Dr Sterne had no reason to apologise, yet she was acting like she had just run over our pet cat. But a stray tear showed just how heartfelt the sentiment was.

We were both just stunned into silence, possibly more bemused than anything else.

'We have just one last push, and I hope I can, in turn, make you all proud too. I failed so many of you, but I'm here now.'

I felt I understood her apology. She wasn't sorry to us, not really. We were her proxies. Proxies for the others who didn't make it this far, the ones she couldn't beg forgiveness from.

The burden of a leader.

We each instinctively bowed our heads.

But something was off.

I had focussed on her right hand. It was clutching a white cloth and was trembling slightly. The pale fabric was stained with brown blotches.

'Are you okay?' I asked.

She simply smiled. 'Don't you worry dear, I'm fine. We have bigger problems. Where is Aribert?' she asked, an unfamiliar rasp to her voice as she said the name. 'I heard what that animal did to you, and to that defenceless security agent. He has become even more unhinged than before, and I fear we may be partly to blame.'

'What do you mean partly to blame?' Styx landed the question I was thinking.

Dr Sterne sighed heavily.

'He was always troubled as I told you before. But

what I didn't tell you, was that the brother he lost was his twin, Aidan. He went missing just before their 21st birthday. A hiccup. Devastated, of course, he threw himself into researching the slipway. He was maybe one of the most brilliant physicists I had ever met. His theories on slipways alone, his tie-ins with string theory and conservation of mass principals, it was fascinating to see.

'But he was always cruel. To interns, research assistants, post-doctoral researchers, it didn't matter. Nobody could keep up with him. He debunked almost every reason ever given for a hiccup to occur. And the further down the rabbit hole he went, the more his ideas turned to conspiracy theories. He knew before anyone else what was happening, but nobody believed him. I didn't believe him. Not really. Not until he sent me that corrupted document, lending more reality to his delusions.'

I had never even thought to ask where they had gotten the information originally, the origins of our doubts about BioDev. Just an excerpt of a memo about our Mr Ghost that lead to our group's founding.

My gut wrenched a little. 'And we sent him the real document.'

'Unfortunately, yes. He believed it to be true already, but in confirming his beliefs, he has clearly taken on a new, much crueller roll in all this.'

'Shit,' said Styx.

Dr Sterne continued, 'To him, we had just validated

everything he had done, no matter how terrible. And freed him to become even more callus.'

She looked to me as she talked, reaching out her free hand and placing it on mine. I stared at her for a moment. Her eyes looked apologetic, maybe even more so than before.

'Meribel, we really have to finish.'

A head poked around the doorway.

Dr Sterne didn't remove her hand for a few moments. 'I'm sorry, Leon. We'll have to continue this another time.' It was strange, but the way she phrased it, it was like both sentences weren't related. Like the apology was for something different, and directed at me.

Styx and I rose as the entourage re-entered the room.

Just as we reached the door, Dr Sterne called out, 'Don't trust that man, Leon. He would set the world ablaze to prove himself inflammable.'

She didn't need to warn me.

We headed back downstairs.

'She's sick you know.' Styx mumbled.

'I guessed as much.'

'Adult T-cell leukemia-lymphoma. It's aggressive, and quite rare. She's forgoing her treatment to be here. Sam and the others had a hell of a time getting her out of the ICU with half the staff trying to intervene. Luckily hospitals tend to have gates pretty much everywhere, emergencies and all that, you know.'

'Will she be okay?'

'Hard to know. She won't show it, but she's frail right now. A few hours away from her treatment won't kill her, but the stress on her body isn't going to help.'

'We'll just have to make it worth it then.'

We landed downstairs and moved to the lounge where I'd hoped the rescued commuters were recovering. They were still unconscious.

'Where's Frank?' I asked of the few who tended to our comatose guests and walking wounded teammates.

'He went upstairs. Sam wanted him to help with the control room.'

No wonder they needed Dr Sterne ready. This was it. Take the control room first, so that the broadcast won't be cut. Then invade the newsroom itself, the occupants of which should be unaware of our presence.

'Oh shit.' The radio on my headset crackled. 'We have a problem here.'

'Where?' I didn't even recognise the voice.

'Main foyer, now. We have company, and lots of it.'

I knew it wouldn't be long before one of those fleeing civilians alerted the police.

'Styx, you need to wake these people up or drag them up that stairs, one way or another they're going on that broadcast. You, you, and you,' I pointed at anyone who looked capable, 'you're coming with me.'

We all sprinted back towards the main foyer. We hadn't reached it before we saw the typical blue and red flashing lights of the law. They weren't from any automobile; there wouldn't be many of them available to local law enforcement. And the sound coming from outside was unmistakable.

A helicopter.

You knew you were in trouble if they deployed a helicopter. They were only used by armies and the more serious emergency response agencies. Except for the fact that I had attended a bunch of air shows as a kid, I don't think I would have even recognised the sound.

They would never have come through the slipway gates in the foyer. It would be like shooting fish in a barrel. They likely deployed to every building in the nearby area and converged on our position.

Arriving at the foyer, we ducked down behind the closest cover we could find. Several others were there already, clearly tasked with watching our backs. I was thankful at that moment that Aribert had somewhat militarised his group. I don't think many of what was left of ours would have held their nerve in the situation.

Lights flooded the entranceway, beams coming in from every side of the large glassy front of the building.

'Shit, can anyone see how many there are out there?' I asked, squinting as I popped my head above the countertop.

'There must have been about forty before the lights came on,' one of the others shouted. 'Probably more now. I think I heard something rumbling up to the front of the building.'

'We just need to keep them out. We don't have to go looking for a fight,' I called out to my fellow defenders. Not only did we not want a fight, but there was also no way we would survive one. 'Styx, you hearing this? Are there any other gates in the building? Can they get in another way?'

'No,' she said over the radio. 'We shut them all down. Last stand, like you said.'

So outside of any secret underground sewer passages, or just an actual back door, we were right where we needed to be.

'Any bright ideas, boss?'

I was almost certain it was sarcasm, but I went with it.

Shock and awe would mean little to those outside. There weren't that many of us, and even our advanced weaponry would be nothing compared to the firepower they could pull down on us.

'We need to show them we're here, let them know we have the area covered.' I scanned the space closest the doorways. There was nothing save for the two gates.

They would do.

'Take out the gates. Use the rifles' secondary mode, those burning green incendiary rounds. We don't need them now anyway, and I'm pretty sure they'll make for a distracting light show.'

Everyone raised their rifles. In sequence, they changed to secondary fire mode, altering the colour of the lighting along the length of the barrel. It was something I had forgotten to ask how to do. The familiar green pulsed furiously while they aimed.

'Now,' I yelled.

The air around us tore as the molten projectiles burst out of the rifles, clearing the foyer in an instant and drenching the central gate in their bright emerald blaze. It was a frightening display. But some of the projectiles missed. One glanced the second gate, and another crashed into a piece of wall beside the largest pane of glass looking out to our assailants. The last, however, tore right through the main glass doorway, nowhere near the gate, and onto something just out of view.

There was no way it was an accident.

The gate doubled over on itself. Firework sprays of sparks shot across the floor towards the doorways, and the stench of burning hit us almost immediately. There was no way their attention wasn't gasped firmly, for better or worse.

'Who the fuck did that?' I began.

The foyer burst into a quick flash of orange, then white.

There she was.

Every one of the many displays in the foyer had the same picture. It was Dr Sterne, looking as calm and regal as every other time she appeared to the public, her illness well masked.

I couldn't believe my eyes. It was happening.

For better or worse, we had nearly done it.

The shrill shattering of glass brought us all back

into the present, as almost every window pane exploded inwards, carrying a multitude of metal canisters that bounced across the floor towards us.

Blue gas began spewing from them as they spun, drenching the air in an opaque nightmare.

'Back!' I screamed, struggling to put my helmet back on. 'Back now!'

The helmet provided some filtration, but I had already taken a full breath of the gas, and my throat felt like it was on fire.

'Back, back now!' I continued to shout, unsure if everyone had cleared the area. But visibility was almost completely gone, and further smashing glass signalled the assault was underway.

I turned tail and sprinted, nearly choking as I ran, back to the lounge. All of the others we had left behind were gone, and it seemed most if not all of my team had arrived uninjured. I hadn't time for a head count.

'They have to come down this hallway to get to the stairway behind us, right? Is that the only way up?'

'Not a fucking clue!' one of the others screamed.

Sounded about right. None of us knew the building well enough, and I didn't know what type of building would have a single central staircase to the next floor. There would be an emergency path of some kind, no doubt.

Their attention needed to be kept there.

'Who has non-lethals?'

'Are you fucking kidding me with this shit again?'

a man shouted, pulling off his helmet. I recognised the prick almost immediately, no doubt the same one who had fired out at the armed responders.

Doug or Lenny, it didn't matter which one it was.

'What the hell are you doing? Why did you do that?!'

'You wanted to show them we meant business. So, I showed them.'

The arrogant idiot. He had forced their hand. We could have maintained the stand-off for long enough for the entire message to go out.

He had clearly been all too eager to drink Aribert's kool-aid.

'Where is he?' I asked, grabbing him by the chest plate.

He smirked. 'Don't worry, he's around. Him and your fuckin' BioDev buddies.'

He crashed the butt of his gun into my stomach; I reeled back. Most of the blow was taken by the armour, but it still winded me for a moment.

I stood to retaliate, trying to pull up my sidearm, but it was too late.

He stood out now, away from the others, rifle pointed at me.

'You think we didn't know about your acquaintances over at BioDev? The fucking companions you keep? You're just as bad as them.' He cocked the rifle. 'We don't need you.'

'What the hell is wrong with you? What are you doing?'

'Me? Fuck you, Leon. Aribert was right about you, you're just a sympathiser. You're weak. He was right about the people being abducted, he was right about WormWhole and BioDev, he was right about everything all along! It wasn't until you guys gave up that document that we could truly see just how right he was about everything. And he's right that we need to be rid of you too.'

The weapon began to pulse an angry red.

The smirk returned to his face.

A moment savoured for just too long.

Like a wrecking ball, Styx tore in from behind and tackled him, straight into me.

The three of us tumbled over the couches behind me, twisting and turning in our grapple. His weapon misfired, shredding the vending machine behind where I stood.

Styx wrapped an arm around his throat from behind. 'Sleep time, fucker!'

But he was well armoured. The tackle had done no real damage, and he sprang back into action immediately.

With a tenderising blow from his elbow, he connected hard with Styx's ribs.

But she wouldn't relent. Styx was made of sturdier stuff than nearly everyone.

Again, he elbowed her hard.

And again. I rose to my feet.

His helmet now off, I swung at him, knuckles crunching under the rigidity of his cheekbone.

But with another thundering blow to the ribs, Styx finally crumbled to the floor.

I raised my sidearm and fired.

The projectile smashed on the armour, spewing out the pale grey goo as it harmlessly fell to the floor.

His fist collided with my mask.

Then again, in quick succession.

It nearly knocked the mask from my face.

Disorientated, I swung backhanded, using the frame of my sidearm as a weapon instead of my now throbbing fist.

I caught the right side of his face once more; the hard metal casing drew blood as it split his cheek open. He spun away to protect from a second blow, hunched down onto one knee.

Styx, resilient as a honey badger and now back on her feet, followed up my assault. Holding his dropped rifle by the barrel, like a golf club, she swung.

The blow shattered his jaw.

The crunching sound was nauseating.

He fell to the floor in an ungraceful heap, bloodied and beaten.

'Prick,' she wheezed, holding her side and dropping the newly bloodied weapon.

His little rant had proven to me how far some of Aribert's group were willing to go, and just how deeply radicalised that few had become by now. They really couldn't see any other option than violence now.

Panting, but victorious, I removed my mask, throwing it down on top of him.

But he wasn't the only of Aribert's group here; I looked to the well-armed contingency still kneeling in cover.

Unsure of what to do, possibly too terrified by the incoming horde of emergency response units, the others simply stared.

'What do we do now?' one of the braver of the group asked.

I was firmly in charge now, as they all looked to me for direction.

'Ignore that fool,' I announced. I kicked his rifle away from where Styx had dropped it in case he somehow regained consciousness. 'You fire every non-lethal round you have down that hallway, in short bursts. Don't use lethal rounds. You hurt or kill one of their officers, and they will roll in on you without remorse. Just keep them out as long as you can and keep your heads down. The second you run out of ammunition...you surrender.'

They all seemed onboard immediately, probably wanting to surrender already.

But they would hold, at least for now.

I nodded to Styx, and we left our rear guard to hold the line.

There was only one place I knew Aribert would go. Whatever psychotic plan he had would need an audience.

And we had helped set up the largest audience he could have hoped for.

Chapter 29

With Styx by my side, we charged forth.

Rapidly navigating through the news station, the sounds of weapon fire slowly diminishing behind us, she led me right to the control room.

The room had an all-glass front, with monitors showing every angle of the ongoing broadcast.

Everyone was still inside, all eyes on the central scene that showed Dr Sterne and a young woman talking.

I recognised her. It was the woman I had lifted from the Pod. Now able to stand on her own, and engaging with Dr Sterne, she looked bewildered and sickly. A thick blanket hung around her shoulders, but she was still shivering.

It must have been quite jarring. She entered a gateway, only to pop out in what seemed like a hospital room. Allowing the "physician" to calm her into a false state of security, she would likely have never seen the light of day again had we not intervened. Instead, she had awoken to a dangerous scenario, under-siege and under-informed, trying to help convey a message to the world. A message she knew very little about.

The fact she wasn't in tears was impressive. I almost felt like crying just seeing her there.

'Come on. We have to let the others know what's going on.' Styx moved in to open the glass doorway.

The hallway was dark, so we were likely unnoticed by now. But the newsroom was dark too, save for something in the far corner.

I pulled Styx back.

'What're you doing, Leon?' she barked back at me.

'Shhhh, keep back.' I peered into the large room again, just to make sure. 'There, you see that?'

I pointed towards the corner. Screens flickered on and off in the room, and live monitors gave off random splatterings of light. But a single colour had drawn my attention.

A slow pulsating pink light ran horizontally against the black backdrop of the far wall.

It was one of the rifles. And it was raised, pointed towards the centre of the control room. Each time the pulse came from the base of the firearm, the face above it lit up.

It was Aribert's other henchman.

We took a few steps back, slowly, crouching down to ensure we couldn't easily be seen in the dim visibility of the corridor.

'Fuck, what's he doing?' Styx asked.

'I don't know, but look there.' I pointed out another person of interest. Everyone else was sat back in their seats, away from the controls, but immersed in the scenes unfolding on the screen. All except for Sam.

Sam was standing, looking straight at the man with the raised rifle.

I cursed at myself.

I had nothing but the electrifying sidearm, and its projectiles could never pierce the thick glass of the control room. Even worse, as I had recently found out, they would do nothing if I hit the armoured tactical gear.

We were completely incapable of helping.

But as infuriating as that was, and as worried as I was for Sam and the others' safety, immediate action wasn't required.

'If they wanted to cut Sterne off they would have by now,' Styx said. 'Maybe he's making sure we don't cut the signal?'

If Aribert were to appear on the monitors, I was certain Sam would have cut the feed.

Styx was right. He was just playing at guard duty, and the people in the room were likely safe until the broadcast was completed.

Aribert must have been close by, ready to enact his plan.

Muffled, distant, and unclear, someone howled.

It was a roar of pain, echoing through the corridors.

Styx and I rose, not missing a beat, and tore off in the direction of the sound. Someone was hurt, badly, and nearby.

Blasting through one last set of double doors, we found the epicentre of the commotion.

Upright, head down and back against the wall, was Frank.

The stench in the air was both familiar and terrifying.

'Frank!' Styx tried to pull him towards her to see what was wrong. He held his arm so tightly in at his front that we couldn't see the damage.

He howled again.

Small bits of oozing black dripped away from his front and onto the ground, where there was already a trail of similar stains.

'Frank, let me see!' Styx pulled at his arm again, assuming him to be hiding the true injury from us. Maybe he was just applying pressure, to ease the pain or stop the bleeding.

But he hadn't hidden anything.

He released the pressure ever so slightly, only for Styx to realise she couldn't help.

There was nothing to help.

From just below his right elbow, there was nothing.

The wound was still burning; black mixtures of cloth and flesh dripped to the floor.

Frank vomited, nearly collapsing as he looked straight at the injury.

'Holy shit!' Styx exclaimed, trying to catch him, and looking to me. 'What do we do?!'

I was struggling to hold back the vomit myself. The vile aroma of the melting flesh was so pungent.

The wound was still burning and threatened to take even more of his arm as it ate into his tissue.

Frank was beginning to wane.

'Leon!' Styx was beyond panicked, most of her energy poured into not dropping Frank on the floor.

'Right, shit, right. He's burnt, burning, whatever. What do you do for a burn?' I racked my brain for a moment. I had burnt myself plenty throughout the years, what did I typically do? 'Cold water! We need to stick it under cold water!'

It seemed the best option. Whatever the composition of the projectile, the incendiary component ate through material for quite a while after its initial impact.

The wound was being cauterised and attacked all at once. We had to put it out.

I helped to pick Frank up, and we followed the closest signs to a toilet.

Kicking in the door, we almost threw him into the sink.

He was out cold by now.

We gushed the water over the still smouldering stump.

I tore the belt from my trousers, wrapping it tightly around his bicep.

Slowly, the water began to work, washing away all traces of the corrosive substance. The impromptu tourniquet seemed to do the job too, as the bleeding dropped to a trickle.

'Fuck, what do we do with him now?' I asked.

'You don't do anything,' Styx snapped, not looking away from the wound. 'You need to get out there and stop that fucking lunatic.'

She was right. There was no doubt who had done this.

Which meant he was likely in the studio now.

Everyone was in danger with him there. He had clearly become too unhinged to be allowed roam free any longer.

I cocked both sidearms, making sure they were powered up and ready for action.

I rushed off down the hallway to where we had found Frank. The smell of sterile burning still hung in the air, but I followed the black stains on the floor.

I arrived in a wide hallway, likely the point of the altercation, given the large burn mark on the furthest wall.

The largest doorway had a light above the door, "On Air" projected across it.

I didn't take the time to plot or plan, or peer through the small viewing window. I had worked up such a flurry of rage that I simply burst through the doorway, making a beeline towards the cameras and lights.

The small crowd around the filming area shrieked as I burst through.

The only one not to flinch, standing with his arms raised to the cameras, was my target.

The crowd—a combination of some of our collective group, actual news staff, and a few extras still draped in large blankets and hospital gowns—parted on my rapid approach.

I raised my weapons, their lighting pulsing to life along the barrels, ready to take him down before he had a chance to try and talk his way out of anything.

I stood out, ready and eager to finish things.

And in what could have been a moment of victory, I faltered.

He hadn't looked at me or reacted to my arrival. He didn't have to.

On her knees, eyes red and teary, and staring directly at me, was Jessica.

But not just her. Dr Ross was also by her side and on his knees, bloodied and barely able to look up at my arrival.

'You animal!' I shouted, aiming both weapons at Aribert.

'No! Leon please!'

The words split me from my rage. The familiar voice as always brought a slight flutter to my chest. But it was drenched in terror now, shrill and shaky.

I looked to her as she pleaded, tears now streaming even more heavily down her cheek. 'Please stop, please.'

'Yes, Leon, please don't interrupt.' Aribert, as calm as ever, waved a small remote. 'Nobody likes to skip straight to the finale.'

I paused. Something was off. Everyone was frozen to the spot, and all looked frightened.

But none as frightened as Jessica.

I took a step closer, keeping my weapons trained on Aribert.

Under Jess's coat was a dark, heavy chest plate. Bulky and with wires dangling, it wasn't until the first flash of an LED that it became obvious.

She had a bomb strapped to her.

It was that day all over again. Flashbacks of Worm-Whole flooded my memories. He had turned her into an unwilling weapon.

Every muscle and sinew in my body tried to react the same. To pull back, step away, put ground between myself and the explosive.

But I did the opposite. I moved towards Jess, kneeled, and put my hand on her shoulder.

I couldn't have stepped back. The slightest hesitation, or show of fear, would have led her to believe the situation was irreversibly dire. It was a movement made to encourage hope.

'It'll be okay,' I whispered to her. 'Promise.'

I had no reason to believe it was true. I hoped she didn't feel the tremor in my hand before I removed it, turning to face Aribert.

'You have had your eyes opened, to the vile corruption at the heart of our civilised society, to the injustices made in the name of progress.' I had missed the beginning of his broadcast, but Aribert was in full preacher mode. 'And here before you, I have the man responsible for this most heinous program. A program that could only have been imagined by a sick mind. He has operated in the shadows for decades, feigning progress through the sheer brilliance of technology. But you all now see, thanks to my work, that it was all a ruse. A placebo to quell the masses into a blind state of acceptance. There is no magic computer, no programmable saviour. There is only the mutilation and torture of the innocent. You are all but kindling to them. Kindling to fuel the fire of their demonic experiments.'

He seemed singularly focussed on Dr Ross. Jess was likely just in the wrong place at the wrong time, but Aribert wouldn't be one to miss an opportunity to inflict maximum misery.

'Now,' he continued. 'In case any of you on the out- side are currently planning to raid this office, I would beg patience. We wouldn't want things to escalate too quickly.'

I could see the camera feed on the monitors in the back. The bomb on Jessica was clearly visible. There was no way they would risk breaching the studio. For all I knew, the group downstairs had been captured, and we were already surrounded.

'And we have a special guest with us today. My dear friend and brother in arms, Leon.'

The feed switched to me, weapons raised, and now that I could see it, face heavily bruised.

'Fuck you!' I spat the words out, although it felt strange to be knowingly cursing on the air live. I hoped my mother would forgive me.

'As feisty as ever, I see.' He began to laugh, turning towards me, placing the trigger in his breast pocket.

'But I have you to thank for this. That little AMI of yours had some very interesting destinations programmed in. You made it easy to visit your friends here. It's a pity your little love interest tried to protect him, she could have just been a good girl and stayed put. But isn't this much better? The big reunion? It warms the heart that I could bring you together this one last time.'

Nobody else was playing negotiator, so the responsibility had fallen to me.

'What do you want, Aribert? Everyone knows what's going on now, the whole world knows. You don't have to do any of this.'

'Oh? How very naive, even for you Leon. Do you think they will really stop? Do you really believe those at the top don't already know exactly what's going on in BioDev? No. There's only one sure-fire way to ensure the system comes crumbling down. And that is for me to tear it down.'

Aribert raised the rifle and pointed it at Dr Ross's head.

Jess roared in terror, trying to move in and protect her father, but he did his best to push her away.

'Back the fuck off!' Aribert screamed at her.

And there it was again. The same chink in his armour as before.

He wasn't as calm and collected as he pretended, his anger always pushing him to the point of losing what little control he had.

I had to draw his attention away from the two.

Goading him was easy before, but he knew he had an audience now, and couldn't back down on his mission. Nothing could convince him to back down at this stage. If I fired on him, he would still be able to pull the trigger. I had nothing to trade, nothing to bargain with. He was holding all the cards.

All I had was his disdain.

'You've done it Aribert.' I spoke as dismissively as I could. 'You've finally validated all your crazy conspiracies. So what?'

'So what? So what? So now I finish this. I don't expect you to understand; I'm doing this for everyone. I will save this world, and there's nothing you or your flock can do to stop me.'

'It's just a pity, is all. All this effort, all the sacrifices. But it doesn't matter really, does it?' I tensed, bracing myself. 'You still failed Aidan. He's still dead, isn't he?'

For the first time, Aribert's unblinking eyes showed the smallest bit of emotion. Momentary sorrow at the mention of his brother's name, followed by a flash of rage.

The outcome was as expected.

I now stood looking down the barrel of the huge rifle. The crowd gasped.

'How dare you say his name!' he roared, the rifle shaking in his hands. 'How fucking dare you! You know nothing about him. You don't get to say his name!'

I found myself almost expecting backup in that

instance. Sam, Styx, Frank, someone. They had been there when I needed them so many times before.

But they were all held up with their own problems.

It was just an unhinged psychopath and me. Easy.

'What would Aidan think of you now? Big man with a big gun, scaring all these innocent people.' I pointed at the onlookers, trying to hide the nervous tremble in my hands.

'I told you not to say his name!' The gun shook again. 'And how dare you, you of all people look down on me! Brother killer!'

I didn't even want to know how he knew about that story. He could have beaten it out of Dr Ross, interrogated him for everything he knew. It didn't matter. It was an unexpected blow.

But despite the accusation, and the knot in my stomach, I wasn't prepared for what came next.

He calmed down almost immediately. The gun stopped shaking, and he started to grin.

'Oh, actually, that's not completely true.' He pushed the gun against my head as he leant in a little closer, trying to hide his words from the cameras. 'You may have me to thank for that. I'm surprised you don't recognise Jessica's new custom chest piece. I made it myself. In fact, I've made a few in recent times. And it turned out I have you to thank for my delivery men reaching the very heart of the enemy operations. You see, Leon, what did I tell you? We work well together.'

I turned my eyes, looking back at Jess as best I could. The bulky uncomfortable vest, the explosive.

And it all made sense.

He had started this. All of this.

The day of the attack. Every building damaged was BioDev.

The fake WormWhole clothing Styx was wearing, supplied by Aribert's men, just like the ones the men wore that day.

Why Scaife had referred to him as a "fucking ter-rorist" when I mentioned him, and why she seemed genuinely concerned at the thought he was coming for her.

He had started this. All of this.

He killed Dan.

'I can see the cogs moving,' he joked. 'Too little, too late.'

He engaged the rifle's secondary fire mode, crank-ing the power up to maximum capacity. The barrel lit up bright green.

'This is where we part ways.'

He pulled the trigger.

But his ego had cost him.

He believed so truly that he had the upper hand, that his position was invincible. He was trying to make a spectacle of my execution, one final violent act before his terrible revenge on BioDev.

He had clearly never seen the weapon used on full power.

Or known about the delay.

On the first clunk, I grabbed the barrel.

On the second, I pushed it up and away towards the far ceiling.

On the third, I brought my firearm up to his neck, the only exposed bit of skin outside his face.

Both weapons fired in unison.

The rifle let tear an almighty projectile, exploding on the ceiling, raining green fire down close to where many of the others stood. They all leapt away from the corrosive raindrops as they fell.

My projectile buried into his neck. The skin bulged out as the foam expanded quickly around his throat.

The spasms were almost immediate as he convulsed and spat uncontrollably.

He dropped the weapon, desperately clawing instead at his breast pocket.

But he was too far gone.

I relieved him of the trigger mechanism as he fought to maintain consciousness.

Drooling, retching, and struggling to breathe, he faltered, falling to one knee.

But true to form he never blinked, eyes locked onto mine for the last few moments of his free life.

The news feed to the outside world must have been almost instantaneous, as once I had taken the triggering device from his pocket, every doorway and several ceiling compartments burst in and the studio flooded with emergency responders.

I handed the trigger to Jess, still bawling and holding her bloodied father.

Kneeling, I placed my hands behind my head. I had

come this far without getting shot, and I wanted that to continue.

We had done our best. There were no plans left now.

I hoped they would see what we did was right.

Chapter 30

It was two months since the news station.

Two months of questions and interrogations. Two months of picking and questioning every decision I had made in the lead up to our broadcast. Where we were, what we did, who we did it with, over and over and over again.

I didn't feel I needed to hold back any truths. I didn't feel like I had done anything particularly wrong. The whole point of what we did was because we felt we were in the right. But they made some good points during the bouts of information gathering. I suppose, technically, I had broken a few laws.

The occasional break-in? Maybe.

Trespassing? Kind of goes with the first one.

Assault? It wasn't like I tried to hurt anyone.

Abduction? Well, yes, they had me there. But in my defence, BioDev started it.

On occasion, they would be nice enough to feed me some information too. Most of our bunker group had survived our forced exodus from Achterhuis. The people who never showed at the rendezvous point had been picked up while on the run by police agencies across the continent.

Lucy had been hurt badly when they were captured, but it was thanks to her knowing someone in the BioDev security team that allowed for them to surrender, despite the kill order. She had already made a full recovery apparently; the woman was a machine.

Dr Sterne was back in hospital too, and responding well to treatment, but was still touch and go. From what my parents had told me on their visit, she was being hailed the world over as a sort of hero of the people.

My face time with the studio cameras had very much worked in my favour too. Although not the intention, it looked a lot like I saved an entire news station from another terrorist attack. So, I had garnered support from the public.

We all had, considering the importance of the broadcast.

Even more, we had gained unusual favour from some divisions within BioDev themselves. Namely, the security forces. I had been right not to trust Aribert when we left his facility. He had rigged the building to blow a few minutes after we had left. When rescue crews finally arrived to find the missing tactical teams, they found the building had been raised. But luckily, also waiting for them was a slightly underdressed assortment of weary combatants.

Knowing his unrestricted animosity, I had sent Styx away on a secret task of sorts. She was to find and untie the woman whom I had saved from execution when I first arrived at the facility.

It was a dangerous gamble. Nothing was stopping them from trying to overthrow us again. But thankfully they had listened to Styx, and without control of the outer gate, they simply untied each other once we left and escaped the facility with time to spare.

I hoped word had made it to whatever hole Aribert was being kept in that I had thwarted yet another of his plans.

He had not made a full recovery from my attack. Vocal cords damaged beyond repair, I was told. No more preaching for that psychopath. I couldn't have been more pleased about it.

But still, we were incarcerated. I hadn't seen the others and was only allowed few family visits.

They said it was for our own protection.

I didn't believe a word of it. They wanted to keep us to themselves until the trial. Which had already begun.

An intercontinental Supreme Court had been specially convened, considering the magnitude of the offence and the contingency of BioDev sites around the world. It turned out that Aribert wasn't wrong; it did go higher than just BioDev. High-ranking government officials were on the chopping block too. It had been a well-kept secret the world over since its inception. And that's where a lot of the trouble with the trial was coming from.

Unwilling and inhumane human experimentation

had long been established as a no-no in medical science. Dating back as far as something called the Nuremberg Code, things had been pretty straightforward on the subject.

But this had created and ethical black hole.

Results gained from illegal human experiment were "not to be used in general medicine and should be destroyed" was how they explained it to me. But BioDev's innovative treatments and medicines were based on the experiments. They were so widespread and frequently used by everyone the world over, that it was being argued that it would set humanity as a whole back hugely to stop using the medicines and treatments. It was put forth that we could land back in the situation that preceded the inception of the experiments, with human kind on the cusp of a pandemic of biblical proportions.

But by continuing to use them, it was argued that it would encourage copycat experimentation around the world. Especially in poorer regions where people going missing might be less reported, making those areas even more dangerous.

Did it mean that the people all died for nothing if we did away with all of the medicines they were "used" to create? Or did it only justify their abduction and murder at the hands of the researchers if the world continued to use the treatments?

There was no easy answer, and my mind had been melting ever since the dilemma was brought to the forefront of the trial. Never once had I sat down and considered the ethical implications of all of it. Back and forth I flopped on the issue, all alone in my cell, trying to see both sides. I knew how I felt about it. I was steadfast on that. I think my actions up until that point made my opinions perfectly clear to others too. But I was just one person. I couldn't possibly make a decision that affected the whole world to such a degree.

That's what the trial was for. The decisions had thankfully been taken far away from me or any of the others.

And everyone I met seemed to have an opinion.

I wasn't sure that everyone from our group in the bunker would even have agreed on what was the right side of the fence. Would Sam and I butt heads on it? Would Frank see reason? What would Dr Sterne think, knowing her technology had played such a key role? Would Styx kick my ass if we couldn't find common ground?

And, in one of the more interesting turns in the trial, I was informed I was to be a crucial witness.

I had no idea why. I had no expert opinion on the matters, no insight they were unaware of. I had even volunteered to stand in defence of Dr Ross at his trial. Not for some foolish attachment to Jessica—I didn't know how I felt about her anymore, it wasn't very black and white—but because it was the right thing to do.

He was reviled the world over as the face of this terrible act. But what Jess had said was true. His advancements in the double-blind AOE system had apparently saved thousands of people from losing their lives to the experiments. He had stayed to do the only good he could from within the system, a fact that I don't think anyone would easily grasp. He did what he thought was the best for everyone. He may have been wrong, he could have taken a hundred different routes that may have turned out better, but we'll never know.

Breaking me from my thoughts, the cell door swung open, several people standing to attention outside.

I guessed I would find out soon enough what the judges and jury were thinking about it all.

I stood and moved out, ready to be escorted.

It appeared the whole detention wing was reserved just for me. How nice of them.

I shuffled on, hardly able to move the guards were so closely stacked around me. But it didn't take long to reach the doorway to the court, and they ushered me towards the bench closest the door.

Sitting there, smile on her face, and drawing a similar reaction from my own, was Sam.

I threw myself down right beside her. Our hands were still cuffed, no hug was possible, so an awkward little shoulder to shoulder bump had to do.

'You alright?' she asked. 'Made yourself a boyfriend yet?'

'Yeah actually, my roomie Bill. He looks kind of like you, bit more feminine obviously...'

We shared a laugh, short and sweet.

'What you think is going on in there?' I asked.

'Same thing that's been happening the last few weeks I imagine. Bunch of old farts talking nonsense about a problem they hardly understand.'

'Yeah...'

'We'll be alright,' she followed up. 'They won't be able to hold us much longer. They've got nothing concrete on any of us. Well, apart from you, really. You're pretty fucked. "The face of the revolution" if I recall.'

She roared laughing at my discomfort with the phrase.

'Yeah yeah, laugh it up, Chuckles.' I waited until she had quieted down to continue. 'I just want out of here. I miss just being a bit...free, you know. Miss my parents, my apartment.'

'The bunker?'

'Not even a little.' I smiled at her. 'Miss you a bit too, which is proof that I have been too long on the inside. Next stop, looney bin.'

She smiled. But not a grin, more a smile of appreciation. Like she missed me too.

But people were close by, and she had clearly been working on her hardy reputation.

'Gone a bit soft have we now Leon? I hate when the boys get clingy. Ugh, so unattractive.'

I had missed her banter somewhat, something I didn't think possible. As abrasive as she was at times, she was militantly loyal, and as brave as anyone I had ever met. I had even seen a sweeter side to her. She was an impressive person, and I was lucky to have her as a friend.

'Have you heard from Frank at all?'

She chuckled. 'Far too much! These near-death moments really bring out the romantic side in him. Now he's all full of notions about us, but we'll see. And he has a pretty cool new cybernetic arm too. It's not even a BioDev model so, viva la revolution, right?'

We both shared one last laugh.

'It's time, Samantha.' The booming voice of one of the police officers brought just a hint of anxiety. I would be next up.

They approached to help her up, but in one quick movement she kissed me on the cheek, and hoisted herself up from the bench, making sure to keep her back turned to me as she walked away, lest I point out she had feelings like a normal person.

'Good luck in there Sam.'

She flipped me off, without looking back.

And then she was gone.

I sat pondering for a moment about what lay ahead. More questions, more gawking, more nonsense. And hopefully more air conditioning, as a bead of sweat trickled down the back of my neck.

A few minutes passed in silence.

'You're up, Leon.'

The rabble of police had again gathered to escort me the few steps into the courtroom.

I stood, dusted off my pants, and gave them a nod.

The real trouble lay beyond the door. The circus of ethics versus progress.

Excitement and anxiety in equal measures gave me goose bumps as the door opened.

It was time for the first leg of my new life.

No more being a passenger, Leon.

Dedication

To those who have helped me along the way, family, friends, my online writing community at Scribophile, and everyone who has given up their time to proofread and review the book during its various revisions, thank you so much for your time and patience in helping me finish my little piece of fiction. It's taken me a long time to get to this point where I'm actually happy to release the book, and it never would have happened without the help I received along the way.

I can only hope anyone reading this enjoys it half as much as I enjoyed writing it.

And if you enjoyed the read, please consider giving a review on Amazon (or other online bookstores), a few reviews can be a great way to help the book spread a bit further and engage with more people.

Teleportnation

Milton Keynes UK
Ingram Content Group UK Ltd.
UKHW020705160124
436122UK00016B/325